JUSTICE
in *Paradise*

JUSTICE
in *Paradise*

Terrye Robins

TATE PUBLISHING & *Enterprises*

Published by Tate Publishing & Enterprises, LLC
127 E. Trade Center Terrace | Mustang, Oklahoma 73064 USA
1.888.361.9473 | www.tatepublishing.com

Tate Publishing is committed to excellence in the publishing industry. The company reflects the philosophy established by the founders, based on Psalm 68:11,
"The Lord gave the word and great was the company of those who published it."

Book design copyright © 2009 by Tate Publishing, LLC. All rights reserved.
Cover design by Kandi Evans
Interior design by Nathan Harmony

Published in the United States of America

ISBN: 978-1-60696-635-8
1. Fiction: Christian: Suspense
09.02.12

Other books by Terrye Robins
Trouble in Paradise
Revenge in Paradise

Counsel is mine, and sound wisdom: I am understanding; I have strength. By me kings reign, and princes decree justice.

Proverbs 8:14, 15

Justice in Paradise is dedicated to my aunt, Freda Riggs, who was always interested and supportive of my writing endeavors.

ACKNOWLEDGMENTS

I would like to thank my husband, Dan Robins, for his help in editing this novel. I would also like to thank all the kind people at Tate Publishing for your hard work, instruction, and encouragement. Our joint efforts have made *Justice in Paradise* possible.

CHAPTER 1

"That was a pip of a trip!" Aunt Edith said as she gave me a hug. Some of the strands from the grass skirt she was wearing became wrapped around my knees.

"I don't doubt that at all," I said, shaking first one leg and then the other to allow the strands to fall away. There was never a dull moment when Aunt Edith was around.

I had come to the Honolulu International Airport to pick her up because she was going to spend a couple of weeks with me. I'm Allison Kane, and was one of the mainland teachers chosen to teach summer school during the month of June at Prince Kuhio Elementary on Oahu.

"You can say that again," Michael said, reaching out his arm to draw me into a hug. "I've traveled thousands of miles over the years for pleasure and work, but I've never had a flight like that one!"

"Hey, you," I said, hugging him back. "I'm glad to see you, but what are you doing here?" My cousin, Michael Winters, had followed Aunt Edith off the plane. Seeing him was a complete surprise.

He cocked one eyebrow at me and grinned. "Afraid you might get caught doing something you shouldn't be?" Michael was the oldest cousin in our large family. Though he was only in his early thirties, my other cousins and I often sought his advice and approval.

I mentally did a quick inventory of my actions over the past two weeks since I had been in Hawaii. Overall, things had gone smoothly, if you didn't count the near-fatal encounter I had a few days earlier with a madman. Besides teaching, I was a part-time reporter for the *Hawaiian Star* newspaper. My research had led me to a man who had severed the fingers from several of his relatives who were buried throughout the Islands. When I confronted him, it wasn't pretty.

"Not me," I said, grinning back at him. "I've been as good as gold."

"So I heard," he said. "I wish you'd stick to teaching and leave the crime solving to the professionals."

I had kept the gory details about the experience from my family members back in Paradise, Oklahoma. But since it landed me in the hospital for a couple of days, it only took a phone call from my best friend, Traci Morris, whom I had been staying with, and word spread quickly.

"Were you sent here to help keep me out of trouble?" I nudged him in the ribs with my elbow.

He smiled at me. "In a roundabout way, I guess. Your daddy cornered me in my office a couple of days ago. He told me he's proud of the hard work I've been doing, and then he handed me an airline ticket." Michael was the controller for our family-owned oil and gas production company, Kane Energy. My father was the president and CEO.

"You did need a vacation, Michael," Aunt Edith said. "From what I've seen, you work way too hard."

"Thanks," he said. He looked back at me. "Anyway, since Richard Kahala has been after me to come here and go deep-sea fishing with him, I thought this might be a good time to accept his invitation." Michael and Richard had been friends since they both participated in a student-exchange program in high school.

"Well, I'm sure you'll have a great time," I said. "Now come on, you two. Let's go get my puppies and pick up your luggage."

Another cousin, Doug Blessing, and I shared custody of two young

dachshunds named Rowdy and Precious. Doug was studying to be a pedia-
trician and dates a lot, so the pups live with me most of the time. Though
he had tried to care for them since I had been away, it wasn't working out.
Aunt Edith had kindly agreed to help dogsit them while she was here.

We chatted as we followed the crowd of people walking toward the
baggage claim area. Aunt Edith's grass skirt drew some curious stares.

"Hey, there's Maxie," Aunt Edith said as we entered the noisy room.
"Yoo-hoo, Maxie." She wiggled her fingers at the silver-haired pilot
standing by a nearby luggage carousel. Earlier I had seen the two of
them laughing as he escorted her from the plane to where I was waiting.
She walked toward him, the swishing-sound from the skirt drawing
more attention from those around us.

"So tell me about your flight," I said to Michael. "You mentioned
you'd never had one like it." He reached out and grabbed his black can-
vas suitcase from the carousel and set it down next to me.

"Allie, I love Aunt Edith, but you deserve a gold medal for all you do
for her." He shook his head and grinned. "While we were waiting to board
our flight in Tulsa, I had to convince her not to put on the grass skirt. She
relented when I told her we would have to change planes in Houston, and
it would be a long walk through the terminal in that thing."

I latched on to Aunt Edith's maroon bag while Michael pulled his bag
of golf clubs off the carousel. Over the years I'd had my share of battles with
Aunt Edith trying to talk her out of doing something she had her heart set
on. She was a twenty-something woman in a seventy-eight-year-old body.
To say the least, she spoke her mind and did her own thing.

"After we left Houston, she had a hard time sitting still for very
long," he said. "Thanks to your daddy's kindness, we had plush seats in
first class. But she kept getting up and roaming the aisles anyway."

"Well, in her defense, she does have restless leg syndrome," I said.
"That new medicine she's taking hasn't done much to help control it."

"I know, and I was trying to be patient with her," he continued. "But
one time she was gone for over twenty minutes, and I became worried.
Thinking she might be in one of the lavatories in coach, I asked a flight

attendant to please check them. She turned up nothing, so I got up and started walking toward the back of the plane searching for Aunt Edith."

"At least on the airplane she was in a confined space," I said. "I still cringe when I think of the time we got separated at Woodland Hills Mall in Tulsa."

Aunt Edith and I had been doing some last minute Christmas shopping at Penney's. She was in the lingerie department trying to decide on a nightgown for my Gramma Winters, who is also Aunt Edith's younger sister. Since we were running short of time, I told her I would run down to catalog and pick up the Christmas dresses I had ordered for my two nieces while she picked out the gift.

The crowds were thick, so I was gone longer than I intended. In the meantime, Aunt Edith ran into her good friend, Daisy Johnson, and her daughter, also doing some shopping. Daisy wanted Aunt Edith's advice on a dress she had seen in ladies ready-to-wear, which was located a couple of departments away.

When I returned to lingerie and didn't find her, rather than stand around waiting like I probably should have done, I started searching. Somehow, with the crowd, we must have passed each other between the two departments. At any rate, over an hour passed before we found each other again.

Michael pulled another suitcase from the spinning carousel. "I walked all over that plane and still didn't find her," he said. "I was beginning to get a little frantic when in the back left side of the plane I heard a group singing 'Tiny Bubbles.'"

I started smiling. "Aunt Edith loves Don Ho."

"I know that now," he said. He reached out and grabbed Aunt Edith's large, green suitcase as it came by. "The chorus was gaining strength by the time I managed to get over there. Our great-aunt was conducting the glee club while sitting in a vacant seat between two guys wearing expensive suits. Men and women from across the aisle, as well as in front and in back of her, were singing 'Tiny Bubbles' for all they were worth."

I patted him on the back. "Hang in there. I'll take her off your hands now so that you can enjoy fun in the sun with a rod and reel in your hands."

Aunt Edith walked toward us. I watched the pilot she had been talking to put a piece of paper in his shirt pocket.

"Well, it looks like you got almost everything," she said, looking down at our feet. Just then, Michael stepped toward the carousel and picked up a good-sized cardboard box with "fragile" written on it. "I would have been back sooner to help you with the luggage, but Max insisted on getting my phone number. I told him I'd be busy while I'm here in Hawaii, but he could call me the next time he flies into Tulsa."

I looked at Michael. He nodded toward Aunt Edith. "She sat in the cockpit with him a couple of hours during the flight."

Aunt Edith took the box from Michael's hands and tucked it under her left arm. "Yes, and I sure had fun up there. But since it has been a few decades since I flew a twin-engine plane, Max wouldn't let me take the wheel."

Thank goodness, I thought.

We all grabbed pieces of their gear and put them on a luggage cart that Michael found close by. He maneuvered it down the long hallway as we walked toward the animal quarantine area.

"What's in the box?" I asked Aunt Edith. She had insisted on carrying it rather than placing it on the cart with the other baggage.

"Oh, I brought along my new motorcycle helmet," she said. "It's really spiffy! I had it customized with a two-tone pink metallic paint job then had streaks of fire glazed on each side. It was a bit pricey, but worth it. I brought it with me in case the opportunity to ride a bike along the shoreline presented itself."

"I didn't think about you wanting to ride a motorcycle while you were here, Aunt Edith." I looked at Michael and frowned. He shrugged his shoulders and gave me a "don't get me into this" look. "Since Michael and I don't ride, I'd be afraid you'd get lost cruising here alone."

"Oh, don't worry about that," she said. "Estelene Melton, a new member in the Screaming Eagles, is a whiz on the computer. When she found out I was coming to Hawaii, she got on the Internet and located some bike clubs here."

Thanks a lot, Estelene, I thought. Just what the over-fifties motorcycle club needed—a worldwide web guru. I spotted the information desk in the quarantine area and started leading them in that direction.

"And would you believe my luck?" she continued. "One of the guys Estelene connected with, Pinky DeLeaf, lives in Traci and Tommy's apartment complex. I'm hoping he can hook me up with a company on Oahu that rents bikes by the week."

One of the reasons I was able to come to Hawaii to teach summer school was because Traci taught at Prince Kuhio Elementary. Back in March, she had arranged an interview for me, and I had spent a week here with her and her husband, Tommy. They had just left this morning to spend a few weeks with their parents back in Paradise. While they were away, Aunt Edith and I would be staying in their apartment.

I ignored the sound of Michael chuckling behind me. I handed the paperwork I had filled out to the agent working the pick-up desk. Once he was convinced that everything was in order, he went to another room.

"I hear that you and Simon are getting along pretty well these days," Michael said while we waited for the agent to return. He started humming the "Bridal March" then joined his hands together at his waist like he was holding a bouquet of flowers.

"We're on very pleasant terms," I said with a smile. "Thanks to Simon, my application to bring the dachshunds here was rushed through, so they won't have to be quarantined."

Simon Kahala was a detective for the Hawaii State Bureau of Investigation, or HSBI, on the island of Oahu. The agency assists local law enforcement agencies throughout the Islands with felony person crimes. We had become pretty close since we met in March.

"Yeah, I wondered about that," Michael said. "When I spoke to Richard on the phone yesterday and mentioned we were bringing your dogs to you, he seemed surprised. He told me they have strict rules regarding animals and plants coming to the Islands. He said he figured Simon had pulled some strings for you." Richard was Simon's younger brother.

"Yes, he did. Fortunately, he knows the guy in charge here. I gave Simon the dogs' veterinarian's phone number, and he passed it along to the agent. He allowed the doctor to fax the vaccination records and other pertinent information to him. Normally, it takes about four months to get the okay to bring pets."

I heard Rowdy and Precious barking long before the agent walked through the door carrying their crate. When they spotted me, they began clawing at the door trying to get out. Precious was whining and Rowdy started howling. The folks standing near us were giving them sympathetic looks. Since they were in this department too, I suspected they had faced the same dilemma with their own pets at one time or another.

"Here you go, miss," the agent said. He set the crate on top of the counter. "Looks like these little guys are anxious to get out of there."

I quickly signed for them, then Michael set the crate on the floor. I had missed my puppies as much as they had me, and I couldn't wait a minute longer to hold them. I stooped down and unlatched the cage door. They both bounded out to greet me then jumped into my arms.

"I missed you guys so much!" I said as I cuddled them. Their hearts were pounding as I held them close to me. Rowdy started jumping around licking any spot of skin he could reach. Precious settled into the crook of my left arm and began washing my hand with her tongue.

"Aren't they adorable?" I heard a lady standing behind me say. I looked down at their shining black eyes and wet noses and had to agree with her. Though my dogs had their mischievous spells, right now they were exactly where I wanted them to be.

"Come on, everyone," I said. "Let's go home."

When we reached the airport parking lot, I led the way to the brown Chevy Malibu the school had loaned me. As Michael began putting Aunt Edith's things into the trunk, we heard a car horn. A late model, silver Jaguar pulled up and stopped. Richard Kahala was sitting behind the wheel.

"Hey, hey," he said as he climbed out of the sleek car. He threw his arms around Michael. "Aloha, Michael. Welcome back to Hawaii!" Richard patted his shoulders then took a step back. "I can't believe you actually made it. Since I've been after you for so long to come, I wasn't sure it would really happen."

"It's great to see you too, Richard," Michael said. "You look terrific. I can't wait to meet your family and catch up while we're out fishing on your boat." He held up his hands and started shaking his head. "No, excuse me; I mean yacht."

I looked at Richard. "Hi, Richard. I didn't know you owned a yacht."

He grinned. "Well, along with five other guys and the bank I do," he said. He stretched out his hand to Aunt Edith. "I'm Simon's brother, Richard. Welcome to Hawaii."

Michael stepped forward. "Richard, this is our great-aunt, Edith Patterson."

"Nice to meet you, young man," Aunt Edith said, shaking his hand. "My young niece here sure likes your brother."

I smiled and turned a couple of shades of red.

"Yes, ma'am, I know that. He thinks she's pretty special too." He looked at me. "Yeah, Allie, I'm proud of my toy, but she isn't new by any means. There's no way the guys and I could afford three mil for a new yacht."

Michael sidled up to me and leaned toward my ear. "Richard e-mailed pictures of it to me, and you never saw anything so plush. There are two classy-looking staterooms; a galley that is complete with a full-size refrigerator, stove, and dishwasher; and a main salon that is as big as my living room at home."

Richard was grinning ear to ear. He laid a hand on Michael's shoulder. "Yes, it's pretty great, I have to admit. And lucky for me one of the other guys has a girlfriend and another one has a sister with the same name as my wife. It was easy for us to agree on 'Lady Kim.'"

"Good choice," I said. Though I had never met Richard's wife, Simon had mentioned her to me a few times.

Rowdy and Precious were getting restless. Richard reached over and patted their heads. "I'm here to take Michael off your hands so you can get your aunt and puppies settled in. But if you don't already have plans for the evening, Kim and I would love for you ladies to join us for dinner tonight. She invited Simon too."

I looked at Aunt Edith, and she nodded. "We'd love to come, but I'll need directions to your house," I said.

He quickly jotted down the directions while Michael put the rest of Aunt Edith's luggage in my trunk. The guys loaded Michael's gear into the Jaguar's trunk, and though they protested, I put the puppies into their carrier for the ride home.

I was surprised that Simon hadn't called me. Before I pulled out of the airport parking lot, I checked my cell phone. I always kept it off while I was at school, but I had neglected to turn it on when I left. When it powered up, I saw that I had three voice mail messages—all from Simon.

"Will you please excuse me, Aunt Edith? I need to return a call to Simon."

"Sure, you go right ahead and talk to your fella. I'll just enjoy the beautiful sights as we drive along."

Without listening to his messages, I dialed Simon's cell phone number as Aunt Edith and I headed out of the airport toward Aiea.

"Well, well," he said when he answered. "I was beginning to think you were mad at me and screening my calls."

"You know better than that," I said, smiling. "I just forgot to turn on the phone."

"Where are you?"

"I just picked up Aunt Edith and a surprise guest at the airport."

"Bet I can tell you who the guest is."

I was about to tell him that I'd take that bet, but then I remembered that Richard's wife had invited him for dinner tonight.

"You knew Michael was coming, but you didn't bother to tell me?" I said.

"If you'll listen to message number two on your phone, you'll hear that tidbit of information."

"Oh. Well, I'll do that after I hang up."

"Tell Simon I said hello," Aunt Edith told me.

I nodded at her. "Aunt Edith says hi."

"Aloha, Aunt Edith," Simon said.

"He says aloha," I told her.

She smiled then muttered to herself, "Hello, good-bye, love, compassion."

I gave her an odd look and then focused back on my driving. We were on H-1, one of the three expressways that cross through the island. Traffic in all six lanes had stopped.

"Something's happened on H-1," I said to Simon. I could see flashing lights from several police cruisers and a fire engine. The vehicles were blocking the way ahead.

"Yes, that was my suggestion in message number three on your voice mail," he said. He cleared his throat. "Take another route to Traci's apartment. About an hour ago, someone dropped a large rock off the pedestrian bridge that crosses H-1 near Exit 16. It hit the hood of a delivery truck then bounced off and crashed through the back glass of a car. Dave and Marshall are already there, and I'm headed that way." Dave and Marshall were two detectives with the Honolulu Police Department who often assisted Simon with his investigations.

"That's terrible!" I said. "Was anyone hurt?"

"Not this time, thank goodness. But it's the second incident like it today, and the first guy wasn't as lucky."

"Traffic is starting to move over there, Allie," Aunt Edith said, pointing toward the two left lanes.

I looked in that direction. Cars were beginning to creep forward.

"I guess they're letting some of the vehicles through now," I said. In my rearview mirror, I saw a break in the lane closest to us. "I'm going to see if I can get over there."

"You'd better get off the phone so you can concentrate on driving," Simon said. "I'll tell you more about what happened tonight at dinner."

"Okay. I'll talk with you later," I said, then hung up.

I maneuvered the car into the nearest moving lane. As Aunt Edith and I drew near the crime scene, I spotted Marshall. We had crossed paths numerous times since I had met him and Dave in March. I had "helped" them solve a couple of crimes. Marshall and Dave had accepted me as part of their team early on.

He spotted me and waved. The reporter and amateur detective in me couldn't resist the chance to get a closer look. I pulled into an empty area a short distance from the mangled car. "Aunt Edith, would you mind waiting here a minute while I try to get some more information about this?"

"Sure. Go ahead."

I pulled out a small tape recorder from my purse. "I'll leave the car running with the air conditioner on so you won't get too hot," I told her. I opened the car door and climbed out.

Marshall started walking toward me. "Hey, Allie."

"Hi, Marshall," I said. I motioned toward the wrecked vehicle. "Simon told me that someone is causing a lot of trouble for motorists today. Can I ask you a few questions about it?"

"I can't really tell you much." He nodded toward the nearby pedestrian bridge. "Dave and a couple of other guys are up there talking to people. We're hoping that someone saw the person who threw the rock."

I looked toward the car. "Can I take a look at the rock?"

He shook his head. "It's already been taken to the lab for analysis. But it's similar to the one dropped in Kalihi this morning. They were both black lava rocks about this big." His hands formed a circle the size of a large cantaloupe. "That type of rock can be found all over this island."

I looked at the bridge. A small crowd had gathered on each end of it. Spectators were standing behind crime-scene tape that had been looped across both ends.

"If I promise not to get in Dave's way, is it okay if I go talk to a couple of people up there?" I nodded toward the bridge.

"It's okay with me," he said. "Can't miss a chance to get a story, huh?"

I grinned at him. "I'm sure Mr. Masaki already has someone covering the Kalihi incident, and this one might not even be connected. But you never can tell."

Marshall motioned toward my car. "Looks like your aunt arrived from the mainland. Simon told me she was coming to Hawaii for a couple of weeks." I looked in that direction. Aunt Edith waved at us. We both waved back.

"Yes, and this type of thing is right up her alley. I'm surprised she stayed in the car." Traffic on both sides of us was moving now. "I guess we'll head up there. I'll talk to you later."

"Okay. Good luck with your story."

I watched him walk toward his car, and then I headed back toward mine.

"Is that one of your detective friends?" Aunt Edith asked as I buckled my seatbelt.

"Yes, that's Marshall. He said it would be all right for me to go up on the bridge and talk to a few people." I pulled out into traffic and headed toward the exit ramp. "I know you're probably tired from your flight, so I'll hurry. I just hate to pass up this opportunity to question some possible witnesses for a piece for the *Star*." I found an empty parking space in a nearby church lot.

"Oh, I'm not that tired," Aunt Edith said. She glanced at the crowd that was growing larger by the minute. "How about if I take the group on the left side and you question the people on the right?" She started unbuckling her seatbelt.

Oh boy. I knew I was pressing my luck expecting her to stay out of this. "Well, why don't you stick with me so that we don't get in the detectives' way," I said.

She nodded. "You're right. Things probably work differently here than back home in Paradise. Frankie and the officers there don't seem to mind it a bit when I help out."

I did a mental eye roll. Frankie Janson, a cousin on the Kane side of the family, had just been promoted to Chief of Detectives with the Paradise Police Department. At only twenty-eight years old, he was the youngest person in northeastern Oklahoma to ever hold a title like that, and he deserved it. Over the years, Aunt Edith and I had gotten into several scrapes trying to help the department solve crime in Paradise. It was a good thing for us that Frankie and his fellow officers were tolerant.

I turned around to check on Rowdy and Precious in the backseat. They were curled up together in their carrier sound asleep. Since I intended to only be a short distance away, I rolled down all four windows. Aunt Edith and I climbed out and headed toward the crowd. Her grass skirt was giving her a little trouble, so I walked slowly so that she could keep up. Dave noticed us and waved, then he turned back to the man he had been talking to.

"Let's go interview those two women standing over there," I said.

Aunt Edith followed me to the elderly women standing together near the bridge railing. One was dressed in a yellow muumuu and had on a bright yellow sun visor. The other one had on pink-and-white flowered slacks and a white sleeveless top.

I introduced myself and Aunt Edith to them. They told me that they had been shopping at the grocery store across the street from the bridge when the incident occurred. They had heard tires screeching, but by the time they gathered up their groceries and walked outside, all they saw was the wrecked vehicle. They said they hadn't seen who threw the rock but heard someone say it was a kid.

I jotted down their names and thanked them for their time.

"Let's go interview those guys over there," Aunt Edith said. She was pointing toward a group of young Oriental men standing nearby. There were five of them, and they were all wearing sunglasses and had backpacks on. One of them was wearing a St. Louis Cardinals ball cap.

A couple had on University of Hawaii T-shirts. There were four Honda motorcycles parked near them—two black, one blue, and one green.

We walked over to the nearest boy. He was lanky and several inches taller than the others. I took him to be their leader. "I'm a reporter with the *Hawaiian Star*," I said. "Do you guys mind if I ask you a few questions?"

The boy was chewing gum and leaning on the green motorcycle. He turned toward the others and said something to them in Chinese. Some of them started laughing. One of them, who was smoking a cigarette, started coughing.

The leader stepped toward me. "I don't mind talking to the press," he said with a slight accent. He nodded toward Aunt Edith. "Or to hula dancers." A couple of the boys behind him snickered. "What can I do for you?"

I motioned toward the scene below the bridge. "Did you fellas see what happened here?" Everyone except the one wearing the cap shook his head.

"Don't know a thing about it," the lanky boy said. "We live nearby and just happened to be riding by. We saw the commotion and thought we'd check it out."

"I see." I glanced toward his T-shirt. "Are you a student at the university?"

"Used to be, but not anymore." He looked toward the other boys. "We've got too many other things going on right now." With the smirks still in place, they nodded in agreement.

Aunt Edith walked toward the person wearing the ball cap. His hand was resting on the seat of the green motorcycle. "So you like Hondas, huh?" she said. "I've got a Harley back home."

The boy smiled and started to respond but was stopped when the leader said something to him in Chinese. The smile was replaced by a frown.

I reached into my pants pocket and pulled out a business card. Handing it to the leader, I said, "Since you live nearby, if you hear anything about this incident, would you please give me a call? I'd appreciate it."

He looked at the card and nodded. Motioning toward the others, they all climbed onto their motorcycles. The boy in the cap climbed on behind the leader.

As I watched them ride away, I suspected that they knew more than they were telling. I interviewed a few more folks standing nearby but didn't find out much.

Aunt Edith and I walked back toward my car. The dachshunds were howling. As I climbed inside I said, "Sorry about that, you two." I opened the cage door and rubbed their heads. "We'll be home soon." I buckled my seatbelt while Aunt Edith got her grass skirt situated.

"Didn't find out much, did we?" she said once we were on the road again.

"No. I've found that being a *haole* tends to make some people clam up."

"Some folks don't take kindly to foreigners," Aunt Edith said. "But hey, that's their problem. Since I was wearing this nifty skirt, I caught the eye of several men up there, including that detective named Dave." She looked at me. "I wonder if he likes older women?"

I grinned at her. "I don't know. If you want to, you can ask Simon about it at dinner tonight."

She nodded and turned to look out the window. I heard her mutter, "*haole*, white person, non-native, foreign to Hawaii," softly to herself.

I smiled. I realized I had missed Aunt Edith and my puppies a lot since I had been gone. It was going to be great having them here with me.

CHAPTER 2

When we reached Traci and Tommy's apartment complex, I stopped in front of the tower and helped Aunt Edith unload her things by the front door.

"Before leaving this morning, Tommy told me they have a couple of luggage carts inside the closet in the laundry room," I told her. "I'll park the car then go inside and get one of them."

I pulled into my visitor's space in the parking garage. I opened the door then reached for the dogs' carrier. "Come on, you two. It's time to see your home away from home." They yipped in agreement.

As I walked toward the tower, I saw Aunt Edith standing by one of the luggage carts, her things already on it. She was holding the box containing her helmet.

"Where did you get the cart?" I asked.

She pointed toward a hefty guy climbing onto a Harley that was parked at the end of the garden apartments near the tower. "Allie, is this fate or what!" she said. "That's Pinky DeLeaf, the guy I was going to call to ask where I could rent a bike." I looked in the direction where she was pointing. The guy weighed at least three hundred pounds and seemed at home on the huge machine roaring beneath him. "Pinky was coming out of the building about the time you pulled into the garage. He went back inside and got the cart for me, then loaded my stuff onto it." Aunt Edith waved at him as he turned his bike around. He nodded at us and headed toward the exit.

"That was nice of him," I said, setting the dog carrier on the ground. "I'd better give the puppies a potty break before we go up."

I opened the cage door, and the dachshunds bounded out. They started sniffing every leaf and bush they came to then followed me to the large grassy area where the biker had been parked. Aunt Edith followed us.

I pointed toward the gated pool area. "You're welcome to use the pool while you're here," I told her. Several sunbathers were stretched out on loungers. Two young children were splashing in the water while their mother kept watch nearby.

"I plan to do that," she said. "I brought along that new swimsuit I was telling you about that I found at Mary Jane's Boutique." She sighed. "I considered buying one of the new string bikinis that had just arrived, but I settled on a fuchsia one-piece instead."

Thank you, Lord, I thought. I glanced down at the puppies snooping around near my feet. "If you all are ready, let's go up and get you settled."

The puppies followed us to the front door of the building. I set their carrier on the empty end of the luggage cart then wheeled it inside into the elevator.

When I opened the door of the apartment, the dogs beelined to the kitchen and found the food and water I had set out for them earlier. Aunt Edith walked toward the sliding glass door leading onto the lanai.

"Boy, will you look at that!" she said. Traci and Tommy lived on the seventeenth floor. They had a spectacular view of Pearl Harbor on one side and the Ko'olau mountain range on the other. "Wouldn't it be wonderful to wake up to this every morning?"

I joined her on the balcony. "It's pretty neat," I said. Despite the bright, sunny day, a bit of gloom tried to overshadow me. "Though I miss everyone back home, I'm going to be sad to leave here when summer school is over."

Aunt Edith put her arm around my shoulders. "That handsome beau of yours might not let you leave." The sadness intensified at the thought of leaving Simon behind.

I smiled and changed the subject. "We're going to leave for Richard's soon. Do you want to freshen up and unpack?"

"Point me to my room."

I picked up a suitcase in each hand and led her down the hall to Traci and Tommy's bedroom. Though I told them that Aunt Edith and I could share the guest room that I had been using, they insisted that one of us use their room while they were away.

"Traci made some space in their closet for you to hang your clothes," I told her, setting her suitcases next to the bed. I pointed toward a closed door. "There's a bathroom through there with a shower. Feel free to set out your things and make yourself at home."

Precious wandered into the room and starting pawing my feet. I leaned down and picked her up.

"It's so nice of your friends to let me stay here with you," Aunt Edith said, setting one of the suitcases on the bed. "And don't you worry one bit about trying to entertain me. I know you have school and your work at the newspaper." She patted the box containing her helmet. "Pinky lives in 1409. He said to come down in the morning and we'll go check out some bikes."

I was about to lecture her on being careful around strangers that she met on the island when I heard Rowdy howl. "What's your brother into?" I said to Precious. Carrying her with me, I hurried to the living room. I looked around but didn't see him. "Rowdy, where are you, boy?" He howled louder. The sound was coming from the kitchen. I rushed in and turned on the light. I still didn't see him. "Rowdy?"

I heard a rustling sound then saw the covered trash can in the corner topple from side to side. All at once, it hit the wall and fell over. The swinging lid clanged to the floor. Dragging the trash can liner and garbage with him, Rowdy came running toward me.

"Oh no you don't," I said, scooping him up. I caught him before he reached the carpet. He had eggshells and coffee grounds sticking to his nose and ears, and a piece of limp lettuce was caught on a front paw. The liner was wrapped around his back paws. Precious was looking at her brother with distaste. Despite the mess all over the kitchen, I couldn't help smiling. "Didn't take you long to get into trouble, did it?" With the goo all over his face, he looked pitiful.

Aunt Edith stepped to the door. "I guess the dog food you gave him didn't fill him up," she said. "Doug told me that lately Rowdy has been getting into the kitchen trash can at his place looking for food scraps. Guess I should have warned you." She walked past me and started picking up the mess on the floor.

I set Precious on the counter and carried Rowdy to the sink. Knowing the messes my dogs got into, I had stopped at a vet clinic the day before and bought a small bottle of doggie shampoo. Still holding Rowdy, I reached into the cabinet below the sink and pulled it out.

"Don't worry about that, Aunt Edith," I said as I turned on the water. "I'll pick up the mess and mop the floor." I untangled the liner from Rowdy's paws and set it on the floor next to me. Knowing a bath was coming, he started howling again.

Aunt Edith ignored me and walked to the small pantry by the stove. She pulled out a broom and dustpan, then set to work picking up the debris.

"You be quiet," I said to Rowdy. "You got yourself into this mess." I put a few dots of shampoo on his back then starting rubbing. Precious was watching us, and she looked like she was glad it wasn't her in trouble this time. She had had her own mischievous moments in the past, like when she chewed off the toe of a man buried in my neighbor's flowerbed.

By the time I toweled off Rowdy and cleaned up the bathing mess, Aunt Edith had the kitchen spick and span. While she went to freshen up, I changed my wet clothes and touched up my makeup. By 5:30, we were all on the road to Richard's house.

"How's it going with Bubba Phillips?" I asked as I turned onto H-3. The road was the newest expressway on the island and was a direct shot across the mountains to Kaneohe and Kailua.

"Oh, we've been having a fine time going skating and to the movies," Aunt Edith said, gazing out the window. Bubba was the new owner of the Caterpillar store in Paradise. I knew that he and Aunt Edith had been going out occasionally. "But he's trying to rush things. I told him that we needed some 'apart' time and that he was free to date someone else while I was here in Hawaii."

"Getting too serious too fast, huh?" I said.

"For me it is. Bubba was pouting when he took me home after church last night. He wanted to go get a pizza and come over to watch *The Tonight Show*, but I told him I had an early flight this morning and needed my rest."

I remembered her telling me about the last time they ate pizza together. The top plate of Bubba's dentures had gotten stuck in some pepperoni, and his teeth had popped out and landed on the table.

"And then there was that other thing," Aunt Edith said. "He was ticked because I couldn't go to Altus with him this weekend for the Tinker Intertribal Pow Wow. Bubba's one-fourth Cherokee and a veteran from the Korean War."

"I've heard that event is a big deal," I said.

"Oh yeah. Every year thousands of people gather down there to honor Native American warriors. I would have probably gone with him if I hadn't been coming here. But hey, I went with him to the Red Earth Festival in Oklahoma City a couple of weeks ago. Bubba's just going to have to get along without me for a few days."

We had crossed over the mountain range, and the aqua-colored ocean loomed ahead of us. Rays of light were reflecting off the tips of the waves, and it was gorgeous.

"What do you think about that?" I said.

"Words can't describe it," she said. She reached over and squeezed my hand lying on the console. "And there's no other person I'd rather share it with than my favorite niece."

"Thanks. I'm glad you came, even if Mr. Phillips has to do without you for a while. It sounds like he's pretty sweet on you."

"One person who wasn't sad to see me leave Paradise for a couple of weeks was Freda Mitchell. You know I told you that she has had her eye on Bubba." Ms. Mitchell was about Aunt Edith's age and sang in the choir at church.

"Yes, but as I recall, you said you could 'handle Freda.'"

She nodded her head. "But I decided to let her have a whirl with Bubba if she wants to, and then we'll see what happens later." She smiled. "Dating him has come in mighty handy, though. I learned how to run a backhoe and front-end loader years ago, but Bubba has been giving me some refresher lessons. They're going to come in handy when I get back home."

Uh oh! I had hoped that Aunt Edith's days of operating heavy equipment were long gone. "What do you mean?"

She smiled. "Your Grandpa A.J. said that when I return home, he's going to let me help clean out the two big ponds in the east pasture on the Circle K. That big storm a couple of weeks ago really churned up the water. Now there's a lot of silt and debris in all the ponds."

Grandpa A.J. and Nana Kane owned an eleven-hundred-acre ranch called the Circle K. There were several thousand head of cattle roaming on it, and numerous ponds were there. Somehow I couldn't imagine Grandpa allowing Aunt Edith to run his backhoe. I intended to corner Michael later and find out what was going on.

Since I had been attending Traci and Tommy's church in Kaneohe, I didn't have any trouble finding Richard and Kim's house in nearby Kailua. When I turned into the driveway, Simon pulled in right behind me and tooted his horn. I waved at him then climbed out of the car.

"Just in time," he said, walking toward me. He reached for my hands then gave me a warm kiss. "I've missed you today."

"Me too," I said.

Aunt Edith walked around the back of the car toward us. "Come here, young man," she said. "Give your favorite Oklahoma aunt a hug."

Simon smiled and put his arm around her shoulders. "It's good to see you, Aunt Edith. Welcome to Hawaii."

"It's great to be here," she said, looping her arm around his waist. "I've wanted to come here for years but never did."

Rowdy and Precious were in their carrier in the backseat. They both started barking. Simon glanced into the back window of the Malibu. "Looks like you brought your buddies with you," he said. They were bouncing around in their crate causing it to rock back and forth.

"Since we've just been reunited, I couldn't stand to leave them on their first night in a new place," I said. "But I don't want to impose on your family by taking them inside the house. I'll let them run around in the yard for a minute or two then put them back into their crate and set it on the front porch."

Simon reached into the car and pulled out the carrier. We all headed up the sidewalk. "Richard and Kim have a fenced backyard and a very friendly Pekinese," he said. "I'm sure they'll all get along great."

Aunt Edith stopped and gazed toward the ocean in the distance. "Isn't that the prettiest sight you ever saw? I plan to travel every road and see as much of this island as possible over the next two weeks."

"Well, I know Allie will be working a lot while you're here, but I'll be glad to show you some sights when I'm free," Simon said.

"Oh, I appreciate it, Simon, but you're a busy crime fighter. I'm planning on renting a motorcycle and hooking up with some members of a club here." She nodded toward his vehicle. "Besides, bikes can travel on trails that even Jeeps can't muster."

Simon looked at me and frowned. I shrugged and shook my head. "She's already met a guy that lives in Traci's building who is part of a motorcycle club here," I said.

From the look on his face, I figured Simon was about to launch into a "watch out for strangers" speech when Aunt Edith interrupted.

"Pinky DeLeaf owns a Harley Heritage Softail just like mine," she said. "I saw it today. It's red and silver and loaded with chrome, a real beauty."

We reached the porch just as the front door opened. "Aloha, everyone," Richard said, stepping out to greet us. Richard's four-year-old son followed him out, and Michael was right behind him. Kim, who was holding their two-year-old daughter in her arms, came out last.

"Thanks for having us," I said. "It's great to finally meet you, Kim." I stretched my hand toward her. She ignored it and gave me a hug. The little girl was squeezed between us.

"Welcome to our home, Allie. I've been anxious to meet you too." She stepped back. "This is our daughter, Bethany." The little girl was stretching her arms toward Simon.

"Come here, baby doll," he said to his niece. He set the dog crate down then took the child from her mother.

Kim looped her arm through Simon's and looked at me. "It's like pulling teeth to get my brother-in-law to come visit us. I'm surprised that Bethany went to him so easily."

"Now, I dropped by just a few days ago," Simon said. He nuzzled the dark-haired child under her chin. She giggled and leaned forward for more.

"You mean when Charlene guilted you into bringing me that luscious strawberry cake to take to the PTA meeting?"

He looked at me and puffed out his chest a bit. "See what a great brother-in-law I am?"

Kim cleared her throat. "Well, that was four weeks ago, and you stayed for about five minutes. I have to bake cookies for this month's meeting tomorrow."

I felt the need to come to Simon's defense. "When I arrived a couple of weeks ago, my friend Traci told me that Simon and her husband, Tommy, went deep-sea fishing with Richard not long ago."

Simon snapped his fingers and looked at Kim. "That's right; we did." She grinned at him. He made an attempt to draw the attention away from himself by changing the subject. "Uh, Kim, you haven't met Allie's great-aunt, Edith Patterson."

Kim turned toward her. "Welcome to Hawaii and to our home," she said, stretching out her hand.

"Thrilled to be here," Aunt Edith said, shaking it.

"And thanks for chaperoning Michael on the trip over," Richard said, slapping Michael's shoulder.

I leaned down in front of the little boy. He was holding on to one of Richard's pants legs and had been staring at me ever since we had arrived. "I'm Allie. What's your name?"

He eased away from his father. "Charlie," he said. He looked at Simon then back at me. "You sure are pretty. Are you going to be my new aunt?"

The question surprised me. I looked up at Richard. He had a big grin on his face. Michael was giving me a "thumbs up" sign.

Simon leaned over and scooped Charlie up with his free arm. "You're right, sport; Allie's very pretty." He looked at me. "And you never can tell about the other part."

I know my face was as red as a beet. The dachshunds chose that moment to introduce themselves by howling and sticking their noses through the wire. Charlie bent down and smiled. "Look, Mama. She brought her puppies with her."

I looked first at Richard then at Kim. "I hope you don't mind, but we've been separated for over two weeks, and I couldn't bear to leave them yet."

"Of course we don't mind," Richard said. "Our dog, Mitzi, is very friendly, and I'm sure she'll love them." He reached down and picked up the carrier. "I'll go let them loose with her in the backyard."

We all walked into the house. Wonderful aromas were coming from the kitchen.

"Make yourselves at home," Kim said. "I'm sure everyone is hungry, so I'm going to start putting things on the table."

"I'll help you," I said.

We brought heaping bowls full of tropical fruit, rice, mixed green salad, and two meat dishes–grilled mahi mahi filets and beef pepper steak laced with Maui onions—into the small dining room. Kim carried in a basket full of homemade rolls while I set drinks on the table. Once we were all seated, Michael said grace, and then we dug in.

"Marshall told me you were talking to some people near the H-1 bridge where that rock was thrown today," Simon said to me. He took the bowl of fruit I was passing to him. "Did you find out anything?"

"I talked to several people but didn't come up with much. I gave my name and number to one guy, but I don't expect anything to come from it."

"What rock?" Richard asked. He was spooning rice onto Charlie's plate.

Simon told everyone about the two incidents that had occurred.

"Where was the first rock dropped?" Kim asked. She was buttering a roll for Bethany.

Simon glanced at me. "Off the Kalihi Street bridge."

I stopped dipping the beef pepper steak from the platter I was holding and looked at him. "Marshall told me it happened in Kalihi, but I didn't realize the rock was dropped off that particular bridge." I frowned. "It stretches over the back road I sometimes take home from Prince Kuhio Elementary."

"That was voice mail message number one," he said. "I take it you never listened to the messages I left on your phone."

"Oops," I said. "Sorry, but I never got around to it."

"I guess you're forgiven." He smiled at me. "In the message I told you that we'd have traffic running again before you got out of school."

I made a mental note to keep my phone on vibrate from then on while I was in the classroom.

"Do you need some help, Simon?" Aunt Edith asked. "You know, I'm not busy tomorrow if you'd like me to come down to the station and lend a hand." She stuck her fork in a juicy piece of fresh pineapple lying on her plate. "This is the best pineapple I've ever tasted, Kim."

"Thanks, Ms. Patterson," Kim said.

Michael and I looked at Simon and grinned. It looked like he was trying to come up with some kind of excuse why Aunt Edith's assistance wouldn't be needed.

"I appreciate your offer, Aunt Edith, but you need to enjoy yourself while you're on the island. I wouldn't want to take up your time with work."

"Well, if you change your mind, just let me know. I wouldn't mind getting to know that fella Dave a little better. He was a cutie!"

I coughed into my napkin. Simon was shaking his head and grinning.

We discussed Michael and Richard's upcoming fishing trip. Though he had only had a couple of days notice, Richard had already secured the provisions on the boat. Everything was set for them to launch first thing in the morning.

"I hope you know what you're getting yourself into with this sea captain," Simon said to Michael. He grinned at his brother.

"Very funny," Richard said to Simon. "You and Tommy didn't seem scared when we went fishing a while back."

Simon shook his head. "No, we had a great time, and you did a terrific job navigating. Skimming the water at twenty-three knots with the fresh sea air and warm sunshine was a joy. I'd put my life in your hands any day."

"How big is your yacht, Richard?" I asked.

"It's seventy-five feet long and has three decks."

"Good grief!" I said. "That's a floating house!"

He grinned. "I have to admit, it's pretty luxurious. All the decks are made from teakwood, and it has two staterooms. The galley is state of the art. Kim, the kids, and I joined one of the other guys and his family for an overnight trip last month. We had enough room to easily accommodate another small family."

"Tell her about the Jacuzzi," Kim said.

Richard looked at his wife and smiled. "That's one of Kim's favorite amenities. Not only does the master stateroom have a 'his and her' bathroom, there's a luxurious Jacuzzi tub that she likes to relax in."

Kim was nodding her head. "Light a couple of candles, turn on some soft music, and I can kill an hour in it very easily." She patted her husband's leg. "Of course, I have to depend on my sweetie here to watch the kids while I'm in there."

"I hope Michael catches a marlin while you boys are out fishing," Aunt Edith said, setting down her fork. "You can't beat the high you get fighting with a fish."

"Well, I'll give it a shot," Michael said. "And this time I'm bringing along plenty of sunscreen. Gramma Winters won't be here to doctor us if we get too much sun."

Kim looked from Michael to Richard. "What's he talking about?"

Richard smiled. "Back in high school when I stayed with Michael and his folks, his Grandad Winters and Uncle Clarence took us out on the lake to fish for crappie." He looked at Aunt Edith. "And speaking of fighting fish, I had my work cut out for me bringing those dudes in that day." Aunt Edith nodded at him. "Anyway, Michael's relatives had sense enough to wear long sleeves and hats out on the boat. Though they told us we needed caps too, we were big, tough teenagers and didn't heed their warnings. We were burnt to a crisp when we got home. We were in so much pain we couldn't sleep that night. Michael's grandmother doctored us with aloe gel."

Michael grinned at him. "And it sure felt good, didn't it, buddy?"

Richard nodded his head. "I swear by it now. We keep it in the kitchen cabinet, the bathroom medicine chest, on the boat, and I've got a bottle of it at work too. That aloe is a cure-all for lots of things."

While Michael and Richard continued reminiscing about their time together as exchange students, the rest of us enjoyed the luscious coconut dessert that Kim had made.

She began wiping the baby's face and hands with a wet washcloth. "Richard, I'm going to let you take care of the kids while I start cleaning up the dishes."

Richard took the washcloth from his wife and started wiping Charlie's hands with it. "Will do, sweetheart." He scooted back his chair then lifted Bethany out of her highchair.

I began stacking Simon's dishes together with mine. "I'll help you, Kim," I said.

Aunt Edith scooted back from the table and began gathering up empty glasses. With everyone pitching in, the kitchen was soon clean and back in order.

Aunt Edith wanted Kim's recipe for the beef pepper steak, so the two of them sat back down at the table to discuss recipes.

The guys had all wandered into the living room. Richard rocked the baby, and she was soon asleep in his arms. Simon was down on the floor building a fort out of Lincoln logs with Charlie. I saw my chance to be alone with Michael, so I motioned for him to follow me onto the porch.

"What's this I hear about Grandpa telling Aunt Edith that she can run his backhoe to clean out some of the ponds?"

Michael started grinning. "She's telling the truth. I was sitting at the table out there last Sunday when Grandpa, your dad, Grandad, and Uncle Clarence were discussing what a mess all the ponds are in." Most Sundays, members from both sides of our family gathered at either Gramma and Grandad Winters' house or at Grandpa and Nana's house for dinner after church. "Aunt Edith had been in the kitchen visiting with Gramma and Nana and some of the aunts, when she headed into the dining room. She said she'd like to help with the pond cleanup, and I nearly fell over when Grandpa said she could run his backhoe."

I shook my head. "What can he be thinking?"

He shrugged. "I don't think he was really hearing her, Allie. He didn't actually say anything to her; he just nodded his head. He was peeved because his tailgate was stolen the night before, and I don't think he realized what he was agreeing to. Besides, have you ever known Aunt Edith to take no for an answer when she had her mind set on something? Remember the chainsaw incident a few weeks ago?"

I shuddered at the thought. The same storm that did a number on the Circle K ponds also did a job on the huge pecan tree in Aunt Edith's front yard. Instead of waiting for help, she had climbed the tree with her chainsaw and cut off some of the mangled limbs herself.

"Yes, I know she's headstrong," I said. "But surely he'll do something to keep her off that backhoe." I frowned. "Grandpa's tailgate was stolen?" His black, one-ton Ford pickup was his new baby. He had only had it a few months.

"Yes, along with three others in town," Michael said. "On Sunday,

Frankie said they were stepping up late-night patrols to try to catch the thieves in action."

"Do they have any suspects?"

Michael sighed. "Not anyone solid, but Frankie said he thinks Tack Dunbar is involved."

So what else is new, I thought. Tack had been a troublemaker ever since we started kindergarten together. His mother left when he was only three years old, and his father was a drunk. Their small, rundown ranch joined the Circle K on the west.

"I'll ask Frankie about it the next time I e-mail him," I said.

"Oh, Riley and DeLana told me to tell you hi," Michael said. Riley was his six-year-old daughter. He and DeLana Miller had been dating ever since she accidentally hit his car at a traffic light in downtown Tulsa.

"I miss Riley," I said. "I assume she's staying with Gramma and Grandad while you're here." Michael had had sole custody of his daughter ever since he and his wife divorced four years earlier. Riley often stayed with our grandparents when he was away on business trips.

"Yes, for a couple of days, and then she leaves for church camp on Sunday. Kristin and DeLana are taking a vanload of kids down to camp. Since Kevin returned to Iraq on Tuesday, Kristin can use the diversion." Kristin Sinclair was another cousin who was also twenty-five years old. Her husband, Kevin, was a chaplain in the army and was serving in Iraq. He was coming home for a two-week visit the day after I left for Hawaii.

"I need to give Kristin a call," I said. "Are the kids still playing T-ball?" Riley and Kristin's son, Joey, were both on the Champions' T-ball team.

"I wouldn't have considered coming on this trip if the regular season hadn't just ended. With all the rainouts in May, a lot of the teams have makeup games. Tournament play won't begin until the first week in July, and I'll be back by then."

Simon and Richard stepped out onto the porch. Darkness had fallen and a cool breeze was blowing. I could taste salt from the air on my lips.

"Where are Aunt Edith and Kim?" I asked.

"I think your aunt is still working her way through Kim's recipe box," Richard said. "Charlie is getting sleepy, so his mom is giving him his bath."

"I need to round up Aunt Edith and the pups so we can head home soon," I said. "I have some papers to grade tonight." I nudged Michael's arm. "Besides, you need your beauty sleep before your big voyage tomorrow."

Michael grinned. "I have to beat off the girls with a stick now, Allie. I'd never have a moment's rest if I was anymore good-looking."

"I know what you mean," Simon said. He draped his arm around my shoulders. "Women just can't resist a handsome authority figure."

I looked at him and smiled. "Oh really? And just how many girls do you have chasing after you, Detective?"

He looked me in the eye and cocked one eyebrow. "Are you jealous?"

Though I *was* feeling a twinge of jealousy at the thought of other girls clamoring for his attention, I took the easy way out. "I'm pleading the fifth," I said.

"Take it from me, Simon; she wouldn't like it one bit," Michael said. He dodged when I attempted to punch his arm.

Kim joined us on the porch. "Charlie is tucked in but needs a kiss from his daddy and Uncle Simon," she said. She looked at me. "And he specifically asked if you would come tell him good night."

"Let's go, everybody. My boy needs his rest," Richard said.

We all trooped back through the house to Charlie's bedroom in the back. It was decorated much like Joey's room back in Paradise in hues of blue, red, and cream. But unlike Joey's room, which had wallpaper with baseball equipment printed all over it, Charlie's room was decorated with sailboats and schooners. A model of Richard and Kim's yacht was hanging from the ceiling. Charlie's head was lying on a light blue pillowcase covered in white and silver speedboats.

Simon knelt down next to his nephew's bed and gave him a kiss. "Good night, sport. It was good to see you tonight."

The little boy looped his arms around Simon's neck. "Good night, Uncle Simon. Come back soon." Simon nodded then stepped back.

We all took our turns telling Charlie good night. He insisted that

I give him a hug. While he had his little arms wrapped around me, he said, "You can come back anytime you want to, Allie." He lowered his voice. "And I hope you and Uncle Simon get married."

I leaned back and grinned at him. "I'll try to come back soon, Charlie. Sleep tight."

When we all walked back into the living room, Aunt Edith came out of the kitchen. She had her purse hanging over her shoulder, and she was folding a sheet of notebook paper in half.

"I'm ready any time you are, Allie," she said. "I copied off the beef pepper steak recipe, and Kim's letting me take home a few of her other cards. I told her I'd find a Kwik Copy place somewhere and make some copies of them. She said I could send the originals back by Simon." She stepped closer to me and nodded toward Simon. "She wants him to visit their kids more, and returning the cards will be a reason he'll have to drop by."

I smiled. Simon was only standing a couple of feet away, so he heard every word.

Richard let the three dogs in from the backyard. The dachshunds bounded over to greet me. I scooped them up into my arms. "Did you two have fun with Mitzi?"

They acted like they were glad to see me, but they kept looking down at the Pekinese sitting by my feet. They seemed reluctant to leave their new friend behind.

Simon retrieved the dog crate for me, and I put the dogs inside it. Aunt Edith reached up and hugged Michael. "You two boys take care of yourselves out there in that boat," she said. "And be sure you take lots of pictures of your catch."

I walked over and hugged Michael too. "That goes double for me. Gramma would have a hard time forgiving me if something happened to her favorite grandson."

Michael's parents, Joshua and Sylvia, had died in a car crash when Michael was only twelve years old. Michael moved in with Uncle Josh's twin brother, Jake, and his wife, Debra, and their family. Gramma and

Grandad Winters took the loss of their son very hard. It was understandable that Gramma would dote on Michael.

He grinned at me. "I notice you didn't say favorite *grandchild*."

"Well, of course not," I said, smiling, "because that would be me!"

He put his arm around my shoulders. "Richard and I will be careful."

Aunt Edith and I thanked our hosts for having us over and for the delicious dinner. Simon reached down and picked up the dog carrier, then walked over and put his hand on Richard's arm. "May you have fair winds and following seas. *Semper paratus*."

Richard smiled at his brother. "Always prepared. We will be."

We all said good night and then headed for our cars. Aunt Edith climbed into the Malibu while Simon put the dogs in the backseat. He pushed the door closed then put his arms around me and pulled me close. "I believe Michael's right," he said.

Though I was pretty sure I knew what he was referring to, I gave him an innocent look. "Right about what?"

He put his forehead against mine. "I don't think you'd like it one bit if other girls chased after me."

The soft scent of his cologne encircled us, and my heart was beating double-time. "Is there someone specific I need to be worrying about?"

He kissed me gently then took a step back. "What do you think?"

I was about to tell them that there better not be any competition, but then he kissed me again. Nothing mattered more at that moment than being in his arms.

He squeezed my hands then headed toward his car. He opened the door and turned around. "As Charlie would say, 'Sleep tight, Aunt Allie.'"

I liked the sound of that.

CHAPTER 3

The next morning, Aunt Edith was fixing breakfast when my alarm went off. I could smell bacon cooking. The dogs had slept on a blanket at the foot of my bed but were nowhere around. I figured they were in the kitchen begging for a handout.

I quickly got ready for school then walked into the kitchen. "Good morning," I said. The dachshunds looked up at me and then went back to eating their kibble. I noticed that it had been mixed with some meat scraps.

"Good morning," Aunt Edith said. She picked up a knife and began spreading butter on toast. "I assumed the groceries in the fridge and cabinets are for the taking, so I helped myself. I plan to leave some money to replace the food and other things we use while we're here."

"Oh, don't worry about that," I said, picking up a slice of bacon from the plate where it was stacked. "Traci received a nice stipend for my room and board from the grant that allowed the school system to hire me. I haven't eaten many meals here because Simon and I go out a lot." Rowdy had noticed that I had bacon in my hand. He put a paw on my leg and started whining. I leaned down and handed him my last bite.

Aunt Edith picked up the saucer full of toast and plate of bacon and started walking toward the dining room. "Well then, I'll be sure the apartment is clean as a whistle before we go home," she said. "I also plan to buy a nice baby gift for them." Traci and Tommy's first child was due in early October.

The dogs and I followed her into the dining room. "They'll appreciate that," I said, sitting down. I helped myself to a slice of toast. "With the high cost of living here, their budget has always been tight. Traci has been putting furniture for the nursery and other things in layaway and paying on them a little at a time."

Aunt Edith nodded. "I had to do the same thing before Bennie was born." Bennie was her only child and had recently moved his wife and two sons from Alaska to Paradise. "But most young couples today want everything right now. They have two or three credit cards maxed to the hilt." She laid a slice of bacon on her plate. "I admire Traci for not putting her family in debt."

I looked at the clock on the wall. "I need to get a move on," I said. I picked up my dirty dishes and started walking to the kitchen. "Besides meeting Pinky later, what are your plans for the day?"

She started stacking the rest of the dirty things. "I want to check out the pool this afternoon and get in a few laps. Also, I thought the dogs and I would walk around and explore the neighborhood." She set the dirty dishes in the sink. Two slices of bacon were left on the plate. She put one in each of the puppies' dishes.

I reached inside the pantry and pulled out the two leashes I had bought the day before. "You'll need these then." I laid them on the counter by the sink. "I'm going to brush my teeth and get on the road." I reached down and patted the dogs' heads. "You two be good for Aunt Edith today." They looked at me with innocent expressions on their faces.

When I pulled into the parking lot at school, I noticed that Miss Kahala's parking spot was empty. She was the principal at Prince Kuhio Elementary and also Simon and Richard's aunt. I wanted to ask her if the school would purchase an ant farm for my classroom.

I had ten students in my class—seven boys and three girls. Their appearance was as diverse as night and day. The ringleaders of the group, Mareko Folora and Seth Morgan, were part-Hawaiian. Mareko was a smart kid, but his parents fought a lot. He and his sister had been placed in foster care more than once.

When they started summer school, they all had reading difficulties. Over the three weeks we had been together, everyone had made great strides. Though I didn't presume to take all the credit, I had tried to come up with interesting units that would entice them to read fun, informative books. So far so good.

As I headed for the building, I noticed the wind had picked up since I had left home. The clear blue sky was now dotted with large, puffy cumulus clouds.

I went to the office and signed in. I asked the secretary to please leave Miss Kahala a note that I'd like to see her for a minute, if possible, before I left at noon. She said she'd pass the message along to her.

I walked down the hall to the school library. Once inside, I headed for the non-fiction section and started pulling out books about insects. Many of the books ranged from second to fourth-grade reading levels. Since all the students were now at or close to reading at third-grade level, I knew they would appreciate both the ease and challenge of these books.

After checking out fifteen of them, I headed toward my classroom. The students soon began arriving.

We said the pledge of allegiance, and then I showed them the different books I had selected. I let each child choose one. I gave them a couple of minutes to peruse it then asked them to share why they chose that particular insect. There were all kinds of explanations ranging from "I want to find out more about how caterpillars change into butterflies" to "I saw some kids get stung by fire ants on the playground" to "Bees are fun to watch" and more.

I looked at Mareko, who had mentioned the fire ants on the playground. I recalled the day when I had been told that I had received the position here. Miss Kahala had been out there checking on some students who had been stung while playing in an ant pile.

"Mareko, would you please tell us more about the ants?" I asked.

He motioned toward the boy sitting across from him. "Well, one day at recess, Seth and I were playing near some first graders. One of them started yelling. There's always a lot of screaming and hollering at recess, so we didn't think much about it. But all of a sudden, this one kid started running toward us whooping and hollering. In just a couple of minutes, another kid started jumping up and down yelling. Seth and I ran over there and saw that they had been sitting in the middle of a pile of fire ants."

Seth's eyes were wide, and he was nodding in agreement. "We felt sorry for those little kids, Miss Kane," he said. "Mareko and me …"

"Mareko and I," I said.

"Yeah, Mareko and I started brushing the ants from the two boys' legs. Another kid got the playground teacher."

I smiled and shook my head. Mareko gave me a puzzled look. "They were really hurting, Miss Kane," he said.

I realized he had misunderstood. "Oh, I'm sure they were, Mareko. I'm not smiling about that. Fire ant bites really sting, and they can be dangerous if someone gets bitten several times." I leaned back against my desk. "I'm smiling because of a similar thing that happened to one of my students in Paradise. His name was Rufus."

A dark-headed boy named David raised his hand. "Did your kids in Oklahoma study about fire ants too? I thought just Hawaii had them."

I walked over to the blackboard and pulled down a world map that was rolled up above it. I pointed to South America. "No, you can find fire ants in many places throughout the world," I said. "They originated in South America. Over the years they traveled up through Mexico into Texas then into other states on the mainland." I thought about the strict rules Hawaii had regarding people bringing animals or plants to the Islands. "I imagine they were brought here accidentally by some travelers."

"Well, the very next day, Miss Kahala had some pest control guys out there destroying those mounds," Mareko blurted out without raising his hand. "Those critters didn't come back the rest of the school year."

An Oriental girl named Annie raised her hand. "What happened to that boy named Rufus, Miss Kane?"

"Well, Annie, one day I took my class outside for a nature walk, which is what I plan for us to do today too." They all started cheering. "Rufus and another student spotted the fire ant mound while we were out there. He had always wanted an ant farm, but his mother couldn't afford to buy him one." I replayed the scene about how Rufus had smuggled ants in from the playground and the chaos that occurred after they got loose in the classroom.

"Well, Miss Kane, you won't have to worry about anything like that happening today," Mareko said. "That exterminator blew that mound to smithereens!"

I smiled at him. "Okay, everyone, during our walk, I want you to write down every kind of insect you see. If you don't know the name of it, ask another student or me, or just draw a picture of it. Now please get a pencil and a sheet of paper, and then line up." They didn't waste any time.

When we walked outside, the wind was stronger than it had been earlier, but it didn't seem to bother the children. They paired up and had a great time racing around the playground searching for insects. After about an hour, we walked back inside.

"Before we settle down to read the books you chose, we're going to take a bathroom break," I said. I could tell that for a few of them, this was good news. "When we return to the classroom, I'll list on the board the names of all the insects you spotted outside."

They hurried to the door, and then I led them down the hall to the restrooms. While I waited for them, Miss Kahala came walking toward me.

"Good morning, Allison," she said. Usually every strand of her thick, black hair was in place. Today it was a bit disheveled. "I had a meeting at the state superintendent's office this morning and just arrived." She patted both sides of her head with her hands. "That wind is something else. I was headed to the lounge restroom to straighten my hair when I saw you. Diane said you needed to see me about something."

"Yes, we just came in from outside too." The students were lining up along the wall. "We're starting a unit on insects. I wanted to ask you if it would be possible to get an ant farm? It doesn't have to be a big one or anything elaborate."

"I think an ant farm is a great idea," she said. "My sisters and I had one when we were in elementary school. Ants are fascinating creatures."

"I was at a pet store in the Pearlridge Center on Wednesday picking up some things for my dogs, and they had some in stock."

"Fins, Feathers, and More? Yes, that's a nice shop." A couple of my students had walked up and were hugging the principal. She hugged them back while continuing to talk to me. "I'll tell Diane to call and give the manager a purchase order number. You can go buy whatever you need for your unit."

"Thanks, I appreciate it, and I'm sure the kids will too."

She waved at my students and then walked back down the hall.

"Okay, everyone, let's go back now," I told them. "Are you ready to learn about bugs?"

They started cheering.

When the students left at noon, I straightened the room then walked to the office to use the computer. An e-mail account had been set up for me on the first day of school, and I had been corresponding with several of my relatives back home in Paradise.

I logged on and found that I had two messages: one from Doug and the other one from Kristin. Doug was asking if the puppies had made the flight all right. He thanked me again for letting them come. He also assured me that he was still driving my Mustang around the block a couple of times a week and was caring for my peace lily like it was his own.

Yeah, right, I thought, smiling. Though my mother, both grandmothers, and others in my family were terrific gardeners, Doug and I weren't great with plants. My peace lily had survived many mishaps while living with me. It had been dropped twice while being lugged back and forth between our duplex apartments and been nearly decimated when Rowdy couldn't find a bone he had buried in the pot. I figured that if Doug just watered it a couple of times during the month, it would be fine.

I wrote back to let him know the dogs were okay, that Michael and Richard had left on their fishing trip, and that I appreciated him taking care of things for me.

Kristin was also checking in. We both taught at Elliott Kane Elementary and had always been close. She wrote:

> Dear Allie,
>
> Kevin is back in Iraq now. I hope you'll continue to pray with me that he'll stay safe. I already miss him something awful!
>
> Michael may have told you that DeLana and I are taking a load of kids down to church camp Sunday afternoon. Well, guess what? I'm going to be a counselor! It won't be the same as when you and I attended as campers, but I'm really looking forward to it. (Since I'm married now, I won't be kissing any boys behind the water tower.)
>
> Tell Michael that Riley is tickled that I'm going. She told me she's bringing some super-sized balloons and a new water pistol Grandad bought for her. She said she plans to douse me good.
>
> Take care of yourself, and write when you can.
>
> Love, Kristin

I smiled. Though I wasn't an angel during my years as a camper, I never sneaked behind the water tower with a boy. When we were fifteen, the camp director caught Kristin and Tony Lawson behind the tower one night after church. They both had to wash dishes after every meal for three days straight. Kristin said it wasn't too bad except for the breakfast dishes—campers didn't always scrape all the eggs off their plates.

Several times while she was washing dishes, fried eggs came floating to the top of the dishwater. Yuck!

I'll have to tell Michael about Riley bringing the balloons, I thought. Toward the end of camp, on Friday afternoon, everyone has a big water fight. It's campers against counselors, teachers, cooks, the evangelist, and any other staff that is there. Everyone always packs lots of balloons and water pistols prepared for the big event.

Grandad once told Doug, Kristin, and me that Michael was the king when it came to winning those water fights. The three of us were spending the night at Grandad and Gramma's, and we got into a water fight with the hose. Doug was stronger than we were and usually soaked us pretty good. But this particular time, Kristin and I ganged up on him, and he ended up the loser. Grandad said that even though Doug was soaked, it didn't compare with the shape most of those counselors were in when Michael finished with them.

I smiled as I thought about all the fun I'd had at church camp through the years. I wrote back to Kristin and told her that I hoped she had a great time. I also told her that the day before I left to come to Hawaii I had seen some giant balloons at Wal-Mart that she might want to check out. I ended the message saying, "Girl, you've got to defend yourself!"

Before I logged off, I wrote to Frankie. I told him that Michael said Grandpa's tailgate had been stolen, and I wanted details! Frankie wasn't the best letter writer in the world, so I knew it was a one-in-a-million chance that he would respond before I flew home in ten days. But it was worth a shot.

I shut down the computer then headed out the door.

On the way to the *Hawaiian Star*, dark, gray clouds were rolling in from the south. The wind was stronger than it had been when the students and I were on the playground. I had to keep both hands on the steering wheel. The friendly skies from early morning now looked ominous.

By the time I reached the office, large drops of rain were splattering on the windshield. I grabbed my umbrella from the backseat then ran toward the building. I saw my boss, Mr. Masaki, talking on the telephone as I walked past his office. He waved and I waved back.

Since I hadn't stopped for lunch, I headed to the vending machines. I chose a can of cranberry-grape juice and a package of Doritos. Though the chips weren't the most nutritious fare, I decided I'd try to eat better later.

Thinking of dinner, I realized that Simon hadn't mentioned going out when I had seen him at Richard's house. I pulled my cell phone from my purse and turned it on. I had one new message, but not from Simon—it was from Frankie. He said, "Call me, Miss Priss. I'm at work."

I figured the threat in my e-mail to him did the trick. I dialed the Paradise Police Department.

Rita, the dispatcher who had been there for over ten years, answered the phone. "Good afternoon, Paradise P.D."

"Hi, Rita. It's Allie." I looked at my watch. It was nearly 6:00 p.m. in Oklahoma. "What are you doing working so late?"

"Hi, Allie." She sighed. "Oh, I'm still here because of that thief who's stealing tailgates. One more went missing early this morning."

"I'm sorry to hear that," I said. "That's the main reason I'm calling Frankie. Michael told me that Grandpa A.J.'s was stolen the other night. I intend to give my cousin a hard time about it." I grinned. "I'm going to tell him that if I'd been there, it probably wouldn't have happened."

"Uh huh," she said. "Well, then you'd better leave your swimsuit lying on the beach and get back here pronto. I'm tired of fielding all these calls with tips about who might be doing it." Rita was familiar with both Aunt Edith's and my crime-solving skills. There were times that we helped bring criminals to justice. But in other cases, we ran a close second to looking like the Keystone Cops.

"No, I'm just kidding about razzing Frankie," I said. "I know he's probably bummed about this latest crime spree. Is he around?"

"He sure is. Hold on a minute."

While I waited, I hummed along with the song that was playing on the line. It was "Maneater" by Hall and Oates. Just as Frankie picked up the phone, I belted out one of the lines from the song, "Watch out boys, she'll chew you up!"

"That about sums it up, Allie," he said. "I just left the new chief's office a few minutes ago, and I feel like a chunk of me was left in there." Paradise had recently hired a woman who was the former assistant chief in Edmond, a suburb of Oklahoma City. I had heard she was having a hard time adjusting to small-town life.

"Sorry," I said. "I've heard from several sources that you're having a rash of tailgate thefts in Paradise. I wish there was a way I could help." I paused a moment. "I tell you what; when you catch whoever is doing it, put him in the pokey, and then I'll beat him up for you as soon as I return."

He started laughing. "Thanks for the offer. Right now it sounds pretty appealing. I can always count on you to cheer me up."

"Why is the chief riding you so hard?" I knew that Frankie always gave every case his best efforts.

"The tailgate stolen this morning belonged to the mayor. The chief had just hung up from talking with him when I walked in."

"Uh oh. So she's feeling the heat from her boss, huh?"

He sighed. "To put it mildly."

"How's Grandpa taking his loss?"

"Not well," he said. "He's hot about it."

"I'll bet. I wouldn't want to be in the thief's shoes if Grandpa gets hold of him before you do."

"You and me both." He paused. "Do you want to hear some good news totally unrelated to this case?"

"Sure. Lay it on me."

He lowered his voice. "Kailyn and I are having twins."

"You're kidding! Frankie, that's fantastic!"

"We're pretty psyched about it. Kailyn has been putting on weight big time, so her obstetrician ran another ultrasound yesterday. Sure enough, there are two little people in there. The middle of October is still the due date, but her doctor said that twins often come early."

"Gramma is going to love this!" I said.

Gramma was elated when my mom's younger sister, Emily, had identical twin girls fifteen years ago. For several years she sewed adorable, matching outfits for them. Though Gramma had never shown any favoritism with her grandchildren, I always suspected that she was glad when Angel and Amber came along. It may have somehow helped to fill a void that was left after her twin son, Joshua, died.

"Yes, I can't wait to see the look on her face when we announce it at dinner on Sunday," Frankie replied.

"I'd like to be there to see it too. I'm having a great time here, but I sure miss everybody at home." The thought of leaving Hawaii and Simon was painful, but I was also starting to get homesick for my family.

"Well, now that Aunt Edith and Michael are there, you'll have your work cut out for you."

I smiled. "Yes, I'm sure they'll keep me on my toes."

"Well, I need to wrap up some things and try to get home before 7:00," Frankie said. "I don't want Kailyn throwing out my dinner."

"I doubt that she would, but I need to get to work too. Take care and good luck on this case."

"Thanks, I need it," he said, then we hung up.

I had completed a serious story earlier in the week, so Mr. Masaki had given me a fun assignment. The annual King Kamehameha Hula Competition was coming up next week. He had been pleased with my work so far and wanted me to try to put an interesting spin on this annual story.

I pulled out the folder containing my research. While my computer booted up, I scanned the articles that had been written by other *Hawaiian Star* reporters. Though well written, most of them were short and contained very little about the history of the hula dance. I decided to start from that angle.

For centuries before Captain James Cook arrived in Hawaii, the natives had been using hula in their religious practices. Laka was the goddess of hula. Men did more dancing than women did, and grass skirts were not used until years later. The skirts in the early days were made of *kapa* cloth. *Kapa*, or *tapa* as it was sometimes referred to, was made from the bark of the paper mulberry tree that was native to the Islands. Sometimes men wore a *malo*, or loincloth, instead of a skirt.

I jotted down more notes about the early traditions of hula then went to a Web site where articles written by university students were posted. I found that not only was hula used in religious dances, it was a part of every aspect of life—births, deaths, warfare, and even surfing.

I smiled when I thought of Simon wearing a *malo*. Since I knew he had participated in surfing competitions before I had met him, it was easy to picture him on a surfboard. My smile quickly changed to a frown when I realized that adoring female fans had probably enjoyed seeing it firsthand.

"No time for jealousy, Allie," I said aloud. I turned back to my note-pad and starting writing again.

The art of hula was nearly wiped out when Western missionaries arrived in the early 1820s. They were shocked by the open dancing and convinced Queen Kaahumanu that it was lewd. But the people refused to let the custom die. In the 1870s, King Kalakaua made it popular again.

I was immersed in my work when the phone rang.

"Hello?"

"Hi, Allie," Aunt Edith said. "Sorry to bother you at work."

I glanced at the clock and saw that it was nearly 1:30. I had intended to call and check on her and the pups but had forgotten it.

"You're not bothering me at all," I said. "How is your day going?"

"The dogs and I are having a blast!" she said. "We took a nice, long walk this morning and then stopped by Pinky's apartment. He told me he'd take me to a place on Nimitz Highway that rents motorcycles. I'm supposed to meet him in the lobby at 2:00. The reason I'm calling is to ask you if there is something I can put over the kitchen doorway to keep the puppies in there while I'm gone. I hate to stick them back in that carrier."

I hadn't thought of how to keep the dogs confined when we weren't there. "No, but I'll work on it. I'll try to leave here a little early so that they won't be pinned up too long. Go ahead and put them in their crate before you leave. I don't want them tearing up something."

"Okay, will do."

"What else did you do today?"

"Well, the pups and I went down to the pool. I swam some laps while they explored nearby." She started chuckling. "One of the tenants, a woman named Evelyn, was stretched out on one of the loungers when we arrived. She wasn't a bit happy to have our company."

"That must have been Evelyn Hunter," I said. "She's not crazy about me either. A few nights ago, she walked up and caught Simon kissing me good night by the elevator. Traci said she's a troublemaker."

"Well, she let me know right off the bat that she was used to having the pool *alone* from eleven to noon every day. She was also ticked because the dogs were snooping around. We might have left her alone and come back later if she hadn't made a snide comment about my new bathing suit."

Uh oh. When it comes to Aunt Edith's fashion choices, people who are acquainted with her know better than to make derogatory remarks.

"I was trying to be cordial," she continued. "Then Evelyn had to insult me by saying that fuchsia should *never* be worn by anyone over thirty years old. Well, that's when I had to *advise* her that she might want to try wearing a pair of knee-length knickers to the pool in the future. Those varicose veins running up and down her legs look like roads on a map!"

Oh boy. "So I take it she didn't hang around much longer," I said, hoping that was the case. I was considering whether or not I should bake Evelyn a cake to try to make amends.

"No, she stalked off back into the building. Precious was snarling at her, and Rowdy was nipping at her ankles as she skitted back inside."

No, a homemade "truce" cake isn't going to get it, I thought. *This is going to take a fancy bakery cake. Better have a nice "I'm sorry" message written on it too.*

"Yeah, that Rowdy is a great judge of character," Aunt Edith said, chuckling. "But his bark is worse than his bite. Too bad he's not a Doberman."

CHAPTER 4

I popped a couple of Tums into my mouth after I hung up with Aunt Edith and then called a bakery a few doors down from the *Hawaiian Star*. I needed to head this off before my aunt and dogs were banned from the apartment building. As I hung up from ordering a twenty-dollar cake, plus another fifteen to have it rush delivered to Evelyn this afternoon, I heard a knock on my door. I looked up and saw Mr. Masaki standing there.

"Hi, Allison," he said, stepping inside. "I heard you on the phone and didn't want to interrupt."

I leaned back in my comfy chair and stretched my legs. "Oh, that's fine. I had to try to resolve a little personal problem." I motioned toward the files on my desk. "I've been working on the King Kamehameha Hula Competition assignment. The history of the dance is very interesting."

Mr. Masaki smiled and nodded. "I thought you might take that approach. The event has been going on for thirty-five years now. Only a small part of how hula originated has been presented in past articles. If you come up with something unique, I'll allot more space than I usually do for your article."

I smiled. "I know that the *Hawaiian Star* is primarily read by people living throughout the Islands. But with the influx of *haoles* moving here,

I'm sure that many are like me and don't know much about the traditions." I leaned forward and placed my hands on my desk. "From what I've discovered so far, I believe I can make this story interesting for young and old readers alike."

"That's what I wanted to hear," he said. "Now, there's another matter I'd like to discuss with you." He sat down in the chair across from my desk. "Since you have connections with Honolulu P.D., you may be aware that someone has been throwing rocks off bridges and hitting cars."

I nodded. "You were busy when I arrived, but I was hoping to share with you what I've found out so far. Have you already assigned a reporter to cover the cases?"

"No, but I don't want to overload you. Since your previous partner didn't work out, would you like me to pair you up with someone else?" My former partner, Kyle Messenger, had been fired for a myriad of reasons, including charging extravagant lunches to the paper and seldom being at work.

"No, that's okay," I said. "I know my way around the island pretty well now, and I kind of like working alone."

"That's fine with me, then," Mr. Masaki said. "Now tell me what you have so far regarding the two rock incidents."

I relayed what I had picked up during my interviews at the H-1 scene and what I had learned from Simon regarding the Kalihi area crime. After my boss left, I wrote the article for the next day's edition of the paper. After revising the copy and getting Mr. Masaki's approval, I e-mailed it to the copy editor.

As I shut down my computer, Simon called.

"This is a nice surprise, considering I'll be seeing you in about an hour," I told him.

He sighed. "Yeah, about that."

Uh oh. This didn't sound good.

"I was looking forward to taking you and Aunt Edith to dinner tonight, but around 4:00, a rock was thrown off a pedestrian bridge near the Koko Marina Center in Hawaii Kai."

Now it was my turn to sigh.

"The rock hit a Toyota pickup traveling on Highway 72. Fortunately the driver wasn't hurt."

"Well, that's a blessing."

"Yes, the first point of impact was on the roof of the cab, then the guy told us that it hit the windshield. There was a hole about the size of a tennis ball knocked out of it."

"I'll bet it scared the daylights out of him," I said. "I jump a mile when a little bug hits mine."

"No doubt it was a shock. It's a miracle the rock didn't come right on through the glass. The guy said it bounced off the windshield, onto the hood, then off onto the side of the road." He chuckled. "He told Marshall and me that he'd complained to his wife this morning that he didn't have time for their usual ten-minute devotion. After what happened today, he said he'll never complain *or* leave for work again before they've finished morning prayers."

"Sounds like he's a believer in divine protection now," I said.

"Sometimes it takes a jolt to wake us up. Anyway, the team and I are going to have to work late questioning some more witnesses here, so I can't make dinner."

"Well, I hate it for you, but I understand." A rumble of thunder shook the window behind me. "Try not to get wet."

"I hear you. Talk to you later."

I picked up my purse and headed home. I barely made it into the apartment building foyer when the sky seemed to explode. Torrential rain fell for over an hour. According to the newscast on television, flooding was being reported in many areas on the island. High waves had driven some residents living near Eva Beach inland. Weather forecasters were encouraging viewers to stay tuned for updated reports.

The next morning the skies looked like lead. The wind had howled all night and deposited leaves and debris onto the lanai. Aunt Edith was

Justice in Paradise

sitting out there trying to read the latest *Good Housekeeping* magazine that she brought with her. The pups were sleeping at her feet.

I was sitting at the dining room table doing next week's lesson plans for school. Simon was coming for us at 10:30 a.m., and we were going to Queen Emma's Palace. After that we were going to take a drive on the other side of the island. I looked out the window and hoped it didn't rain us out.

"Whew, that wind is something!" Aunt Edith said as she walked inside. The puppies scampered in, and then she pulled the sliding-glass door closed. "The pages of my magazine are getting torn." She flipped on the lamp that was sitting on the end table next to the couch. "Maybe in here I can sit and finish this article in peace."

"Yes, debris peppering my bedroom window kept waking me up last night," I said. "I hope Michael and Richard are battening down the hatches."

"Oh, I'm sure the boys are fine," Aunt Edith said. She glanced back down at her magazine. "Did you know that the birthday for the 'Happy Birthday' song is coming up? On June 27, 1859, 'Happy Birthday' was sung for the first time."

"No, I didn't know that."

"It says here that two Louisville sisters, who were both teachers, came up with the four-line ditty. Mildred was an authority on Negro spirituals and composed the melody. Her sister, Patty, who was a professor at Columbia University, wrote the lyrics."

"That's nice," I said, only half listening to her. *Kids always enjoy learning about sea life,* I thought. I made a note in the margin of my plan book to go to the school library first thing on Monday morning to check out books for the unit.

"My mother, your great-grandma Jennie's birthday was on June 22," Aunt Edith said. "She was tickled when Maggie was born the same day."

At the mention of my mother's name, I snapped to attention. "Oh no! I forgot all about Mom's birthday." I looked at the calendar at the top of my lesson plan book. June 22 was next Wednesday.

There wouldn't be time to shop for a gift and mail it to her before then. Since she owned Paradise Petals, the busiest flower shop and

61

nursery in the three-county area around Paradise, sending a bouquet or plant was never an option for a gift. I looked at the clock on the living room wall and saw that it was 9:30. With the five-hour time difference, it would be 2:30 in Paradise. Since my older brother, Jamie, didn't usually work on Saturday, there was a chance I'd catch him at home.

I walked over to Tommy's recliner and picked up the phone. "Thanks for reminding me about Mom's birthday, Aunt Edith. I'm going to see if Jamie will shop for me."

On the third ring, my six-year-old niece, Brittany, picked up the phone.

"Hello, Kane residence," Brittany said.

"Hi, punkin. What are you up to today?"

"Hi, Aunt Allie! I'm helping Daddy babysit Ryan while Mommy is in the shower. But it's not easy."

I had no doubt about that. My twenty-month-old niece, Ryan, could be a handful even when two or three adults were trying to watch her. "What are you doing to keep her busy?"

She sighed. "We've been playing with the zoo you bought me a couple of Christmases ago. So far so good."

The Duplo block zoo set had hook-together red, yellow, and green blocks. The plastic wild animals were molded with slats on the bottom to fit onto the blocks. I knew it had served Brittany well.

I heard a loud crash in the background. "Uh oh," Brittany said. "Ryan just ran into my bedroom, so I'd better go see what she's into."

The sooner the better, I thought. "Okay, sweetie. I'll talk to you later."

"Daddy, Aunt Allie's on the phone," she yelled. The telephone receiver clunked against the floor, and I heard Brittany's fleeing footsteps.

"Hey, you," Jamie said.

"Hey, yourself. It sounds like Ryan is exploring again."

"That girl is a menace. Yesterday she wandered into Brittany's room and rubbed red finger paint on her carpet."

"Oh no! Were you able to get it out?" I knew that the bedrooms had just recently been recarpeted.

"Not a chance," Jamie said. "Nicole and I have tried every kind of cleaner made, and though it's faded a bit, the pink on beige is pretty much set."

"Gosh, I'm sorry to hear that."

"Yeah, we have two choices to hide the damage. We can move the bed into the center of the doorway to cover the spot."

"I don't think that's an option," I said, smiling.

"No, we really don't want to have to climb over the headboard and mattress every time we enter the room. The other choice is to cut out the ruined area and then try to sew in another piece of carpet." I heard him sigh. "I don't suppose I could slip that kid into a box and send her to you in Hawaii, could I?"

I started laughing. "Well, I'd love to see her, but I don't think that's a solution. Besides, Mom and Dad would be unhappy with her gone." Our parents couldn't make it more than a few days at a time without having their granddaughters for an overnight visit. "Speaking of Mom, you know her birthday's coming up next week, don't you?"

"Already on top of it," he said.

"Really?" Jamie often forgot birthdays and anniversaries. It dawned on me that he must have had a reminder. "Nicole told you, didn't she?"

He sighed. "Got me figured out, don't you?"

"Always," I said, giggling. "I was hoping we could go in together on something. Jeff might want to contribute too." Jeff was our single, twenty-year-old brother.

"Well, Nicole suggested sending Mom and Dad to Branson for a weekend getaway. If you and Jeff want to contribute, they could stay an extra night and maybe see an additional show."

"I'm in," I said, "and I'll bet Jeff will be too. Since he's on a limited budget, I'll pay for the motel room for all three nights, if you guys want to take care of show tickets and meals."

"I'll call him later tonight," Jamie said. I heard a door slam and Brittany hollering for her daddy. "I've got to go. Ryan just ran into the bathroom. If I don't get in there, she's liable to flush down half a roll of toilet paper and flood the bathroom again like she did a few days ago."

"Okay. I'll talk to you later. Love you."

"Love you too. Tell Simon I said hi."

"Will do." As I was about to hang up, I heard him yelling Ryan's name. I smiled and shook my head.

"Is Jamie's family doing okay?" Aunt Edith asked. She put her magazine down on the end table.

"Yes, and we settled what to do for Mom's birthday. We're sending her and Dad to Branson for three days."

"Oh, that's nice. They'll love that." She stood up. "I'm going to go take a shower and get ready."

I glanced at the clock. Simon would be arriving in less than an hour. "I guess I'd better do the same."

Right on time, Simon was there to pick us up. We headed east on H-1 to the Pali Highway. The Queen Emma Summer Palace was on the east side of the road and nearly hidden by tall trees and large shrubs.

"Here we are, ladies," Simon said. He pulled into the small parking lot and stopped.

Aunt Edith gazed at the white wooden structure. "Isn't that pretty?" she said.

"The natives of Hawaii are proud of it," Simon said. He walked around the front of the Jeep and helped Aunt Edith out. "It was built in 1848 by a man named John Lewis. The frame and siding were shipped here from Boston."

"My, my," Aunt Edith said. "So was this guy Lewis part of the monarchy?" We all started walking toward the front of the palace. I knew that Aunt Edith was as fascinated as I was when it came to the former kings and queens.

"No, John Lewis was part-Hawaiian and a businessman here, but not royalty. A couple of years after the palace was completed, he sold it and the sixty-five acres surrounding it to Queen Emma's uncle, John Young, for six thousand dollars. The uncle was a friend and advisor of

Kamehameha the Great and didn't have any children, so he left it to her when he died."

We climbed the front steps to the porch. I was admiring the tall, white columns. I nearly bumped into Simon when I turned around to follow them inside.

The ornate front door was standing open. Inside the front hall, a young woman was sitting at a small desk. "Aloha," she said. She stood up. "Welcome to Queen Emma's Summer Palace."

"Aloha," we all replied.

Simon paid our admission fee, and then we all signed the guest book.

"I'm Salena, and I'll be your guide today," the woman said, handing each of us a brochure. She looked at Simon. "I heard you telling these ladies some things about the estate. Feel free to interject any comments or ask questions during the tour."

"Simon has been living here all his life," Aunt Edith told her. "If he wasn't so busy fighting crime and keeping the streets safe on this island, he'd make a good hand for you here."

I smiled at Simon and saw him blush. "Thanks, Aunt Edith," he said. The guide was grinning at him.

Where we stood in the entry hall, Salena told us about the gold davenport and other various items there. She said that the tall feather standards standing in the corner were used by the ruling class as fans and often during celebrations as well. There was a royal coat of arms over the front door inscribed with the Hawaiian motto. Salena said that in English it meant "The life of the land is perpetuated in righteousness."

Emma had married royalty. She and Alexander Liholiho Kamehameha IV, King Kamehameha the Great's great-grandson, married in 1856. They only had one child, Albert Edward, and he died when he was only four years old of a sudden illness. The cradle he used and his porcelain bathtub, a gift from a Chinese emperor, were in the front bedroom. In the back bedroom, Queen Emma's bed, made from koa wood, stood beside Prince Albert Edward's four-poster crib. A cabinet nearby held the prince's red fireman's jacket, silver cup, and other personal effects. My heart ached for the queen who had lost her child at such an early age. It made me want to hug my two nieces.

"If you'll come this way, you'll see Queen Emma's grand piano and some other pieces of furniture the family used," the guide said.

We followed her into the parlor. A splendid baby grand piano was off to one side, and a large dining table and chairs made from koa wood sat in the middle of the room. A china hutch and other pieces made the room feel cozy. I roamed across the room toward the piano.

"Allie is a talented musician," Simon said. "Since the queen also played the piano, I'm sure that she and Allie would have enjoyed each other's company."

The guide smiled at me. "You're welcome to play something, if you like."

I couldn't resist the invitation. I sat down on the cushioned bench and began playing my favorite classical piece, "Moonlight Sonata," by Ludwig van Beethoven. The song was written in 1801 but wasn't copyrighted until much later. Still I wondered if it might be possible that Queen Emma had also played it on this piano. I closed my eyes and became one with the rich, mellow tones coming from the instrument.

When I finished playing, the room was silent. I opened my eyes and saw that Aunt Edith and Salena looked as peaceful as I felt. I saw a look of appreciation and pride in Simon's eyes. It made me feel wonderful.

We concluded the tour of the house in the Edinburgh Room. A red recliner used by King Kamehameha IV sat in the middle of it. A Victorian settee covered in green velvet sat near the center hall door. It was believed to have been a gift from the Duke of Edinburgh.

"Thanks for a great tour," Aunt Edith told the guide. "I sure enjoyed it."

"I did too," I said. Simon agreed.

"You're welcome to walk around outside before you leave," Salena said. "There are a variety of unusual trees and flowers on the grounds."

"Thank you; we will," Simon said. He led us past the small gift shop around to the front of the palace.

The lush grounds were well cared for. Simon pointed out some of the trees and plants mentioned in the brochure. Many were not only beautiful but useful too. The Hawaiian state tree, the *kukui*, or candlenut tree, provided a black dye. The oily kernels were burned to create light, and the nutmeat was used for medicinal purposes. The dark brown shells were polished and strung to make necklaces.

"I assume that since this is called the 'summer palace,' the royal family lived somewhere else on the island the rest of the time," I said to Simon.

He nodded and motioned toward the highway and buildings beyond. "It's hard to imagine with all the traffic, houses, and businesses around here now, but this was once just trees and fields as far as the eye could see." He turned and pointed toward the mountains behind us. "It was cooler here during the summer months. Queen Emma lived here until she passed away in 1885."

Aunt Edith had pulled a pocket-sized Hawaiian dictionary from her purse. I heard her murmur to herself, "*kukui*: lamp, light, torch."

"Is anybody ready for lunch?" Simon asked.

"I'm game," I said.

"Me too," Aunt Edith replied.

"Mr. Omura's deli is not too far from here," Simon said as he helped Aunt Edith into the backseat of the Jeep.

"He has wonderful food, Aunt Edith," I said. I climbed into the front passenger seat.

"Well, I'd like to try some real island food," she said. "Does he have any of that?"

Simon and I looked at each other and grinned. Since I had been on Oahu, we both had enjoyed several meals from Mr. Omura's deli. It offered some of the finest cuisine around.

"I think you'll find some things you like," I said to her. I looked at Simon. "We're ready when you are."

❊   ❊   ❊

The deli is a favorite stop for many. Working people crowd the small place from 10:30 to 2:00 on weekdays. There's often a full house for dinner on weeknights, and on Saturdays it's even busier. I guess people who work too far away or are busy through the week stop by on weekends.

When we walked inside, we squeezed our way into one of the two lines of people waiting their turn at the counter. Mr. Omura and Berta, his red-haired helper, were greeting customers and dishing up food as quickly as they could.

Aunt Edith sniffed the air and smiled. "Boy, oh howdy, I smell teriyaki, ginger, and something else good that I can't put my finger on." She lifted her head higher and sniffed again. I caught Mr. Omura's eye and waved. He smiled and waved back at me.

He motioned toward a new helper behind the counter to come over and take his place. I was surprised to see that it was Sammy Cho. Sammy and I had first met when I came to interview for the summer school position. He had had his share of run-ins with the law but was now working two part-time jobs and trying to better himself. He waved at us.

Mr. Omura made his way through the crowd to where we were standing. "Simon, Miss Allie," he said with a smile. He shook Simon's hand.

"It's good to see you, Mr. Omura," I said. "This is my great-aunt, Edith Patterson. She's here visiting for a few days."

The man turned and stretched out his hand to her. "Welcome to the Islands, Ms. Patterson," he said.

She shook his hand. "Oh, call me Edith. It's great to be here." She sniffed the air again. "Am I smelling tarragon, or is that oregano, Mr. Omura?"

He grinned. "Please call me Luu. In which dish, Edith? There are many fine choices today."

The line was moving closer to the counter, and I was trying to decide whether I wanted the crab salad or the caldereta, a dish made with goat meat and spicy vegetables. I had first tried some at Simon's grandparents' house and had fallen in love with it. Simon was busy checking out the menu too.

Aunt Edith reached for Mr. Omura's hand and started leading him to the counter. Berta had been keeping a close eye on the two ever since their conversation had begun. She was a plus-sized woman who would make three of Aunt Edith. She didn't seem too happy to see my aunt holding her boss's hand.

When they reached the case filled with different salads, soups, and sandwiches, Aunt Edith started pointing at first one dish, then another. Both she and Mr. Omura were talking with their hands as well as their mouths.

When Simon and I reached the counter, Aunt Edith was giving Mr. Omura an earful about how she rolls catfish and crappie in cornmeal and then fries it to a golden brown. He was nodding his head but arguing that you couldn't beat grilled or poached ono or moi, which were both delicate white fishes with a flaky flesh.

Aunt Edith looked around at the people still coming into the small deli. "Well, I can tell by this crowd that you must be a fine chef," she said to him. "But I'll make you a deal."

Oh no, I thought.

She put her hands on her hips, and I knew from past experience that trouble was brewing.

Mr. Omura continued grinning at her. "And what kind of deal are we talking about, Edith?"

"I'll come in here on Monday and sell more fried ono, or any other kind of fish you choose, than you will the grilled or poached variety." She had a triumphant look on her face.

"Well, I'll take that bet," he said. He glanced toward the counter. "Berta will be gone on Monday, and I can use the extra help. We start cooking lunch at 9:30 each morning."

I felt like I needed to intercede somehow but was at a loss. I looked at Simon. He just shrugged and grinned. I looked at Aunt Edith and said the first thing I could think of. "I thought you and Pinky DeLeaf were going to get together on Monday?" *And that's a better solution, Allie?* I gave myself a mental head slap.

"Oh, that's right," she said. She looked at Mr. Omura. "I'll tell you what. I'll call Pinky tonight and tell him we'll have to ride Monday afternoon instead of that morning."

Since I would already be at school, how she was going to get to the deli had yet to be resolved. She looked at Simon. I guess he took the hint.

"Would you like me to pick you up and bring you here Monday morning, Aunt Edith?" he said. Aunt Edith had a way of getting people to do what she needed.

"Why, thank you, Simon. I'd appreciate that." She turned and looked at Mr. Omura. "Luu, you can expect me here by 9:30 sharp on Monday."

Mr. Omura nodded his head. The twinkle I saw in his eye told me that he was taking this fish-cooking challenge seriously, and he didn't intend for Aunt Edith to win.

"Now that we have that settled, how about lunch?" Simon said.

We drove around the North Shore of the island. When we passed the Polynesian Cultural Center, I told Aunt Edith about some of the things Simon and I had seen there in March. Several miles on up the road, Simon stopped for gasoline at a little Mom-and-Pop grocery store/gas station. I bought us all a can of pop.

A little way down the road, he pulled into a crowded beach park. More than a hundred people of all ages were in the water snorkeling, swimming, and surfing. Many more sunbathers were making good use of the sandy beaches.

"This is Ehukai Beach," Simon said. He pointed toward the water. "In the winter, Vans Triple Crown, the world's greatest surfing competition, is held here."

"So this is the location of the Banzai Pipeline?" Aunt Edith said. She gazed out at the royal blue water.

I looked at her in surprise.

"I did some homework before coming here, Allie," she said. "I thought I might learn to surf, so I wanted to find the best beach to do it."

Simon smiled at her. "Well, it looks tame out there now, Aunt Edith. But when the tubular waves start rolling in, only the most experienced surfers try them. The waves are steep and powerful. Many surfers have wiped out on the Banzai Pipeline, and some didn't live to tell about it."

We watched the surfers a while longer then headed back to the Jeep. Simon drove near Haleiwa then headed south through the center of the island. It was a great afternoon.

He dropped Aunt Edith and me off at the apartment around four. When we walked in the door, only Precious was there to meet us. Rowdy was nowhere around.

"How did you get out of the kitchen, sweetie?" I leaned down to pat her head then looked over the partition I had placed in front of the kitchen door. "And where's your brother?" I was starting to get an uneasy feeling in my stomach.

"Probably hiding under the bed," Aunt Edith said. "You'd better take a look at this."

My heart sank to my knees when I walked into the living room. A gorgeous arrangement containing four feet tall exotic feathers that Traci kept just inside the patio door was lying in ruins all over the carpet. Silk berries and tropical flowers that once filled the brass pot were strewn from the door to the couch.

"Rowdy!" I yelled. Precious had already skittered under the dining room table in anticipation of the showdown that was about to occur. "Rowdy!"

I marched down the hall and looked under my bed. No dog. I glanced into the closet but knew from past experience that it was a waste of time. Whenever Rowdy got into mischief, he always hid under things. I walked on down the hall toward Traci and Tommy's bedroom. I knelt beside their bed. "Boy, are you in trouble, mister!" I said as I looked under it. Still no dog.

Hmmm. I was running out of low furniture to check under. Just then, I heard a whine followed by some scratching sounds. "Rowdy?" I said. The whining grew louder, and I realized it was coming from the connecting bathroom.

I stood up and walked to the door. "Rowdy? Where are you, boy?" The whining was muffled. I looked behind the toilet; no sign of him.

"Okay, pup, you're going to have to give me some help here." He started barking. In the small bathroom, there weren't many hiding places, but he had found a unique one. I opened the cabinet door beneath the sink. There he was.

"Did you find him?" Aunt Edith said, walking up behind me. Precious was at her heels.

"Yes, but I don't have a clue how he got in there." I stooped down for a closer look. "And I'm not sure I can get him out."

Rowdy's muzzle was wedged between the sink drain pipe and the U-shaped trap. It was rigged differently than anything I had ever seen. Within the confined area, the plumber had to perform some extra twists and turns to get everything to fit right.

I stood back up. Rowdy started howling. I guess he thought I intended to leave him in that mess. "Don't worry, boy. I'm just trying to figure out what to do."

"I guess I forgot to close the cabinet door after I got ready in here this morning," Aunt Edith said. "I was looking for another roll of toilet tissue in there."

I sighed. "It's not your fault. Rowdy knew he'd be in trouble about the mess he made, so he started looking for a hiding place." I was stumped. "I guess I'll go call the super and see if he can come up and help us."

"Before you do that, let me have a look," Aunt Edith said. I moved closer to the shower stall. She knelt down and peered under the sink. "You know, I saw a pair of expansion pliers along with some other tools in the pantry. I bet I can take off the trap and get Rowdy out of here."

My head was starting to pound. Was I ready to let my aunt start taking apart the plumbing in my best friend's bathroom? It was Saturday afternoon, and I knew there was a good chance the super wouldn't be available to help. Rowdy started whimpering. It was possible he was in pain.

"I know you're pretty good with chainsaws, heavy equipment, and have other skills, but have you ever done anything like this before?" I asked her, pointing toward the sink.

She stood back up. "Oh sure. I've taken several self-help classes down at the Senior Citizens Center. One of them was in basic plumbing."

I smiled. "I wish I had known that. A week before I came for summer school, my bathroom sink at the duplex got clogged with hair and gunk. I tried commercial-strength drain cleaner, but it didn't solve the problem. I drug Doug over and made him tear it apart and clean it out." I smiled again. "It took him over two hours, and he wasn't happy about it."

"Well, it's a pretty simple procedure. If you'll go get the pliers for me, I'll get started."

I hurried to the kitchen with Precious hot on my heels. I found the expansion pliers then grabbed a stew pot from the storage cabinet. I knew there was bound to be water and goo in the trap, and I hoped that the bulk of the mess would land in the pot.

"Here are the pliers," I said when I returned.

She had laid a bath towel on the tile next to the vanity and was kneeling on it. "My knees aren't what they used to be," she said, motioning toward the towel. "Oh good. I'm glad you brought the pot too."

She took the items from me then positioned the stew pot beneath the trap. With the pliers, she began unscrewing the ring that connected it to the drainpipe. Once the ring was free, she carefully pulled the curved trap off the pipe. Rowdy's head was still caught, but when she moved the trap away from the drainpipe, he was able to move his head.

"Okay, Rowdy," Aunt Edith said. "Just give me a second to dump this trap, and then you're a free dog."

Though not too happy about the delay, he did what she said. Within a few seconds, the water was in the pot, the pot was shoved over to the side, and Rowdy was free.

He came bounding toward me. I bent down and scooped him into my arms. "I hope you learned a lesson from all of this," I said. He was licking my face. I gently took his muzzle in my hand. "You were lucky we had Aunt Edith here to bail you out, or you might have had a long night under the sink."

I could tell he wasn't a bit worried that I would have left him under there. We had been through enough scrapes together that he knew he had his bluff in on me.

"Well, that's that," Aunt Edith said. "Can you give me a hand up, Allie?"

"Sure thing." I stretched my hand toward her and pulled her to her feet. I glanced under the sink. The pipes were reconnected, and aside from a few wet spots on the floor of the vanity shelf, it looked as good as new.

"You're a real pro at this," I said. I took the pot of yucky water from her. "I'll go get rid of this in the bathtub."

I set Rowdy down on the floor. "You stay with me," I said to him.

We all headed toward the living room. I stopped in the other bathroom long enough to dump the pan of water. After that, I led Rowdy back to the scene of his crime in the living room. Aunt Edith was putting the feathers and other items back into the brass pot. I leaned down to help her. Just then, the phone rang.

"Hello?" I said.

"Aloha," Traci said. "How are things with you, Aunt Edith, and the pups in paradise?"

"Hey, it's good to hear from you," I said. I glanced at the mess on the floor. "But it's probably good that you're not here at this very moment. Aunt Edith, Precious, and I are fine, but Rowdy is in deep trouble right now."

"Let me guess," she said. "Rowdy is making himself at home in our apartment."

I smiled. "In every sense of the word."

I relayed how the pups got out of the kitchen while Aunt Edith and I were out sightseeing and what a plumbing pro Aunt Edith turned out to be.

I looked at the drooping arrangement now back in its pot by the door. "I'll pick up some new feathers and flowers for you before we leave here," I said.

"You certainly will not," Traci said. "I never have liked that arrangement. The only reason it's still there is because one of Tommy's aunts gave it to us for a wedding present. I felt like I needed to display it. This will give me a chance to get something new." She paused. "Besides, when the baby starts crawling, I was going to have to do something with it anyway. If she likes to eat as much as her daddy does, the berries in that arrangement would be too tempting."

I realized she had said "her" daddy. "So when did you find out your baby is a girl? You saw the doctor several times before you left here but didn't say anything about knowing if it was a boy or girl." Traci had had some mild cramps off and on since I had been in Hawaii.

"Well, I don't know for sure, but I have a feeling it is. My mom is convinced that because I'm carrying the baby high, it's bound to be a girl. And face it, girls run on both sides of the family, so that adds to the probability too." Traci had two older sisters and Tommy had three.

"I assume your parents were tickled to see you and that you're having a great time back home," I said.

"It's wonderful! Mom is pampering me, and I'm eating that up. Tommy and Dad went fishing with your Grandad and Uncle Clarence yesterday and caught a mess of crappie. Mom fried it for supper last night, and I ate three fish all by myself!"

I giggled. "If you're not careful, you're going to gain a bunch of weight eating your mom's good cooking for three weeks."

"Yes, but it's *so* good! I forgot how great it is to be waited on. She and I met Kristin and Marilyn for lunch at the Pink Cottage today. That caramel nut pie was to die for!" Kristin's mom, Marilyn, and Traci's mother had been friends for years.

I smiled. Traci seemed so content and happy being back in Paradise. Though I knew she loved her home here in Hawaii, it was always a treat for her to get back to her Okie roots.

She said she had run into Frankie and that the "Tailgate Bandit," as he was being called by everyone in town, was giving the officers fits. When Traci started yawning, I told her she needed to hang up and get to bed. It was almost 11:00 in Paradise.

"It's been good talking with you," she said.

"For me too," I said. "Enjoy every minute of your vacation."

"Believe me, I will."

I had no doubt that she would.

CHAPTER 5

The sun shining through my bedroom window the next morning woke me. I turned to look at the clock on the nightstand and was relieved that it was only 7:15. I could go back to sleep for another hour before I had to get up to get ready for church.

While plumping my pillow, I heard Aunt Edith talking in the other room. I figured she was either speaking to the dachshunds or was on the phone to someone back home.

I turned over and adjusted my covers but couldn't get comfortable. I had always had trouble sleeping late, even when I had the chance. While in high school, Traci and my other friends wouldn't get up until noon on Saturday. I was lucky to sleep past 8:30.

I heard Aunt Edith say something, and then Rowdy barked twice. Precious bounded onto my bed and began licking my hand that was lying on top of the blanket.

"Are you trying to get me up, little missy?" I said. I started rubbing her head. The sound of my voice brought Rowdy running into the room. He jumped onto my leg then made his way past my stomach to my chest. I could feel his breath on my face. I knew he wouldn't budge until I opened my eyes and acknowledged him.

"You're gaining weight," I told him. I nudged him off me. "Okay, you two, I'm up."

They bounded off the bed as I reached for my robe lying on the bedspread. Aunt Edith was talking on the phone when I walked into the living room.

"It's a disgrace, that's what it is," she said to the person on the other end. She wiggled her fingers at me. I mouthed a "good morning" to her.

"When I get back from my vacation, if Frankie and his squad haven't found it, I'll help you search." From the tone of her voice and the way she was curling and uncurling a strand of her hair, I could tell she was upset.

She sighed. "I know he is," she said. The curl was getting a brief reprieve from her tormenting fingers. The person on the other end must have been saying something to calm her down. "I'm enjoying myself. Allie and I had a great time yesterday." She proceeded to tell the person a little about Queen Emma's Palace and other things we had seen.

I walked into the kitchen and poured myself a glass of orange juice. A box from the bakery in Pearlridge Center was sitting on the counter by the stove. I lifted the lid then helped myself to a blueberry Danish I found inside. Rowdy was sitting on my foot whimpering. I saw that the dogs' food dishes were empty, but their water bowls were brimming with fresh water.

"Aunt Edith already fed you breakfast, little man," I told him. Though his tummy was getting too round, I couldn't resist his pitiful look. "Okay, just a nibble." I pulled the corner off the roll and leaned over to give it to him. He snatched it from my fingers and didn't drop a crumb.

"Okay, have a good afternoon, and I'll talk to you later," Aunt Edith said. She hung up the phone and looked at me. "That was Clarence. Oh good, you found the Danish."

"Yes, and it's yummy." I popped a blueberry-covered piece into my mouth. "You must have taken a walk this morning."

"I got up about six." She stood up. "The sun was just coming up. The pups and I walked a lap around the outside of the shopping center, and then we went inside to finish up."

Rowdy had followed me into the living room and wasn't taking his eyes off my roll. I looked down at him. "Forget it," I told him. "You've had a taste already."

Aunt Edith reached down and patted his head. "He and Precious ate their food in about two minutes, so I gave them a cherry Danish to split for dessert."

I shook my head. "You're going to spoil them more than they already are."

"I know," she said. "I guess I'm just missing Samson." Samson was a tomcat that Aunt Edith had owned since I was in high school. He was one of the many kittens that had been born to Sassy, the old barn cat that Nana Kane had had for almost ten years.

"What's going on with Uncle Clarence?" I licked some filling off my fingers then took a swig of orange juice.

"His tailgate was stolen last night."

Uh oh. Uncle Clarence's 1984 red Dodge pickup was like a friend to him. Over the years, it had experienced lots of mishaps. There were rusted dents and scrapes that had been there since I was kid. One side mirror had a big piece of gray duct tape across it, and the running board on the driver's side had rusty baling wire holding it on. The afghan that Gramma gave him when I was in the sixth grade still covered the tattered seat.

"Grandpa's was stolen, and now Uncle Clarence's? I wouldn't want to be in Frankie's shoes when they have dinner today at the Circle K."

"Well, Clarence is upset, that's for sure," Aunt Edith said. She had refilled her coffee cup and was walking back in from the kitchen. "And I don't blame him. But he said he felt better since he came in from church. The pastor spoke this morning out of Psalms 89 about justice and judgment belonging to God. It reminded Clarence that the Lord watches out for His children. We need to do what we can, then let God do the rest. What goes around comes around."

I nodded. "But the tough part is sitting patiently waiting for God to do the rest."

"You said it."

We met Simon at church in Kaneohe. Traci and Tommy had been attending services in the small, white building since they had moved to the island. I had felt right at home there too. The furnishings were simple, and no air conditioning was needed because the windward breezes were often blowing through the slatted windows. Since Simon, Traci, and Tommy had become friends too, he attended regularly now. I really liked the music director and had become acquainted with others my age.

I introduced Aunt Edith to Pastor Wells and to a couple of older ladies I'd met. She hit it off with them right away. The ladies were widows about Aunt Edith's age. As they walked together toward the seniors' Sunday school class, they were chatting away. Simon and I went into the young adults' class.

The lesson was about standing strong and trusting God through adversity. Since I often found myself needing help in that area, I welcomed the refresher course. The scripture text was from Acts 16. I had taught a simpler version of the lesson to the children in my Sunday school class back in Paradise.

It talked about Paul and Silas traveling to various cities in Greece. In one place, a girl possessed with an evil spirit followed them around and kept disrupting their services. After a few days, Paul became fed up with her actions and cast out the spirit. However, the men who had been profiting from her fortune-telling ability weren't about to let Paul get away with it. Even though it was the right thing for him to do, when you start messing with someone's livelihood, you're likely to get into trouble. That's what happened to Paul and Silas. The men took them to the authorities, who had them beaten and then thrown into jail.

Simon leaned over and whispered, "The jails back then were dark, damp dungeons. Prisoners today get a lot better treatment than Paul and Silas did, but they still gripe about every little thing."

I looked at him and nodded. "If the authorities stuck them in a filthy hole like they used in those days, I bet they'd keep their mouths shut when they got back to the nice, clean cells they're staying in now."

He grinned at me. "I bet you're right."

Despite the raw state of their bodies and the despairing conditions in the prison cells, at midnight Paul and Silas started praying and singing. I liked to think about them singing one of my favorite choruses, "What a Mighty God We Serve," or maybe, "Awesome God." Whatever they sang did the trick. An earthquake resulted, all the cell doors burst open, and everyone there, even the jailer and his family, were saved.

Our teacher's wife was sitting beside me. "I became upset when the electricity went off Friday night," she whispered to me. "The storm knocked it out for eight hours. I was too worried about things spoiling in the fridge to even fall asleep."

I cocked my head toward her. "We're all pretty spoiled in this day and time, aren't we?"

She smiled and nodded her head.

After class was dismissed, Simon and I joined Aunt Edith in the sanctuary for the worship service. She told us she had enjoyed her class. When the main service was over, the three of us followed the crowd to the back. The minister and his wife were at the door shaking hands with everyone as they left.

"Wonderful sermon, Pastor Wells," Aunt Edith said as she shook his hand. "You're a bit younger than our minister back home, but I like your style." She winked at him.

The pastor smiled at her. "I'm glad you joined us today, Ms. Patterson. I hope you'll come back often while you're visiting the island." He nodded toward Simon and me. "We've become attached to your niece and Simon. They're great people."

She beamed. "Yes, they are, and they're good for each other."

I started blushing. Simon was holding my hand. He gave it a squeeze.

Aunt Edith took a step closer to the minister. He was at least a foot taller than she was, so she motioned for him to lean down. "They might be getting married some day. Don't you think they'd have pretty babies?"

Several folks standing near us were smiling. I felt like crawling beneath the nearest pew. Simon was nodding his head. I elbowed him in the ribs.

The pastor grinned. "I believe they would. And you know, we have a wonderful nursery and children's department here at the church."

Aunt Edith looked at him and nodded. "I get your drift, Pastor. You and I are on the same wavelength."

I reached out and took her elbow. "Come on, Aunt Edith. These other people are waiting to shake his hand too." I turned her toward the steps leading from the church. "Great message today, Pastor," I murmured as I led her down the steps. Simon shook the minister's hand then followed us to the car.

Since we were going to take Simon's Jeep to Sea Life Park, he followed us back to the apartment. While Aunt Edith and I changed out of our church clothes into more comfortable things, Simon put on shorts and a T-shirt that he had carried in from his car. When everyone was ready, we drove over to the Pearlridge Center food court for lunch then headed to the park.

"It looks like we're going to have some company there today," I said. The two-lane road to the aquarium was crowded with buses, cars, and motorcycles.

"Sea Life Park is always busy," Simon replied. "They're constantly adding new exhibits and improving on the old ones, so it's one of the top attractions on Oahu." He turned the Jeep into the parking lot and pulled into an empty space. "Is everybody ready for a fun-filled day?"

"You betcha," Aunt Edith said.

"Me too," I said. I climbed out of the car. Simon gave Aunt Edith a hand out of the backseat.

We all started walking toward the main entrance. Aunt Edith pulled her wallet from her purse. "I'm paying for everything we do today, and I don't want an argument from either of you about it."

"That's kind of you, but since I'm a government employee, I get an annual pass," Simon said. "I don't have to pay to get in."

We reached the ticket window. "That may be so, Simon," she said, "but I'd like to treat us to that fancy luau they're having here tonight." She pulled several travelers checks from her wallet and handed them to the person sitting in the booth. "Kristin went online and printed off some Oahu tourist attraction brochures for me the other day, and Sea Life Park was one of them." The lady in the booth handed her some change and three park maps. "Since you guys have been kind enough to let me tag along with you, the least I can do is pick up the tab."

"We want you with us," I said to her. "Don't we, Simon?"

He nodded. "You brighten my day, Aunt Edith. You always have."

"Well, that's sweet of both of you to say, but I know what it's like to have an old fogie hanging around when you'd like to be alone with your sweetheart." She stuffed her wallet back into her purse. "That's why Daisy, Clarence, and I keep our distance from each other when one of us has a date." She handed each of us a map. I glanced at it and saw that times for the shows, exhibits, and tours were listed on the back.

Simon had been to Sea Life Park many times and rarely glanced at his map. He proved to be a great guide. We began with the Hawaiian reef tank, which was a 300,000-gallon aquarium filled with over two thousand specimens. Among the mix were sharks, rays, moray eels, and many types of fish. A short distance away was the sea turtle lagoon, and a show was about to start. We found a spot to stand among the hundred or so other people waiting.

"Several thousand Hawaiian green sea turtles, or *honu*, have been hatched here in the park then released into the wild," Simon told us while we waited. "Two of the captive-bred turtles, Jia and Johnson, were recently let go. Satellites have tracked them. You can go online and see the tracking maps for them, as well as the other four adult turtles that were released from here."

"That's cool," I said. "I bet my students would love to find out more about that."

Simon nodded. "Just go online to the Sea Life Park Web site, then click on the 'turtle tracking maps' icon."

A sea-turtle expert gave a presentation and demonstrated the feeding procedures. The more I learned, the more I was sure that my students would love finding out more about the endangered species.

Next we headed to the Hawaiian Ocean Theater. We had just settled into our seats when the dolphin performance began.

"Aren't they beauties?" Aunt Edith said, gazing at the sleek animals sliding through the water.

"And intelligent," I said. "Did you see how synchronized that dance was? They did a far better job than most humans would."

Simon leaned toward me. "They offer dolphin swim adventures here," he whispered. "Care to take a dip?"

I looked at him and grinned. "Not on your life," I whispered back. "I'll just enjoy them from afar, thank you."

Aunt Edith leaned across me. "Simon, did you say that they let people swim with the dolphins?"

Simon cleared his throat. "Well, they do, but it's pretty expensive, and you have to provide your own swimsuit and towels."

Aunt Edith started digging around inside her purse. She pulled out a royal blue one-piece bathing suit and a plastic bathing cap. "Well, I'm half prepared," she said. She looked at some of the staff working by the pool. "I bet I could slip a ten-spot to one of those trainers down there and sweet talk him into finding me a towel." She proceeded to pull a ten-dollar bill from her wallet.

Simon must have discerned that I was a bit uneasy. "You know, they have a dolphin encounter that isn't quite as interactive, but still fun, about fifty bucks cheaper, and I bet you'd love it."

She frowned. "What do you get to do?"

My breathing slowed down a bit.

He pointed to the massive tank. "You sit on that platform down there where the girl with the long braid is sitting now." We both followed the direction of this hand. "The dolphins come right up to the platform, and you can stroke them, pat their noses, that type of thing.

Also, with a trained professional, you can get into the water and actually swim with the animal."

Her frown changed to a smile. "I like that idea," she said. For a couple of minutes, she watched the girl work. "The money is no big deal, because after all, you can't take it with you."

I saw an opening to push her toward this new idea. "But fifty dollars is fifty dollars. It would probably pay for all the gasoline you would use in the motorcycle you're renting tomorrow."

She thought about that for a moment then started nodding her head. "You're right, Allie." She looked at Simon. "Now, where do I sign up?"

We convinced her to let us finish watching the performance, and then we walked down to inquire about the dolphin encounter. By the time she paid the ninety-nine dollars and had her swimsuit and bathing cap on, it was her turn in the pool.

She seemed to have a blast. You could hear her laughing all over the area. I took several pictures of her with her digital camera and promised to upload them at school and e-mail them to Daisy and Uncle Clarence. Gramma wasn't into the "computer age," so she probably wouldn't see them until Aunt Edith showed her the prints after her vacation. At least then she'd be sitting next to her in one piece.

"So how was it?" I asked her when she rejoined us.

She started chuckling. "I haven't had that much fun in years!" She fluffed her silvery curls where the swimming cap had flattened them down. Her wet swimsuit was in a tiny, plastic zipper bag, so she stuffed it back into her purse. "If I lived here, I'd buy myself one of those annual passes and come out often just to swim with the dolphins!"

I looked at Simon and smiled. He squeezed my hand.

"From what I saw, the dolphins and trainers were having as much fun as you were," he told her.

"Yeah, that young man, Tandy, who gave me instructions at the start, said I ought to apply for a job here. Wouldn't that be one of the best jobs in the world?"

I did a quick evaluation of a couple of the occupations Aunt Edith had had over the years. Working at Sea Life Park would score somewhere near the top.

Great-grandma Jennie had wanted her three children to play musical instruments, but couldn't afford them. Gramma longed to take piano lessons from a woman who taught lots of kids to play. Being the older of the two girls, Aunt Edith washed dishes at the local diner to save money to buy a flute for herself and a used upright piano for Gramma. Uncle Clarence worked in the hay fields to buy both a violin and alto saxophone, then taught himself how to play them.

She married Uncle Ben in 1943 when she was seventeen years old. World War II was in full swing, so while her husband was off at war, Aunt Edith worked in a factory that produced rubber tires.

"So where do we go from here?" Aunt Edith asked, looking at her map. Simon and I were studying our maps as well.

"How about going to see the rays and then the sea lion discovery?" Simon said. He glanced at his watch. "It's almost 3:15. I'm sure you'll want to see the bird sanctuary and the new baby wholphin too, before the exhibits close at five."

"Well, let's get a move on," Aunt Edith said. "The bird guy starts talking soon." She headed down the trail toward the bird sanctuary.

I tugged on Simon's arm. "Our leader has spoken."

As we followed her to the exhibit, Simon received a phone call from Marshall. I figured our nice afternoon was about to be interrupted.

"Well, that's good to hear," Simon said to him. "Let me know if anything changes." He hung up.

"No rocks today, I hope."

"Not so far, but it's not 4:00 yet," he replied.

"There weren't any incidents yesterday, were there?"

"Fortunately, no."

"Maybe the rock throwers are taking the weekend off," I said.

He put his arm around my waist. "That's just what Marshall said. But just in case, he and Dave and some other officers are patrolling near bridges around the island this weekend."

I noticed Simon looking at his watch several times during the afternoon, but Marshall never called back.

All the shows and attractions we saw were amazing. Many of the birds, which had been injured or in poor health when brought to the park, had been lovingly nursed back to health and were thriving. Though we missed the trainer talk at the penguin habitat, we watched the majestic birds and looked at the breeding site that was instrumental in helping the endangered Humboldt penguins repopulate. The sea lions were fun to watch, the docile stingrays slicing through the water were enchanting, but for me, watching the young baby wholphin was the highlight.

"Isn't she adorable?" I said.

We watched the grayish-black youngster frolicking around her mother. Every minute or so, she would swim to the platform, snatch capelin, a sardine-like fish, from the hand of a trainer, then slide back near her mother.

"Kawili'Kai is one-fourth false killer whale and three-fourths Atlantic bottlenose dolphin," the trainer said. She tossed another fish to the waiting baby. "Her mother, Kekaimalu, which means 'from the peaceful ocean,' was born here in Sea Life Park twenty years ago. Kekaimalu was the offspring of a fourteen-foot, two-thousand-pound false killer whale and a six-foot, four-hundred-pound dolphin. Her mom and dad were the lead performers in the popular water show then." She smiled. "It was a bit of a surprise to the staff that they were also romantically involved."

The crowd laughed. "It just proves the theory that opposites attract," Simon said, squeezing my hand.

Several hands shot up in the audience. The trainer pointed toward a hefty man wearing a yellow-flowered aloha shirt and straw hat.

"Since the mother was a hybrid, how was she able to give birth?" he asked. "If a horse and donkey have offspring, the mule can't reproduce."

"Sir, that's a very good question," the trainer said. The baby was circling in the water near the platform waiting for another fish to be thrown. "Although Atlantic bottlenose dolphins and false killer whales are different species, scientists still classify them in the same family. Leading experts who study marine mammals tell us that the two species are close in terms of taxonomy, or in other words, their natural relationships."

The trainer pointed to a lady sitting in the row in front of us. She was wearing a purple-print sundress and had a pair of binoculars hanging around her neck. "Yes, ma'am?"

"Is Kekai, uh, Kamlu…" She looked at her husband sitting next to her for help. He looked down at the floor and ignored her. "Uh, is Keke…"

"Oh, good grief, Martha!" the man barked at her. "Just say 'the mother.'" He shook his head then leaned toward the man sitting next to him. "I've taken almost fifty years of this."

Simon and I looked at each other. "Guess fifty years together has been a little trying for them," I whispered.

"Or perhaps the quality of their time together hasn't been as special as ours," he whispered back. "If we're lucky enough to be married fifty years, would you promise me that we would still hold hands and get along?"

My eyes grew wide. *Did I just hear what I thought I heard?*

Simon winked at me then looked back toward the trainer.

My pulse was racing. He had some explaining to do when we were alone. Though it wasn't easy, I tried to focus my attention back on Martha and the trainer.

Martha sat up straight and pulled back her shoulders. "As if you were such a prize and had so many other choices, Marvin!" she said to her husband. The man's face turned red. Martha looked back at the trainer. "Before the baby was born, was Kekaimalu the only wholphin in the world?"

The audience started clapping. Martha had said the mother's name perfectly. She glanced at her husband with a look of victory on her face. He pulled the brim of his baseball cap lower over his eyes and slumped down in his seat.

The trainer gave Martha a "thumbs up" sign. "There have been some reports over the years of wholphins being spotted in the wild." She motioned toward the animal. "But lucky for us here in Hawaii, Kekaimalu is the first one ever born in captivity."

After a few more questions, the show was over, and we followed the crowd out of the arena.

"I could use a cold drink," Aunt Edith said. "How about you two?"

"Me too," I said. I pulled my wallet out of my purse. "But I'm buying."

Before either of them started arguing with me, I walked the few yards to the snack bar and ordered three large frozen lemonades. While I watched the young girl fill the glasses, I thought about what Simon had said earlier. Though it wasn't an actual proposal, it showed me that the prospect was there. I started giggling. The girl fixing our drinks gave me an odd look, but I didn't care. I was on cloud nine!

"Here, Allie, have a taste of this!" Aunt Edith said. She was holding a forkful of shoyu ginger potato salad toward me. I ate the yummy bite.

"Mmmm, it's wonderful, but I'm stuffed." I had just finished the last of my Kalua pig, poi chicken, long rice, and second sweet potato dinner roll with butter. Though my stomach was saying no, my eyes were telling me to try the coconut cake and bite of apple cobbler that Simon had set down next to my plate. I looked at him. "I told you just a tiny slice of cake."

His mouth was full of grilled mahi-mahi. He just shook his head and shrugged.

"My clothes are getting so tight, I'm having trouble zipping my slacks," I complained. Though I wanted to blame someone else for my dilemma, it wasn't Simon's or anyone else's fault that I had put on a few pounds since arriving in Hawaii. *Better start taking the stairs again and walking more,* I thought.

Simon swallowed and wiped his mouth with his napkin. "You don't look like you've gained an ounce, so stop fretting about the dessert," he said. He put his arm around me and pulled me to him. "Besides, if I fatten you up before you go home, maybe the cowboys around Paradise will leave you alone." He kissed me before letting me go.

"Hey, I think the show is about to start," Aunt Edith said. Some servers carried off our dirty dishes, and we settled back to enjoy the performance.

Beautiful Polynesian girls dressed in brightly-colored skirts, leaf headdresses, and puka-shell leis danced their way onto the stage. They performed the hula to slow slack-key guitar music, and then the action sped up when the drums hit a Tahitian beat. I loved every song that was sung. The show was topped off by the fire dancers' performance. As I expected, the whole evening was spectacular.

The three of us walked across the parking lot to the Jeep. "You know, Allie," Aunt Edith said, "I need to get one of those coconut shell bras like those dancers were wearing." She glanced down at her chest. "I could use a little help in that area."

Simon started coughing. I patted his back several times until he was able to control himself again. I had to bite my lip to keep from laughing at her remark, but she was deep in thought and didn't seem to notice.

"Thanks for a great weekend," I said. We had arrived home. Aunt Edith had gone upstairs leaving Simon and me in the car talking. He was cuddling me in his arms, and his cheek was resting against my hair.

He pulled me closer and kissed the top of my forehead. "My pleasure. It looked like both you and Aunt Edith had a great time, and I did too."

I was trying to think of a way to broach the subject he had brought up at the wholphin exhibit. I was about to say something when he interrupted.

"You know, Allie, this isn't a pleasant subject for me, but there's only nine days left until summer school is out." I felt his chest sink a bit as he let out a sigh. "Have you been giving any thought to *us* and your final days here?"

Boy, had I ever. "Yes, but I've tried not to dwell too much on the leaving part." Though we were already close, I snuggled in tighter.

"Yeah, me too."

We were both quiet for a while. I was enjoying the peace and security I felt being wrapped in Simon's arms.

"Though we talked on the phone and e-mailed each other a lot before you arrived, it sure has been nice knowing I could run by here and see you face-to-face just about anytime."

I smiled. "Yeah, I've come to depend on the nice routine of having you at my beck and call."

He started laughing. "Beck and call, huh?"

The rise and fall of his chest felt wonderful. I pulled the arm that was wrapped across my waist tighter around me.

"No, just kidding. With the heavy caseload you've had at work, I'm thrilled to have had as much of your time as I've had." I intertwined my fingers with his. "I've enjoyed the chauffeuring, fine dinners, great sightseeing and entertainment, help in writing pieces for the *Hawaiian Star*, and everything else more than you'll ever know." A lump rose in my throat. I cleared it a couple of times before plowing ahead. "But none of it would have been as special as it was if I hadn't been with you." I dabbed at my eyes before the tears started falling on my cheeks.

For a minute or two, Simon didn't say anything; he just hugged me tighter. I was starting to have some trouble breathing when he finally spoke.

"Allie, I feel like I'm in heaven when I'm with you. It tears me apart thinking how empty it's going to be around here when you go back to Oklahoma." He paused and seemed to be weighing very carefully what he was about to say. "We both have our own professions and homes, which unfortunately are 4,000 miles apart. I know you love Paradise and are committed to your family. It would be difficult for me to ask you to leave all that to move here."

The lump in my throat was now the size of a baseball. More tears were threatening to start falling. I didn't want to embarrass myself, so I didn't say anything for a minute while I tried to gain control of my emotions.

"Well, you're pure Hawaii *aina* through and through," I said. "You're part of the land, nature, and spirit here. You'd be like a fish out of water in a land-locked place like Paradise."

He brushed aside some strands of my hair that had fallen on my face. "I loved my visit to Oklahoma," he said softly. "Though in a different way than Hawaii, it was beautiful." He sighed. "But I just can't imagine living there."

I sat up, brushed the wrinkles from my shirt, and then looked at him. "I can't imagine it either."

He leaned over and wrapped his arms around my shoulders. Looking deep into my eyes, he pulled me toward him and kissed me. My fingers clung to his shirt. I didn't want him to release me—ever.

CHAPTER 6

The next morning, I woke up before the alarm went off. I needed a few minutes in the school library before the kids arrived, so I jumped up and hit the shower. While the pulsating spray massaged my shoulders, I thought about my conversation with Simon from the night before. Little had been resolved regarding our future together. However, we both agreed to give it some serious thought over the next week, as if I hadn't been already.

After I was dressed and nearly ready to go, my cell phone rang. Surprised that anyone was calling so early, I quickly picked it up.

"Good morning, sunshine," Michael said.

"Good morning to you too, sailor." I plopped down on the end of the bed. "Caught anything yet?"

"As a matter of fact, I wrestled a ninety-pound marlin to the deck on Friday afternoon. The wind was blowing a gale and whipping the boat back and forth, so it wasn't easy. Despite all the high-tech equipment Richard has on that boat, it still came down to brute strength bringing in that fish. I was wet with sweat by the time I hauled it in, but believe me, it was worth it!"

I smiled. "I bet. The connection sure is good. Since you're out on the open sea, I'm surprised it's not garbled."

"Well, it probably wouldn't be as clear, but Richard and I have been staying at Amanda and Rob's since Friday night." Simon and Richard's sister, Amanda, and her family lived in Hilo on the Big Island and owned a helicopter tour company there. "The ocean waves were enormous, and the yacht was taking a beating, so we headed closer to the shoreline. Amanda had been tracking our movements with their GPS. She radioed Richard and invited us to stay with them until the water settled down a bit. Over the weekend, they took us all over the island."

"That's cool. How do you like Amanda and Rob?" Though I had heard Simon mention his sister and brother-in-law several times, I still hadn't met them.

"Very friendly," Michael said, "and their house is as neat as a pin, even though Denny is all over the place. That kid talks like a little adult. I've never heard a youngster that small have such a large vocabulary." Denny was Amanda and Rob's eighteen-month-old son.

"Yes, Simon has mentioned that Denny is gifted. At first I thought it might just be the proud uncle in him talking, but Denny was tested last month and found to have an I.Q. of 144."

"Well, that explains a lot then. He and Amanda came along when Rob took Richard and me on a helicopter ride Saturday. We flew all over the Big Island and got a bird's eye view of the Kilauea volcano flaring up. When we saw the fresh lava flowing out, Denny began telling us how magma comes up through the earth and is forced out through openings in the crust." He paused and started chuckling. "I didn't know that kind of stuff until at least the third grade. I don't know which was more amazing—Denny knowing the big words and facts about it or seeing that burning lava river flowing into the sea."

"I'd love to see that too," I said, "but with school and the newspaper, I'm sure I won't make it to another island before I go back home." A little bit of sadness hit me again. "But that's okay. Simon, Aunt Edith, and I had a pretty great weekend ourselves."

"Yeah, besides checking in, I wanted to see how it was going with Aunt Edith. Is she behaving herself?"

"She's being a very good girl, as well as being helpful too."

I filled him in about how she had rescued Rowdy and that she rented a motorcycle and planned to go riding with Pinky later today. I finished by telling him about our visit to Queen Emma's Palace and that Aunt Edith had swam with the dolphins at Sea Life Park.

"I'll bet she had a ball doing that," he said.

"Oh yeah. We also saw the new wholphin baby, stingrays, and tons more."

"It sounds like you had fun," Michael said. "I saw some manta rays myself. On Saturday night, Amanda and Rob treated us to dinner at a hotel in Keauhou Bay. The hotel is built on a rocky cliff, and the mantas come there every evening to feed. Rob said that plankton are attracted by light, and the mantas feed on the plankton."

"Boy, it would be neat seeing them swimming free in open water."

"They were gorgeous! The wingspan on those delta-wing-shaped creatures is at least seven-foot wide. They dart through the water, make a U-turn, and then glide back in for more food."

"So you had your own mini sea life adventure."

"Yes, even though the original fishing plan had to be modified, it's been great being with Richard's family."

"I was afraid you might be having trouble out there," I said. "On Friday evening, rain fell here like it wasn't going to quit, and the wind was really getting with it. Special reports kept coming on television telling people near Eva Beach and another place or two on the island to evacuate because of the flooding danger."

"Richard has been monitoring the tropical storms for several days now. That's another reason we headed to Amanda's when we did. With one right after another forming, they're causing havoc in the ocean. We decided to stay on land and give the waters time to settle down a bit."

"Wise decision. So when are you heading back out?"

"We're leaving in about an hour."

"And Amanda will be keeping an eye on you with the GPS?"

"Yes, but I'm glad that God has a bigger eye on us."

"Amen. I've been praying for a safe journey for you guys."

"Thanks. I appreciate it."

Aunt Edith stuck her head in the door. "Oh, sorry," she whispered when she saw that I was on the phone.

"That's okay. I'm talking to Michael. I'll fill you in about his escapades so far as soon as I'm off here."

She nodded. Her fluffy white curls bobbed up and down. "Tell him *palekana malu* before you hang up."

I raised my eyebrows. "I don't know what that means. You'd better tell him." I handed her the phone.

"Hi, Michael. This is your Aunt Edith. I wanted to tell you *palekana malu*. I'm wishing you safety and protection on your trip." Though I couldn't hear Michael's response, she started smiling and nodding her head. "Yes, I've been working more on my Hawaiian words, and I stumbled across that phrase when I was looking up something else." He said something to her. "Oh, so Allie told you about that, huh? Yes, Simon is picking me up soon and taking me down to a deli run by this handsome Japanese man named Luu." She looked at me and grinned, then proceeded to give Michael the details about her fish-selling bet. Her eyes were bright and she started blushing. "I know I'm bound to sell more of my cornmeal-rolled fish, but even if I lose, it will be fun working with Luu. He's a dandy and single to boot!"

I was grinning bigger when she said good-bye to Michael then handed the phone back to me.

"Well, like Aunt Edith said, *palekana malu*, Michael," I said. "Call me again if you get the chance."

"Will do. You two have a great day," he said, and then we hung up.

When I reached school, I signed in at the office then headed to the library to check out books about sea turtles. I also found some books on manta rays and dolphins, as well as a couple of great ones about wholphins. I added all of them to the growing stack.

I knew that the school librarian had accumulated a wealth of great teaching materials over the years, so I headed to the "Teachers Use Only" bookshelf hoping to find some guides on various types of sea life. I wasn't disappointed. I pulled out and scanned several manuals, then spotted a bound copy of a research paper on the captive-bred green turtles release program. Two professors, who taught at the University of Hawaii, had recently published it. I added the paper to my stack then gathered all the materials and walked to the classroom.

All the students were in their seats ready to go before the first bell rang. They were eager to find out what was on the agenda this morning.

"Boys and girls, I went to Sea Life Park yesterday and saw some wonderful animals. How many of you have been there?" Not surprisingly, everyone raised his or her hand. "Well then, you may already know more about the Hawaiian green sea turtle release program than what I learned yesterday. Can someone tell us about it?"

Several of them raised their hand. I called on Annie.

"My big brother did a report on Jia and Johnson last year," she said. "I watched him chart some of Jia's movements along the coast of Oahu."

I smiled at her. Annie had made great strides lately. She was not the same timid little girl who had told the class at the beginning of June that she would rather clean the bathroom than have to try to read a book. Now she was one of the first to volunteer to help another student with a hard word or give her opinion about a topic we were discussing.

"Okay, Annie, tell us what you know about them."

She stood by her chair and told the class that Jia was about eighteen months old when she was released into the wild. The turtle had moved all along the southeastern coast of Oahu, never venturing more than five miles from the shoreline. She migrated northward, finally reaching Kaneohe Bay. She continued swimming about twenty miles out into the Pacific and was still in that area today.

"Very good," I said. "Now, how would all of you like to do your own research on marine animals and perhaps do some charting of some of the other turtle hatchlings?"

"That would be cool!" Mareko blurted out without raising his hand. All the others nodded in agreement.

Annie smiled and started clapping her hands. "I can do it, Miss Kane. I've been going to some of those reading game Web sites you told us about, and I'm a whiz on our computer now." I had encouraged the students with home computers to go to sites promoted by the PBS network and other educational sources. I was glad to hear that Annie was using the list I had provided.

"Not any better than me, I bet," Mareko said to her. "I've checked out every site Miss Kane gave us at least twice."

"That's wonderful, Mareko," I said. "I'm proud of you, but please remember to raise your hand and wait to be called on before speaking."

"Sorry, Miss Kane," he said.

I pointed toward the books I had spread out on the activity table at the back of the room. "I'd like you all to go pick out one book. Ladies first." I watched the three girls walk to the table and select their books. "Now, boys, it's your turn, and please don't run." They clamored back with Seth and David in the lead.

I watched Seth thumb through a couple of the easier picture books then settle on a harder one about bottle-nosed dolphins that had fewer pictures and more text. He turned around and held up his choice for me to see. "I love learning about dolphins, Miss Kane," he called out. "Did you see the wholphins when you were at Sea Life Park?"

I smiled and nodded my head. Seth had also come a long way since summer school had begun. He was reading more difficult books and wasn't intimidated by them.

"The wholphins were beautiful," I said. "I hope a couple of you choose to do more research about them."

"I will, Miss Kane," Danielle said. I noticed she had already picked one of the two books I had found on the wholphin mother and baby.

"Thank you, Danielle. I'm sure you'll do a great job."

I gave some brief instructions on what I wanted them to focus on for their reports, and then everyone settled down to read their books. We went to the computer lab to use the computers for Internet research. By the time the noon bell rang, they all had several pages written.

I drove to Mr. Omura's deli for lunch. Besides craving one of his scrumptious tuna salad sandwiches, I was curious how Aunt Edith was doing. I had to park my car a block away because there weren't any closer spots available.

People were backed up to the door, so I had to wait a couple of minutes before I could squeeze inside. Though it was often crowded at lunchtime, I had never seen so many people here at one time. Once I was inside, Aunt Edith spotted me. She waved then went back to dishing up food for the customers. All the chairs were occupied, and people were standing along the wall holding plates of food.

Mr. Omura saw me and motioned for me to make my way to the counter. I excused myself a half-dozen times as I maneuvered through the crowd.

"Isn't this great, Allie!" Mr. Omura said when I reached him. He leaned toward me then pointed toward Aunt Edith, who was lifting a basket of fried fish from the deep fryer. "After talking to your aunt on Saturday, I had a feeling this would be a good thing. I had a hundred flyers printed up that afternoon then had Sammy and his friend distribute them to the businesses around here this morning."

I smiled at him. "I'm a little confused, though. I heard you bet Aunt Edith that your poached and grilled ono would outsell her fried fish."

He nodded his head and grinned. "Oh, I knew as soon as I met her that she needed a challenge, so that's why the wager was made. I figured she was a good cook, but she was also a cutie, and I wanted to get to know her better." He winked at me.

What people do for love, I thought. "Well, it looks like sales are brisk. I assume she's winning the bet."

He didn't have time to answer because Aunt Edith walked up next to him. "Allie, can you believe this?" she said, nodding toward the crowd.

"I've been mixing batter and rolling fish ever since Simon dropped me off at 9:30 this morning. People began coming in at 10:30, and I started falling behind. Luu had Sammy start doing all the frying around eleven so that I could do the prep work." She pointed toward Sammy then brushed a white curl from her forehead with the back of her gloved hand. "I like him. He and I make a great team."

Sammy must have heard his name because he looked toward us and nodded. I smiled and waved at him.

"I'm trying to get your aunt to agree to come back and work tomorrow," Mr. Omura said to me. "But for pay, of course." He looked at her. "Please, Edith?"

She shrugged. "Sure, why not? But I don't come cheap, Luu."

"How about fifteen dollars an hour and all the lunch you can eat?" he proposed.

I thought that was a generous offer.

Aunt Edith puckered her lips. "Well, that's not too bad, but I had twenty dollars an hour in mind."

He frowned, and then he spotted more people coming in the door. "Okay, Edith, you've got a deal. Twenty dollars an hour it is."

"And still all the lunch I can eat?"

He smiled. "Sure."

I saw him look at her small frame and figured he thought she wouldn't eat much. Boy, was he in for a surprise!

They had to get back to work cooking and serving folks, so I took my tuna sandwich, cookie, and drink and headed to the *Hawaiian Star*.

After eating lunch, I called the King Kamehameha Hula Competition coordinator to get some information about this year's event for my article. Among other things, he told me that over five hundred dancers had registered and that talented musicians from Hawaii would be accompanying most of the groups. While we talked, I wrote down a page full of notes then thanked him for his help.

I put away that file then pulled out the folder containing my notes about the lava rock crimes. Aside from being able to report the days and locations where the crimes had occurred, I only had a measly amount of materials to work with. Thinking about the charting that my students had been doing, I decided to get a map of Oahu and do some plotting myself. I didn't have one in my office, so I walked downstairs to bum one from one of the other reporters. The only soul around was my boss.

"Hi, Allison," Mr. Masaki said when I stuck my head inside his office. He had his feet crossed on top of his desk and was finishing a hamburger. "Come in; have a seat."

I sat down in one of the chairs in front of his desk. "I didn't mean to interrupt your lunch," I said. I watched him wad up the burger wrapper and toss it into the trash can.

"You're not interrupting," he said. "I wanted to visit with you today, so this is a good time." He wiped his mouth with his napkin and then tossed it into the can. "Have you found out anything new regarding the rock-throwing incidents?"

I shook my head. "Not really, but I thought I'd try to find an Oahu map and chart where the crimes have occurred. Would you happen to have a map around?"

"Sure do." He stood up and walked to the four-drawer file cabinet sitting near the door. "I've got several maps somewhere in here." He pulled out the top drawer, didn't see what he needed, then proceeded to the next drawer down. Still not finding a map, he tried drawer number three, then finally the bottom one. He reached into the back of it. "Here's some." He pulled out a thin magazine, closed the drawer, and then handed it to me.

"Thanks." I quickly thumbed through it and found that there were eight different maps inside—one showing the entire island, then seven more detailed maps that showed different regions of the island. Communities, bodies of water, police stations, and more were listed on it. "This is perfect. Not only can I chart the crimes' locations, I can become more familiar with the island too." I stood up to leave.

"Let me know if you need anything else," he said.

I nodded then walked back upstairs to my office.

I was familiarizing myself with the spots where the crimes had occurred when my office phone rang. It was Simon.

"Busy working?" he asked.

"Not really earning my keep today. I don't suppose you've learned anything new about the rock incidents, have you?"

"Not enough to help you with your article, if that's what you mean. Like you suggested yesterday, whoever is doing them took the weekend off."

"Thank the Lord," I said. "Do you think it's over? Maybe whoever was doing it is too scared to try it again. With more citizens on the lookout and pressure from law enforcement, they might be afraid to try it."

"Yes, my team and I can be pretty intimidating," Simon said, chuckling. "But seriously, I hope you're right and there won't be any more rocks thrown."

"Thanks for dropping Aunt Edith at the deli this morning. I stopped by there for lunch, and that place was packed!" I filled him in on the success of Aunt Edith's fish venture and about Mr. Omura offering her the job.

"I'm glad to hear they're hitting it off," Simon said. "Speaking of food, would you like to go out for dinner tonight?"

"I'll do you one better. You come over around 6:00 and I'll cook."

He was quiet for a second. "Really?" Since I had never cooked for him, I guess he had a right to be skeptical.

"Yes, I really do know how to cook," I said, giggling. "Just don't expect a five-course meal. How about spaghetti and salad?" I heard a phone ringing in the background. "I might even throw in some French bread."

"You're on," he said. "Can you hang on a sec? I've got another call."

My cell phone started ringing. "Go ahead. Mine is ringing too. I'll meet you back here in a minute."

When I answered, Aunt Edith was on the line.

"Allie? I'm with Pinky, and I'm using his cell phone." Her voice sounded a bit panicked.

I glanced at the clock on the wall. It was 4:20. "Are you okay?"

"Yes, I'm fine. We've been out riding…Kaneohe and Kailua, and we…back through the Pali tunnel…" She was fading in and out.

"I'm sorry; I didn't hear what you said after Pali tunnel."

"I said you need to call Simon, then…here…you can…" She dropped out.

"Aunt Edith?" No response. I looked at the display. She was gone. I scrolled to recently received calls then called the last one that came in. *Why did she want me to call Simon?* I began shutting down my computer. *Was she in some kind of trouble?*

She picked up after the second ring. "I lost you," she said.

With my free hand, I stuffed my notes back into the file folder. "Yes, you dropped out." I stood up and reached for my purse. "I'm leaving right now. Tell me where you are, and I'll come pick you up." I had all these awful images going through my mind that Pinky had taken advantage of her.

"Calm down, Allison; I'm fine. I was calling to tell you that some-one just dropped a rock off the pedestrian bridge that crosses the Pali Highway." She said something else, but her voice was muffled.

"Where on the Pali? I didn't catch your last sentence."

"Oh, I was asking Pinky where to tell you to come. He said we're about a half mile east of Queen Emma's Palace. Can you let Simon know?"

"Yes, I was talking to him on the office line when you called. I'll let him know then head that way."

"Good deal. See you soon," she said, then hung up.

I picked up the receiver on the other phone. "Are you back yet?" I asked.

"Yes, but I've got to go. There's been another rock thrown on the Pali."

"That's what Aunt Edith just told me. I'm heading out too. I'll see you there in a few minutes." I hurried toward the parking lot, jumped into my car, then raced toward H-1.

I could see red lights flashing before I passed Queen Emma's Palace. As I pulled up to the scene, I saw a red Nissan sedan with the back glass broken out sitting on the side of the road. A middle-aged guy was leaning against the driver's door talking to Marshall. Dave was a short distance away talking to a young black couple.

I climbed out of my car and started walking toward the group. I spotted Aunt Edith and Pinky standing together a short distance away from the mangled vehicle. I waved at them and headed their way.

"That rock sure did a number on that car, didn't it?" Aunt Edith said when I reached them.

I looked at the sedan again. "It sure did. The driver looks okay, though."

"Your aunt and I came out this side of the tunnel about five minutes after it happened," Pinky said. He was wearing an orange T-shirt that had had the sleeves ripped off. It looked to be an extra, extra large size, but it still wasn't covering everything. One of his arms could make two of mine. "I wish we had arrived sooner. I would have loved to get my hands on the twerps who are pulling these stunts. They'd have been crying for the police to rescue them by the time I got through with them."

From the scowl on his face, I had no doubt that would be true. In the distance, I saw Simon's car winding its way toward us. He parked behind the damaged car then climbed out and waved at us. I waved back. He walked toward Marshall and the driver.

"Pinky and I met a couple of motorcycle riders just as we came out of the tunnel," Aunt Edith said. "They were riding Hondas, one blue and one green."

"Really?" I pulled my notepad from my back pocket. "Did they look like any of the kids we talked to the other day?" I flipped to a blank page.

"I couldn't tell. The face shields on their helmets were dark."

"They couldn't have been the ones that threw the rock, though," Pinky said. I looked at him. He pointed toward the pedestrian bridge. "Whoever threw it would have had to ride or drive away from up there. Even a dirt bike couldn't make it down those steep sides."

I looked up at the bridge. It spanned the highway and was about fifty feet above it. The slopes of the hills on both sides were at least forty-five-degree angles. The jagged rocks and small trees clinging to the dirt would have also made the trek down very dangerous, if not impossible.

"Even if they didn't do the crime, they might still be involved," I said.

A few minutes passed, and then Pinky suggested that they leave. I told Aunt Edith I had invited Simon over for supper. Since I'd probably be here for a while, she offered to go on home and get things started. I watched them ride off, then I wandered over to Simon.

"How about a scoop for the local paper?" I said, giving him a charming smile.

He grinned. "I'd like to help you, Miss Kane." He motioned toward the sedan that was being loaded onto a tow truck. "Unfortunately, there's not much more to report than at the other three sites. No one saw the rock coming until it hit the Nissan." He pointed toward the couple that Dave had been interviewing. They were getting back into their car. "Those people were about a hundred feet behind the Nissan. They told Dave they saw the rock coming off the bridge just before it hit. By the time they stopped, they were focused on the accident rather than where it came from." He sighed. "Pretty much the same story as the others, only the names and places have changed."

"What about motive? Do the victims have anything in common?"

Simon shook his head. "Not that we've determined so far. We know the perpetrator is getting away on a motorcycle; witnesses have told us that. There were skid marks at both the H-1 and Kalihi locations, but we don't know yet if they were made by the thrower's bike." He motioned toward the top of the bridge. "Marshall and some other guys are up there now scouting around. Maybe they'll turn up something useful."

"I hope so. Wish I could help, but so far I'm as lost as you seem to be."

He nodded. "Don't worry; we'll catch them, and you'll get a great story when we do."

I looked at my watch. "I guess I'll go on home. Aunt Edith was going to start supper, but since I promised you I'd be cooking, I need to at least help her."

He smiled. "I'll be there soon."

I waved good-bye then headed to my car. Once inside, I glanced at the still open notepad lying on the seat beside me. Only two sentences were written on the sheet. I sighed. "You'd better come up with something quick, Allie," I said as I started the car, "or your boss is going to find someone else to cover this story."

When I arrived home, the smell of fresh basil, oregano, and rosemary filled the air. I realized Aunt Edith had made her own special spaghetti sauce, which certainly beat the jar kind I had planned on using.

"It smells heavenly in here," I said. Rowdy and Precious were clamoring for my attention. I leaned down and rubbed their heads.

"Yeah, Pinky grows fresh herbs in some pots on his lanai. When he heard you say you were planning on spaghetti tonight, he offered to give me some sprigs."

I could see some of the cuttings still lying on the countertop. "That was nice of him. I hope you invited him to join us for supper." I lifted the lid on the pot containing the simmering sauce. A fresh, spicy aroma filled the air.

"Yes, I did, since he was contributing to the meal." She reached for the spoon lying next to the pot and began stirring the sauce. "He's also bringing dessert." She put the lid back onto the pot. "I understand he's quite the pastry chef. He told me he gets calls to help with the fancy wedding cakes at that bakery where I picked up the pastries the other morning."

"Really? I wouldn't have pegged him to be a chef. A sumo wrestler, mechanic, or some other job that requires a lot of physical strength, yes; a baker, no."

Aunt Edith smiled. "Believe it or not, though Pinky bakes and dabbles in fixing motorcycles, he has a college degree in secondary education. He taught chemistry at one of the high schools here for fifteen years."

I arched my eyebrows. "That's great. I've got a bad habit of pigeonholing people."

Aunt Edith walked over and put her hand on my shoulder. "It's not a bad habit, Allie. That's what has helped make you a good detective."

Someone knocked on the door. I walked over and opened it. Both Pinky and Simon were standing there.

"How did you get inside the building?" I asked Simon. Visitors had to buzz the occupants from an intercom system located outside the front door of the tower.

He pointed to Pinky. "My new friend here was walking up to the door just as I drove up. He recognized me from the Pali scene."

While Aunt Edith and I prepared the rest of the meal, the two guys visited in the living room. When we were all seated at the table, Aunt Edith said, "Will you *pule*, Simon?"

Pinky and I both looked at Aunt Edith. She had bowed her head and closed her eyes. We looked at each other then at Simon.

He grinned at us. "Ask the blessing," he interpreted.

We both smiled then bowed our heads. After the prayer, we all dug in.

Among other things, we talked about the rock-throwing incidents, the crazy, wet weather, and the new Garden of Eden at Diamond Head. I told Pinky and Aunt Edith that I had become friends with Maynard Desmond, the landscape artist who was designing and constructing it. When I reached the part that some of his inspiration had come after I told him about the garden back in Paradise, Aunt Edith insisted on seeing it. I told her I'd take her there the next afternoon.

CHAPTER 7

The next morning I awoke to another gray, dreary day. It had rained all night. Water droplets clung to the bedroom window.

I didn't feel like dressing up, so I slipped on some comfortable slacks, a coordinating plaid top, and navy-blue loafers. I brushed my hair, pulled it into a ponytail, and then tied a navy-blue ribbon around the rubber band. After a breakfast of cereal and juice, I was out the door.

At school, the students kept busy working on their marine-life reports. We used the computer lab most of the morning, and they gathered a wealth of useful information.

While driving to the *Hawaiian Star*, wind gusts were strong. Palm trees along the roadway were whipping back and forth. I switched on the car radio to see if I could get a weather report. It didn't take long to find out that another tropical storm was forming near Kauai and would be working its way over the rest of the islands by nightfall.

My plan for the afternoon was to do some work at the *Star* for an hour or so, then meet Aunt Edith at Mr. Omura's deli. She would be finished with her shift by then and planned to follow me to the park at Diamond Head on her motorcycle. Though I wasn't sure if Maynard would be there working, I knew she'd enjoy a tour of the garden. Since my students had planted apple trees there and I had contributed a bit during the excavation process, I was prepared to play tour guide.

When I was about a mile from the newspaper, the guy on the radio said that during the night a mild earthquake had hit near San Francisco. Measuring 3.8 on the Richter scale, only slight damage had occurred within the city. He reported that some people in nearby communities had also felt the tremors, but little or no damage was sustained.

I knew that since the entire west coast of the mainland sits on a major fault line where constant convergence and divergence of the tectonic plates is occurring, you never knew when an earthquake was going to happen. And even if you did, where could you go?

The announcer went on to remind his listeners that 80% of earthquakes occur around and within the Pacific plate. With the Hawaiian Islands smack dab in the middle of the region and some tourists likely listening to his broadcast, I wasn't sure why he was pointing out that fact. Not good tourism public relations if you asked me.

I looked at the radio and shook my head. "I'll take Oklahoma tornadoes over earthquakes any day," I told the announcer. "At least you get some advance warning and can take cover from them." He started talking about tsunamis then, so I reached over and switched off the radio. That was enough gloom and doom for now.

As I turned into the alley leading to the parking lot behind the newspaper, I saw Sammy Cho walking toward his car. It was parked behind his uncle's laundromat, which sat adjacent to the *Hawaiian Star* building. I tooted my horn, and he waved at me.

"Not working at the deli today?" I hollered as I climbed out of my car.

"Working the evening shift," he yelled back. "I had a couple of classes this morning at the university."

We walked toward each other. "I'm glad to hear you're going to school," I said. "What kind of degree are you pursuing?"

"I'm leaning toward marine biology."

I nodded. "Though I'm partial to teaching and journalism, the world needs lots of good scientists. Besides the deli, are you still working at the show on Kuhio Beach?" Recently Simon and I had seen him perform at the Torch Lighting and Hula Show there. It featured a conch shell ceremony and had plenty of Hawaiian music, hula dancing, and other entertainment.

"Oh yeah. It doesn't pay a lot, but I love doing it. I'd like to give up the twenty hours a week I'm putting in at the gas station, though, but school isn't cheap."

"There are grants and scholarships available," I said. "Would you like me to check into some for you?"

"It's nice of you to offer, but my sister has been looking into some programs for me," he said. "And the financial aid counselor at school is also working on it."

"Well, it sounds like you've got it covered then." I nodded toward the building. "I'd better get to work. It was nice seeing you."

"Yeah, you too," he replied. "See you around."

Since I hadn't stopped for lunch, I hit the vending machines on the way to my office. While sipping on cranberry-apple juice and eating peanut butter crackers, I wrote my article for Wednesday's paper. With limited progress on the cases so far, my notes were sparse. Less than two hundred words later, the piece was finished.

I e-mailed the article to the copy editor then walked downstairs to stretch my legs and dispose of my juice can in the recycling bin. Mr. Masaki wasn't in his office. I scribbled a note on a scrap piece of paper telling him I was going back to the Pali Highway scene to do some snooping. It was time for more legwork.

When I arrived back in my office, the copy editor had replied to my e-mail. He said that my piece had been accepted without changes and was set to run. I shut down my computer, grabbed my purse, and was out the door by 1:45.

When I arrived at the deli, Aunt Edith was removing her apron. "You timed that just right," she said. "We just got the kitchen cleaned up after the masses cleared out."

Mr. Omura said hello to me then walked over to stand beside her.

"Another record day in lunch sales, Edith." He smiled at her. "What can I do to sweet talk you into staying in Hawaii?"

I was surprised to see Aunt Edith blush. "Oh, you'll continue to do fine after I'm gone home, Luu."

"I doubt that, but it might help if you give me your secret batter recipe." He winked at me.

"You may have your work cut out getting her to give up that recipe, Mr. Omura," I said. "I'm pretty sure no one knows it but my Gramma and her." Since it was Great-grandma Jennie's recipe, they had guarded it like it was gold.

"We'll see, Luu, we'll see," Aunt Edith said. She smoothed the front of her hot-pink T-shirt then bent down and picked up her motorcycle helmet, which was sitting on a shelf behind the counter. "I'll see you in the morning." With her free hand, she grabbed her purse. I waved good-bye to Mr. Omura, and then she and I were out the door.

Aunt Edith's rented motorcycle was a smaller, less flashy version of the Harley she owned. In my rearview mirror I watched her weave in and out of traffic like a pro. When we stopped at a red light, I noticed that the sun's rays were bouncing off her two-tone pink helmet, and she was catching the eye of surrounding motorists.

At the next intersection, I signaled that I was turning left, and she followed me up the entry ramp to get on H-1. Traffic was heavy on the expressway, but I caught a break and merged into the flow. Aunt Edith stayed right behind me.

We had only traveled a short distance when I realized I was following a black stretch limousine. In front of it was another one. I gasped when I saw that a hearse was leading the way.

Oh boy. Aunt Edith and I had barged right into the middle of a funeral procession! I knew from my past experiences in Hawaiian cemeteries that Polynesians took funerals and after-death traditions very seriously. I didn't want to risk offending anyone.

I glanced in my side mirror. There was a long line of cars with their lights on behind us. Vehicles on both sides of the freeway were pulling over to the side of the road to show respect.

It was another six miles to the park near Diamond Head. My island map was back at the office. I wasn't sure if I could find the park using city streets. I decided to just stay put until we reached the exit I knew. Hopefully no one in the procession would take offense.

A quarter mile from our exit, I flipped on my turn signal. In my rearview mirror, I saw Aunt Edith stretch out her right hand. We exited H-1, and I breathed a sigh of relief.

At the stoplight, I turned right onto Twelfth Avenue, which was a straight shot to the park. I glanced in my mirror to be sure Aunt Edith was still with me. The scene behind me nearly gave me a heart attack! Not only was Aunt Edith following me, but the rest of the cars from the funeral procession were following her!

I started gasping for air and trying to figure out what to do next. Vehicles all along Twelfth Avenue were pulling to the side and stopping. Even a city bus pulled over. People on it had their heads bowed in reverence.

I made myself start breathing more slowly. A traffic light up ahead turned red, but cars were beginning to back up behind Aunt Edith. I wasn't sure whether to stop at the red light and risk more congestion or just go on through it. Fortunately, the decision was taken out of my hands. One of the motorcycle cops who had been escorting the procession must have seen everyone exit behind me. With his lights flashing, he pulled ahead of me. He looked at me and frowned, then motioned that I should follow him.

I was totally lost by the time we reached the cemetery in Hawaii Kai. Inside the entrance, the policeman jumped off his motorcycle and took control. He motioned for the cars behind Aunt Edith to turn left onto a narrow road that led to the gravesite.

I parked my car and climbed out. Aunt Edith stopped her bike right behind me.

She took off her helmet. "Well, that's a first," she said, fluffing her curls with her hand. "I guess those people behind me didn't know the way to the cemetery and thought they'd better follow us."

"I feel terrible that we got right in the middle of the procession," I said. Family members, who had been riding in the two limousines, were staring at us. I didn't know whether to tuck my head or wave.

"Oh, don't worry about it, Allie. Worse things than that have happened." She smiled. "Just think. Following us gave all these people a 'remember when' story to laugh about and tell their grandchildren some day."

"Let's hope it turns out that way," I said.

Finished with his traffic duties, the cop walked over to us. After he removed his helmet, I recognized him. He had been at the rock-throwing scene on H-1 on Thursday.

"Kind of got sidetracked back there, didn't you, Miss Kane?" he said. I figured he recognized me from that day or from seeing my picture in the *Hawaiian Star*.

I shrugged. "I didn't realize it was a funeral procession until we were right in the middle of it. Sorry about that."

"It's okay. No real harm was done. Where are you headed?"

"I'm taking my aunt to see the new park near Diamond Head." I looked in the direction where we had just come. "I'm turned around, though. Can you give me directions?"

"I'll do better than that; I'll take you there."

It turned out that the park was only a mile from the cemetery. The policeman waved and went on straight after we turned into the parking lot.

I sighed. Simon was bound to know about our little sidetrack adventure before the tour of the Garden of Eden was done.

Aunt Edith and I walked over the small hill to the area where the garden was being created. I was glad to see not only Maynard there, but also Nathan Nowicki. Another man was with them. Maynard was pointing to batches of plants in pots sitting on the ground all over the place.

Nathan and the other man were both leaning on their shovels listening to what he was saying.

"Well, it looks like you guys are hard at it," I said as we drew near them. The three men looked at us.

"Allie!" Nathan dropped his shovel. He loped over to me and then threw his arms around my shoulders.

"Hi, Nathan," I said, hugging him back. "It's good to see you." Over his shoulder I saw Maynard wave at us.

Nathan let me go, and he stepped back. "Boy, I sure have missed you!" My first two weeks on Oahu, I had given Nathan a ride to work each morning. We had become good friends.

"I've missed you too." I motioned toward Maynard. "It looks like you're in good company, though."

He grinned. "Yes, Maynard and Uncle Hiram are the best!" He grabbed my hand. "Come on! You haven't met Uncle Hiram yet, and I also want to show you what we've been doing here!"

I motioned toward Aunt Edith. "Come on. I'll introduce you."

Nathan dragged me to where the two men were standing. She followed us.

"Allie, this is Maynard's uncle and my great-uncle, Hiram Song. Uncle Hiram, this is my good friend, Allie."

I stretched out my hand to Mr. Song. "I'm Allison Kane. It's so nice to meet you." I nodded toward Maynard and Nathan. "You've got a couple of fine nephews here."

He shook my hand. "Please call me Hiram." He stepped back and put his arms around each of his nephews' shoulders. "I couldn't be prouder of these two guys. Words can't tell you how happy I am to be here with them." Both Maynard and Nathan were smiling.

Though related, the three men had just recently become acquainted. They were descendants of a wealthy Hawaiian landowner, Kawana Kahuku. He was Hiram's grandfather, Maynard's great-grandfather, and Nathan's great-great-grandfather. Just like with many families, parents didn't always agree with their children's choices for mates, resulting in estrangements and disinherited offspring. Because of Nathan's brother, the three men had been brought together. Regardless of hard feelings and mistakes made by their ancestors, they had become close friends.

I put my hand on Aunt Edith's arm. "Gentlemen, this is my aunt, Edith Patterson," I said. "She's here on vacation and wanted to see this marvelous exhibit."

She stepped toward the men. "Boy, this is something!" she said, stretching out her hand. "It's *makalapua*." They all nodded then shook her hand.

"*Makalapua?*" I said.

Maynard smiled at me. "It means 'beautiful' and 'to blossom forth.'" He turned to Aunt Edith. "I'm impressed that you're learning the Hawaiian language."

"I'm working on it," she said. "From what Allie had already told me about your garden here, I expected it to be beautiful. That's why I looked up that word this morning."

Maynard nodded his head. "Well, you two ladies are just in time." He pointed to some young trees sitting in pots. "We were discussing where to put the carob and cassia trees." He pointed toward some small bushes that had recently been planted. I could smell the light, minty fragrance coming from the hyssop. "The three of us agreed on the best place for those henna and myrrh bushes, but we're still undecided about where to put the Rose of Sharon bulbs."

"I love the way you've arranged the lilies," Aunt Edith said. She walked toward that section of the garden. "I'd suggest putting the Rose of Sharon in front of the lilies. When they flower, the colors will complement each other."

We stood around talking for a while, and then I led Aunt Edith to the section designated "The Orchard." I showed her the apple trees my students had planted.

She looked down at the sign posted in front of the cluster of trees. "Planted by students from Prince Kuhio Elementary," she read. "That's something they'll always remember, Allie."

I nodded. "Thanks to Maynard, it was a very special day for all of us."

I showed her the rest of the exhibit, and then we walked back to where the men were busy working. They stopped what they were doing.

"We don't want to keep you from your work, gentlemen, so we're going to go," I said.

"It was good seeing you, Allie," Maynard said. "And it was nice meeting you, Ms. Patterson. Come back anytime."

"Please call me Edith, young man," she said. "I've enjoyed meeting all of you and seeing your project today."

"It was nice having you," he replied. "Don't be a stranger, Allie."

"I won't. You guys have a great day!"

Hiram and Nathan waved at us, and then Aunt Edith and I walked back to the parking lot.

"So, where are you headed now?" Aunt Edith asked.

I pulled out her helmet from inside the trunk of my car. I had locked it up so that she hadn't had to carry it with us.

"I'm going back to the pedestrian bridge where that rock was thrown yesterday," I said. "See if I can scrounge up some clues."

Aunt Edith put on her helmet then straddled the seat of the Harley. "Do you want some help?"

"No, that's okay. Why don't you go home and swim or do something fun this afternoon."

She nodded. "I think I will. I'll probably take the pups on a little walk first, and then we'll hang out by the pool." She started the motorcycle. "See you this evening."

I watched her zoom out of the parking lot. I climbed into my car and headed toward H-1. After exiting onto the Pali Highway, I located the side street that led to the pedestrian bridge. Modest homes lined the left side of the street. There was a sharp drop-off on the right side. When I reached the top of the incline, the street veered off to the left. A narrow strip of blacktop led to the bridge. I parked, grabbed my purse, and then climbed out of my car and walked onto the bridge.

It was about eight feet wide and had steel handrails running waist high on both sides. The footpath was made of crisscrossed steel. Solid aluminum plates came up knee high on both sides and were topped with metal rails.

I could see the cars racing by on the highway below. Every time one passed, a *swoosh* of air sent dead leaves and dirt flying. I stood for a moment and watched traffic traveling toward Honolulu. Just like the victims, everyone was going about his or her business. It made me angry to think of the self-centeredness and evil inside whoever had committed the crimes.

"They need some lessons in compassion," I said to myself.

I looked over the railing. Though I had never been afraid of heights, watching the cars racing below made me dizzy. An eighteen-wheeler rumbled by, and I felt the bridge shake. Instinct made me grab the rail.

Well, it's time to get this done if I'm going to, I thought. Still gripping the handrail, I walked across the bridge to the other end looking for clues. On my way back, I spotted a cigarette butt sticking out of a clod of dirt. I reached inside my purse and pulled out a red pen and piece of white scrap paper. After folding the paper into a V-shape and cupping it in my hand, I fished out the butt with the pen then pushed it into the paper. I folded the paper and slipped the package inside my purse.

On the day of the incident, several detectives had searched the area, but I was hoping to find something they might have missed. My heart skipped a beat every time a big truck passed below causing the bridge to shake.

Years of dirt had accumulated where the side panels met the footpath. Much of it had hardened. I kicked a loose clod, and it bounced like a rock. If the holes in the floor grid had been larger, it would have fallen onto a car passing below.

The panels attached to the sides had been christened by graffiti. Some of the words had bled through the silver paint job.

It takes more than one coat, I thought. When my brother Jamie was a senior in high school, some of the football players had climbed up and spray-painted graffiti on the water tower in Paradise. Uncle Clarence was on the town maintenance crew at the time. I remember hearing him complain that it took two coats of the metallic paint to cover up the mess.

I pulled off a fleck of loose paint from the panel. It crumbled, and the pieces floated through the holes in the floor behind me and dispersed in the wind. Next to the bridge panel near the spot where it fell through, I noticed something yellow intermingled with dried leaves. I took a step back then leaned down to get a closer look. It was a couple of Juicy Fruit gum wrappers wadded together. The foil inner wrappers were still flat and were laying about a foot away.

I reached back inside my purse and pulled out the pen and the paper containing the cigarette butt. After unfolding it, I worked the yellow balls out of the leaves with the tip of the pen then rolled them onto the paper. I also pushed the two foil pieces into the package.

I scanned the area but didn't see anything else worth retrieving. As I started to walk on across the bridge, my right shoe was stuck. I looked down and pulled on it. A big glob of gum was stuck to it.

"Eeewww." The recent showers had kept the yucky blob of chewed gum moist. Long strings were hanging from the sole of my loafer. A couple of strands had wrapped themselves over the top.

I set my purse down. While holding on to the rail with my left hand, I pulled off the shoe with my right. The floor of the bridge wasn't the cleanest, and I wasn't crazy about getting my sock dirty. I tried to balance on my left foot while I fished my red pen out again. I figured I could scrape off enough of the gooey gum to keep from getting it all over the floor mat in my car.

Just then, another eighteen-wheeler flew by underneath, sending up another *whoosh* of air. A cloud of dust blew through the holes in the bridge floor. I started coughing and teetering back and forth on my left foot. The next thing I knew, I fell into the railing. I barely caught myself before I toppled over the edge.

I heard the squeal of tires. On the highway below me, I saw a car screech to a stop. Another car coming up behind it swerved to miss the back end. He pulled over to the edge of the road and stopped.

On the other side of the highway, the same thing was happening. People were stopping along the side of the road, getting out of their cars and pointing at the bridge. When one man started yelling at me, I realized I was the reason.

Uh oh. It hadn't dawned on me that people driving by might see me and wonder if I was the rock thrower. When I saw two police cruisers with their lights on pull up behind my car, I knew I was going to have some explaining to do.

The officers climbed out of their cars. One of them was talking into the microphone clipped to his shoulder. The other one, with a hand on his revolver and a frown on his face, was slowly advancing toward me.

Still holding my sticky loafer in my hand, I said, "Sir, I can explain."

He held up his free hand. "Miss, I don't want you to get excited." He continued toward me. "We're not here to hurt you."

I heard sirens on the highway. I glanced down and saw two more police cars pulling to the side of the road.

"We're not here to hurt you," he said again, "and we don't want you to hurt yourself either." He continued walking toward me.

Hurt myself? Did they think I was planning to jump off the bridge?

I started shaking my head. "No, you've got this all wrong. I would never hurt myself." I started to panic. "My name is Allison Kane, and I'm teaching summer school at Prince Kuhio Elementary."

He was still frowning and didn't look like he believed me.

"I'm also a part-time reporter for the *Hawaiian Star.*" I started digging inside my purse for my press I.D. "I've just been up here looking for clues."

The other officer walked up next to the first one. He muttered something to him. The first officer stopped frowning and dropped his hands to his sides.

I don't know what the other cop told him, but I breathed a sigh of relief when the one talking to me moved his hand away from his gun.

"I'm sorry, miss," he said. "I didn't realize you were Detective Kahala's girlfriend."

Oh no.

"He's on his way here."

First the funeral procession and now this, I thought. *Simon wasn't going to be very happy with me.*

The policeman pointed to the houses along the side street. "Besides numerous other callers, three of the people living over there called 911. Each report was about the same; there's a strange-looking woman with a blonde ponytail walking back and forth on the bridge. Some of them thought you were a jumper, and the others seemed to be afraid you were up to no good." At least a dozen people were standing in the yards of the two houses nearest the bridge. They were all looking at us. He cleared his throat. "After the incident here the other day, I'm sure you can understand their concern."

I dropped my gummy shoe onto the bridge floor and slid my foot inside it. "I'm sorry about all of this," I said. "I was just trying to get information for my newspaper article. I didn't mean to cause such a ruckus."

Just then Simon pulled up. He parked behind the second police car. I felt like a heel.

Both officers looked his way. The one I'd been talking with motioned toward Simon. "Well, it looks like you're in good hands now, Miss Kane. We'll be on our way." They turned to leave.

"Thanks a lot," I said, somewhat sarcastically.

I suspected they were glad it was me who had to deal with Simon and not them. I watched them nod at him as they passed each other. He was shaking his head as he walked toward me.

"Before you get on to me, I can explain," I said.

He grinned at me. "I hear you went to a funeral today."

I rolled my eyes. The grapevine in Hawaii worked even faster than the one back in Paradise. "No. Aunt Edith and I just led everyone to the gravesite."

He leaned forward and gave me a kiss. "You really keep things hopping around here, Allie." He motioned toward the bridge. "The 911 circuits have been jammed for thirty minutes. Every driver with a cell phone passing under this bridge must have called it in."

I nodded toward the still growing crowd in the yards across the street. "Not to mention the neighbors," I said. "But I take offense to being called *strange-looking*."

Simon reached out for my hand. I picked up my purse then put my free hand inside his.

"When I heard that the suspect had a blonde ponytail, I had a hunch it was you," he said. He dropped my hand and looped his arm around my waist. We walked toward our cars in step with each other. "Fifty feet above the highway with blonde hair, folks probably took you for a *haole*."

"Well, it doesn't mean I'm *strange-looking*." My feelings were hurt.

He pulled me closer to him. "People on the island hate to think that these rock throwers are locals, so they're secretly hoping they can pin it on an outsider." He stopped and turned me to face him. "Of course, it would be easy to make you a permanent resident here. Just say the word."

The word. I knew what he was referring to—love. Neither of us had launched out and said it yet.

I looked deep into Simon's brown eyes. There was a sparkle there that I had seen a lot lately. His long, thick eyelashes couldn't hide it.

I smiled at him. "Easy?"

He grinned. "Well, maybe that was a bad choice of words." We continued walking toward my car. "One thing I discovered when I visited you in Oklahoma was that you and your family members have very strong ties."

I nodded. "My parents and grandparents would be heartbroken if I considered leaving Oklahoma."

We had reached my car. Simon nodded toward the bridge. "Did you find anything useful while you were over there?"

I opened my purse and took out the folded paper containing the cigarette butt and gum wrappers. I unwrapped the package so that he could see the contents.

"I don't think the wrappers have been lying there very long," I said. "They aren't brittle or faded from the sun."

Simon took a handkerchief from his back pocket. He picked up the cigarette butt with it. "I'm surprised the detectives missed this."

"Well, to their credit, all this stuff was partially covered with dead leaves.

The way the traffic below whips the wind around up there, they could have been completely covered when they were looking for evidence."

"I'll send this stuff to the lab." His cell phone started ringing. "Kahala," he said. Within seconds, he was frowning. "I'll be right there."

"I take it the call wasn't good news," I said.

He put the phone back into his shirt pocket. "Another rock has been thrown off a pedestrian bridge."

I looked down at my watch. It was 4:10 p.m. "Where?"

"Not far from the Byodo-in Temple on Kahekili Highway."

"I want to come with you," I said. "Can I follow you over there?"

"Sure, let's go."

Simon opened my car door for me then hurried to his cruiser. I turned my car around and followed him down the side street to the Pali Highway entrance ramp. He turned on his lights and siren, and we were on our way.

After exiting the Pali tunnel on the Kaneohe side, we curved around onto Kamehameha Highway. Though I had traveled all around Kailua and Kaneohe since being on the island, Simon led me down an unfamiliar road that branched off from the main highway. For several blocks, we traveled in a densely populated residential area then turned onto Haiku Road.

Up ahead I could see an ambulance and several police cars with their lights on. The pedestrian bridge spanned the divided road and wide drainage ditch that split the lanes in two. Beneath the bridge on the right side of the road was a Ford Fusion. The back glass had been shattered and part of it was gone.

Simon pulled in behind one of the police cars, and I parked behind him. We climbed out and began walking toward the scene. Marshall was talking to a young woman. As we drew closer to them, I could hear her crying. The paramedics working close by supplied the answer why. A tiny form, barely three feet long, was wrapped in sheets lying on the gurney.

I gasped. "Oh, Simon! A baby's been hurt this time!" Not a sound was coming from the child.

Simon's eyes were blazing with anger as he marched toward the attendants. Two of them were working on the child. I held back—I wasn't prepared to see if what I feared was true.

My attention turned toward the young mother. She was sobbing uncontrollably, so Marshall wrapped an arm around her. My heart ached for her, and I wanted to do something to help.

"Don't worry," Marshall said to the woman, patting her shoulder. "We're going to get whoever did this to you and your baby."

I could tell that Marshall was upset himself. With a flick of his chin, he motioned for me to come over. I walked over to them then placed my hand on the mother's shoulder. With tears streaming down her face, she looked at me. My heart wrenched, so I put my arm around her and drew her close. She laid her head on my shoulder. I started praying silently that God would help and comfort her.

Just then, in the direction where the toddler lay, I heard a whimper. Both the mother and I looked that way. There was another whimper, then an all-out wail. The baby's little feet were kicking under the sheet, and one arm was beating the air for all he was worth.

"My baby!" the mother yelled. She broke from me and ran the short distance to the gurney. She leaned over and cupped the baby's head between her hands. "Mommy's here, sweetheart. Mommy's here!" She started stroking the child's chest and tummy with one hand and talking to him softly. Though he wasn't happy to be to be confined—and he was letting all of us know it—with his mother near, he started calming down. His shrill cries soon turned into gurgles and coos.

Simon walked back to where I was standing. Though much of the anger in his features had been replaced by a look of relief, he was still agitated.

"Do they think the baby's going to be all right?" I asked.

"Hearing him cry out was consoling," he said. "The medics said his heart rate and blood pressure were good, but they couldn't wake him up. Apparently he was knocked unconscious when the rock broke through the back window."

I brushed a tear from my eye. "Poor little guy."

"He has a couple of cuts from flying glass that may require a stitch or two." The attendants were loading the toddler into the ambulance. The driver was helping the mother inside. She seemed more in control than she had been earlier. "Marshall and I will follow them to the hospital. When the mother's up to it, we'll see if she can tell us what she saw."

I looked toward the bridge. Beneath it, Dave and some other detectives were talking to several people. "This makes me sick, Simon." My sadness was quickly turning to anger. "What is this wacko trying to prove? How long before he kills somebody?"

Simon had a grim expression on his face. "Chances are getting better with each new attack. Over a hundred tips have come into the hotline since last Thursday, and we're investigating them all, leaving no stone unturned."

I felt helpless but wanted to sound encouraging. "Well, there's bound to be a break soon."

He smiled. "I hope so." The ambulance was turning around. "I've got to head to the hospital. I'll call you later tonight, okay?"

I nodded. "I think I'll go talk to a couple of those people over there before I head home."

I watched Simon get into his car. He fell in behind the ambulance as it drove by. Marshall was close behind him.

Hoping for a lead, I talked to each of the eight people still at the scene. Unfortunately, all of them had arrived after the incident occurred. One person, who was the first to arrive, said someone riding a Honda whizzed by him when he turned onto Haiku Road. Aside from noticing that the driver was dressed in black and had a dark face guard on his helmet, he hadn't seen anything else distinguishable.

The crowd dispersed, and a tow truck came for the mangled Fusion. I talked with Dave for a while and watched a couple of the other detectives do a plaster cast of some tire marks near the bridge. With the rain the previous night, there were some good impressions in the mud. After that, I drove home.

CHAPTER 8

"That's one of the saddest things I've ever heard!" Aunt Edith said. While we ate dinner, I had told her about the event at the bridge. "Boy, would I like to get my hands on whoever hurt that baby!"

"Me too," I said, setting down my fork. Though the mouth-watering mushroom steak Aunt Edith had prepared was as great as always, I had only been able to eat a few bites. I was still too upset about the mother and child at the scene. "Thank goodness he wasn't hurt worse than he was."

Aunt Edith started stacking our dirty dishes. She hadn't eaten much either. "Are Simon and his team any closer to catching the person doing this?"

I picked up the two bowls containing the remaining mashed potatoes and leftover broccoli. "I don't think so. Today I gave him a couple of things I found near the Pali Highway crime." I set the two bowls down on the kitchen counter. "But who knows if it will lead to anyone."

Aunt Edith started loading the dishwasher. "I just can't stop thinking about that poor baby's mother," she said, shaking her head. While holding a dirty plate in midair, she turned toward me. "You know,

Allison, we should go to the hospital and take that baby something. The mother too."

I put the margarine in the refrigerator. "Oh, they probably have family there with them," I said, closing the door. "Besides, Marshall and Simon were going to talk to the mother."

Aunt Edith put the dirty plate down. "All the more reason to go," she said. She started loading the dishes faster. "You said that the mother seemed to be comforted by you. She might be able to tell you something that she won't think to tell Simon and Marshall."

I thought about that. "You know, you might be right." I started wiping down the counters to hurry the cleanup along. "It's worth a shot."

I called Simon to tell him that Aunt Edith and I were coming. He told me that the only family member there with the young mother was the baby's father. Apparently they had recently moved to the island from Japan and had no other relatives living here.

Just before dusk, Aunt Edith and I left the apartment to head to the hospital. It was sprinkling when I pulled onto H-1, but it quickly turned into a downpour. The hospital was eight miles away from Aiea. For a few miles, my wipers had a hard time keeping the water off the windshield. About a mile from the facility, the rain stopped.

Since I had been a patient at the hospital myself, I knew the location of the gift shop. Aunt Edith and I bought a teddy bear for the baby and a lotus plant for his mother. We both thought that a plant from her native homeland might make her feel better.

We found the baby's room in the pediatric ward on the fifth floor. He was in a semi-private room, but no one else was in the other bed. The inner wall was made of glass to allow for easier monitoring by the nurses. I could see the child's mother standing on one side of his bed. She watched Aunt Edith and me approach. The child's father was standing with his back to us on the other side.

Simon was standing at the doorway. When he saw us, he came to meet us. "You made it fast," he said. He leaned over and kissed my cheek. "You didn't speed, did you?"

I smiled and shook my head. "In that pouring rain? Not a chance."

Simon arched his eyebrows. "Has it been raining again? Inside these thick walls you can't hear much."

I looked around him at the family inside the room. "How's the baby?"

"The doctor said his CT scan looked good. We figure the rock may have grazed the baby's head because there is a scrape on one temple." He glanced toward the room. "If it had been a direct hit, he wouldn't have fared as well." When he looked back at me, I saw a flicker of anger in his eyes.

"Did Marshall find out anything from the mother today?" I asked.

"Not much. Marshall is always very thorough when questioning people, but this time, the mother was so distraught it really upset him. He's got a slew of young nieces and nephews, a couple of them infants. He told me a while ago that all he could see when he was trying to comfort that mother was his two younger sisters' kids."

"I know just how he feels," I said. "I kept thinking about Ryan, who's about that baby's age."

"After Allie told me about what happened, neither one of us ate much dinner," Aunt Edith said.

"It stole my appetite too," Simon said. He looked at the clock on the wall by the nurses' station. "I'm glad you two decided to come. Marshall left this with me to go back to the scene to scout around before dark. Even though Dave is thorough, Marshall doesn't want to take a chance that something will be overlooked. I told him about the stuff you found today at the Pali bridge."

"Oh gosh, Marshall doesn't think I'm trying to show you guys up, does he?" I said, frowning.

Simon put a hand on my shoulder. "Of course not. Though you've gotten yourself into some tight scrapes, we're grateful for your help. Marshall is just antsy to follow this up. Dave called him and wanted him to drive down to the office when he could. He wanted to show Marshall what he and the other guys gathered at the scene today."

"Yeah, I saw them do a plaster cast of some tire tracks," I said. "It was pretty cool."

He smiled. "I don't suppose you turned up anything, did you?"

"Well, one guy I talked with said he saw someone riding a Honda whiz by him when he turned onto Haiku Road. He said the rider was dressed in black and had a dark face guard on his helmet." I heard a distant rumble of thunder.

"Yeah, Marshall got the same information."

The baby's mother walked to the doorway of the room. She stood looking at us.

I looked at Simon. "Why don't you go try to talk to her," he said. "Maybe she'll open up to you."

Aunt Edith handed the teddy bear to me. "Go ahead, Allie. If you come bearing gifts, she might feel more comfortable."

Simon gave me a quick kiss on the forehead. "I'm going downtown to find out how the lab's coming along with the cigarette butt and gum wrappers. I had a patrolman come by here and pick them up. I'll call you later to see if you find out anything from the mother."

"Okay, I'll talk to you later."

Aunt Edith stepped toward Simon and raised her head as high as she could. "I'll take one of those too," she said.

I grinned and so did Simon.

"Sure, Aunt Edith." He leaned down and kissed her forehead.

She smiled and patted his cheek. "Thanks, I needed that."

He waved good-bye then walked toward the elevator.

I guess I made a good connection with the baby's mother, because she told me everything she could remember. Though her attention had been on her child, she remembered hearing a motorcycle zoom off. She had already relayed that much to Marshall. She told me that she looked through the broken back glass of her car and saw the rider. Her description of him was much like the one I had received from the other guy. But there were some additions. She had noticed red and yellow flames of fire painted on the side of his helmet. Also, she had seen gold tassels hanging down on each side of the handlebars. She said she hadn't thought to tell Marshall about either of those things.

"I've thought about getting some of those snazzy tassels for my bike," Aunt Edith said on the ride back home. "They really spruce up the handlebars."

I smiled. "I'll tell Simon what I found out when he calls later." I took the Moanalua Road exit off H-1. I glanced at Aunt Edith. She was looking out the passenger window. "So, what did you do the rest of the day after you left the Garden of Eden?"

She looked at me. "Well, the pups and I took a walk on the shady street around the corner from the apartment. Then we came back home and went down to the pool."

"That sounds like fun." I was quiet for several seconds. "Anybody else there?"

The day after I had the bakery cake delivered to Evelyn Hunter, she slipped a thank-you note under the apartment door. Luckily I had found it before Aunt Edith did.

"Yes, there was a young mother with her two children down there," she said. She cleared her throat. "And Evelyn Hunter was there too."

I mentally calculated how much cash was in my wallet. I let out a sigh—not enough to pay for another cake.

"It seems that Evelyn isn't so bad after all," Aunt Edith continued. "In fact, she can be downright hospitable when she's backed against a wall."

I looked at her. "I take it you gave her no choice but to be more civil to you this time."

"Well, it was the dogs that broke the ice. Evelyn was lying on one of the loungers when we arrived. She ignored us at first, but then when Precious walked over and started licking her fingers, she warmed up a bit. She sat up and started scratching the pup's head. Not to be left out, Rowdy jumped up in her lap and demanded the same attention."

Good dogs! I thought.

"Yeah, I figured that if the pups could forgive her snotty behavior the other day, I could bury the hatchet too."

"Well, I'm glad you got that settled," I said. "You're bound to run into each other once in a while."

"We swam for a while, and then she invited me and the puppies to her apartment for some cake."

I stared straight ahead, very intent on where we were going.

"Yes," Aunt Edith continued, "Evelyn has quite the sweet tooth. She has been eating on a tasty, half-white/half-chocolate bakery cake for several days now. The piece she served me had the letters S-O-R-R spelled out on it."

I was terrible at keeping secrets, especially from my family. We had stopped at a red light. I dropped my head and stared at my lap. "So I guess Ms. Hunter told you I sent her the cake." I raised my head and looked at her.

Aunt Edith smiled and nodded. "I appreciate it, Allison, but you don't have to clean up my messes. I realized I goofed right after I said those mean things to Evelyn the other day. On Sunday morning, I took a couple of those blueberry Danish rolls to her. I had the bakery clerk put them in a separate sack, and then I set them down by her apartment door. I wrote 'Sorry' on the sack and signed it."

"Good for you," I said. I pulled into the apartment complex and headed to the parking garage.

"I think she's lonely," Aunt Edith said. "Her apartment is decorated beautifully, but it lacks that homey feeling. While we had our cake, I mentioned to her that I'd like to put together a little album for Sarah and Daisy using some photos I'm taking here. You know, dress it up with some of those fancy doodads like your mother uses for your book." Mom made scrapbooks for my brothers and me, as well as for Brittany and Ryan.

"That would be a nice souvenir for them," I said. "Gramma's crazy about that sort of thing."

Aunt Edith nodded. "After we had our cake, Evelyn took me back into her bedroom to show me a scrapbook she had put together. There were only a few pages in it, and the photos were of her parents and an older sister. The pictures had been taken decades ago. She didn't have anything current."

I pulled the car into my parking space and turned off the key. "Has she ever been married?"

Aunt Edith shook her head. "She said she came close one time when she was in her thirties. She was still living with her parents, who were both sickly. From what she said, they tried to sabotage the relationship from the beginning. They did very little for themselves. After two years of waiting, her beau got tired of it and found somebody new."

"How awful for her," I said.

We climbed out of the car and started walking toward the tower. The air was heavy with moisture.

"When her parents died, she inherited their home and a tidy little nest egg. But she said the house held so many sad memories for her that she sold it to a couple who moved here from Maui. That's when Evelyn moved here."

I knew that real estate throughout the Islands sold for exorbitant amounts if you didn't possess Hawaiian blood. "Besides taking care of her parents, did she have any kind of job?"

"Well, I noticed in her bedroom that she had a curio cabinet full of Avon cologne and aftershave bottles. Some of them dated back to the early 1960s. Ben and I were big into using Avon back then, and every time they'd come up with a new car bottle or some other nifty design, I'd buy it. I was 'Unforgettable' and he was a 'Wild Country' man." She laughed. "We had bottles of that stuff running out the wahzoo. Anyway, Evelyn told me that she sold it to her neighbors, mainly just to get out of the house once in a while."

"It sounds to me like she needs a friend like you to break her out of her shell," I said. If there was a butterfly waiting to be released from its cocoon, Aunt Edith was the one who could do it.

"That's what I thought too. After I left Evelyn's and got back to the apartment, I called Mildred Wells."

I thought for a minute. I knew that was someone back in Paradise, but I couldn't place her. "I don't think I know her," I said. I looked at Aunt Edith and frowned. "Besides, after leaving Ms. Hunter, why the sudden urge to contact Ms. Wells?"

"You know her, Allie. She's the queen of the Red Hot La De Dahs. Daisy and I went with her to a few Red Hat luncheons last spring. We had a great time."

"Oh yeah. Now I remember." I unlocked the outside door of the tower, and we walked into the foyer.

"Anyway, I called Mildred to ask her to track down some Red Hat chapters here in Hawaii. It turns out they have over thirty groups on this island alone. I thought that if I could hook Evelyn up with a group here, she could meet some women her age, get out more, and have a little fun. Mildred gave me the phone numbers for a few of the queens here, and I made some calls."

"It sounds like a good idea to me, but are you sure Ms. Hunter will think so?"

I had heard some funny stories about various Red Hat groups around Paradise. My neighbor, Mrs. Googan, belonged to one of the chapters. She had told me about some crazy things that had happened at their all-night card parties, during their excursions to Red Hat teas and banquets in Oklahoma and beyond, and a lot more. They were always on the go to places like Branson, Las Vegas, and other exciting destinations. Mrs. Googan traveled with several other ladies last summer on a ten-day cruise around the Hawaiian Islands. They spent time on four different islands, took a helicopter tour, attended a couple of luaus, and did tons of other neat things.

Aunt Edith smiled. "Well, I took a leap of faith that Evelyn would be interested. I couldn't reach the first two queens I tried, but then I spoke with the one who heads up the group in Haleiwa. I was very impressed with her. She reminded me of Mildred. It turns out they're having a 'Roaring 20s' luncheon tomorrow, and she invited Evelyn and me to come."

"Have you told Ms. Hunter yet?"

"I called her, and she said she'd think about it and let me know."

From what I knew about her and from what Aunt Edith had described, I had my doubts that she would want to go.

We reached the seventeenth floor. When the elevator doors opened, Evelyn was standing there waiting to get on.

"Well, hello, ladies," she said, just as cordial as could be. She had a big smile on her face. She didn't look like the same woman who made me feel like a heel when she caught Simon and me kissing in the hallway a while back. "I baked some molasses cookies this afternoon, and I thought you two might like some." She motioned toward our apartment. "Since you weren't home, I just set the package down by the door."

"Thanks, Ms. Hunter," I said. It looked like the waters were peaceful now. "I love molasses cookies."

We stepped off the elevator. "Yes, thanks, Evelyn," Aunt Edith said. "I haven't baked molasses cookies in years. Would you like to come over? I'll fix some coffee to have with them."

She shook her head. "No, sorry, I can't, Edith. I have to get ready for that Red Hat meeting tomorrow." She was bubbling over with excitement.

"I'm glad you decided to go with me," Aunt Edith said. "I'm sure it will be a blast." She looked at me. "Allie, when I was over in the Pearlridge Center the other morning, I saw a costume shop. I wonder if they'd have some 1920s clothes we could rent?"

Evelyn started shaking her head again. "Oh, Edith, don't worry about that. I've got all kinds of long skirts, beads, and fufu hats that belonged to my grandmother. When she passed away, she left all kinds of things to my mother. The clothes were packed away with a bunch of my parents' other things in a storage building not far from here. I went over there this evening and carried home a few boxes full of '20s stuff. If you want to come down to my place later, we can go through it and pick out some things to wear."

Aunt Edith nodded. "Sounds good. I'll be down in a few minutes."

Evelyn got onto the elevator. "See you after while." She waggled her fingers at us.

Aunt Edith and I walked to the apartment. It was hard to believe what

I had just witnessed. Who would have imagined that Evelyn Hunter, the busybody in the building who often complained, stirred up trouble, and caused other tenants to dislike her, could have such a turnaround? Whether she wanted one or not, Aunt Edith had a new friend.

At 10:15 p.m., Simon called. "You weren't in bed yet, were you?" he asked.

"No, I'm just lying on the couch watching the news on television."

"I wanted to let you know that the lab technician lifted a partial fingerprint from the Juicy Fruit wrapper you gave me," he said. "They got a hit on AFIS too."

I sat up on the couch. "Really?"

"Yes, it belongs to a former University of Hawaii student. He was convicted of petty larceny a few months back. He stole a couple of Playstation games from a shop in Mililani Town."

"That's good," I said. "Not the part about him stealing the video games, but that someone has been tied to the bridge incident."

"He's a possibility," Simon said. "But other than that one charge, he hasn't been caught doing anything else illegal."

I sighed. "It's quite a stretch then, isn't it? Why would someone who committed petty larceny start throwing big rocks off a bridge? It doesn't sound very logical, does it?"

"There's nothing logical about crimes that hurt others. We've been trying to determine a motive. What's in it for the person or persons doing it? The victims seem to be random; some are hurt and some aren't."

"I've been thinking about it too," I said. "But so far, I've come up with zilch."

"Well, it's the first connection we've had, so we're checking out this student. First thing in the morning, Marshall and Dave are going to talk to him."

I told Simon that the baby's mother saw the motorcycle rider wearing a flashy helmet. I also told him about the gold tassels on the handlebars. It was new information, so he jotted it down.

We hung up about 10:30. I was tired, so I started getting ready for bed. While I brushed my teeth, a huge clap of thunder rattled the windows.

Aunt Edith wasn't home yet, and I debated about waiting up for her. But since she was in the building just a few floors down, my sleepiness won out. I said my prayers, putting in a special request for Simon and Frankie to catch the criminals they were after. I also asked God to protect Michael and Richard, as well as all my other family members and friends. I turned out my bedroom light and was asleep when my head hit the pillow.

A lot of rain fell through the night. While I dressed for school, I could hear cars splashing through puddles on H-1 below. Normally the water drained off the expressway quickly, but a lot had accumulated on it and was causing some traffic problems.

When I walked into the living room, the television was on. The weather girl said that a tropical depression was hanging over the Hawaiian Islands. Though the sun was shining now, she said to expect more rain that afternoon.

Aunt Edith was in the kitchen making toast. "Good morning, Allie," she said. Two more slices popped up from the toaster.

"Good morning. I see you made it home all right. Sorry I didn't wait up for you last night."

"Oh, that's fine," she said, buttering the toast. "I got in about 11:00. Evelyn had so many nifty clothes and accessories to browse through that we both had a hard time deciding what to wear to the Red Hat tea today." She picked up the saucer of toast and a pitcher of orange juice and started walking toward the dining room table. "I also told her about visiting the Garden of Eden, and we got to talking about flowers and such. She'd like to go out there and see it. Even though it's still under construction, do you think Maynard would mind?"

I shook my head. "I don't think so." I finished putting some mango jam on my toast then took a big bite. When I looked across the table,

Aunt Edith was staring at me. "What? Do I have jam on my face?" I picked up my napkin and started rubbing my chin with it.

"No, I was just thinking about that baby and his mother," she said. She drummed her fingers on the table then took a swig of her orange juice. "Allie, I know you're doing what you can as a reporter, and Simon is too. But I'd like to offer my assistance to help find whoever threw that rock at that sweet woman's car." She set her juice glass down hard. "Yes, sir, it's something I really *need* to do."

I had seen that determined look before. She had "assisted" the Paradise Police Department several times. Among other things, Aunt Edith was the head of the neighborhood watch for her block, and Daisy Johnson was her helper. She and Daisy took their positions seriously. They both kept an eye out for unusual happenings in their area. Since there were several children in the neighborhood, they wanted to be sure they had a secure place to play. Most of the parents seemed grateful for Aunt Edith's and Daisy's astute attention.

One incident stuck out in my mind. Every weekday morning, Aunt Edith got up at 5:00 a.m., fixed coffee, and let her tomcat, Samson, outside. On Monday, Wednesday, and Friday, there is an additional part to her ritual. She puts a white, linen scarf around her hair to hold it back then puts beauty cream on her face. It's a heavy, white, cold cream that she has used forever. She watches *Six in the Morning* on television until around 6:00 a.m. By then Samson is back and ready for breakfast. Once he's back inside, Aunt Edith opens the living room mini-blinds.

A nice, young couple named Lewis lives across the street from Aunt Edith. They have two children. One Monday morning, Aunt Edith noticed the dome light in the Lewis' Volkswagen, which they park in the street, going on and off. The husband, Ron, leaves for work at 7:45, with little Ronnie, their seven-year-old son, in tow. Aunt Edith knew that Ron dropped Ronnie off at Elliott Kane Elementary, and then he goes on to work in Tulsa.

When the dome light in the Volkswagen flicked on, Aunt Edith saw a man wearing a baseball cap inside it. He leaned over the steering wheel then bent down farther, like he was trying to find something on the floorboard.

Aunt Edith decided the guy was trying to hotwire and steal the Lewis' car. Instead of calling Ron or 911, she put on her neighborhood watch vest over her white nightgown and grabbed a shovel from her back porch. She trotted across her front yard, gown flapping in the breeze, white cream on her face, and scarf on her head.

Evidently Ron awoke about that time. He looked out the window and saw a "ghost" flying across Aunt Edith's yard. While watching the scene in the street, he called 911. Frankie was on his way to work and just a few blocks away. When he turned onto Aunt Edith's street, he also saw the white, billowing form. He told me later that he was a bit spooked himself before he realized it was Aunt Edith.

According to her side of the story, she yanked open the car door and caught the teenage boy inside by surprise. She asked him what he was doing in there then ordered him to get out of Ron's car.

"I had to bop him on the shoulder with the shovel a few times to get his attention," she told Frankie. "Not enough to hurt him, just enough to let him know I meant business."

Frankie told me that when he walked up on them, the kid was yelping and yelling, "Quit, you crazy, old lady!" He was trying to escape through the passenger door, but it was locked. She continued poking him with the shovel handle until Frankie made her give it to him.

I looked at Aunt Edith sitting across the table from me. "Well, since you're just visiting Hawaii, the police here might not be as open to your help as they are back home," I told her. I picked up my dirty saucer and juice glass. "But let's give it some thought. Maybe together we can come up with something."

As I hurried to get ready for school, I thought about Aunt Edith's desire to help find these criminals. Heading out the door, I wished that I was accomplishing more myself.

CHAPTER 9

When I arrived at school, I headed to the library to check out books about volcanoes and earthquakes. Today the students would share their reports about the sea animal they had chosen to research. After that I wanted to shift the focus to how the Hawaiian Islands were formed.

I was pleased with each child's report. Several had gone beyond what I had asked them to do and had drawn pictures to accompany it. Mareko and David had constructed a diorama complete with scenery, plastic fish, and a small bowl of water set in one corner of the box. Together we added new sea life words to the word wall. Over twenty new terms had been added during the unit, and they were using the words in their conversation and reports.

"I'm proud of you guys," I said, smiling. "You're all doing so much better with your reading, and you've lost much of the shyness that you came here with."

"It's because we're studying fun stuff, Miss Kane," Mareko blurted out.

Sitting at the desk behind him, Annie reached over and nudged his shoulder. "You forgot to raise your hand!" she hissed.

"Oops!" Mareko shrugged then raised his hand in the air. "Sorry about that."

I smiled at him. "That's okay, Mareko. I'm glad you're enjoying the subjects we've been studying." I turned around to my desk and picked up a book that had an exploding volcano on the front cover. "How would you like to read about how Hawaii was formed?"

"Yahoo!" Mareko shouted. Annie reached forward and nudged him harder this time. "Ouch! Stop punching me, Annie." He started rubbing his shoulder. "I'm just excited; that's all."

"It's okay, Annie," I said. After my announcement, all the children were excited and had started talking to each other about the new topic. "Okay, settle down, everyone, so I can tell you more."

After a few seconds, all mouths were closed, and their eyes were turned toward me. "You'll have a choice of books to pick from." I turned around and picked up the stack lying on my desk. "You need to decide whether to choose a book about volcanoes or earthquakes. Since both subjects deal with rock formations, and I know that some of you have rock collections, I'm going to give you an opportunity for show-and-tell. I'd like you to categorize and label your rocks. The science textbooks on the shelf at the back of the room will help. There's also a special dictionary here in this stack that will assist you too. Tomorrow we'll go back to the computer lab so you can use the Internet."

David raised his hand. "Should we bring our rock collections tomorrow?"

"Yes, please bring them so we can all work together to identify and label as many as possible. Don't worry if you don't have any rocks to bring." I started walking toward the back of the room. "I'll pair you up with someone who brings some." I spread out the books on the activity table. "In a few minutes, I'll let you come back and choose a book. How about having show-and-tell on Friday?"

I heard a few "sounds good to me" and "I'll be ready" among other positive replies.

"Okay, then. Girls, come on back and pick out a book."

"Not again," a couple of the boys groaned. Since the three girls in the class had to compete against seven boys, I tried to give them a little special treatment once in a while. Getting to choose things first was often part of it.

Once everyone had his or her book in hand, they settled down to start reading. I had purposely chosen books containing colorful illustrations in them. Though it was essential to have accurate facts too, the artwork added some flair. For eight- and nine-year-old children, flair was important. From the looks on their faces, I had scored an A+.

I didn't stop for lunch, so when I arrived at the *Hawaiian Star*, I headed for the vending machines. Since many on the staff ate sporadically, Mr. Masaki had recently had sandwich and hot soup machines installed. When I reached them, another reporter named Mia was standing there looking at the various selections. From the sad look on her face, it looked like she was facing the toughest decision in her life.

"Hi, Mia," I said as I walked up beside her.

She looked at me, and then her face crumpled. Tears started streaming down her cheeks.

At first I was at a loss as to what I should do. Aside from an occasional hello in passing, we rarely encountered each other. Wanting to offer some kind of comfort, I stepped over and put my hand on her shoulder. She lowered her head and began sobbing.

"Mia, what's wrong? Can I do something for you?"

She started trying to get control of herself, so I just stood quietly waiting.

"There's nothing you can do," she said, wiping the tears away with her fingers. "It's just been a rough day; that's all." She pulled a tissue from her pocket and blew her nose. "I should have stayed in bed all day. First thing this morning, my husband and I got into a silly argument over the cat. We both left the apartment mad at each other. Then on my way here, over on Kalakaua Street, a guy not paying attention to his driving ran into the back of my car."

"Oh, Mia, I'm sorry. Were either one of you hurt?"

She shook her head. "No, but my left brake light was broken, so that will mean a trip to the repair shop. On top of all that, I just found out that one of my sources for a piece I've been working on for the last two weeks wasn't truthful with me. Now I have to go tell Mr. Masaki that I'm back to square one on it."

There wasn't much I could do to correct any of the things that she had faced, but I wanted to say or do something to help brighten her day. I patted her shoulder. "If I can help you with your article, I'd be glad to," I said. "I'm not making much headway on my own assignment right now, so a diversion might help. And you know that our boss is a sympathetic guy when it comes to sources. I'm sure he's faced similar situations over the years." Mia wasn't looking as forlorn. I motioned toward the vending machines. "And it would be my pleasure to buy your lunch today. How about a cup of hot tomato soup and a pimento cheese sandwich?"

She grinned at me. "Sounds good," she said, dabbing her eyes with the tissue one last time. "But I'm buying dessert. Will it be a Hostess Twinkie or chocolate cupcake?"

"I'm partial to the cupcakes myself. Let's split a package."

We made our purchases then headed toward the employee lunchroom. Chatting while we ate, I think we both felt better when we were finished.

When I reached my office, the phone was ringing. I hurried to unlock the door and picked it up on the fourth ring.

"I was beginning to think you were playing hooky," Frankie said.

"Well, isn't this a nice surprise," I said. "I don't usually hear from you this much when I'm at home."

"I admit it; you're privileged this week. But there's a purpose to this call. I stopped by Paradise Petals this morning to give your mom a birthday card. She told me she hadn't heard from you in a few days." He cleared his throat. "You didn't forget her birthday, did you?"

"No, Jamie was supposed to arrange a weekend getaway to Branson for her and Dad. It was going to be a joint present from him, Jeff, and me. I was going to call Mom later this afternoon and sing 'Happy Birthday' to her and find out how she liked the gift." I started worrying. "I guess I'd better call Jamie first."

"Well, Jamie will probably see Aunt Maggie tonight. He's dependable, so I wouldn't worry about it if I were you."

"I'll check with him anyway, just to be safe. How's the Tailgate Bandit case progressing?"

"Fair. Tips are coming in and we're checking out each one. Rita's about to pull her hair out, though. She had to work a double shift yesterday because the night dispatcher called in sick. Along with a dozen other people, a gal named Estelene Melton kept calling her."

I grinned. "Yeah, I heard about Estelene from Aunt Edith. She's a new member of the Screaming Eagles, and apparently she's also a computer whiz. She tracked down a motorcycle club here on Oahu for her."

He sighed. "Don't tell me Aunt Edith is going to be trekking all over Oahu on some kind of monster machine?"

"She already is. Estelene hooked her up with a guy named Pinky, who lives in Traci and Tommy's apartment building, and he took her to a shop to rent a bike."

"Well, she's a big girl," he said. "Anyway, some of the Eagles decided that they ought to patrol the neighborhoods to help watch for the Tailgate Bandit. Estelene kept calling Rita every two hours with a report. Most of the time she stated that 'all was quiet on the western front.' I guess she likes old war movies. But, believe it or not, a couple of tips we got from the group may help us."

"That's great!"

"Yeah, about 10:00 last night, one of the club members was patrolling over on Maple Street. He spotted an old, gray Dodge pickup without the headlights on pulling out of a driveway. The club member rode on past the house but became suspicious when he glanced in his rearview mirror. The driver still didn't switch on his lights even after he was in the street. The Eagle turned around to check it out, but the guy took off."

"Did he get the license plate number?"

"No. The streetlights are out over there, and he couldn't make out the numbers. But he did notice that on the driver's side, the door was painted red."

"Hmmm. That sounds like Tack Dunbar's truck."

"Bingo."

"Well, I'm not one to defend Tack, but maybe he was visiting someone at that house," I said. Tack had girlfriends all over Paradise.

"That was a possibility. But this morning the owner of the house called the station. He's a fifty-nine-year-old house painter who just moved here from Springfield, Missouri, and he hasn't met anyone in town except his realtor."

"Maybe Tack was just pulling in to turn around." I couldn't believe I was making excuses for him. We had had our share of run-ins over the years. While we were in high school, at one of the spring dances, Tack kept bugging me to dance with him. I finally relented, but before I knew what was happening, he started groping me. I slugged him upside the head and knocked him on his rear end right in the middle of the dance floor.

"The painter reported that the tailgate from his Silverado was missing," Frankie said. "Rita passed the call to me because the guy was really upset. I don't blame him, either. A new tailgate costs about a thousand dollars."

"Did you go question Tack?"

"Yes, but he has an alibi. Peggy Sue Murphy lives one street over, and she claims they were together until 4:00 a.m."

"And you believe her? Peggy Sue isn't the most reliable person in the world."

"Yeah, I know."

Peggy Sue once accused one of our other cousins, Noel Kane, of taking advantage of her. Noel was my age and lived with his family on a large ranch just outside of Wall, South Dakota. Noel had been riding broncs and bulls in rodeos since he was nine years old. He and his brother, Tate, and sister, Summer, always spent a part of their summer vacations with Grandpa and Nana at the Circle K.

When Noel and I were sixteen years old, Peggy Sue set her sights on him and enticed him into taking her out. He wasn't big into dating girls as wild as Peggy Sue, so after a couple of dates, he didn't call her anymore. She got mad about it and retaliated by telling her daddy that on their last date, Noel had forced her to do some improper things. It could have gotten out of hand if Traci and another girl hadn't overhead Peggy Sue bragging to some other girls at Wal-Mart that she planned to get Noel into big trouble. They heard her say that she had tried to get Noel to do those things, but he had rebuffed her. She intended to make him pay for it.

"I know that Peggy Sue's word isn't gospel," Frankie said. "But until we can find someone else who saw Tack out that night, she's his alibi. Now let's talk about more pleasant things. I guess Michael is having a great time fishing."

"He is," I said. "I spoke with him Monday morning. They left Friday, and he caught a ninety-pound marlin that afternoon off the Ka'anapali coast."

"I'll bet he had a ball hauling that thing in," Frankie said. "He could always outfish the rest of us boys whenever Grandad and Uncle Clarence took us up to Grand Lake."

"He said it put up a fight. The ocean waves were giving them fits too, so they took a detour to the Big Island late Friday night. They spent a couple of days there with Simon and Richard's sister, Amanda, and her family. They're part owners of a helicopter tour company. Amanda's husband, Rob, flew them all over the island. They even got a bird's eye view of the Kilauea volcano flaring up. Michael was tickled to see some fresh lava flowing out of it."

"Man, I'd love to see that too!" Frankie said. "I've never had a big desire to travel to Hawaii, but volcanoes have fascinated me since I was a kid."

"Yeah, I remember the model you made for the science fair in sixth grade." I started giggling.

"Well, that explosion was a freak accident," he said, defensively. "The three tries the night before went perfectly. If Donnie Lambert hadn't put in so much baking soda, it would have worked fine."

"Anyway, I plan to grill Michael for every detail of what they saw. It had to be magnificent!" I said.

"When are they due back on Oahu?"

"Sometime late tonight."

"Well, it sounds like he's enjoying his vacation. After we catch this Tailgate Bandit, I plan to take off a couple of days."

"I hope it's soon."

"You and me both," he said. "Well, it's time for me to head home to my wife and a hot dinner. I'll talk to you later."

"Tell Kailyn I said hello."

"Will do," he said, then hung up.

I glanced at the clock. It was 1:30. That meant it was 6:30 in Paradise. I called Mom and Dad's house. The phone rang and rang. Figuring Dad may have taken Mom out to dinner, I tried her cell. She picked it up on the third ring.

"Hello?" she said.

"Happy birthday to you, happy birthday to you, happy birthday dear Mom, happy birthday to you!" I sang to her.

"Well, thank you very much," she said, laughing.

"I'm sure I'm not the first to sing to you today, but I was saving the best for last," I said, giggling.

"That was beautiful, sweetie. I'm so glad you called."

"I tried the house first. Did Dad take you out for a birthday dinner?"

"As a matter of fact, we're at Red Lobster right now having crab legs and shrimp."

My stomach started growling. "Mmmm. That sounds yummy." The Red Lobster restaurant had always been one of my favorites. "Well, since you're eating, I won't keep you long. I just wanted to be sure you knew I hadn't forgotten your birthday. Jamie has our present for you."

"He called me this morning and said that he would see me at Gramma's later tonight for cake."

My stomach started rumbling again. "I suppose Gramma made you an orange chiffon angel food cake." *Man, this was torture!*

Mom laughed. "She told me at church Sunday that she planned to. Want me to mail you a piece?"

I considered it. "I'd sure like some, but it would probably be a gummy mess when it arrived. Maybe I can talk Aunt Edith into making us one."

"There you go. How's she doing?"

I relayed some of what had been going on with Aunt Edith. I also talked with Dad for a couple of minutes. He promised to tell everyone at Gramma's that I said hello, and then we hung up.

I sat in the quiet of my office feeling a twinge of homesickness. Birthday celebrations were a big deal in our family. On the Winters' side, Gramma always made a special birthday cake for her children. She invited their spouse, kids, and grandkids, if they had any, over to celebrate. On the Kane side, since there were fewer members, Nana cooked dinner on her child's birthday and invited all the Kanes over. Since I was related to both sides, I lucked out.

Mom's birthday celebration was the first one I had missed since being in Hawaii, but I was feeling left out. Needing a little pick-me-up, I decided to get out of the office. I had accomplished about all I could anyway.

I pulled out the Oahu map that I had been using to plot the rock-throwing locations. Since I hadn't been out there, I decided to go to the bridge near the Koko Marina Center in Hawaii Kai to take a look around. Maybe I would find something that the police had missed.

When I walked downstairs to tell Mr. Masaki I was leaving, he wasn't in his office. I pulled a red pen from my purse, then picked up a scratch pad lying on his desk. I scribbled a quick note to tell him where I was going, and then left it on his desk. Often finding myself needing something to write on, I tucked a couple of clean sheets from the pad into my purse.

I took H-1, which turned into Kalanianaole Highway to Hawaii Kai. While driving along the shoreline, I switched off the air conditioner and rolled down the windows on both sides of the car. The warm ocean breezes blowing in pushed the melancholy feeling away. Traffic was light, so as I drove along, I was able to steal glimpses of waves rolling in and crashing on shore. The scene was soothing.

I pulled into the Marina Center parking lot and turned off the car. I sat quietly for a few minutes soaking up the sun and watching two sailboats in Maunalua Bay. It was mesmerizing seeing them bob up and down like toy boats in a bathtub. One of them had red and magenta striped sails. It was gliding along at a fast pace. The other one had turquoise and white sails. At first it seemed to be glued in place, but as I continued watching, it grew smaller as it floated farther out to sea. For a few minutes, all seemed well with the world.

Time to get to work, Allie, I thought. I rolled up the windows, stuffed my purse under the driver's seat, and then climbed out. After locking the car, I walked the short distance to the elevated walkway crossing the two-lane Kalanianaole Highway.

Unlike the other pedestrian bridges I had seen so far, this one was a swinging bridge. With all the earthquakes in the region, it seemed to me to be a good choice. It had steps leading up to it. The first six were natural stones that had been set into the grassy hillside. The remaining ten formed the staircase and were made from concrete. The bridge itself was suspended by guy wires held by tall, steel girders on each end. The heavy, wire mesh flooring was similar to the one crossing the Pali Highway.

While I was up there snooping around, a few people carrying shopping bags walked over it. The whole area was teeming with people. I suspected the bridge was used often by not only the residents living on the ocean side of the road, but by tourists as well. With all this activity going on, it was hard to believe that the detectives hadn't found a witness willing to talk about Friday's crime.

I walked from one side to the other but didn't notice anything unusual. With the heavy foot traffic, chances of finding anything that the detectives hadn't already seen was probably moot anyway. By now any evidence missed would either be contaminated or destroyed. I decided to take a look along the highway below.

Despite the busy shopping center a half block away, this section of the road was less traveled. The main highway continued on to the eastern tip of Oahu then circled back north to the Kailua/Kaneohe side of the island. This bridge spanned the section of highway that veered off toward Koko Head.

I didn't know from which direction the car that was hit had been traveling. The detectives would have cordoned off the highway and searched the area within thirty to thirty-five feet of where the rock came down. I decided I'd take a second look within that radius then branch out another ten to twenty feet beyond it.

Starting on the left side of the road, I walked slowly along, looking for anything that may have been touched by humans. I pushed aside grass and weeds with my shoe in case something may have fallen below my line of sight. It took me about thirty minutes to cover that area, but I didn't find anything worth keeping.

I crossed the road and started walking back on the other side. After several minutes, I began getting frustrated. So that the trip wouldn't be a total loss, I decided to gather some seashells for my nieces. I had passed some real beauties in a variety of sizes along the way. Being this far from shore, they had probably washed up sometime when the region had flooded.

Though the area was pretty much litter free, about ten feet back, I had noticed an aluminum piepan lying in the grass. I walked back to retrieve it, picking up a couple of small shells along the way. A few feet off the road, I spotted a larger shell that was a couple of inches long. Near it were two smaller ones.

I picked up the piepan, dropped in my treasures, and then turned to walk back toward the bridge. That was when I saw it.

A jagged piece of glass from a broken windshield was lying on top of a clod of dirt. It was partially covered by weeds, but from that angle, the sunlight was causing it to sparkle.

I knelt down and parted the grass with my hands. The chunk of glass was about the size of a silver dollar. Something black was stuck to it. I picked it up to take a closer look, being careful not to cut myself on the glass splinters. A piece of lava rock was embedded in the center of the shard. I bet my nieces' seashells that it was the point of impact on the victim's vehicle.

"Good job, Allie," I said aloud. I placed the glass fragment in the piepan. There was still a chance I might find something else I had missed, so I continued searching along the side of the road as I made my way back to my car. By the time I reached it, the only things added to the piepan were some more seashells. But that was okay—I had an offering to bring Simon.

As soon as I unlocked the car door, I could hear my cell phone ringing. I pulled my purse out from under the seat and answered it.

"I just got a call from your Aunt Edith," Simon said. He sounded out of breath. "Someone just threw a rock off a bridge near Wahiawa."

"Oh no, not another one!" I started my car. "Did Aunt Edith see it happen?" The joy from my recent find turned to alarm. "She didn't try to intercede, did she?"

Simon was panting. "I'm afraid so." I heard him take a deep breath. "She said she tried to stop a guy speeding off on a motorcycle."

"Stop him? How?"

"Hold on a second," Simon said. I heard him cough a couple of times. There were loud traffic noises in the background. "Okay, I'm back."

"How in the world did she try to stop him? And why are you out of breath and coughing?" I could feel my heart beating doubletime.

"I'm running," he said. He coughed again, then I heard a car door slam.

"Running? Who are you running from?" I pulled out of the parking lot onto the highway. "Where are you?" I was really getting concerned now.

"I'm in my car now at Honolulu P.D." I heard the loud rev of an engine then the squeal of tires. I figured it must be Simon peeling out. "Today was my day to take the annual medical exam required by HSBI. Besides giving blood and going through all the other crummy tests men have to endure, I had to take a stress test." He wasn't breathing quite as hard now. "I was on the treadmill when the 911 dispatcher tracked me down to take Aunt Edith's call."

I was coming up to a traffic light. There were no other vehicles on the cross street in sight. I was debating about running the red light.

"So you just ran off in the middle of the test?" I said. I saw a police car rounding the corner. I stomped on my brakes. Through his windshield I could see the officer wagging his finger back and forth at me. I smiled at him and shrugged my shoulders.

"That's exactly what I did," Simon said. "As I ran out the door, I hollered at the dispatcher to call the Wahiawa police station. I'm streaking that way now."

"Streaking?" I could hear his siren blaring.

"As in eighty miles per hour on H-1," he said. "Which would work great if everyone would get out of my way!" I heard him lay on his horn.

I wanted to find out more about what Aunt Edith had done, but while driving at that speed, it was too dangerous for Simon to be on the phone. "I'm heading that way too," I said. "I want to find out *everything* when I see you there."

"Me too," he said. "See you soon."

My mind was going in a thousand directions as I entered H-1. I glanced at the clock on the dashboard. It was 4:20. Assuming the rock was thrown around 4:00 like the others had been, Aunt Edith would have been with Evelyn Hunter coming back from the Red Hat tea in Haleiwa. As determined to help as she seemed to be when we talked that morning, no telling what she would do to try to stop whoever had hurt that baby boy.

"Lord, Lord, Lord," I said, and then I stomped on the gas pedal.

I made the trip to Wahiawa in record time. Fortunately, I didn't come across any more policemen on the road. Though I know God doesn't condone speeding, He probably made an exception for me this one time. I figured my quick prayer earlier must have helped pave the way.

As I pulled up to the scene, I spotted Aunt Edith talking to Simon. She was dressed in a floor-length black skirt covered in sequins and a red, slinky, silk blouse with a scooped neck. The red pillbox hat she was wearing had small feathers sticking out the top. She was also wearing red pumps. The ensemble fit the 1920s to a tee.

I pulled my pen and the scratch-pad paper from my purse, then climbed out of the car and started walking toward them. Aunt Edith seemed to be doing all the talking. I saw her point a finger toward the bridge, then sling both her arms in the air, and then kick up one leg. Simon was nodding his head. As I drew nearer, I could see that Simon was frowning. He looked my way, and relief swept over his face. Aunt Edith saw me too.

"Allie!" she said. "You should have seen me! Talk about an adrenaline rush!"

I could tell that Simon didn't share her excitement. "I'll be over there with Marshall and the van driver," he said to me. "I'll fill you in when I'm finished." He held up his hand. Between his fingers he was gripping a long, dark hair. "And thanks for this, Aunt Edith."

I watched him walk toward a maroon van sitting sideways in the far right lane of the highway. "Sam's Dry Cleaners" and an address for the facility was painted on the side panel. The hood was caved in, and there was a lava rock the size of a bowling ball sitting on it. Marshall was talking to the red-headed driver.

I turned toward Aunt Edith. "I pulled that hair off the head of that kid riding the bike," she said. She was bubbling over with excitement.

"Simon told me on the phone that you tried to stop the rider," I said.

"Not *tried*; did," she said. "If Evelyn and I had left the Red Hat tea, which was a humdinger by the way, at 3:15 instead of 3:30, I'd have caught the punk *before* he threw that rock off the bridge." She reached up and adjusted her hat, which had tilted to one side. "She and I were cruising along on Kamehameha Highway looking at the sights and had just passed the Dole Plantation when an ambulance sped past us headed this way. A couple of minutes later, a police car roared past us. He was followed by a fire engine. All three of them were running red."

I looked around. "Speaking of Evelyn, where is she?"

Aunt Edith pointed behind me. "Over there in the blue Crown Victoria."

I turned around. On both sides of the road, several cars had pulled off. The drivers were trying to catch glimpses of the action ahead. Parked three cars behind mine, I saw Evelyn's Ford. Only the top of her head was showing.

"What's she doing in there?" I asked. With the sun beating down, it was too hot to be sitting in a closed, parked car.

"She's resting," Aunt Edith said. "She has the air conditioner on full blast and the seat tilted back all the way. When I grabbed the steering wheel so that we'd fishtail in front of that motorcycle, it was a bit much for her to take."

I rolled my eyes toward heaven then looked back at Aunt Edith. "You're telling me that you took control of her car while *she* was driving, then spun it in front of an approaching motorcycle?"

"Yeah, that's about it." She raised her arm and waved. I assumed Evelyn was watching us.

So much for the new butterfly, I thought. After this, Evelyn was bound to claw her way back into that nice, safe cocoon she just left.

"Oh, it got more exciting after we stopped him," Aunt Edith went on. "I jumped out, which wasn't easy in this tight skirt, and then I ran around the front of the car and grabbed the guy's arm. He thought he was going to get away, but I had news for him. Holding tight to his sleeve, I swung my leg up, just like I used to when I was trick riding, then I settled my bottom in behind his. Man, was he surprised!" In her younger days, Aunt Edith used to do all kinds of stunts on horses at the annual Paradise rodeo.

"I'll bet he was," I said. I was feeling a headache coming on.

"Evelyn was watching all this with her mouth hung open. The guy revved up his bike and did a wheelie trying to buck me off. That's when my barrel-racing days paid off. I was stuck to him like white on rice. He started bolting and swerving trying to get rid of me. I hollered at Evelyn to back up the car. She caught on quick. She threw it into reverse and laid some rubber. He tried to swerve around her car, but had to climb that hill over there before he could get away. That's when I climbed off."

I put my fingers on my temples and started massaging them. "You climbed off a moving motorcycle?" I could understand Evelyn's need to lie down.

"Oh, it was no biggie," she said. "When I was a kid, we had a pony that hated fireworks. One July Fourth, I was out riding him, bareback of course, and firecrackers were going off all over the place. He got scared and shot off like a bullet! I just raised one leg and slid off and let him go. When he grew tired of running, he came back home."

I started to argue that a runaway pony was a lot different than a six-hundred-pound motorcycle, but I changed my mind. Actually, there wasn't much difference.

"Could I borrow your pen and a sheet of that paper you have there, Allie?" Aunt Edith asked.

I handed her the two items. She bent her knee so that her thigh became a type of desk. I watched as she drew a circle then some squiggly, snake-like images inside it. After she was finished, she handed the drawing and pen to me.

I raised my eyebrows. "What's this supposed to be?"

She pointed to the drawing. "It's a picture of the tattoo that the kid had on the back of his neck." She reached over and pointed at the swervy lines. "Those snakes were red, but the outline of them and the circle was dark blue, like you often see in most tats."

I held it closer. The symbol meant nothing to me. "I'll give this to Simon. He might recognize it. Maybe it's a gang sign or something."

Evelyn had walked up to join us. She still looked a little gray around the edges.

"How are you feeling?" Aunt Edith asked her. "You look better than you did earlier."

"I'm better now," Evelyn said. "A little cool air and I was good as new." She smiled at me. "Your aunt is quite the feisty one. I guess she told you what happened."

I started to apologize to her, then decided against it. Aunt Edith had told me I didn't need to clean up her messes. I'd let her take this one.

"Yes, she jumps right in the middle of things sometimes," I said.

Evelyn's smile grew bigger. "Well, I think it's great! I've had more fun today than I've had in ages." She looked down and smoothed the front of her clothing with her hands. The black, lacy blouse and fitted skirt was an improvement over the frumpy-style clothing I had seen her wear around the building. "If it hadn't been for Edith, I wouldn't have dressed up and gone to the Red Hat tea today, and I certainly wouldn't have involved myself in trying to stop a criminal." She nodded at Aunt Edith. "Thank you, Edith, for a memorable day."

Aunt Edith shrugged her shoulders. "Thanks for the help. That guy should have thought twice before messing with a couple of cool babes like us." She winked at her.

Once again, Aunt Edith saved the day!

CHAPTER 10

Since the motorcycle rider had been covered from head to toe, aside from the tattoo, Aunt Edith hadn't noticed anything else distinguishing about him. Other witnesses told the detectives that he was riding a black Honda with lots of chrome. However, Aunt Edith did tell Simon that there was a rip on the side of the bike's seat. She had hiked up her skirt before jumping on with the guy. The torn strip of leather had scratched her thigh.

A couple of police cars from Haleiwa had chased the rider up Highway 99. Simon received word that they lost him when he cut through a sugarcane field. The stalks were tall, and the officers lost sight of him. Several Wahiawa policemen blocked off two roads that jutted up against the field, but the guy never rode out. A police helicopter flew over it, but to no avail. The guy had vanished. They figured he had escaped on the trail leading to another plantation.

Aunt Edith and Evelyn drove back to Aiea. In my car, I followed Simon and Marshall to the field. Other detectives were already there looking for evidence. We got out and walked the path where the rider had cut through the stalks. Many were broken or lying on their sides.

One of the crime scene investigators was preparing to take a cast of the tire tracks in the mud.

We were all walking carefully through the field so that any possible evidence lying there wouldn't be destroyed. However, with the massive foliage and sheer size of it, it was like looking for a needle in a haystack. We poked around for over an hour. Around 6:00, it was starting to get dark, so Simon called a halt to the search.

Walking back toward our cars, Simon said, "Thanks for your help, Allie. Another pair of eyes is sometimes helpful."

"But not this time," I said. "I didn't find a thing."

"We didn't know if there would be anything to find," he said. "But you never know."

We were nearing the front of the field where the rider had cut through from the road. The toe of my shoe caught on a chunk of root that was hidden in the shadows. I looked down and pulled it free. That was when I spotted a piece of yellow paper.

I leaned over for a closer look. "No, Simon, you just never know." I pointed to the scrap. "Take a look at this."

He bent over and pulled a handkerchief from his pants' pocket.

"What is it?" Marshall asked. He was a few feet ahead of us but had stopped walking when we did.

Simon stood up with the paper cupped in the cloth. "A Juicy Fruit gum wrapper. And it's not wadded up this time."

Marshall smiled at me. "Good goin,' Allie. At least a dozen of us lead-footed guys have tramped through here and passed over that wrapper today."

"Well, don't give me too much credit yet," I said. "It may not amount to anything."

Simon tapped his forefinger on his temple. "Think positively, Allie. We need a break in these cases."

"Oh! That reminds me," I said. We had reached the edge of the field. I walked to my car and opened the passenger door. "Aunt Edith drew you a picture." I picked up the paper that she had drawn the symbol on and the glass fragment I had found. I walked over and handed the shard to Simon.

"I found this in the grass at the Hawaii Kai crime scene. It might be one more piece to our puzzle."

Marshall shook his head. "I can't believe we missed that!"

Simon smiled. "Guess we're going to have to add Allie to the payroll, Marshall." He looked at me. "I'll get it to the lab. Now, what's this picture you were talking about?"

I handed the drawing to him.

He looked at it and frowned. "Looks a little like the symbol you see at doctors' offices," he said.

Marshall leaned over to take a look. "No, that's from 'Sage Master,'" he said.

Both Simon and I looked at him. "Sage Master?" I said.

He nodded. "It's a popular new Playstation game. One of my teenage nephews asked me to buy it for him for his birthday. Before I did, I thought I'd run it by my sister to be sure that she or someone else hadn't planned to get it for him. She nixed it real quick! Said it was gory and too violent for anyone to be playing, regardless of his or her age."

"Hmmm. The guy today must not think so, if he has it tattooed on his neck," Simon said. "At least it's a way to help us identify him. It's not easy getting rid of a tattoo."

By the time I left Wahiawa, it was too late to get ready for church and make it on time. I had been looking forward to a reprieve and could have used a spiritual boost. When I walked into the apartment, I saw Aunt Edith sitting on the couch reading her Bible.

"Sorry I didn't make it home in time for us to go to church," I said. The dachshunds ran to meet me. I bent down and rubbed each of their heads.

"Oh, that's okay," she said, closing her Bible. "I'm sure you've been busy doing the Lord's work today. I've got some burgers keeping warm in the oven for us." She patted my arm as she walked past me into the kitchen.

"Well, I don't know about that," I said. I walked to the sink to wash my hands.

Aunt Edith pulled some buns from a package and began slathering mustard on them. "Knowing you, I'm sure you have," she said. "First you went to school, and I'd wager my hamburger here that you said a prayer for all those kids before you arrived."

I nodded. "I do every morning."

She plopped a thick piece of meat onto each of our buns. "Secondly, you probably witnessed to someone today, either by an act of kindness or with words."

The thought of how upset Mia was at the vending machines popped into my mind.

"I did get better acquainted with a girl at the paper who was having a bad day," I said. "She seemed to feel better after we talked and had lunch together."

"And I can tell that Simon appreciates your support and help on this case they're working on. You've been an asset to him several times lately." She added some spicy mango relish to the burgers, then put on some lettuce leaves.

"After that motorcycle rider took off today, he cut across a sugarcane field," I said. "I found a gum wrapper like the one that was on the Pali bridge. I'm hoping it will have a useful fingerprint on it."

She added a slice of cheese to each burger then put on the top bun. "See? And I'm sure you called your mother to wish her a happy birthday."

I smiled and nodded.

"Just like I said, you've been doing the Lord's work all day." She put each of the finished concoctions on plates then added a large spoonful of macaroni salad on the side. "Now let's go eat."

I grabbed a bag of Doritos from the pantry and followed her to the dining room table. She said grace, and then we started eating.

I told her I had talked with Frankie earlier in the day. She said she had called Uncle Clarence, and he was still upset about his missing tailgate.

"I started reading through the book of Proverbs this evening," Aunt

Edith said. "Just before you arrived, I read one of my favorite passages found in the third chapter. 'Trust in the Lord with all your heart; and lean not unto your own understanding. In all your ways acknowledge Him, and He shall direct your paths.'"

"I've always loved that passage too," I said, wiping mango relish from my mouth.

"Like Pastor Wells said at church Sunday morning, though we may not understand why, sometimes bad things happen to good people. Both your grandpa and Clarence fit into the 'good people' category, and they're both praying men." She smiled. "I'd sure hate to be in that thief's shoes when he gets caught. And mark my words, he *will* be caught."

The phone started ringing. I had just popped the last bite of hamburger into my mouth. I walked over to answer it.

"Hello."

"It sounds like you're eating dinner," Simon said.

I gulped down the remaining food in my mouth. "Sorry about that. Aunt Edith and I were just finishing. Have you eaten yet?" We had planned to have dinner together, but the Wahiawa incident threw a wrench in it.

"I'm at Honolulu P.D. One of the guys called in a pizza, so I'm eating while I work."

"Did you send the gum wrapper to the lab?"

"Yes, but they're backed up down there, so it will be sometime tomorrow before I get a report." He was quiet for several seconds, and then he cleared his throat. "I just got a call from Amanda."

"Oh? How's she doing?"

"Not too well, I'm afraid. Last night there was a big storm off the southern coast of the Big Island."

"Yes, there have been a lot of those lately." He didn't say anything. "Simon, did something happen to Amanda or to her family during the storm?"

"No, they're all okay." He grew quiet again.

I sensed that he was trying to break something to me but was struggling with what words to use.

"Well, what was she calling about then?" All kinds of bad things started running through my mind. That's when it hit me. "Something's happened to Michael and Richard, hasn't it?"

"Now don't jump to conclusions," Simon said. "Richard is an excellent seaman. Amanda lost contact with them early this morning, but they've probably just been thrown off course a bit."

"But with the state-of-the-art radios and tracking equipment she and Richard both use, how can that be?" My stomach was rolling. "And what about their cell phones? Has anyone tried to call them?" As soon as that came out of my mouth, I realized the foolishness of the question.

"Out on the open sea, cell phone service is iffy at best," Simon said. "But don't worry. Amanda notified the authorities, and the Coast Guard is already on it. Also, Rob and his brother are in a chopper searching the area where Amanda last saw them on the screen."

I put my hand on my aching stomach. "Would Richard's high-powered yacht stay afloat and weather a storm, even a big one?"

"In normal circumstances it would."

I was starting to get it. "But these aren't normal circumstances, are they? What aren't you telling me?"

He took a deep breath then let it out. "The earthquake off the coast of San Francisco has wreaked havoc on the ocean floor, stretching to the Islands and beyond. Along with the tropical storms that keep popping up around here, the water has been churned up big time." He paused. "Around midnight, the weather service spotted a rogue wave about five hundred miles east of the Big Island."

"A rogue wave? What in the world is that?"

"It's a freak of nature. I don't have the statistics, but maybe one in every 10,000 waves becomes extraordinarily high."

The *Poseidon Adventure* movie popped into my mind. A massive wave had struck that ship and capsized it. "So if a rogue wave hit their yacht, it wouldn't stand a chance, would it?" A wave of despair washed over me. My cousin was lost at sea! Tears sprang to my eyes.

"Now don't get all upset," Simon said. His voice was soothing. "Richard watches the instruments closely, and if that wave was coming toward them, I'm sure he would have steered them out of harm's way. There could be other reasons why they dropped off Amanda's screen, like a malfunction in her GPS equipment."

Or if they've been dragged to the bottom of the sea, a little voice mocked. I tried to push the worry away and take comfort in Simon's words. The hamburger I had just eaten was threatening to come up.

Trust in the Lord, a different small voice said. "Well, I'm believing that Michael and Richard are going to be found and will be just fine," I said to Simon.

"Good girl," he said. "And I'm believing it with you. Now get some rest. I'll call you when I get more information."

After we hung up, I filled in Aunt Edith. Though I knew she cared for the boys, she didn't seem to be as upset about the situation as I was. Before we went to bed, we knelt together by the couch and prayed for Michael and Richard's safekeeping. We also prayed for the people searching for them, that they would find them soon.

After I was ready for bed, I took my Bible from the nightstand. I slid between the sheets and held it to my chest and closed my eyes. "Give me the scripture I need right now, Lord," I prayed.

I set the Bible on my lap and let it fall open on its own. I looked down and saw Psalm 89. Reading the first few verses, I was reminded of the strength and faithfulness of God. When I reached verse nine, I felt a wonderful sense of peace sweep over me. "The Lord rules the raging seas. When the waves rise, He stills them." I read the verse aloud a couple of times, and then finished the chapter. After setting the Bible back on the nightstand, I fell asleep.

The next morning, I woke up before Aunt Edith. I took the pups outside to do their business. After they finished and we were back inside, I fixed some pancakes for breakfast. By the time they were ready, Aunt Edith was up and dressed.

"Well, isn't this a nice surprise," she said when she walked into the kitchen.

I put the last pancake from the griddle onto the stack. "It's not too fancy, but at least you didn't have to do the cooking this time." I reached up and took the bottle of syrup from the cabinet.

"Oh, I enjoy cooking for someone besides myself," she said. She poured herself a cup of coffee. "Man, I slept like a rock last night. I guess working at the deli and all the running around I've been doing caught up with me."

We carried the food and condiments to the dining room table. "How's it going at the deli?" I asked. "Are you enjoying working there?"

"Oh, I'm having a blast," she said, sitting down in her chair. "Luu is fun to work with, and Sammy is a hoot. He keeps us laughing while we're preparing the mountain of food for the lunch customers."

"Good. I'm glad to hear that. I want you to enjoy your vacation." I took a bite of pancake. "I'm sorry I've had to work so much. Among other things, these rock-throwing cases are keeping me really busy at the newspaper."

"Don't worry about it. I'm having a great time." She poured a big glob of syrup onto her half-eaten stack. "I don't always take the same route to work, so I'm seeing a lot of the island every day." Since I wasn't available to drive her around, her motorcycle was proving to be valuable transportation.

"Well, I'm covering the King Kamehameha Hula Competition that starts tomorrow night for the paper. How would you like to come along with me?" I started stacking the dirty dishes. "I thought I'd invite Simon too."

"I'd love to!"

"From what I've researched so far, it's bound to be lot of fun to watch. Dancers from the mainland and Japan come here and are joined by others from the Islands to compete. They have male groups, female groups, combinations of both, and groups of senior women competing."

"*Kupuna wahine*," Aunt Edith said. "I fit right into that category."

I set the dirty dishes into the sink. "I know *wahine* means woman. I take it *kupuna* means senior?"

"You got it," she said, putting the syrup bottle back into the cabinet. "It will give me a chance to wear my grass skirt again."

Oh no. "Well, I'm afraid it may be too late for you to enter the competition. Besides, they have their groups already established. Most of them have been practicing together for years."

She thought about that for a second. "Well, I'll take it along just in case."

I decided to let it go. I hurried to get ready for school then left.

Many of the students brought different types of rocks to class. Several of them were unique. The books they had read helped in the labeling process, and Internet searches filled in the gaps. Mareko brought an unusual lava rock full of holes. While on a picnic with his family, he had found it on a beach near Makaha. He told me that he had fished out tiny seashells that were buried inside two of the deeper holes. When the noon bell rang, everyone was prepared to give their reports and show their collections the next day.

On my way to the *Hawaiian Star*, I stopped by Duke's Tator Shack and picked up a baked potato topped with chili, cheese, and sour cream. The spicy aroma coming from inside the sack made my stomach do flipflops during the rest of the drive. I tried to settle it down by taking sips of Dr. Pepper.

When I arrived at the newspaper, I hurried to my office, turned on my computer, and then started eating. Well into finishing off the spud, the phone rang. I swallowed most of the bite that I had in my mouth before answering it.

"I caught you eating again, didn't I?" Simon said.

I wiped my mouth with my napkin. "Believe it or not, I do others things besides eat," I said. "I'm working at the same time." At least I had turned on my computer. "Any word yet about Michael and Richard?"

"The Coast Guard has been searching the area where they were last picked up on radar. They haven't found any debris from a wrecked vessel, so that's good news. Also, I contacted the National Oceanic and Atmospheric Administration in Boulder, Colorado. The guy I talked to told me that there could have been a glitch in Richard's GPS due to space weather interference. He said that people from around the globe have been experiencing all kinds of crazy things with their systems lately. They report the problems to their carriers, and then the carriers contact NOAA. "

"Space weather? It's bad enough having to deal with storms right here on Earth without having weather in outer space playing into the scenario."

Simon chuckled. "Space weather refers to what happens to us during stormy times on the sun. Last spring I read an article about it in the *Hawaiian Star*."

"Hmmm. I never heard of it."

"According to the article and from what the guy at NOAA told me this morning, we're in what they call a 'solar minimum.' Solar flares and storms are really cranking up. They cause all kinds of problems for global positioning systems. Apparently electromagnetic surges during the storms are too much for our transformers to handle."

"So all of us earthlings, who have become dependent on electronic gadgets that get their signals from satellites, are going to start having problems," I said.

"That's about the size of it. It's likely that the one on Richard's yacht was affected."

"I hope it is a simple GPS malfunction," I said. "I don't like thinking that a rogue wave may be the cause of their disappearance."

For several seconds Simon didn't say anything. "Have you told Mr. Masaki that Michael and Richard are missing?"

I sighed. "No, but I'm sure he's picked it up from the newswire services. The reporter in me knows the story has to be covered, but the closeness I have to the two guys is screaming that it's not true." I couldn't bring myself to call Richard and Michael victims.

"I'm sure Mr. Masaki will understand," he said. "He'll probably assign another reporter to cover it."

"I imagine he already has. Still, I'll go down and tell him that I'll help with it if he wants me to." I glanced at the calendar on my wall. "On a lighter note, I was telling Aunt Edith this morning that I'm supposed to cover the King Kamehameha Hula Competition at the Neal S. Blaisdell Center Arena tomorrow evening. She's coming along with me. Would you like to come too?"

"I wouldn't miss it. I love watching beautiful women in grass skirts."

I cleared my throat. "Is that right?"

He caught on quickly. "Oh, I didn't mean *other* girls. *You're* going to wear one, aren't you?"

I giggled. "Nice save, but you know better than that. Aunt Edith plans to bring hers along, though."

"I'm sure she'll be the belle of the ball. What time should I pick you two up?"

"It starts at 6:00, and I'd like to get there ahead of time to try to get a few interviews from some contestants. Is 4:30 too early?"

"Four thirty it is," he said. "But I'm leaving *my* grass skirt at home."

I started laughing. "I'm sure you'd look adorable in it, but I don't blame you. The guys at the police department would probably razz you to death if they saw you in it."

"Yeah, they're jealous. I have prettier legs than they do."

"I don't doubt it."

"Well, as much as I'm enjoying this banter, I've got to head to a meeting with the brass. How about dinner out tonight? Pick you and Aunt Edith up about 6:30?"

"Sounds good. See you then."

I called Aunt Edith to tell her that Simon wanted to take us out for dinner. She told me she appreciated his invitation, but she had a date with Mr. Omura. She sounded excited about it. I was glad for her and for myself too. Simon and I hadn't had much alone time lately.

I pulled out the folder containing the Oahu map and my notes on the rock-throwing incidents. Red X's marked the spots where incidents had occurred. I tried to determine if there a pattern. Studying the map, the locations appeared to be random. Two of the drop points were close to popular tourist attractions. One had been dropped near the Koko Marina Center in Hawaii Kai. The other three rocks had been dropped from bridges spanning busy highways. I drummed my fingers on the desktop.

I reached inside my top desk drawer and pulled out a ruler. Using the scale at the bottom of the map as a guide, I laid the end of the ruler on the Kalihi dot and measured the distance to the H-1 Exit 16 bridge where the incident took place the next day. As the crow flies, they were about twenty-five miles apart. Then I moved the ruler and measured the distance between the bridge crossing the Pali Highway near Queen Emma's Palace to the bridge near the Koko Marina Center. Again, approximately twenty-five miles apart.

"Maybe you're on to something here, Allie," I said to myself.

Encouraged, I measured the distance from the Marina Center bridge to the bridge crossing the Kahekili Highway where the baby had been hurt. Twenty-five miles, give or take a mile or so. I was getting excited now.

I measured the others, and most of them were about the same distance from each other. The one in Wahiawa was the only sticking point. It was about fifty miles from all the other bridges. *Maybe the guy messed up that time*, I thought. *Or maybe he's just not finished yet!*

I started searching for other pedestrian bridges on the map. Though I couldn't be sure that the map maker had marked them all, I circled the ones that he had. When I was finished marking, sixteen red circles were staring back at me.

"Shoot!" I said. With only a one-in-sixteen chance of catching the rock-thrower in the act at one of the remaining bridges, I needed some help. "This calls for reinforcements."

I knew that Simon would be in his meeting, but I decided to leave him a voice mail. When I called his cell phone, it went directly to it.

"Hi, Simon, it's me. I've been studying a map and have marked pedestrian bridges from where rocks haven't yet been thrown." I paused a moment. What was I going to do, tell him how to do his job? "Uh, being the conscientious detective that you are, you probably already have officers watching those bridges, but I'm planning on taking a shot at it too." I paused again. Since I didn't know for sure where I was headed, I decided to leave it at that. "See you tonight."

I folded the map and stuck it inside my purse. After shutting down my computer, I went downstairs to talk to Mr. Masaki.

"Knock, knock," I said as I tapped on his open door.

He looked up from the sheet of paper he was reading. "Come in, Allie. Have a seat."

First I told him about Richard and Michael's disappearance. As I figured, he was already aware of the situation. I was relieved when he told me that he had assigned the story to Mia Cunningham.

"I know that it's hard, but I hope you won't worry too much about your cousin and his friend," he said. "We have highly trained Coast Guard personnel stationed here, and they are experts when it comes to rescue procedures. Nearly every week, at least one sailor or yachtsman gets into a distress situation somewhere out there in the Pacific and needs their help. Their recovery success rate is very good."

"That's reassuring," I said. "I'm trying to stay positive and believe for the best. I did want to tell you, though, that if I can help with the story in any way, I will."

He smiled. "I'll tell Mia."

I told him that I had been plotting the locations where the rocks had been thrown so far. I wanted to stake one out with the hope of catching the perpetrator in the act. Mr. Masaki wasn't enthusiastic about my plan.

"I admire you for wanting to try to catch these guys," he said. "But it's a long shot that you would be at the right bridge at the right time. Besides, I'd be concerned for your safety if you were there. These criminals aren't concerned about hurting innocent people with the rocks, so I doubt that they would mind hurting you either."

I knew he had a valid point. "I guess you're right. I'm just tired of the walls I keep running in to."

"I understand, Allie. I really do. Every reporter faces the same thing at one time or another." He stood up and walked to his file cabinet. "I forgot to give you a folder of clippings on past hula competitions. Since you're covering it this year, why don't you spend some time this afternoon going through it? There are some funny interviews and pictures in it that are bound to cheer you up." He pulled a thick manila folder out of the second drawer then handed it to me.

"Okay, I'll look through it." I stood up to leave. "Thanks for your advice about the stakeouts."

He nodded and smiled. "I imagine you would have figured it out on your own."

I walked back to my office with the file in hand.

CHAPTER 11

Over dinner at one of the local diners, Simon told me that around 4:00 that day, a rock had been thrown off a bridge near Kahuku Town. It had missed the back of the driver's car by mere inches. The motorist said the motorcycle rider's helmet had red and yellow flames painted on each side.

I pulled the map from my purse. No bridge near Kahuku Town was marked on it.

"I got your voice mail today," Simon said. "I hope you didn't waste your time staking out a bridge." He reached into the bread basket that was sitting on the table between us and helped himself to another dinner roll.

"No, Mr. Masaki talked me out of it." I reached into the basket and took out the remaining roll. "It ended up being a worthwhile day after all, though. I'm better prepared to do the hula competition story, and I also got to talk to your sister."

Simon raised his eyebrows. "Really?"

I nodded. "She called on my office line. If I had gone out on the stakeout, I would have missed her."

He stopped buttering his roll. "Uh, what did she have to say?" He had a slight frown on his face. "If you don't mind sharing."

"She said she was checking to see how I was doing in regard to

Michael and Richard's disappearance." I set my roll down on my plate. "I told her I was trying to keep the faith that they would be found soon safe and sound."

Simon nodded his head. "That was nice of her to call you." He took a bite of his roll then picked up his salad fork. "Did she say anything else?"

I put both elbows on the table and clasped my hands together, then rested my chin on them. "She told me not to be too concerned that they were last sighted near *Kiapolo Lua*."

Simon sighed and put down his fork. He wiped his mouth with his napkin, then laid his hands on the table.

"I wish she hadn't mentioned that to you," he said. "*Kiapolo Lua*, or the 'Devil's Pit' as it's called in English, came from an old Polynesian myth."

"Amanda said that some people compare it to the Bermuda Triangle," I said.

Simon shook his head. "I think that's an exaggeration."

"So you don't think some mysterious force caused the yacht to be drawn into the abyss?" I smiled at him.

"The entire Pacific is an abyssal plain. A few ships have gone down in that particular area under mysterious circumstances." He picked up his fork again. "Any loss of life is tragic, but with the number of people that sail those seas, it could just be coincidence."

"When I told Amanda I had never heard of *Kiapolo Lua* and that you hadn't mentioned that it was where Richard's yacht dropped off her screen, I could tell that she realized she had put her foot in her mouth. I downplayed it like it was of no consequence, and then we talked girl stuff for a while." I reached my right hand across the table and patted his free hand. "After I hung up with her, I did a little research regarding that area on my own. From what I discovered, there's a lot of volcanic activity going on around there."

"Yes, lava flows are prevalent, and new sections of land are added to the ocean floor all the time." He speared a bite of meatloaf with his fork. "In that particular area, magma comes up through cracks in the earth's crust, and chimneys form. Methane gas bubbles up through the chimneys, or 'black smokers' as they're sometimes called, causing unstable conditions for boats." He stuck the meat into his mouth.

I began shaking my head. "So what you're telling me is that if you combine space weather with rogue waves and add in these black smokers, not counting severe storms or other complications, any of these things could have contributed to the yacht going off course?"

"That's about it."

"Well, then why in the world would *anyone* want to subject themselves to those kind of conditions?"

Simon started smiling. "For sport, adventure, thrill? When you get into your car in Paradise and drive to Tulsa, you're taking a chance. Regardless of how great a defensive driver you are, there's always a chance that, God forbid, you'll have a wreck. Drunk drivers are a menace on the road, and they're becoming more of a hazard every day. And you know what they say, more accidents happen to us within ten miles of our own homes than anywhere else."

"Okay, I get your drift." I scooped the last bite of my mashed potatoes onto my fork. "Michael and Richard, like most men, thrive on adventure. Michael was very excited about getting to go fishing for marlin and to hang out with Richard on his yacht." I sighed. "I just hope it will be worth it."

"Don't worry. Like I told you, Richard is an excellent seaman, and I believe they're going to be found soon. Now let's finish our dinner."

The rest of the evening, I didn't let myself dwell on negative things. I just enjoyed Simon's company. Our time together was running out, and I wanted to make the most of every minute.

We arrived back at the apartment before 9:00. He stayed a while and we watched *C.S.I.* on television. I told him it was one of Aunt Edith's and Uncle Clarence's favorite shows. Though he endured it, he couldn't help making fun of the drama in the lab.

"There's no way those superglue vapors are going to bring out that perfect fingerprint," he said. "The culprit would have to have motor oil on his fingertips to leave such a remarkable print."

I just ignored him and watched the show. I had always been a fan of it myself.

When the program was over and Simon was ready to leave, Aunt Edith still hadn't returned from her date. I walked Simon to the elevator. We took our time kissing good night.

After he was gone and I was back in the apartment, I grabbed a root beer from the fridge. I walked onto the lanai and sat down in one of the chairs. A cool breeze was blowing off Pearl Harbor. The night lights up and down Moanalua Road and beyond were beautiful. I sipped my drink and enjoyed the glory of the Hawaiian night.

I started thinking about the baby that had been hurt and wondered how he was doing. My thoughts wandered to the other victims too, then drifted to Michael and Richard.

Michael's favorite Bible verse popped into my mind. "He that dwells in the secret place of the most High shall abide under the shadow of the Almighty," I said aloud.

"I will say of the Lord, He is my refuge and my fortress: my God; in Him will I trust," Aunt Edith said.

I looked up and saw her standing at the door. "I didn't hear you come in. I guess I was so engrossed in this gorgeous scene, someone could have come in and carried me off. Come out and join me."

Aunt Edith walked out and sat down in the other chair. "This is such a magnificent place," she said, looking out over the balcony's railing. "It's reassuring to know that the Almighty is just as comfortable watching out for us here as He is back home in Paradise."

I nodded.

"You know, Allie, Michael lives by those two scriptures we just said. I've heard him quote them many times."

"Yes, I have too."

"Michael trusts God to meet every need," she said. "One time I heard him talking to your cousin Noel at the Circle K. It was the summer after he had just graduated from high school. That day Noel received a rejection letter from one of the South Dakota colleges."

I remembered that day. Noel had always wanted to be a veterinarian, but school had never been easy for him. Though he studied hard, his grades were mediocre. He received rejection letters from three different colleges in one week.

"We were just sitting around on the porch, and no one was really saying much," Aunt Edith continued. "All at once Michael laid his hand over on Noel's shoulder and quoted those two scriptures. He looked at Noel and said, 'You're going to be hearing from a great school soon. And you're also going to get a good part-time job when you get back home.'"

I looked through the darkness at her. "The next week, I remember Uncle Tom calling Noel to tell him that a new veterinarian had just moved to Wall and needed an assistant," I said. "He worked for him while he attended classes at the University of South Dakota."

Aunt Edith stood up. "Those scriptures are words to live by, Allie." She winked at me. "There's no better shelter than under the Almighty's wings. And mark my words, wherever Michael and Richard are right now, they're both under that shelter."

She walked inside the apartment and closed the sliding glass door. I looked down at the traffic below moving on H-1. *Everyone is going about their own business*, I thought.

I looked up at the sky. "Michael and Richard are under your wings, aren't they, Lord?" There was no audible answer, but within my spirit I felt peace. I winked at the sky. "Thanks."

When I walked outside to the parking garage the next morning, it was a gorgeous day. The birds were singing and the sun was shining. As I drove to school, I gave Simon a call.

"Good morning," he said when he picked up.

"And how are you this fine, sunny day?" I asked. Just hearing his voice made me smile.

"Much better now that you've called. What's up?"

"I forgot to ask you yesterday if the lab found any prints or other useful evidence on that piece of glass I gave you."

"I'm afraid not. I meant to tell you, but with everything else, it slipped my mind."

"Bummer," I said. I could see up ahead that the lane I was driving in was being diverted to the left. A couple of road workers were filling potholes. The rocky, black material they were using reminded me of the rock that Mareko had brought to school. "I know they probably already checked, but would you please ask the technician who tested it if he dug down into the holes in the rock? Maybe our perpetrator got careless and some skin cells scraped off and fell into one of them."

"They're pretty thorough down there, Allie."

"Yes, I'm sure they are, but would you mind humoring me on this? Call it a hunch, or just wishful thinking, but I was hoping that we'd get something off that rock."

"Okay, I'll ask him to take another look."

In the lane beside me, a car horn blared. I glanced in my rearview mirror. A Toyota pickup had cut in front of a Mercury Sable.

Simon cleared his throat. "I hope you're not talking on your phone while you're trying to drive in rush-hour traffic."

Oops! "Not for long," I replied. "See you tonight about 4:30. Have a safe day!" I disconnected before he had time to admonish me further.

The students all did a fantastic job on their reports. Several had drawn or printed off pictures they had found on the Internet and used the art in their rock displays. Show-and-tell was a huge success.

"Boys and girls, I'm very proud of you and the great job you did with your reports. Let's give each other a hand." I started clapping and they followed suit. Some of the boys starting whooping and patting each other on the back.

Mareko raised his hand. "It was fun doing that research on the computer, Miss Kane." The others nodded in agreement. "I wish I had one at home to use this summer."

I knew that most of their families were struggling to make ends meet, and a computer was a luxury most didn't have at home. "Maybe someday, Mareko," I told him. "But there are other resources available to you, which brings up my next point. With only two days of school left, I've decided not to give you any more reading assignments." There was a mixture of cheers, frowns, and "ahs." It surprised me that Mareko and David were among those disappointed that I wasn't introducing more books. "Instead, this weekend, I'd like you all to start thinking about how you feel about reading now and what your favorite book or subject was during summer school."

"Oh, that's easy," Seth said, without raising his hand. "Rocks and Native Americans."

Jennifer was sitting behind him. "That's two subjects, Seth," she said softly to him. "Miss Kane said your *favorite* book or unit." I was impressed that she had substituted the word unit.

"Oh yeah, thanks, Jen," he replied. "Hmmm. I'll have to give that some thought."

Jennifer smiled at me, and I smiled back. She gave me a look as if to say, "He's getting it now, but I'll watch out for him later."

"Well, it's Native Americans for sure," I heard Annie tell the boy behind her. He nodded. David and Mareko agreed together that it was the sea life unit. The others were quietly discussing among themselves what they had enjoyed most.

I smiled at the group. It felt good to see them so animated about the books they had read and subjects they had studied. A bond had developed among them. They had seen each other struggle, but like Jennifer and Seth, they were now respectful of each other and anxious to lend a hand.

"There's something else I'd like you to think about," I announced. "Though you're all too young for jobs now, someday you'll probably want to make some spending money." I had no doubt that they would probably have to get some kind of part-time job in their early teens if they wanted to enjoy the same luxuries that other kids their age did.

"So, in addition to what we've already discussed, I'd like you to think about what professions interest you."

I saw David frown, then he raised his hand. "Miss Kane, there aren't very many jobs for kids."

I smiled at him. "I know that you have to be at least sixteen years old for many jobs, David, but I'm talking about things you can do for neighbors or grandparents to earn some money." He still looked at little confused. "For example, I know that most of you have pets. You might want to consider having your own dog-walking service. Or if you enjoy small children and have helped with your younger brothers and sisters, babysitting might be an option."

Annie raised her hand. "My sister is a lifeguard at the public pool in our neighborhood," she said. "I heard her tell a friend the other day that she makes decent money every summer."

I nodded at her. "There are lots of opportunities out there if you seek them out. Maybe you'd like to mow lawns in your neighborhood. I just want us to toss around some ideas. On Monday we'll see what everyone came up with regarding all the things I mentioned."

The bell was about to ring, so we started straightening the room.

After the students were gone, I walked to the office. I knew that many of them were already making occasional trips to the public library, but I thought it might be fun to have a guided tour. I called the library closest to the school and arranged a tour for Monday morning. After I hung up, I checked my e-mail.

I had a friendly note from Kristin. She was using a computer that was set up at church camp. She said that after dealing with seven-year-old kids all week, she needed some adult interaction and wanted to hear about Hawaii.

I told her that school was going well and that Aunt Edith was enjoying her new job and her visit here. I touched on the rock-throwing crimes then debated if I should mention Michael's disappearance. Since Kristin was at camp, I doubted that she knew anything about it. I decided not to say anything. A subject that serious isn't something you put into an e-mail.

The only person I had called about it was Mom and Dad and Michael's girlfriend, DeLana. Mom had told me that she would break it to Gramma and Grandad. I was glad she was telling Gramma—she was a real prayer warrior. DeLana hadn't taken it well, which was understandable. I should have had Mom go over and tell her in person. Before we hung up, DeLana said she was calling the airlines to get a ticket to fly here. I called Dad back and told him what she had said, and he insisted on paying for her flight. I knew it would be a relief for her. Like me, she lived on a tight budget. She was supposed to arrive around 8:00 tonight. Richard's wife, Kim, was going to pick her up and let her stay at their house.

The only other e-mail I had was from Doug. He was asking about the dachshunds and letting me know that things were fine at home. "I'll be glad when you get back," he wrote. "Your peace lily is missing you."

I replied back telling him to hang in there just a few more days. I also relayed most of what I had told Kristin.

After logging off and signing out in the office, I walked outside toward my car. I stopped in my tracks before I ever reached it. Lying in the middle of the hood was a lava rock the size of a basketball!

I looked around the parking lot, but no one was in sight. The other summer school teachers hadn't left yet, so I figured I was the first one to see it.

Taped to one side of the rock was a white piece of paper. I walked closer so that I could read what was written on it. I got a little weak in the knees when I read the message. "Back Off!" was written in bold, red letters. Beneath the phrase in smaller print, it said, "And the same goes for your white-headed cohort!"

I read the message a second time, and then I started to get peeved. *Guess my articles rubbed you the wrong way, buddy,* I thought. If he was perplexed by Aunt Edith's actions, I figured it must be the guy she had bushwhacked at Wahiawa. I took my phone from my purse and called Simon.

"Guess what's lying on my car?" I said when he answered.

"Well, this one's a first. Do I really want to know?" he said.

"Probably not, but it may help with the case we're working on. Someone put a big lava rock in the middle of the hood." I stepped closer and looked around the edges of the rock. "I hope the car's not scratched."

"You're taking this calmly," Simon said. "I'm more concerned that this person knows where you work than if the school district's car is scratched."

I hadn't thought of that. "Yeah, you've got a point there." I looked around the parking lot again, then toward the playground.

"Don't touch it; I'll be right there," Simon said.

I glanced at my watch. My time was going to be cut short at the newspaper since Simon was picking Aunt Edith and me up at 4:30.

"Can't I just bring it to you?" I opened the car door. There was a crumpled Wal-Mart sack lying on the back floor mat. "There's a plastic bag here that I can wrap around it before I pick it up."

He was quiet for a few seconds. I figured he was debating whether that was a good idea. "I guess that will be okay. Just be careful not to drop it. Even though lava rocks are porous, it might be heavier than you expect."

"Okay, I will. Meet you at the *Star*."

I put my phone back into my purse, then tossed the purse into the passenger seat. After smoothing out the sack, I wrapped it around the rock. Since it was lying in the middle of the hood, I had to lean over the car. My arms had to do most of the lifting. The first time I tried, the thing *clunked* back onto the hood. "Well, if the car wasn't scratched before, it probably is now," I said to myself. I braced my legs against the side of the vehicle, and then gave it another shot. That time I was able to lift the rock high enough to slide one hand beneath it.

When I had it in my arms, I noticed that one edge of the duct tape holding the note in place was loose. *Maybe the pain in the neck that left this also left a print on the gummy side of the tape.*

I laid the rock on the seat next to my purse then headed to the newspaper. Simon was already there when I arrived. While I was parking, he climbed out of his car and walked toward me. I pointed toward the sack. He walked around to the passenger side, and I opened the door for him.

He reached inside and picked up the rock. "This is bigger than some of the others have been," he said. He read the message taped to it. "I may need to assign a patrolman to follow you around."

I slid out of the car. "Oh, that's not necessary. I'm seldom alone except when I'm going to and from my car into a building." I walked over to him. "I'll be more watchful and stick close to another teacher or co-worker in parking lots until we catch this guy."

Simon was frowning. "But that won't help when you're driving around the island," he said. "Since whomever left this knows that you work at Prince Kuhio and here too, he might be waiting on a bridge somewhere along the way holding a big rock with your name on it."

I could see his point. "I'll be extra careful; promise."

Some of the tenseness seemed to leave him, so I suspected that I had won this battle.

"Okay, I'm holding you to that promise. Let me get rid of this thing." He walked over to his car and put the rock in the backseat. "I wanted to let you know that your hunch was right," he said as he walked back toward me. "The lab technician swabbed the holes again inside that rock-embedded glass you gave me. He found a few skin cells."

"Yes!" I said. "Man, am I good or what!"

Simon grinned. "The crevice was jagged, so he had missed them the first time. The DNA matched the strand of hair that Aunt Edith gave me at Wahiawa."

"Good deal! Does it match anyone in AFIS?"

From his expression I could tell that it didn't. "Sorry, no hits. But when we do get a suspect in custody, at least we'll have some evidence to try to match up with him."

"This is frustrating," I said. "We have bits and pieces of this-and-that, but no warm bodies."

"I know it's not easy," Simon said, "but don't get discouraged." He kissed my forehead, then he put his fingers beneath my chin. He tilted my head up so that he could look into my eyes. "Now you need to go inside and bang out a super article that will reassure the public that we're working overtime to catch these guys." He nodded toward his cruiser then back at me. "These thugs aren't fond of you, and I suspect it's because you're putting too much pressure on them. Don't let up now."

I nodded at him and put my hand to my forehead in a salute. "Aye, aye, sir."

He smiled then kissed me again. "See you at 4:30."

I walked into the building and headed straight to my office. I knew that everyone was probably glued to their computers trying to grind out their stories before the 8:00 p.m. deadline.

I took Simon's advice. After thumbing through my notes, I started typing. The anger that I felt after finding the rock on my car found its way into my article. Anyone reading it would know that the police were determined to catch these criminals. I insinuated that the entire force was hot on the trail.

Though I knew Mr. Masaki would have the final word, I chose a headline that I felt summed it up—"Watch out...we're coming to get you!"

CHAPTER 12

Simon was there to pick up Aunt Edith and me right on time. I tried to convince her not to bring along her grass skirt, but it was useless. She insisted that having it with her at the competition would "get her in the mood." I'm not sure what "mood" she meant, but I didn't argue with her. We both climbed into Simon's Jeep, and we were off. He turned east onto Moanalua Road. The Neal S. Blaisdell Center Arena was just a few miles away.

"This is going to be great!" Aunt Edith said. She patted the folded skirt that was lying on the seat beside her. "I sure hope I get the chance to use this baby tonight."

I glanced back at her. "Well, like I already told you, it's doubtful."

"I know, but I wanted to have it with me just in case." She started humming and patting her foot to the beat.

Simon looked at me and grinned. I grinned back.

Aunt Edith stopped humming. "Hey, Allie. Three of the kids you talked to on the bridge the other day just rode past us on the other side of the road."

I turned around. She was looking out the back window. I saw two motorcycles resembling the ones the riders that day had been standing beside. Their shirts were also the same beige color.

"I never forget a bike," Aunt Edith said, turning to face the front again. "Plus, that one kid riding on the back with that other boy had on a St. Louis Cardinals cap."

On our side of the road, we were in bumper-to-bumper traffic. We had stopped, and nothing was coming toward us on the other side. Simon looked into his side mirror. "Well, there's no way I can turn around and catch them now. They're already out of sight." He rolled down his window and stuck out his head. "Something's happened up there." Just then, his cell phone began to ring. "Kahala," he said when he picked it up.

I saw a frown crease his forehead.

"Believe it or not, I'm less than a mile away," he told the caller. He cut the steering wheel to the left and maneuvered the Jeep into the other lane. "I'll be there in a minute." He closed the phone then reached beneath his seat and pulled out a red light. "You girls need to hang on." He slapped the light on top of the car, flipped a switch on the dashboard that started a siren, and then hit the gas.

Stopping the car near the entrance of the Blaisdell Arena, he said, "You can breathe now, Allie."

After traveling at seventy miles per hour on the wrong side of the road, we had reached the location in less than a minute. I let out a sigh of relief that we hadn't hit any cars along the way.

"Man, what a ride!" Aunt Edith said, laughing. "You're my kind of driver, Simon!"

He grinned at me. "Your knuckles are white. If you don't let go of that armrest, your hands are going to go numb."

I glanced down and saw that I still had a death grip on the car door. "I was sure we were going to hit that Volkswagen van that didn't yield the road to us back there," I said. My fingers were tingling. I shook them to stir up the circulation.

"We weren't in any real danger," Simon said. "People here are good about yielding to emergency personnel. The fines are stiff if they don't."

I saw Marshall and Dave standing in the arena parking lot talking to a young man. He was wearing a University of Hawaii T-shirt.

"Marshall is the one who called me," Simon said. "That kid he's questioning over there had a good-sized lava rock in his backpack. He tried to enter the building. I want to ask him a couple of questions, and then Marshall and Dave can take it from there."

"Do you want Aunt Edith and I to stay put?"

He glanced in the rearview mirror. Aunt Edith had already unbuckled her seat belt and was fidgeting in the seat.

"You need to get inside for your interviews," he replied. "You can both come with me."

I climbed out of the Jeep then gave Aunt Edith a hand out. I had borrowed a camera from the newspaper and had laid it in the seat beside her skirt. She handed it to me. I took the small tape recorder that I carried with me from my purse, then put the camera strap around my neck and slung the purse over my shoulder. The three of us walked toward the small crowd that had gathered around the detectives.

Dave looked our way. "Hey, Simon," he said as he walked toward us. "Allie, I'm sorry we interrupted your evening. I'll make this quick."

"How are you, Dave?" Aunt Edith asked. She gave him a big smile.

He smiled back. "Just fine, Ms. Patterson."

"What's the kid saying?" Simon asked him.

"Oh, he claims he was just coming to the competition for a nice evening out," Dave said. "He says he doesn't know how the rock got inside his backpack. He insists he's by himself, though we have witnesses stating that three others on motorcycles rode in with him."

"Probably those riders on the two bikes that whizzed by us on the highway," Aunt Edith said. Dave raised his eyebrows then looked at Simon.

"I didn't see them, but Aunt Edith and Allie did. They were long gone when I received your call." He nodded toward the arena. "The three of us are going to spend the evening here. Allie's covering the event for the *Hawaiian Star*." He nodded toward the guy with the backpack. "I'd like to ask him a couple of questions before we go in."

"He's all yours," Dave said.

The four of us walked toward Marshall and the boy. As we drew closer, I recognized him. He was one of the boys in the group that I had talked with after the incident on H-1.

He had a bored expression on his face, but something changed when he saw me. "Well, if it isn't Miss Reporter and her old lady sidekick," he said.

Marshall grabbed the boy's arm and shoved him up against the cruiser. "Hey, watch your smart mouth, kid," he said.

Simon walked over to the boy, and then he turned and looked at us. "Do you all mind giving us a minute here in private?" He looked at Marshall and nodded our way.

"Sure thing, boss," Marshall said. "Allie, will you and your aunt step over here with me?"

I had seen that expression on Simon's face once before. It was like the calm before a storm. Danger rested there, and I was thankful it wasn't directed toward me. Aunt Edith and I followed Marshall a short distance away.

Simon stepped in front of the kid with his back to us. His nose was just a couple of inches from the boy's. I couldn't hear what Simon was saying, but I saw the boy's knees go limp and his face turn pale. The smirk was replaced with a look of fear.

The boy nodded his head then shook it back and forth. He nodded it once more. Simon stepped back. "Allie, Aunt Edith, our friend here has something to say to you before he accompanies Marshall and Dave downtown."

We both walked toward him.

"Miss Kane," the boy said, "I'd like to apologize to you and your aunt for my rudeness. Please forgive me."

Surprised by the apology, I didn't know what to say. I just nodded at him.

"Apology accepted, young man," Aunt Edith said.

Marshall turned the kid around and handcuffed him. Dave walked over, opened the back door of the cruiser, and then helped the boy inside.

"I'll call you later tonight, Marshall," Simon said. "You can fill me in then."

"Will do. You all have a nice evening, and enjoy the hula show."

While Simon, Aunt Edith, and I walked toward the building, I asked Simon what he had said to the young man.

"Oh, I just told him he needed an attitude adjustment."

I looked at him. "An attitude adjustment, huh?"

Aunt Edith chuckled. "It looked to me like you put the fear of God into him."

Simon grinned. "Well, in a manner of speaking, I may have." He took hold of my hand. "I mentioned that Allie has divine connections with the Big Guy upstairs."

I stopped walking and turned to look at him. "Divine connections? And that's all it took, huh?"

Simon glanced down at the pavement then looked at me and smiled. "Well, I also might have mentioned that in the last three months you've been instrumental in putting two murderers behind bars." He squeezed my hand. "And that they were sent away for a very long time."

"Woo-hoo," Aunt Edith said. "Way to go, Simon!"

"So that kid thinks that I'm some kind of avenging angel? As in having special insight and a mainline to God and judges?" I frowned at him. "Powers that reach beyond the human realm?"

He grinned at me. "In a manner of speaking."

"Call Him up, call Him up, tell Him what you want; Jesus on the mainline now," Aunt Edith sang. The song was a favorite with the congregation at our church in Paradise.

I smiled at her then looked at Simon. "Well, in those two situations you referred to, I did figure out who the guilty parties were, and they are going to spend a long time in jail. Unfortunately, both times I came close to losing my life." The thought still gave me goose bumps.

"But it all came out in the wash," Aunt Edith said. "And you're a better person and reporter because of it."

"She's right," Simon said to me. "Now let's go have some fun and forget about criminals."

Aunt Edith and I sang a little more of "Jesus on the Mainline" as we walked through the gate of the building. There were a couple of people who gave us odd stares, but several others just smiled. One man started clapping and singing along. It was going to be a fun evening!

I had an hour to talk to different group directors and some of the dancers before the competition was set to begin. The tape recorder was a big help. I was able to cover more ground than if I had had to take notes.

Ten minutes before the contest was set to start, I heard the announcer out front.

"Ladies and gentlemen, *wahines* and *kanes* of all ages, welcome to the Thirty-fifth Annual King Kamehameha Hula Competition." The crowd started cheering. "We are proud to announce that we have twenty different groups participating this year, ranging in age from fourteen to eighty-five. Half the groups will be performing the *kahiko*-style dance, as our ancestors did, and the other half will be performing the more modern *auana* style." He gave more background about the competition. When he held up the handsome, carved bowls that would be given out as trophies, the crowd cheered again.

I recorded all of his speech. When he concluded, I needed some clarification on part of what had been said. I saw a group of six young women dressed identically in short hula skirts standing a short distance away. They all had long, flowing black hair and a plumeria blossom pinned on the left side of their heads. Each one also had a lovely orchid lei draped around her neck. I walked over to the group.

"I'm Allison Kane, a reporter with the *Hawaiian Star*," I said. "Do you mind answering a few questions for an article?"

They all appeared shy and didn't seem eager to talk. After several seconds, one of them stepped forward. "I'll help you," she said.

"Thanks, I appreciate it." I turned to a clean sheet of paper in my notepad. "What's your name?"

She hesitated then answered, "Dahlia Hong." After I wrote it down, I held the tape recorder up between us.

"First of all, I've noticed that there are different types and lengths of hula skirts being worn here today," I said. "I also heard the announcer refer to them earlier." I pointed toward her skirt. "Does the style you have on have a particular significance?"

"Yes, we're wearing *kahiko*-style skirts," she said. "They are shorter and are made from ti leaves, woven strands of grass, or some other type of natural material. As you can see, we're embellishing our outfits with leis and flowers in our hair. *Kahiko* means 'ancient' or 'old-fashioned.' We'll be performing the type of hula that our early ancestors used."

"Interesting," I said. Two older women wearing long grass skirts, similar to what Aunt Edith had, walked by us. "Now tell me about the ones those women are wearing."

Dahlia turned her head and looked at them, then turned back to me. "Those are *auana* skirts. That type of dance is slower with more swaying involved. It's a more modern version of hula, though the footwork is almost identical to *kahiko*. Generally, there is less body adornment."

I asked her a few more questions, and then I clicked off the tape recorder. "If you girls don't object, I'd like to snap a picture of you." I stuck the recorder inside my purse and reached for the camera hanging around my neck. "I'll also need each of your names for the caption beneath it."

Though the other girls hadn't been anxious to talk to me, they weren't a bit shy about having their photograph taken. Each one started smoothing her hair, adjusting costumes, or doing other primping before I started posing them for the shot. After three pictures were taken, I asked for their names. A couple of them had to help me with the spelling.

I thanked them all then went to find Simon. Earlier he had told me that he'd try to get some seats near the disabled-seating area so that I could find him easier. He waved his hand in the air when I got close. He had lucked out and found a prime spot in row four. Three seats on the aisle—a perfect place to see everything. When I reached him, he stood up so that I could squeeze by and sit next to him.

The music accompanying the first group of performers cranked up. "I've got two tapes full of interviews," I told him. The music volume increased a notch.

"What did you say?" he hollered.

"I said, I have lots of good material for my article," I hollered back. I glanced at the empty seat beside me. "Where's Aunt Edith?"

The music got louder. He leaned close to me. "She said she needed to go to the little girls' room." He glanced down at his watch. "She's been gone over twenty minutes."

Just then the performance ended, and the crowd was on its feet. Everyone was clapping and whooping. The noise was deafening.

"Where are the restrooms?" I shouted at Simon.

He pointed behind him. "Go straight back up this aisle then turn right," he shouted back.

I nodded, climbed over him again, then started up the aisle.

The crowd was still on its feet as another group of dancers made their way onto the stage. This time the music was from Tahiti. I enjoyed watching Tahitian dancers more than any other kind.

I had reached the back of the arena, so I turned around and leaned against the wall. I wanted to watch the performance before going out to find Aunt Edith.

The dancers were lined up on the stage waiting for their cue. The group was made up of a mixture of both men and women all elegantly dressed in gorgeous costumes. They were all young, mostly in their mid- to late twenties. Their director was standing on the floor in front of them. The drums were going wild!

With all the bright colors, loud music, and emotion from the crowd, the room was electric! During the ten-minute performance, I couldn't help tapping my foot and clapping along too.

When the group finished, they received a standing ovation. The music stopped, and some of the dancers shifted positions. I needed to go hunt for Aunt Edith, but I didn't want to miss a minute of the next act. After everyone was in place, I looked from one end of the line to the other. My mouth dropped open. Aunt Edith was standing between two girls on the left end!

She had on an ornate headdress, a coconut-shell brassiere, and a grass skirt just like they did. Instead of showing her bare midriff like the girls on each side of her, Aunt Edith had put the bra on over her lime-green T-shirt.

The director was pointing his baton toward that end of the line. The girls on each side of Aunt Edith looped their arms around hers. She was all smiles. The drums started their fancy, Tahitian beat, and everyone in the line began dancing.

I had to give Aunt Edith credit. She was gyrating her hips to beat the band! The crowd had noticed her and was going wild. They were cheering, especially when she turned her back to the audience and started moving her hips faster. I didn't know a seventy-eight-year-old woman was capable of that. I doubted that I could last as long as she did.

I glanced down the aisle. Simon was looking back at me. All I could do was shrug my shoulders and smile. He was shaking his head and grinning.

When the performance was over, I walked around to the dressing area at the back of the stage. Aunt Edith was having one of the girls help her remove the bra. She spotted me and waved me over.

"Wasn't that terrific, Allie?" she said. A girl was helping her take off the feather and puka-shell headdress. "Thanks, Cherry."

"You're welcome, Ms. Patterson," Cherry said.

"This is my great-niece, Allison Kane, who I was telling you about."

The girl looked at me and stretched out her hand. "It's nice to meet you. I've read some of your articles in the *Hawaiian Star*. You're a good writer."

I smiled at her. "Thanks. I appreciate the compliment." I motioned toward Aunt Edith. "And thanks for letting my aunt dance with your group today." I looked at Aunt Edith. "I wasn't expecting it."

She grinned at me. "Well, I was sitting up there with Simon wearing my spiffy grass skirt, and I just couldn't let all that bouncy music go to waste. When I left to go to the bathroom, the music just seemed to pull me the other direction. I intended just to take a quick peek behind the stage, maybe catch you while you were doing your interviews. That was when I bumped into Cherry."

Cherry smiled at her. "And I'm glad you did." She looked at me. "Since she had on the skirt, I assumed she was with the *kupuna wahine* group. We walked together to their dressing room, but along the way, your aunt told me she was just visiting the competition with you."

I looked at Aunt Edith. "Then how did you manage to get on stage and dance with the young performers?"

Aunt Edith motioned toward Cherry. "Cherry is the event coordinator's daughter and also the talent director for two different dancing groups in Hawaii. New performers have to try out for her before they ever get to show their stuff to the director. She said that the judges assess the first ten minutes of each group's performance. After the music stops, they can regroup then do whatever they want to for another five minutes purely for the entertainment of the audience."

I looked at Cherry. "So that was when Aunt Edith got to join in and dance?"

She nodded. "She gave me a little preview of her talent backstage, and I knew that the audience would love the addition. I'm sure you heard their response."

"Yes, from their applause, I'd say she was the hit of the night," I said. I looked at Aunt Edith. "You were really shaking your booty."

Aunt Edith smiled. "And it was fun too!"

A young man had walked up beside Cherry. "I'm sorry to interrupt, but Madame Wasuki needs your help."

"I'll be right there," Cherry told him. She turned back to us. "Madame Wasuki leads the *kupuna wahine* group, and they're up soon." She handed a small piece of paper to Aunt Edith. "Give me a call when you're back in Hawaii."

Aunt Edith nodded at her. "Will do. Thanks again."

"It was nice meeting you, Allison," Cherry said. She turned and walked away.

"Cherry said she'd hook me up with Madame Wasuki when I come back to Hawaii," Aunt Edith said. She pushed aside some strands on her grass skirt and slipped the paper inside the pocket in her slacks.

I raised my eyebrows. "You're planning on coming back to Hawaii?"

She nodded. "I love it here! There's no way I'm going to be able to see all I want to on this trip. Not only is there a lot left to see on Oahu, there's a whole chain of islands out there I want to explore!"

I understood how she felt. We're not supposed to envy people, but right then I felt the envy bug bite me.

"But that's for another discussion," she said. "Come on. Let's get back to our seats so we can catch the other performances." She grabbed a handful of grass skirt in each hand then started walking away from me. "I'll bet Simon was surprised to see me out there."

I hurried to catch up to her. "There's no doubt about that," I said. From the shock I had seen on his face earlier, his expression said it all.

Though it was almost 10:00 p.m. when we got home, I called Kim to be sure that DeLana had arrived all right. She assured me that she had. I didn't get to talk with DeLana because with the long flight and time difference, Kim said she was exhausted and had already turned in. Shortly after I hung up with Kim, I hit the sack too.

All night long I dreamed in color. Faceless men holding lava rocks in their hands and wearing feathers, colorful skirts, and coconut-shell bras were dancing all over the place. When the phone rang at 4:45 a.m., I awoke with a start.

"Hello?" I said, nearly knocking it off the nightstand.

"Allie, it's me."

It took me a second to recognize Simon's voice. My thoughts were still in motion from my crazy dream.

"What's wrong?" I asked him. Getting a call in the middle of the night was never a good thing.

"Not wrong…right," he said. "Richard and Michael have been found."

Elation replaced the worry. "Praise the Lord!" In the quiet apartment, it sounded more like a shout. "Are they all right? Where are they?" I tried to shove back the covers, but the sheet was wrapped around my right ankle. I reached down and pulled my foot free. "Was the boat still in one piece? More importantly, are *they* still in one piece?" In addition to the dancing dream, I had dreamed that Michael and Richard were out in the ocean clinging on to a hunk of the yacht. To make things scarier, hungry sharks were circling them.

"Slow down, and I'll answer all your questions," Simon said. "Amanda just called me. She had just gotten off the phone with the representative of the Coast Guard in charge of the search. One of their helicopter pilots spotted a fire on an uninhabited island."

I swung both legs over the side of the bed. "An island?" *No sharks on an island.*

"There are a couple of them southwest of Maui about forty miles from *Kiapolo Lua.*"

Again with the "Devil's Pit," I thought. I knew that there were more than 140 islands in the Hawaiian Island chain, most of them uninhabited.

"The Coast Guard guy said the helicopter passed over that island yesterday evening. The pilot was flying through heavy clouds, so it was difficult to see. He traveled about thirty miles farther north, but something kept nagging at him to go back to that area. By the time he got back, it was nearly dark. He spotted wisps of smoke then saw the orange glow of a fire on the beach."

My heart was beating doubletime. "With all the rainy weather tracking through the Islands, I'm surprised they had anything dry enough around to start a fire," I said.

"Well, Richard was an eagle scout in his teenage years, and he's a whiz at fixing things. If there was any way to get a fire going, I'm sure he figured it out."

"Was there any sign of their yacht?" I still couldn't shake the image of them clinging to bits of it.

"The representative said their boat was damaged, but not beyond repair." He paused for a moment. "Amanda mentioned something about a small family being on the island too, but I didn't get much of the story. She wanted to get off the phone so that she could call Grandma and Grandpa Kahala to tell them the good news about the rescue. She said she'd fill us in later. We won't know the whole story until we see Michael and Richard."

"Where are they now?" I asked.

"The helicopter pilot flew them to a hospital on the Big Island. He said they were both in pretty good condition."

I breathed a sigh of relief. "I'd like to go see them, and I'm sure Aunt Edith will want to come along too."

"I figured you would. Before I called you, I called Hawaiian Airlines and bought five roundtrip tickets. Kim is leaving the kids with her parents in Hawaii Kai. She and DeLana will meet us at the ticket counter at the airport."

"What about Dennis and Charlene?" I hadn't thought to ask Simon before now how his mom and dad had been holding up during all of this.

"Mom and Dad have been at Amanda's since Thursday night," Simon said. "Dad insisted on going up in the chopper yesterday with Rob to search. Mom knows a bunch of people on the Big Island. They've been holding an around-the-clock prayer vigil since she arrived."

"That's wonderful," I said. "On both counts."

"The flight leaves at 8:00 a.m., so I'll be by to pick up you and Aunt Edith around 6:30. Can you both be ready by then?"

"Are you kidding?" I looked at the clock on the nightstand. It was 5:00. "When I wake up Aunt Edith, we'll be ready and waiting by 5:30."

"If it's all right with the two of you, we'll probably spend the night at Amanda's. Is there somewhere you can leave your dogs?"

Precious and Rowdy were rolled up together and lying on the end of my bed. Bleary-eyed, neither of them looked like they appreciated being awakened at this hour.

"I don't know. I've met a lot of people, but I don't know if I'd feel comfortable asking them to keep the dogs."

Aunt Edith appeared in the doorway. Her curly, white hair was sticking out in all directions.

"Hold on a sec," I said to Simon. I covered the receiver with my hand. "Michael and Richard have been found."

Aunt Edith raised her hands toward the ceiling. "Thank the Lord!" she said.

"Simon is coming by to get us, and then we're flying to the Big Island to see them."

"Did I hear you say something about the dogs?" she asked.

I nodded. "We'll be there overnight, so I need to leave them with someone."

She walked to the end of the bed. "I bet Evelyn would come by and feed them and let them out," she said. She started scratching both the pups' heads.

"That's a good idea," I said. "When I get off here, will you call her?"

"Sure." She looked at the clock. "Evelyn's an early riser like I am. I'm sure she's already up having coffee."

I gave her a thumbs up, and then she left the room. "We may have the sitter problem solved," I told Simon.

"Well, if it falls through, we could take the dogs with us," he said. "I'd have to call in some favors to keep them from being quarintined, but it's not impossible."

"If Evelyn Hunter can't do it, I'll call you back. Otherwise, Aunt Edith and I will be down at the front door with our overnight bags by 6:30."

"Okay, I'll see you then," he said, then we hung up.

I hurried to the bathroom to take a shower. I could hear water running, so I knew that Aunt Edith was doing the same thing in her bathroom. After shampooing my hair, I quickly dried it then stuck in a couple of rollers on the crown for some lift. Precious and Rowdy knew something was going on. They both kept getting under my feet. I used a curling iron on my hair then ushered the pups to the kitchen for their breakfast. If they were busy eating, it would be easier for me to get ready.

As Aunt Edith predicted, Evelyn was already up having coffee. She said it would be easier for her to keep the dogs at her place. I was glad for the offer, because I wasn't sure that Traci and Tommy would appreciate me giving a key to the apartment to their neighbor. After Aunt Edith and I finished a quick breakfast, we sacked up the dogs' empty food and water dishes, and then I clipped their leashes onto them. While Aunt Edith finished packing a bag, I took them outside to do their business.

The sun was just coming up. I shuffled back and forth from one foot to the other waiting on the dachshunds to do their thing. Since it was Saturday, traffic was light on H-1. With the reduced noise, I could hear birds singing. It was a joyful sound.

I looked up at the soft, puffy clouds in the distance. They were out-lined in purple as the rays from the rising sun cast their glow. "Thanks, Lord, for keeping Michael and Richard safe out there," I prayed.

Within my spirit I heard a whisper: "The angel of the Lord encamps around them that fear Him and delivers them."

"Thank you, Lord."

As I led the dogs back into the building, I thought about that scrip-ture. I could pinpoint several times in my life when angels surely had been protecting me. It was a comforting thought.

CHAPTER 13

At 9:00, Simon, Aunt Edith, Kim, DeLana, and I arrived at the Kailua-Kona International Airport. Simon's grandparents, Trip and Ella Kahala, had flown over from their home on Maui and were waiting for us at the rental car counter. Trip had already rented a roomy, nine-passenger Chevy van. It was the biggest one they had available. Once we were all seated inside, there was plenty of space for our luggage. Kim had brought along an extra bag containing clean clothes for Richard and Michael.

Upon Trip's insistence, Simon climbed into the driver's seat and told me to ride shotgun. On the way to the Kona Community Hospital, everyone became acquainted. Kim and DeLana were a bit teary-eyed. Though we had all been assured that Michael and Richard were in good condition, from the conversation in the van, the unknown was haunting us all. I wouldn't be satisfied until I had Michael wrapped in a bear hug, and I sensed that DeLana and Aunt Edith were feeling the same way. I was sure that all the Kahalas felt the same about Richard.

When we arrived, Simon led the way to the emergency room. Amanda and Rob, along with Dennis and Charlene and one of Rob's brothers, were sitting in the large waiting room. Introductions and hugs made the rounds, and then Dennis sat back down and gave us an update.

"They found the boys, along with a family of three who had been missing for over four weeks, on a tiny island southwest of Maui," he said. "Apparently the currents flowing through the nearby Alenuihaha Channel have been going haywire due to the high waves and crazy weather around here lately."

"That's over a hundred miles from where they started their excursion," Simon said, "and a far cry from Manuka Bay." For us nonresidents, he elaborated. "Manuka Bay lies near the southern tip of this island. Richard was taking them there because anglers have had great luck catching marlin and other game fish in that area." He looked at his father. "Even with the problems they encountered, how in the world did they get so far off course?"

"When the boys first arrived, they gave us a couple of minutes with them," Dennis said. "Richard told me that the yacht was like a yo-yo in the middle of the ocean. Besides going up and down with the enormous waves, they still kept moving forward. He said the force of the wind was driving them up to twenty knots an hour."

"There was nothing that he and Michael could do but to tie down everything and hang on," Charlene said, wringing her hands. "I'm so thankful they're alive."

She looked small sitting on the seat beside her hefty husband. Dennis outweighed her by more than a hundred pounds. She had dark circles under her eyes. I had no doubt she had lost a lot of sleep since their son had been reported missing.

Dennis placed his big hand over Charlene's small ones. "It's okay now, honey. You saw for yourself that Richard and his friend are going to be fine."

She tried to smile, but exhaustion took over. Tears welled up in her eyes. "Please excuse me, everyone," she said, wiping a tear from her cheek. "It's been a rough three days."

She opened her purse, which was lying on the seat beside her, and started rummaging inside it. I assumed it was for a tissue. Before she found one, Simon, Trip, and Rob's brother had all stepped forward and were pushing their handkerchiefs at her. Their chivalry brought a smile to her face. The rest of the women in our group were looking on. We were all smiling at their gallant behavior and concern for Charlene.

"Well, thank you, gentlemen," she said to them. She took all three of the cloths but only used Simon's. She passed Trip's and Rob's brother's handkerchiefs back to them. "I appreciate it, fellas, but I think I'll use Simon's." She blew her nose into the large cloth a couple of times and then seemed uncertain about what to do with it. She closed her fingers around it and looked at Simon. "I'll wash this then get it back to you, son."

Simon was sitting beside me on a vinyl couch, and we were facing his parents. He glanced at me and grinned, then looked at his mother. "Thanks, Mom. I packed a couple more in my suitcase, so I won't need it back for a while."

She nodded at him. Amanda was sitting between Rob and her brother-in-law. She walked over and sat down beside her mother, then draped her arm around her shoulders. Charlene seemed to be taking great comfort from her family. It was a blessing to watch.

"Hey, sis, do you have any more details about that family they found on the island too?" Simon asked Amanda. "Was it the Jamisons?"

She nodded. "The Coast Guard representative said they had all lost a few pounds but were in pretty good condition considering their ordeal. We'll have to get the in-depth scoop from Richard and Michael."

Simon looked at me. "About four weeks ago, a family named Jamison was vacationing on Maui. One day they took off in a small sailboat from Kihei headed north. The sunny day turned stormy before they returned. Bits of the boat and part of the main sail were found floating about ten miles from shore."

"It's a miracle they were found alive," Dennis said. "That island is nothing but forest and craters. No one ever goes there."

We talked softly among ourselves, being careful not to disturb the other families waiting for reports on their loved ones. About 10:30, a doctor came to the doorway. He looked at Dennis.

"Mr. Kahala? Your son would like you and your wife to come back now."

Dennis and Charlene rose to their feet. Dennis motioned toward Kim. "His wife, Kim, is here too, Doctor," he said. "I know Richard will want to see her also."

"Oh, certainly, Mrs. Kahala," the doctor said to Kim. "Richard didn't know if you would be here yet."

Kim jumped up from her chair and hurried toward the doctor. "How is he, really, Doctor? Is my husband going to be okay?" The moist tissue she had been threading back and forth through her fingers was hanging in tatters. Trip walked over and pushed the handkerchief that Charlene had passed back to him into Kim's hands. "Thanks, Grandpa," she said, looking down at it. She dropped the wadded up tissue-ball into his waiting palm.

The doctor smiled at Kim. "He's had a rough few days and sustained some abrasions and a couple of cuts, but I think he'll be fine."

I stepped toward the physician. "My cousin, Michael Winters, was brought in with Richard. Can my aunt and I come back to see him?"

The doctor nodded. "Mr. Winters is in the adjoining room. If you'll all come with me, I think everyone can fit."

We all followed the man down the hall. He pointed toward the second door on the left. "Mr. Winters is in there," he said to me.

"Thank you," I said. The doctor walked on down the hall with all the Kahalas following close behind.

Simon turned to me. "I want to give you, Aunt Edith, and DeLana some time alone with Michael. I'll go with the others to visit Richard now then stop in to say hello to him later."

I nodded, and then turned to open the door to Michael's room. The door didn't have a round knob. It was a metal lever used in most hospitals that had to be pushed or pulled to move the heavy door.

I opened the door a couple of feet and stuck my head inside the room. Michael was lying on the bed covered with a white sheet. Only his head and sunburned shoulders were visible. His eyes were closed, and I thought he was asleep.

Aunt Edith and DeLana were standing right behind me. I turned around and touched my lips with my index finger indicating that we needed to be quiet. They both nodded at me.

I carefully pushed the large, wooden door open. Sometime during my previous twisting and turning, the strap from my purse had looped over the metal lever. As I stepped into the room, with Aunt Edith and DeLana stuck to me like glue, the strap caused me to stop short. My shoulder hit the door with a loud *clunk*, and Aunt Edith bumped into my back. I lost my footing and tumbled headfirst onto the floor. Since Aunt Edith stopped suddenly, DeLana banged into her. The two of them fell on top of me. All three of us were piled together in the middle of the floor.

"That's quite an entrance, ladies," Michael said. He had one eye open and was grinning at us. "But I'm so glad to see all of you, it's worth the racket." He sat up on the side of the bed.

Ignoring Aunt Edith and me, DeLana stood up and rushed over to him. "Oh, Michael," she said. "I was so worried about you." She touched his cheek. He pulled her to him and kissed her.

Aunt Edith had rolled off of me, and I had managed to stand. I stretched my hand toward her and helped her up. After that, I unwound my purse strap from the door handle.

Michael and DeLana were so engrossed in their kissing they didn't seem to notice that anyone else was around. When they finally separated, Michael looked at us. "Come here, you two. You're also a sight for sore eyes."

"What some people will do to get attention," I said as I walked toward the bed.

He grinned. "Give me a kiss and hug, squirt," he said. "You can't fool me; I know you were concerned too."

I leaned over and kissed his sunburned cheek, and then we hugged each other. "Yeah, I guess I was a *little* concerned," I said, standing back up. "From what Richard told his dad, I take it you had quite a ride out there."

Michael nodded. "You wouldn't believe it, Allie. Think Moses and the Red Sea story, and you'd be close."

"You boys were never far from our thoughts and prayers, Michael,"

Aunt Edith said, walking to the bed. "I was sure you would come out all right." She kissed his forehead, and then stepped back.

"Thanks, Aunt Edith."

I smiled at him. "So you think the waves that you and Richard saw would give Moses and the Israelites a run for their money?"

He nodded. "Aside from seeing a couple of movies and documentaries with walls of water that demolished buildings and took out trees, I've never imagined anything like it. The instruments went berserk, and water was coming over the sides of the yacht too fast to bail it out. I just kept quoting Psalms 91:1 and 2 over and over while the wind and waves had their way with us."

I glanced at Aunt Edith. She winked at me. "Yes, Aunt Edith reminded me last night that she's heard you quote those two scriptures a few times."

"Well, God truly was a shelter for us," Michael continued. "It was like there was a wall encircling the yacht. Though water kept pouring in, it was swept away as quickly as it came in. It was like there was an enormous broom sweeping it back out to sea."

"More like a mighty hand," Richard said from the doorway. We all looked at him standing there. All of his family members were close behind him. "I haven't been big into going to church lately, but Michael made a believer out of me."

"Get in here, buddy," Michael said.

Richard, fully dressed, walked over to the side of the bed. He laid a pair of jeans, a green short-sleeved shirt, and a pair of red polka-dot boxer shorts on the end of Michael's bed. "Since you're taller than me, the jeans may be a bit short, but at least they're clean and haven't been soaked in salt water. I'm ready to get out of this joint, aren't you?" He clasped Michael's outstretched hand and gave it a quick shake. "The doctor has given me my walking papers and said he's heading in here next."

As if he'd been summoned, the doctor walked through the door. All of us stepped aside to give him access to Michael.

"You're free to go too, Mr. Winters," the physician said. He handed him a prescription form. "I'd like you to take this antibiotic for five days to get rid of any infection that might develop due to the scrapes and cuts you sustained. After you're dressed, you can be on your way."

"Thanks, Doctor. I appreciate your help."

As the physician turned to leave, Aunt Edith looked at the roomful of people. "Well, you all heard the man," she said. "Let's scoot out of here so that Michael can get his clothes on and we can split this joint!" She walked toward the door. Everyone smiled, and then we all followed her into the hallway.

Within five minutes, Michael was dressed and standing in the hall with us. Kim had been holding Richard's hand like she'd never release it, and Michael latched on to DeLana's as soon as he joined us.

"To celebrate the safe return of my son and his good friend, I'd like to treat everyone to lunch," Dennis announced.

"The Spotted Pig is just down the street," Charlene said.

"Ooh, I love that place," Amanda said. "Rob does too."

Simon turned to me. "It was voted the number one barbecue place on the Big Island last year."

"I love barbecue," Aunt Edith said.

DeLana and Michael were both nodding their heads. "Sounds yummy and I'm starving," he said.

Everyone else in the group agreed. "Well, let's go to the Spotted Pig then," Trip said. He reached for Ella's hand. "Come on, sweetheart. Our son is treating us to lunch."

As he led her away, I heard Ella softly say, "Before Dennis changes his mind?"

"You got it," Trip replied. He started heading toward the parking lot. Everyone followed him.

Simon and I were behind the others. "Dad isn't big on eating at restaurants or on picking up the tab," he whispered to me. "Don't get me wrong; he's got a kind heart, but he's frugal, and he'll choose Mom's or Grandma's cooking any day over eating out."

I smiled at him. "That sounds like Grandad Winters."

"When we all occasionally meet at a restaurant," Simon continued,

"Grandpa is usually the one who pays. I guess he wants to take advantage of this unique situation."

Once we were outside, Trip led the way to the rented van. Rob and Amanda led his brother and Dennis and Charlene to their late-model, black SUV. Again Trip insisted that Simon drive. Now that Richard and Michael had joined us, every seat was taken. However, with Michael's arm holding DeLana closely and Richard snuggling Kim, the nine-passenger van still could have held a couple more people and not been crowded.

The Spotted Pig was a scrumptious buffet filled with all kinds of barbecue, salads, vegetables, breads, and desserts. Everyone filled both a dinner plate and saucer with the goodies. We sat together at a long, rustic table that seated fourteen.

Aunt Edith was sitting between Ella and me. "You have a wonderful, caring *ohana*, Ella," she said. "They seem to have a lot of fun together like our group does back home."

I looked at Aunt Edith. *I should know that word*, I thought.

"*Mahalo*, Edith. I'm very proud of all my children and grandchildren," Ella said.

I'm going to have to brush up on my Hawaiian. I leaned over toward Simon, who was sitting on my left. "Family?" I asked him.

He nodded. "You got it." He started cutting a piece of roast with his knife. "Hey, little brother, tell us about that family you guys met on the island. I'll bet they were happy to see you."

"You can say that again," Richard said. "The father is an investment banker in New York City and didn't have many survival skills. They were able to pick some star fruit and Japanese bananas and find a few fallen coconuts to eat, but that was about all the nourishment they had had."

"If they were drinking the milk from the coconuts, they were getting lots of vitamin C and potassium," Ella said. "Other people found stranded on uninhabited islands have survived for weeks on coconuts alone."

"I doubt that these people would have," Michael said. "From what the man told us, they live a caviar-and-champagne lifestyle. The wife said they have a maid, and she's used to going to spas and having her nails done twice a week. If you can afford it, there's nothing wrong with that, I guess, but it doesn't help much if you're on a deserted island trying to survive." He was sitting beside Richard. He reached over and patted him on the back. "When Richard rigged up a way to catch some fish then started a fire to cook them for our dinner that first night, they treated him like he was royalty."

Richard wiped his mouth with his napkin. "That scouting experience paid off, didn't it? But you weren't too shabby yourself, old friend. That shaky lean-to they had been living in leaked and was about to fall down. You showed them how to reinforce the walls and make the palm roof more watertight."

"Michael was a great scout when he was a boy," Aunt Edith said. "I still have the macramé plant holder he made for me."

"Well, I may have helped provide the physical comforts, but Michael helped that man and his wife emotionally and spiritually," Richard said. "Their thirteen-year-old daughter, Annie, attends a church near their home, but her parents are agnostics."

"*Were* agnostics," Michael interrupted.

Richard looked at him and nodded. "*Were* agnostics, thanks to you. Annie told us that from their first day on the island, she had been praying that they would be rescued. When her dad caught her one morning, he became pretty upset with her."

"Until she found the stream of fresh water," Michael said. "She had also been praying that they'd find water on the island. On the third day there, she went out to find a secluded place to pray and stumbled on to a small stream flowing with cool, fresh water. Not only was it clean enough to get all they needed for drinking, it was beside a hole that they could fill up for baths."

"God will provide," Charlene said, wiping her mouth with her napkin.

"Yes, He will," Aunt Edith said.

"Anyway, though her dad gave her a hard time about it, Annie never quit praying that they would be rescued," Richard said. He looked at Michael. "She was thrilled when Michael and I washed up on the beach."

"Washed up on the beach?" I said. My dream about the sharks circling them was coming back to haunt me. "You were still inside the yacht, weren't you?"

Richard smiled at me. "Yes, and a good thing too. Tiger sharks swim in that area, and I had already spotted a few."

"Did you know that tiger sharks have caused more human deaths than any other kind?" Michael asked me.

I shook my head.

"Richard shared that tidbit of information with me *after* we landed on the island."

"Well, I didn't see any need to add more worry to the situation," Richard said. "But when we first started having trouble, it crossed my mind that we might be washed overboard and see a few face-to-face. Next to the first aid kit, we keep some shark repellent. We hadn't ever needed it, so it was about three years old."

"And boy, was that stuff ripe!" Michael said, wrinkling his nose. "I had seen the can when we boarded the yacht. It looked like a big can of hairspray."

"Well, if you got some of it in your hair, it would hold it in place, wouldn't it, Dad?" Dennis asked Trip.

"Yes, son, and it would take a dozen shampooings to get it all out." Trip looked at the rest of us. "Sharks don't like the smell of dead sharks. To make the repellent, they take rancid, white shark muscle and boil it down. The stuff is put inside metal cannisters then dropped into the water. The liquid comes out and disperses the sharks."

"Unless you need to put it directly on your body," Michael said. He shook his head. "But let me tell you, when I saw those shark fins sticking out of the water all around the boat, I was ready to take a bath in that stinky stuff!"

"It smelled like you did," Richard said, grinning at him. "Fortunately we weren't washed out of the boat, so the sharks didn't get a taste of an Oklahoma delicacy. The yacht eventually ran up on the rocks. With the size of the wave that hit us, it's a miracle the boat wasn't more mangled."

"There's a famous Coast Guard saying, Richard," Trip said. "You have to go out, but you don't have to come back." He had a solemn expression on his face. "When I heard about you boys, I couldn't stop thinking about the *SS Edmund Fitzgerald*. Back in 1975, a rogue wave brought that ship down, and it was a whole lot bigger than that fancy yacht you two were on. Twenty-nine crew members went down with the ship. When the Coast Guard found it, the thing was split in two pieces."

Ella patted her husband's hand, and then she looked at us. "We've both been pretty upset ever since we heard the news that the boys were missing," she said. "I know it's been a trial for all of us. It was a wonderful relief to see that they are okay."

Richard pushed back his chair and walked over to his grandparents. He squatted down between them and put an arm around each of them. "I'm sorry you were worried," he said.

Trip swiped a tear off his cheek. "Everything is all right now; that's the main thing." He looked around the table. "Now there are way too many empty plates sitting here. You guys need to go back through that line and fill them up again!" Dennis was sitting on his left side. Trip reached over and patted his shoulder. "Remember, Dennis offered to pay for all this good food!"

Several of us started laughing. Simon's dad stood up. "That's right, everyone. Follow me." He led the way back to the buffet.

While we ate second helpings, Richard gave us more information about what had happened prior to landing on the island. He said that the instruments on the yacht alerted him that a huge wave was coming toward them. He turned the boat in the other direction, but the wave seemed to turn with them. The battery died, and the GPS went haywire. When Simon mentioned his "space weather" theory, Richard agreed that it probably contributed to their problems. I told Michael that I tried to keep the faith and not worry too much.

"Jesus wasn't too late for Lazarus, Allie," Michael said. "The rescue plane came right on time for us."

"Lazarus?" Rob asked.

"Rob wasn't raised in church like my brothers and I were," Amanda said.

"Lazarus and Jesus were good friends," Michael said. "Jesus was out of town when Lazarus died. It was four days before the Lord returned. When Lazarus' two sisters, Mary and Martha, told Jesus about the death, He was sad. He told the women to take Him to the tomb."

"Have you noticed there are a lot of Marys in the Bible?" Dennis said. Charlene nudged him in the ribs. "Oops, sorry, Michael. I didn't mean to interrupt your story."

Michael smiled at him. "That's okay. Anyway, Rob, the sisters told Jesus that their brother had been dead too long and that he wouldn't be smelling the greatest, but Jesus insisted. When He reached the tomb, He ordered the stone covering the cave opening to be rolled back. He called out, 'Lazarus, come forth.' Long story short, Lazarus walked out of there, still wrapped in the cloth binding they used back then, and he was as good as new."

"Cool," Rob said. "So even though Lazarus had been dead four days, Jesus still gave him his life back." He paused. "I guess if you and Richard hadn't been found, you'd have still survived until you were."

"Yes, I believe we would have been fine."

Rob looked at Richard. "The pilot who spotted your fire told me that your yacht was sitting in plain sight on the beach."

"Exactly where it washed up that night," Richard said.

"Then how in the world did all of us miss it? Though your dad and I concentrated our search on the southwest side of the Big Island, we flew over the island where you were found a couple of different times. The Coast Guard pilot did too." He shook his head. "I just don't see how we missed seeing that tub of yours. A seventy-five-foot, white yacht sitting on black lava rocks should have stuck out like a sore thumb."

"I believe now that there was a Higher Power controlling *when* we were found," Richard said. "Just put two and two together. Compared to the others in the Hawaiian chain, that island is only a speck. The wind and waves could have driven us twenty or thirty miles farther west, or north for that matter. Instead, we shipwrecked on that particular spot."

"From what the Coast Guard representative told me, if the Jamisons hadn't been found when they were, they probably would have starved to death," Amanda said.

Richard glanced at Michael then back at us. "I believe that my buddy, Brother Michael here, had been commissioned to do a job that we didn't know about when we left port."

Michael smiled. "As it turned out, Richard and I escaped with just a few scratches, and both the father and mother gave their hearts to Jesus." He sighed. "But with all the acrobatics the yacht did on the water, the marlin I caught on Friday came loose and was washed out to sea."

"Yes, and it was a beauty," Richard said.

Talk at the table turned to other things. Since DeLana, Aunt Edith, and I had never been to the Big Island, Trip and Ella suggested that we all venture to Hawaii Volcanoes National Park the next day after church. We were excited about that prospect. Richard and Michael took turns sharing funny and sometimes embarrassing stories about each other. They kept all of us laughing.

As I sat there watching them, I suspected that Michael and Richard would always stay close. Richard had an animated yet peaceful look on his face now. I knew from experience that being with "Evangelist Michael" was a life-changing thing.

After the wonderful lunch, we rode to Amanda and Rob's house. We were all staying overnight there but had different ideas about how we wanted to spend the rest of the afternoon.

Amanda and Rob needed to drive to Rob's parents' house to pick up their son, Denny. They unlocked the house then took off in their SUV to get him. Trip and Ella wanted to go visit some friends they hadn't seen in a while who lived in Honalo, which was just a few miles from Kona. Amanda had told them they could use her Ford Taurus to do that. Rob's brother headed home. Dennis and Charlene retreated to the comfy chairs on the lanai to take naps. Richard and Kim wanted some alone time. They grabbed some lawn chairs and a couple of towels and headed to the private section of beach that ran along the back part of Rob and Amanda's property.

"Well, it looks like the rest of us are on our own," Simon said. He motioned toward the van. "Grandpa's already paid to rent that thing, so how about a tour of some sights around here?"

"I'm game," Aunt Edith said. "Let's go." She started walking to the van.

Michael and DeLana conversed together for a few seconds. "We'd like to tag along too," he said. He started maneuvering DeLana toward the van. "Come on, sweetie, let's get the backseat." He hadn't let go of her arm since we had left the restaurant.

"No smooching while we're driving," I said when they walked past me.

Michael grinned at me. "It doesn't count if you don't see us."

I guess since I was relieved that he was safe, my bratty side was emerging. "Her arm isn't going to escape, Michael," I said. "If you're not careful, you're going to cut off the circulation."

DeLana looked up at Michael and kissed him on the cheek. "Mind your own business, Allie," she said. She looked at me and winked. "I'll gladly suffer numb arms and legs too, just to have him back with me."

I smiled at them as they climbed into the van.

Simon reached over and took my hand. "Come on, Miss Troublemaker," he said. He led me to the front passenger side of the vehicle. Before he opened the door, he kissed me.

"That was nice, but what was it for?" I asked him.

"Just because," he said, smiling. "Just because."

CHAPTER 14

We took off south down Highway 11, which runs along the Kona coast-line. Though we would take the same road the next day to the Hawaii Volcanoes National Park, time would be limited. Simon wanted to show us some special sights along the way.

The ocean view was a treat in itself. The aquamarine color and white-capped waves were gorgeous. Surfers were out in full force. The white-sand beaches were lined with sun worshippers out to get a deeper tan. Instead of running the air conditioner, we all opted to lower some of the van windows to let the cool, salt air drift inside. It was wonderful!

When we reached the town of Captain Cook, Simon turned onto a side road. "If we had stayed on the highway another few miles, we would have come to Kealia," he said. "That's where Rob's helicopter company, Sky Kings Over Hawaii, is located."

The road we were on took us close to the Captain Cook Monument. No one wanted to hike through the high grass down to it. Instead, we just got out and snapped a few pictures. After that we continued on the narrow road to St. Benedict's Painted Church.

When we walked through the front door of the small, white build-ing, we were met by stunning beauty. The scattered columns, painted in muted shades of red and white, resembled candy canes. Pictures of ferns, against a backdrop of a tranquil ocean and sandy beach, were displayed on the arched ceiling. Narrow pews lined the walls.

Aunt Edith walked to the front of the church and sat down on one of them. "This sure is a pretty place to worship," she said. She looked up at the ceiling. "Until you became accustomed to it, I bet it would be hard to focus on the priest."

"Probably so," I said. Simon and I were ambling along hand-in-hand admiring the exquisite wall paintings. Several well-known Bible stories were portrayed.

Michael and DeLana had followed Aunt Edith to the front of the church. They were looking at the sacrament table and other things on the stage. Michael glanced toward the ceiling. "Looks like this building has been around a while," he said.

Simon and I walked forward to join them. "It was built in 1875," he said. "I don't know for sure, but I imagine it was a plain structure until Father John Velge took charge. He told Bible stories to the natives here." Simon ran his hand along the column he was standing near. "In 1899, the interior painting began. It took about five years to complete the project."

We all walked back outside and strolled around the tiny cemetery. Some of the graves had been there since the late nineteenth century. As we headed back toward the van, a priest pulled into the small, gravel parking lot. He waved at us, and we all returned the greeting.

"They have mass here every morning at 7:00 a.m., but they also have a service each Saturday at 4:00 p.m.," Simon said. He glanced at his watch. "Folks will be starting to arrive soon." We all climbed into the van and then headed west toward the Pu'uhonua Honaunau National Historical Park.

When we pulled into the parking lot, Simon said, "In the old days, criminals and defeated warriors traveled here. They came to seek forgiveness from the priests for their sins and safety from their enemies."

We all headed up the long walkway to the visitor center. Aunt Edith, DeLana, and I picked up brochures showing a map of the park and facts about it. Typical of many fortresses, it was built close to water. Simon led the way to the royal grounds then stopped.

"Special permission had to be granted for commoners to enter these grounds," he said. "Even letting your shadow cross this threshold would mean death."

"It would pay to arrive on a cloudy day then," Aunt Edith said. We all looked at her. "You know, your body wouldn't cast a shadow on cloudy days."

We all grinned at her and then followed Simon farther into the compound. He stopped in front of the temple. It had been rebuilt to resemble the structure of ancient times. Branches from mountain apple and *ohi'a* trees were tied together with coconut fiber and crowned with a ti-leaf thatched roof.

Farther along, Simon pointed to a huge rock where holes had been carved out. "The Polynesians have always enjoyed bright, colorful clothing," he said. "Historians think that among other things, those rock-bowls were probably used to hold dye. They may have also been used to let ocean water evaporate for the salt it would leave behind."

Aunt Edith peered down into one of the impressions. "You've got to use what's handy."

Michael pointed to the nearby cove. "Look at those big, green sea turtles," he said.

We all walked to the inlet. The water was gently lapping the white-sand beach. I counted five of the magnificent creatures swimming and eating in the shallow water a few feet out.

"There are a lot of sea turtles in this area," Simon said. "There's plenty for them to eat here." He pointed toward the saltwater pools among the rocks in the ocean a short distance away. "Pools like those were built-in fish holding tanks. The ancients made weighted rope out of ti leaves, and then they'd use them to drive fish into those shallow pools. The method of fishing is call *hukilau*, which means 'seine' fishing."

"In other words, they swept the fish into the pools using large fishing nets," Michael said. Simon nodded. Michael looked at Aunt Edith and me. "If Grandad and Uncle Clarence had lived here, they still would have preferred using poles."

I smiled. "Yes, they probably would have strung together some coconut rope onto a stout stick. When they're fishing, they love the thrill of the fight."

Michael nodded. "It runs in the family. I can't explain the rush I felt when I was hauling in that marlin the other day."

DeLana motioned toward two huts open on each end a short distance from the cove. "I'll bet that's where they dry the ti leaves." Rafters and wooden benches inside the huts were draped with long, green leaves.

"You're right on the mark, DeLana," Simon said.

We started walking that way. I noticed that Aunt Edith wasn't following us. "Are you coming, Aunt Edith?"

She was still watching the sea turtles feeding and snoozing on the beach. "I wonder if the great-grandparents of these guys were turned into turtle soup for the king and the other folks living out here back then," she said.

We all grinned. "Maybe," Simon answered. "Just like you said earlier, they probably used what was handy."

She nodded and then started walking toward us. "That might help explain why they're endangered now." She looked at us and shook her head. "I'd sure hate to have to be the one to clean and cook 'em."

She was standing beside Simon. He draped his arm around her shoulders. "Yes, that was bound to be a chore," he said, "but I doubt that it would have contributed to the declining number of turtles today. I'm sure they had plenty of fish and other good things to eat too."

She nodded her head and sighed. "Too bad the king didn't get a taste of my cornmeal-rolled fried fish. Being born too early caused him to miss out on a treat!" She glanced down at her map, and then she peered up ahead at a tall, stone wall. She started walking away from us. "Well, aren't you all coming?" she hollered over her shoulder. "I want a closer look at that Great Wall over there. It was built way back in 1550. I want to take a look at something older than me."

"We're right behind you, Aunt Edith," Michael hollered back. He and DeLana started following her. He glanced back at Simon and me. "Well? You heard the lady. Let's get a move on, or she's going to go off and leave us."

Simon took my hand, and we started following Michael and DeLana. "I love being around your aunt," he said to me. "There's no way anyone could stay down and depressed around her. She finds something special and unique in everything she sees."

"That's Aunt Edith for sure."

We continued along the trail past the Keoua stone, which reportedly had been a favorite resting place of Keoua, the high chief of Kona. Holes at the base of the massive stone may have been used to support posts for a canopy. We ventured on past other sites, and then walked back to the van.

It was almost 3:00. Simon wanted to take us to the Hulihee Palace in Kona before we drove back to Amanda's house. He gave us a little history lesson about it on the way there.

In 1838, Hawaii's second governor built the palace across the street from Moku'aikau Church, the first stone church on the island. The Hulihee Palace was his primary residence until his death six years later. It was then passed to his adopted son and his wife, Princess Ruth Ke'elikolani, who was also the half-sister of Kamehameha IV and Kamehameha V. A large basement had been hollowed out of the lava rock. Above it a two-story structure was built out of the rock, coral lime mortar, and koa and *ohi'a* wood. Every Hawaiian monarch from Kamehameha III to Queen Liluokalani had resided at the Hulihee Palace.

"I want to warn you," Simon said as he pulled into a nearby parking lot. "The earthquake ten miles off the coast of Kailua-Kona last fall caused massive damage to the palace. The repairs are ongoing, but it's a very expensive process, so it's taking a long time."

"Does the government maintain it?" DeLana asked.

"No, along with other facilities, the Daughters of Hawaii take care of it," Simon said. "But they sometimes run into money problems."

"Are they a non-profit organization?" I asked.

"Yes, and very dependent on donations."

"It's a shame that such an important landmark doesn't get state funding," Aunt Edith said.

Simon nodded. "There's a nominal admission fee, but it would take a lot of visitors to accumulate enough to pay for all the repairs that are going to have to be made."

We had reached the front door of the palace. Inside, sitting at a small table, was a man with a white mustache. He looked to be in his late sixties. His nametag stated that his name was Chester.

"Welcome to the Hulihee Palace," Chester said. Simon handed him a twenty-dollar bill to cover our admission fees. Michael reached into his wallet and pulled out another twenty and gave it to the man.

"We appreciate the help, gentlemen." He handed each of us a brochure. "We're scheduled to close at 4:00 today, but you all just take your time."

"Four o'clock," I whispered to Simon. "The witching hour."

Simon patted his shirt pocket. "Keep your fingers crossed that Marshall won't be calling me about another rock crime," he whispered back.

Chester pointed toward the next room and lowered his voice. "The director's pretty strict about closing time, but my wife is getting her hair done, so she won't be here to pick me up until 4:30." A lady in the other room peeked around the corner at us. Aunt Edith waved at her. "Each room contains antique furniture, paintings, and much more," Chester continued. "I hope you enjoy your tour."

Simon took my hand and started leading the way into the Kuhio Room, which was on the right side of the entry hall. Michael and DeLana followed us.

"Too bad your wife doesn't live in Paradise, Oklahoma," I heard Aunt Edith say. I glanced back. She was still standing by the front door. "You can't beat my hairdresser. Her name is Gladys, and she's an artist when it comes to doing hair." She patted her curls. "One time Gladys gave me hair extensions just like the kind those glamorous actresses out in Hollywood wear."

Chester nodded his head and seemed impressed by her revelation. "So you're from Oklahoma. I heard they were about finished with the USS *Oklahoma* Memorial over at Pearl Harbor."

"Yes, sir, they are," Aunt Edith said. "Our governor and his family came over here last December and broke ground for it. My nephew and his oil company gave a big donation to help build it."

That's news to me, I thought. We had all stopped moving and were listening to their conversation. I stepped toward Michael. Being the controller for Kane Energy, he oversaw all checks written by the company. "How did she find out about that?" I whispered to him.

He shrugged. "You know Aunt Edith. She knows more about this family and its dealings than anyone else I know."

"Well, that's nice to hear," Chester said to Aunt Edith. "Every donation helps."

"That's my great-niece, Allie, standing over there," she said, pointing to me. "It's her daddy that runs the company, and he's always generous when it comes to good causes."

The man smiled at me. Though I had no influence when it came to the family business, I was pretty sure I saw a gleam in his eye. I smiled back at him.

"Well, I'd better join them so we can see this fine facility before your wife gets here," Aunt Edith said. "Nice talking with you."

"Yes, ma'am; me too. You all have a nice tour."

Aunt Edith fell in beside DeLana. We all walked into the Kuhio Room.

"Isn't this a lovely dining area?" DeLana said. There was a long ornate table, china cabinet, and sideboard in it. "This table is one of the most beautiful pieces I've ever seen." She walked over and ran her hand along the top of it. "This wood is gorgeous!"

"It was made from a single piece of koa wood," Simon said. "That china cabinet over there was made by hand out of the same type, then trimmed in another native wood."

I was reading about the room in the brochure. Since I taught at Prince Kuhio Elementary, everything I learned about him intrigued me. "According to this, Prince Kuhio was the last royal owner and resident of Hulihee. He and his wife restored and kept most of the original furniture." I walked over to a large trunk sitting against one wall. It had an inscription carved on the front. Since I didn't have my Hawaiian dictionary with me, I asked Simon what it said.

"It means 'strive for the highest,'" he said. "It was one of six made for Queen Kapiolani. They were used to carry her things to England for Queen Victoria's Golden Jubilee in 1887."

Michael was peering at the huge gaps where the walls met the ceiling. "Boy, that earthquake sure did a number on this room," he said. He walked from one end of the room to the other. "There are major foundation problems here."

"Yes, it's a shame," I said.

We crossed the entry hall into the Kuakini Room. The director was still seated at a small desk positioned in one corner. The same type of damage that we had seen in the other room was also prevalent here.

"This room was dedicated to John Adams Kuakini," the woman told us. "He built Hulihee Palace. Feel free to roam around and look at the contents in the display cases."

Two of the glass cases were filled with stone tools, wooden bowls, and other ancient artifacts. One case contained jewelry and other personal items that had belonged to the royal family.

"Unfortunately, some of the display cases were broken during the earthquake," the director said. "Many of the royal belongings that were exhibited in here have been placed in storage for the time being."

We wanted to go upstairs and look around, but the staircase had been roped off. The director said there had been too much damage to the steps and on the floor above, making it dangerous for visitors. After thanking her and Chester, our group walked outside.

Simon and I, Aunt Edith, and DeLana all strolled around the estate admiring the plants and ocean view. Michael hung close to the palace. In his teenage years, during summer breaks, he had worked with a local home builder in Paradise. He had picked up all kinds of skills in masonry, plumbing, framing, and more. I saw him run his hand over a long, jagged crack in the wall of the structure. The wide crack began at the roof and descended along the side of the wall to the ground.

Michael motioned for us to come closer. "Do you know what kind of corporate donations have been given to help with repairs?" he asked Simon. Money matters were often on his mind. I could almost see the wheels turning inside that financial brain of his.

"There are several companies here on the Big Island that have helped," Simon said. "But every island has its own treasures to preserve, so contributions have been limited."

Michael looked at me. "Since Hawaii has become so important to you, it's important to the family too."

I was beginning to get his drift. I motioned toward the palace. "Do you think Dad might want to help fix this?"

Michael continued examining the building. "I think he would."

Both my cell phone and Simon's started ringing. I glanced down at my purse in surprise. Lately, the only calls I received were from him or Aunt Edith. Since I was standing here with both of them, I couldn't imagine who would be calling. I scrounged around in my purse and found the phone. Simon answered his, then turned his back to us.

"Aloha, sweetheart," a deep, male voice said to me. "Your mom and I were just thinking about you."

I started smiling. "Were your ears burning?" I looked at Michael and whispered, "It's Dad."

Michael grinned at me.

"Hey, Dad," I said. "You couldn't have called at a better time …"

"That's terrific news, Allie," Simon said as we drove back to Amanda and Rob's house. "The Daughters of Hawaii Foundation are going to be thrilled to receive Kane Energy's help."

"I wish your phone call had also been good news," I said.

"Yeah, I was hoping the rock throwers would take the weekend off.

No such luck. Fortunately, a police cruiser came up behind them just as the rock was thrown, so their aim was off. It hit the concrete embankment under the bridge and then bounced into the grass. We'll talk more about it later. I don't want to ruin the rest of our evening with work."

Michael took the hint. From the seat behind me, he tapped on my shoulder. "I told you your dad would want to do something to help with the palace repairs."

"He's a very generous guy," I said. I turned around to face Michael. "And not just when it comes to donating money."

Michael shrugged his shoulders and grinned. "Hey, I offered to be back at work Monday morning as originally planned, but your dad wouldn't hear of it."

I smiled and patted his knee. "Well, you deserve a few days tacked on to your vacation after losing part of it lost at sea. It will be nice having you with us when we fly back on Thursday." A twinge of sadness touched my heart at the thought.

DeLana was cuddled up next to Michael. "Just think of it like this, Allie," she said. "It's in Kane Energy's best interest to get Michael back refreshed and glad to be at work. It would cost them in time and money if he made mistakes getting the quarterly reports done." She winked at me.

"Hey," Michael said, looking at DeLana. "Whose side are you on, anyway?"

DeLana squeezed his arm. "Just kidding, honey. I can't help giving you a bad time now and then."

I was glad to see the old DeLana back. She had always been fun to be around because she often joked and had a smile on her face. Over the last several days, she had been under such stress about Michael I had been concerned about her mental well-being.

When we walked in the front door, it was evident that Ella and Charlene had been working their magic. They were working side by side in the kitchen. Spicy aromas were wafting their way through the room. Pots were bubbling on the stove, and the timer on the oven was dinging.

Amanda was setting the dining room table. It was covered with a pale pink, linen tablecloth. Eight beautiful china plates and crystal goblets sat on it. Another smaller, square table was set up beside it covered with the same shade of cloth. The china and crystal was another pattern, but just as elegant. One spot was set with a plastic Spiderman plate and matching sippy cup for Denny.

"It smells scrumptious in here," Simon said. He walked into the kitchen and kissed his mother on the forehead. Then he turned and kissed his grandmother in the same fashion. Both ladies beamed up at him. Aunt Edith scooted by me and asked Amanda for an apron.

"Simon, get out of there and let them finish supper," Richard hollered from the living room. "I've been sitting in here for an hour smelling all those yummy dishes they've been working on. It's been torture! My stomach won't stop growling!"

Simon and I walked into the living room. Michael and DeLana followed us. Kim was sitting next to Richard on the couch shaking her head. "Don't listen to him, Simon," she said. "We've just been back from the beach long enough to take a quick shower."

Richard looked at Kim. "Don't tell him that. I still need some sibling sympathy after all I've been through."

Kim shook her head again and rolled her eyes at him.

The four of us smiled at them. Simon walked over and nudged Richard's shoulder. "Why aren't you in there helping then, little brother, if you're so tormented?"

"Yeah, that's right," Richard said, rubbing his shoulder. "Push a guy when he's down." He gave Simon a pitiful look, but was fighting back a smile. "Michael and I lived off grubs and beetles for three days, and now you want me to wait longer for the cuisine the ladies are preparing." He was really laying it on thick. "Besides, you know that Mom and Grandma won't let anyone tread on their domain when they're cooking Mexican food."

"Grubs and beetles?" Michael said. He sat down on the couch beside Richard. DeLana sat down next to him. "Your nose is going to start growing, Pinocchio."

"Hey, I'm on a roll here, buddy," Richard replied. He looked around the room. "Okay, so I'm stretching it a little."

"I thought I smelled enchiladas," I said, sitting down on the love seat.

"Sour cream chicken enchiladas," Amanda said, walking in from the dining room. "And Grandma made Maui Gold Pineapple Salsa too."

My mouth was starting to water. I heard a loud rumble. We all looked at Michael. DeLana smiled at him, and then patted his stomach.

"Either Michael is hungry too, or we just had a mild earthquake," I said, grinning.

Simon sat down beside me. "The sound of his growling stomach just overshadowed mine," he said. He sniffed the air. "I smell chocolate too."

"Grandma baked a triple chocolate mousse cake," Rob said, walking in from the patio. Trip and Dennis, who was carrying Denny, followed close behind. "The four of us couldn't take it anymore, so we've been sitting outside on the patio."

There was only one chair in the living room left unoccupied. Dennis started to sit down. Trip, who was standing behind him, cleared his throat. Dennis stepped aside and offered the chair to his dad.

"Thanks, son; don't mind if I do," Trip said, sitting down in the comfy-looking chair. "Come here, Denny. You can sit on Grandpa Trip's lap." The toddler beelined to his great-grandfather and jumped into his lap.

Dennis glanced around the room. He seemed uncomfortable having nowhere to sit. "How's it coming in there, Charlene?" he hollered at his wife.

Before she could answer, Ella appeared at the doorway. "Dinner is served," she said.

"Thank God!" Dennis said. He didn't wait for an invitation. He headed straight for the dining room. "Dad, you sit at the head of the table, and I'll take the other end." No one had to be told twice. We all stood up and made our way to the dining room.

After Trip said grace, bowls and platters were passed around. In addition to two large platters full of enchiladas, Charlene had made homemade tortilla chips for the pineapple salsa. There were huge bowls filled with refried beans, rice, and guacamole. A big, crystal bowl was filled with a mixture of fresh pineapple, papaya, mango, and star fruit.

We all ate to our hearts' content. As usual, I stuffed myself. But I wasn't the only one.

After the dishes were done, Simon and I walked outside and sat in lawn chairs on the patio. The sound of the waves lapping the beach was peaceful.

"So tell me what else Marshall had to say," I said.

Simon sighed. "This time a baseball-sized lava rock was thrown off a pedestrian bridge onto H-1 near the Waipahu Sugar Mill. The policeman who spotted the guy had just gotten off work and was going home. Traffic is always heavy on that two-lane road where it happened. But there's also construction going on in that area, so it's more congested than usual. The officer couldn't catch the motorcyclist before he got away."

"Bummer."

"Yeah."

The others joined us on the patio, so we didn't talk any more about it. The rest of the evening was spent lounging, visiting, and enjoying the cool ocean breezes and good company. Until his bedtime at 8:00, Denny kept us entertained. It was truly paradise!

CHAPTER 15

On Sunday morning, we all rose early and took turns with the two bathrooms. Amanda and Rob attended a church with a membership of about four hundred people, but the facility was too small to accommodate everyone all at one time. Therefore, they had two Sunday morning services. The contemporary worship service started at 9:00, and the more traditional style started at 11:00. We had all voted the night before to go to the early service so that we'd have more time at Volcanoes National Park.

At 8:45, we all filed into the sanctuary. Dennis and Charlene had attended there several times, so they knew some of the folks roaming around visiting. They waved at several people as we walked down the aisle to a couple of vacant pews in the center section.

The music director led the congregation in some lively songs. The last one was a slower tune called "We Are More Than Conquerors." Though I hadn't sung it in years, it was a blessing. While we were singing, I glanced at Simon, who was sitting on one side of me. Michael was on my other side. I could tell they were being encouraged and blessed by the song too. When the chorus was repeated, all three of us harmonized together and gave it all we had.

We are more than conquerors,
Thro' Him that loved us so;
The Christ who dwells within us,
Is the greatest power we know.

After announcements were made and we had prayed together for various needs that had been mentioned, the pastor walked to the pulpit. He was a short man of Oriental descent. Before he began speaking, his eyes roamed the large auditorium. They came back to rest in the area where we were sitting.

"I feel impressed to tell you a little about myself," the preacher said. "Most of my members have heard the story I'm about to tell, but I believe that it will help someone here." Though he continued scanning the crowd, his gaze seemed to keep coming back to Simon, Michael, and me.

"I was born in Thailand just before the Vietnam conflict began. Our family was poor, and we were practicing Buddhists. The war started when I was seven years old. The United States warned our government not to harbor war criminals or aid the Vietnamese soldiers in any way. However, the officials didn't heed the warnings, so the people of Thailand paid the price.

"Because my family had very little money, every morning I would rise before dawn and run to a nearby bakery to buy day-old bread. I'd load as many loaves as I could carry into a big sack, then I took it back to our neighborhood. I'd run from door to door selling the bread. When the sack had only one loaf left for my family, I'd go home. After I was ready for school, I'd run two miles to the schoolhouse."

"And we thought we had it hard when we had to walk a few blocks to Elliott Kane Elementary," Michael whispered to me.

"Yes, and I sold lemonade that time because I wanted to, not because the family had to have the money," I whispered back.

"You two pipe down up there," Aunt Edith whispered to us. She was sitting next to Trip and Ella in the pew right behind us.

Michael and I smiled at each other. When my cousins and I were little, it wasn't unusual for us to get thumped on the head by a grandparent or aunt sitting nearby if we were caught talking during the sermon.

The pastor continued telling us how his father had been arrested and taken away. He and his mother didn't know if his dad was alive or dead. They ran from village to village trying to escape the bombing and turmoil of the war that had filtered into their homeland.

"But, ladies and gentlemen, a few years later we found my dad and became a family again. It was a miracle we were reunited, but I believe in miracles. Buddhism is behind me now, and I'm a born-again Christian. The injustice of war was overcome by a just God."

"Amen" and "Praise the Lord" could be heard all over the sanctuary.

"Now, if you have your Bible, please turn to Isaiah 9:6 & 7." The rustle of pages could be heard throughout the building. "I'd like you to stand and read this passage with me."

Michael's Bible went almost everywhere with him. It had even survived the storm. I looked on with him as we read.

> For unto us a child is born, unto us a son is given: and the government shall be upon His shoulders; His name shall be called Wonderful, Counselor, the Mighty God, the Everlasting Father, the Prince of Peace:
> Of the increase of His government and peace there shall be no end, upon the throne of David, and upon His kingdom to order it and to establish it with judgment and with justice from henceforth even forever. The zeal of the Lord of hosts will perform it.

During the message, I thought about the rock-throwing crimes. According to the scriptures we had read together, justice would be served. I hoped it would happen before I went back to Paradise.

I also reflected on Richard and Michael's ordeal at sea. I snuck a look at Michael and DeLana. Their arms were entwined together. On the other side of DeLana, Kim and Richard were holding hands while listening to the minister. The hearts of the stranded family had been changed after meeting Michael and Richard and being rescued from the deserted island. There had to be some justice in that too.

"Fine sermon," Trip said as we all walked out of the church when the service was over.

"We really like our pastor," Amanda said. "His messages always give you a boost and something to think about the rest of the week."

"Yes, it was a good service," Aunt Edith said. "But now I'm ready to change clothes and head off to see that volcano!" She led the way to the van.

We drove the short distance back to Amanda and Rob's house. Denny had gone home with one of Rob's brothers and his family. They had recently bought a new wading pool for their little girl, and she wanted a swimming buddy.

While the rest of us changed clothes, Amanda, Ella, and Charlene put sandwich fixings on the table. While the three of them went to change, Simon and I fixed drinks, and Aunt Edith put paper plates, napkins, and silverware on the counter. Kim and DeLana had their hands full keeping the men folk out of the way.

After eating a quick meal, everyone headed back to the van. Simon and I were walking together, and Richard and Kim were right behind us.

Simon stopped and turned around. "Here, catch," he said to Richard. He tossed the vehicle keys to him. "I drove to church this morning, and though you may not be the expert driver I am, I'm letting you drive us to the park." He put his arm around my shoulders and drew me closer. "I want some time to sit next to my favorite girl."

I looked at him and raised my eyebrows. "Is that because one of your other girls isn't around?" I couldn't help ribbing him a little.

Before Simon could answer me, Richard spoke up. "I hate to tell you this, Allie, but Simon's so homely and hard to get along with, he probably couldn't get another girl." He grinned at his brother.

Simon stepped toward him and put his arm around Richard's shoulders. "Aren't we cocky today," Simon replied, and then he lowered his voice. "But you'd better be careful, Richie. I know secrets about you."

When he heard "Richie," I thought I saw the smile on Richard's face falter a bit.

"Secrets, huh?" Kim said, looking up at her husband's face. "Anything I need to know?"

Richard started shaking his head. "No, sweetie. He's just trying to start trouble."

Simon looked at the couple and grinned. Sibling rivalry—you've got to love it!

We all piled into the van then headed south on Highway 11. Since the mountains and rift zones ran through the center of the island, going around the southern tip from Kailua-Kona was the shortest route.

We drove through Honalo and Kainaliu. "They sure have some unusual names for their communities here in Hawaii," Aunt Edith said. A sign up ahead said that Kalakekua and Captain Cook were coming up soon. "They use a lot of K's and W's, don't they?"

All the Hawaiian residents nodded their heads. "There are only twelve letters in the Hawaiian alphabet," Dennis said. "All the vowels are used, as well as the consonants H, K, L, M, N, P, and W."

"I see," she said. "Well, we have some doosey names in Oklahoma too. In the county over from Paradise, there's a place called Cocklebur Flat."

"And then there's Tahlequah, Brushey, and Corn," I said.

"Don't forget Quay, Gray Horse, and Bushyhead," Michael added.

Trip, Dennis, and Simon were all smiling. "And some people think Hawaiian names are strange," Trip muttered. Ella nudged him with her elbow.

"I'd call all of them 'unique,'" I said. "Every culture is proud of its own language, and it often comes through when towns are given special names."

There was a lot to see as we continued down the highway. We came upon charred lava fields from flows occurring decades earlier. Huge, jagged rocks intermingled with smooth, black material stretched to the sea below. Between lava fields, Mother Nature had produced lush grasslands thick with new life. In some sections, acres of macadamia nut trees stretched as far as the eye could see.

When we reached the entrance to the park, Trip pulled out his wallet. "I've got a lifetime membership card that lets us into any national park in the country," he said. The ranger at the gate took a look at the card and then handed it back to Trip.

After driving a short distance further, Richard pulled into the parking lot. A ranger and a couple of tourists were standing on the sidewalk in front of the visitor center looking at a map. Several more people were wandering around the area. A group of a dozen or so tourists were huddled together on a covered patio that was connected to the main center. A ranger standing near them seemed to be giving some kind of presentation or instructions to them.

We all climbed out of the van. "Do we want to start here or go across the road?" Trip said.

Ella pointed toward the visitor center. "I suggest going in and finding out the schedule of tours today. We'll want to get our names on the lists." She turned around to face Michael and me. "Both volunteers and rangers give guided tours and talks here several times a day. Though all the members of my family have been here numerous times, we still go away learning something new almost every trip."

"Sounds good," Michael said. "Let's go in and sign up."

We all walked into the building. Ella signed up our group for the tour of the Jaggar Laboratory, which was located across the road from the visitor center, and for one of the ranger talks. We had thirty minutes to kill before the next talk was set to begin, so we browsed around looking at the exhibits and maps. We also watched a short film. While I was in the gift shop, I heard a volunteer calling the names on the list. By the time I paid, the rest of our group had already followed the volunteer and the others outside to the covered patio. Simon was patiently waiting at the front door for me.

"The formation of the Hawaiian Islands is a marvelous thing," the speaker was saying when Simon and I arrived. We scooted in close to Aunt Edith and Michael. "And it's not over yet. We're standing right over a hot spot of magma." Several in the crowd glanced down at the ground. "Below our feet is a massive boiling cauldron, if you will, just waiting to explode."

One woman reached over and took hold of her husband's arm. A couple of teenage girls looked at each other with wide eyes. Thinking about the inferno churning below us *was* a bit unsettling. I took a step closer to Simon.

"I'm sorry, but I'm afraid I couldn't save us if it decided to blow right now," he whispered.

I grinned at him but didn't move away.

"Mauna Loa and Kilauea are two of the world's most active volcanoes," the volunteer said. "From the base on the sea floor, Mauna Loa rises 56,000 feet high, which is twice as high as Mt. Everest. Kilauea has been very active recently and been making the news. Are any of you folks from California?"

Four people raised their hands. "From Los Angeles," one of the men said.

The speaker nodded. "So you're used to smog then." All four nodded. "Well, here in Hawaii, we have our own version of smog. It's called 'vog.'"

"Vog," a little boy said, giggling. "That's a funny name."

The volunteer smiled at him. "Funny name, but not a funny substance, young man. Recently the Kilauea volcano opened a new vent. Toxic sulfur dioxide has been spewing out in massive doses causing thousands of protea flowers on farms around here to shrivel up and die. Many growers on the Big Island are losing their crops, and that hits the pocketbooks of locals and tourists, as well as the mainland shops who depend on us for their flowers. It's a $2 million-a-year business in the Islands. Not only that, some nearby residents have had more respiratory problems due to the polluted air."

The woman who had earlier grabbed her husband's arm put a hand over her nose and mouth.

The speaker saw her. "No need to be concerned, ma'am. The air quality has improved a lot in the last few days. The park was only closed for two days as a precautionary measure."

She nodded at him but left her hand where it was.

We were told a bit more about Kilauea's latest antics, and then the speaker suggested we take the short drive to the viewing area to see it for ourselves. He answered a few questions then the group broke up.

I noticed a woman dressed in an old-time, ankle-length, print dress standing across the road. She was wearing a small hat with feathers and holding a ruffled parasol. She looked to be in her seventies.

"The tour I signed us up for is starting to gather over there," Ella said, pointing in the direction of the woman.

Trip was standing beside Simon and me. He raised his arm and waved at the woman. "Mrs. Maydwell!" he hollered.

She adjusted her wire-rimmed glasses, then looked at us and waved.

"Come on, everyone," Trip said. He grabbed Ella's hand and motioned for us to follow. We all hurried to keep up.

"It's good to see you again, Mr. and Mrs. Kahala," Mrs. Maydwell said. "Did you come in on the train today?"

I looked at Simon. "A train?" I knew that buses were often used on Oahu, but there were no trains on any of the islands as far as I knew.

Simon smiled. "You'll understand what's going on in a minute."

"We came in on the 1:00 train," Trip said to her. "It was a bit smokier today than usual."

Now I was really confused. First the old-fashioned dress and parasol, then Trip telling her we all came in on a train? I looked back at Aunt Edith, who was standing beside Dennis and Charlene. They all seemed to be enjoying the exchange between the two.

Mrs. Maydwell nodded her head then sidled next to Ella. "I'm sure you didn't have anyone get fresh with you today, Mrs. Kahala, not with your fine husband watching over you."

Ella smiled and shook her head. "No, but I had my hat pin out just in case."

Mrs. Maydwell smiled. "Good for you." She reached up and removed a long, silver pin with a pearl on one end from the hat she was wearing. She waved it back and forth a couple of times. "These come in handy to ward off men who overstep their bounds with a lady traveling alone." She pushed the pin back into her hat. "I recognize your son and his wife and their children, but I see you've brought along some new friends with you today."

"Yes, we did," Ella answered. She motioned for Michael, DeLana, Aunt Edith, and me to move up closer to her. "These fine friends have come all the way from Oklahoma to visit." She patted Michael's arm. "This is my son Richard's good friend, Michael, and his fiancée, DeLana."

DeLana started blushing. "Well, good friend at least," she said. She stuck out her hand to the woman.

Mrs. Maydwell stepped closer and shook her hand. "Don't worry, my dear." She glanced at Michael then back at DeLana. "He'll come to his senses soon. I hear that those folks from Indian Territory are mighty smart people."

Michael and DeLana both grinned. "Yes, Mrs. Maydwell," Michael said. He draped his arm around DeLana's shoulders. "And we're getting smarter every day." He leaned his head down and kissed DeLana.

The woman smiled. She stepped closer to Aunt Edith and me. "My, my, aren't you a pretty thing!" she said to me. She gingerly touched my hair. "Golden hair shining like the sun." She glanced at Simon. "And she must be your friend."

"Yes, ma'am," Simon said. He reached for my hand and pulled it into the crook of his arm. "My *very* good friend, Allie." He started gently bending my fingers back and forth.

"I like your hat, Mrs. Maydwell," I said.

She patted her short, gray curls that were hanging below it. "I wouldn't think of going out in public without it," she said. "When I was your age, though, I didn't wear hats much. I had dishwater blonde hair. Never cared for the color, but my daddy thought it was pretty, so that was good enough for me."

"Nothing wrong with dishwater blondes," Aunt Edith said to her. The woman looked at her and smiled.

"Mrs. Maydwell, this is another one of our friends, Edith Patterson," Ella said.

Aunt Edith eyeballed the woman's dress, then her parasol. "That's a fine paisley print you have on there. My mama used to own a parasol similar to that one, way back when." She took a step toward the woman. "Kept her skin looking velvety smooth up to the day she passed away. That was before sunscreen was invented, you know."

Mrs. Maydwell laughed. "Yes, Ms. Patterson, I hear that a lot of fine inventions are being tinkered with all over the world."

Our group followed the woman to a small underground facility behind the Volcano House. It was the original location for the Hawaiian Volcano Observatory, which was established in 1912 by Dr. Thomas A. Jaggar, a scientist from the Massachusetts Institute of Technology. Old-fashioned flasks, beakers, test tubes, seismic monitors, and other paraphernalia were strewn about on long tables inside it.

A man portraying Dr. Jaggar gave a short, humorous presentation. He stressed how important the real scientist's work had been in saving lives. Dr. Jaggar had developed methods to study volcanoes, including the use of seismographs to study the size and number of earthquakes associated with them. He was a successful writer who had published several hundred papers and books. He also gave speeches in addition to posting his volcano updates.

The actor completed his talk by telling us a little about Dr. Jaggar's personal life. When he had traveled to Hawaii, his wife didn't come with him. After working with Isabel Maydwell for many years, he married her.

Before we said good-bye, we all applauded the actors and told them how much we enjoyed the presentation. We went into the Volcano House to look at some of the maps and pictures displayed on the walls, use the restrooms, and get a cold drink from the restaurant. After the short reprieve, we all headed back to the van.

"Along the way to Kilauea, we'll stop at the Jaggar Museum," Richard said as we pulled out of the parking lot. "There are several exhibits there that give the history of some of the Hawaiian volcanoes. There are also seismometers on display that provide real-time data regarding current volcano and earthquake activity."

"After that we'll want to be sure and stop at the Halema'uma'u Crater, Richard," Dennis said. He looked back at me. "I doubt that you and your Aunt Edith have ever seen such a large, deep hole."

"I'm sure it will be a first," Aunt Edith said. "Allie, I'll pay for the pictures if you'll get a set of prints made for me."

"I'll be glad to."

Richard parked the van behind a string of cars near the overlook. Everyone climbed out. We all started walking toward the rim. Over time, volcanic gases had seeped through the ground forming sulfur crystals. They had paved a walkway around the massive crater. Steam was billowing up from deep within it. The smell of sulfur permeated the air.

"The wind is blowing the odor toward us today," Trip said as we continued walking. "It's usually not this ripe."

Simon and I were behind Trip and Ella. "It reminds me of the rotten eggs my cousins and I threw at each other when we were all about ten years old," I said.

Both Trip and Ella stopped and turned around. "I'll bet that was a smelly mess," Trip said.

I smiled. "Doug and Kristin and I were spending a week at Gramma and Grandad's place during summer break. One hot afternoon, we were outside messing around and found a small pail full of eggs. Someone had gathered them from the hen house, but hadn't taken them inside to the refrigerator. Doug started horsing around and accidentally dropped one of the eggs on the ground. The rotten smell that rose from it was sickening."

Both Simon and Trip were grinning at me.

"Doug started threatening to throw one at me, but I beat him to it. I intended to throw the egg past him, but I missed. It hit him right in the forehead! I guess Kristin thought that was what I meant to do, so not to be outdone, she grabbed two from the pail and threw them right at his chest. They hit him just below the chin."

"That poor boy!" Ella said.

"Well, don't feel too sorry for him yet," I said. "I knew I was in trouble, so I started running away from him. That's when he threw one and hit me in the middle of the back. He wasn't about to let Kristin get by either. He started chasing her across the yard. He hit her in the rear end with one, but missed her when he threw the second egg at her. She had ducked just in time. Doug had her down on the ground threatening to dump the rest of the eggs in the pail on top of her head when Gramma came outside."

Ella started smiling. "Being a grandma myself, I bet I can imagine what happened next."

"Gramma made all three of us come stand in front of her. Doug tried to gather some sympathy by telling her that I had started it. He tried to play on her feelings further by acting devastated that I had ruined his shirt."

"Good move," Simon said. "Play the messed-up clothing card."

Ella looked at him.

He stepped toward her and put his arm around her shoulders. "Now, Grandma, you know you always wanted Richard and me to look our very best."

She smiled at him and patted his hand. "Yes, and you usually did, at least when you were around me."

"Sorry to interrupt," Simon said to me. "Please continue."

"Well, Gramma didn't care who started it. She just knew she was finishing it. Doug started gagging as the slimy, smelly mess slid down his shirt onto his bare feet. Kristin was as white as a ghost. I tried to move away from him because I felt like I was going to throw up. Gramma told me I'd better stand still or I'd really be in trouble. She calmly told us that we were going to clean up every speck of broken egg in the yard, and then wash our clothes at the back hydrant." I sighed. "She also made us gather the eggs every morning during the rest of our visit."

"Knowing your Gramma, I doubt that it was long before your parents found out," Simon said.

"That was the hardest part, I think. The three of us knew that our parents would be told, and none of us was anxious for that to happen.

We didn't know if it would be that day or if it might be the following week. Not knowing was as hard as the present punishment."

"But she didn't tattle on you, did she?" Ella said. "I told you I figured I knew what would happen."

"You're right," I said. "As far as I know, Gramma never said a word to our folks. At supper that evening she told Grandad, but he just laughed about it."

"I would have laughed too," Trip said. "If your grandpa was anything like me growing up, he probably got into his own share of scrapes."

The rest of the group had wandered several yards away. We joined them, then looked into the crater again. "This is the heart of the volcano," Charlene said. "Some natives consider it to be a sacred site."

"It's extraordinary, that's for sure," Michael said.

After a short time, we headed back to the van then drove toward the Chain of Craters Road. It would lead us to the Kilauea vent where lava was pouring into the ocean. Before the turnoff, there was an enormous sea of black.

"That's Devastation Trail," Charlene said. "It was the result of the 1959 eruption."

"As you can see, even after almost fifty years, plants are slow to return," Dennis said. Small bushes and flowering plants were pushing up between the ugly ruts left by the flow. Tufts of grass were sparse and scattered.

"I hope we get to see some lava today," Aunt Edith said.

"I have to warn you," Rob said. "We'll probably only be able to see some steam. Even at night, about the only thing visible is the glow from the lava, rather than the flow itself."

"Unless you're lucky enough to get a bird's eye view," Michael said. He was seated next to me.

I knew he was referring to the helicopter ride he and Richard had taken the weekend before. "Bragging doesn't become you, Michael," I said, nudging him.

Even though Michael and I had been speaking softly, Rob heard us. He turned around and looked at me. "How would you like a ride of your own when we get finished here?" I didn't know what to say. I looked at Simon.

"He'll take you up," he said. "Rob's a great eye-in-the-sky tour guide."

"That would be awesome, Rob." I looked at Simon again. "Will we have enough time before our flight back to Oahu?" *Say yes, say yes,* I thought.

Simon grinned. "For a short run. Our flight doesn't leave until 8:10 p.m., and I can rush us through security."

"We'll go up in the six-seater," Rob said. "Anyone else in here is welcome to come along and fill the empty spots." Before we reached the Kilauea overlook, it had been decided who would be coming along.

After parking some distance away, we all walked as far as the rangers would let us. As Rob had predicted, large plumes of steam were billowing up from the ocean. To get the best photos I could, I wandered a short distance away from the group. Jagged rocks and ditches from recent lava flows made the footing precarious. A frown from one of the rangers standing nearby kept me from going any further.

We milled around for about thirty minutes. On the road to the Thurston Lava Tube, Michael's cell phone rang.

He looked at the display and then smiled. "Hi, Gramma."

I was seated between him and Simon. Michael nudged my elbow.

"Yes, Richard and I are both fine," he told her. She said something to him. "Yes, I appreciate your prayers and know that the Lord was watching out for us." He grinned at me as he continued talking.

"Why does he keep smiling at you?" Simon whispered to me.

"Probably because he's Gramma's favorite, and he's pretty sure she hasn't called *me* since I've been here."

After Gramma, Michael talked with Riley for a few minutes. "I love you, darlin.' I'll call you tomorrow night." He stretched his phone toward me. "You can stop pouting now. Gramma tried your phone first, but it went to voice mail. Here, my beautiful daughter wants to talk to you."

I took the phone from him. "Hi, sweetie. How are you doing?" With my free hand, I started rummaging in my purse for my phone.

"Terrific, Allie. Church camp was a blast, and Grandad took me fishing yesterday. On top of that, we have our first T-ball tournament game coming up next Saturday, and I can't wait! Will you be able to come?"

"I wouldn't miss it for the world," I said. I glanced at my phone display. Nothing. The battery was dead.

"Brittany, Joey, and I have really missed you since you've been in Hawaii," she said. "And you're missing out getting to help find the Tailgate Bandits. I heard Frankie say today at dinner that two more were stolen last night. One of them was from our pastor's pickup."

"That's terrible." I looked at Michael and mouthed "pastor's truck."

He nodded, so I figured Riley had already filled him in about it.

"Well, I'll talk to Frankie soon and get all the details," I told her. We had reached the Thurston Lava Tube, and everyone was starting to climb out of the van. "You have a good week, sweetheart. I'll see you at the game on Saturday. Love you."

"I love you too," she said, then hung up.

"The pastor babies his new pickup just like Grandpa A.J. does," I said to Michael as we walked through the huge lava tube.

"Those tailgate thieves are treading on thin ice," he said. "You don't mess with God's men and not get in trouble."

We all enjoyed the trek through the lava tube and the magnificent rain forest around it. The moist air and lush greenery was refreshing. The entire tour had been something I would always cherish.

CHAPTER 16

"I really enjoyed that," Aunt Edith said as we drove out of the park. We were back on Highway 11. She looked out toward the ocean. "That sure is a beautiful *moana* out there."

Trip, Dennis, Kim, and Simon all looked out the window in the same direction. Ella and Charlene looked at Aunt Edith. Michael, DeLana, and I looked at each other.

"*Moana?*" I had heard of the Ala Moana Center and had shopped there several times. However, I hadn't ever thought about what the term meant. Since most of the group was looking out the windows toward the ocean, I did too. I was expecting to see some type of boat or maybe a strange sea animal out there, but I didn't see anything but water. I looked back at Michael and DeLana, and they were also stretching their necks to see out the window. They turned back to me and shrugged. "Well, somebody is going to have to tell Michael and DeLana and I what a *moana* is," I said.

Aunt Edith turned her head around. "Oops, sorry, guys. I'm getting so fluent in speaking and understanding the Hawaiian language I forgot I might need to interpret for you *haoles*."

We're not the only *haoles in here,* I thought, but I didn't comment.

Michael leaned over and whispered to me. "Aunt Edith doesn't know more than fifteen or twenty Hawaiian words, does she?"

I grinned and shook my head. "Thanks for being patient with us, Aunt Edith," I said.

"Yes, we *haoles* appreciate your help," Michael said.

She nodded. "*Moana* means 'ocean.' I was saying it's a beautiful ocean out there." She turned back around, very pleased with herself.

"Good job, Aunt Edith," Simon said. "Together we'll have these *haoles* whipped into shape in no time."

I nudged him with my elbow.

A little after 4:00, we reached Sky Kings Over Hawaii. I had noticed Simon looking at his cell phone several times. He slipped it back into his pocket, and then he and I climbed into the backseat of the helicopter. Michael and DeLana grabbed the middle seat, and Aunt Edith rode next to Rob. We all put on headphones so that we could hear each other talk over the noise of the blades above us.

"No messages?" I asked Simon.

"None so far."

"Good," I said. "Despite their protests, I hope there were no hard feelings that everyone in the group couldn't come along with us." Amanda had driven herself, Ella, Kim, and Charlene back home in her car so they could start supper. Dennis, Richard, and Trip were going to hang out in the maintenance shop until we returned, then ride back in the van with us.

Simon wrapped his hand around mine. "Don't feel badly," he said. "Dad and Grandpa fly with Rob or one of his brothers anytime the notion strikes them. They both love Rob's place. Besides, when they found out that two mechanics were working today overhauling a blown helicopter engine, you couldn't have forced them on to this chopper. They love 'helping' Rob's mechanics and getting their hands greasy."

I smiled. "Sounds like my cousin, Pauley, Doug's brother. He practically lives at the auto body and repair shop where he works. When he's not there, he's tinkering with his motorcycle."

"You guys talking about Pauley?" Aunt Edith said into her headset.

The ear pieces were smashing down her curls. "He's the best mechanic in the state of Oklahoma, if you ask me. He's been able to fix my bike when nobody else had a clue what was wrong with it."

"He's a whiz all right," Michael said. "Pauley made my Lincoln look and run better than it did before my wreck." He looked at DeLana and cleared his throat.

She looked at him. "Okay, so I wasn't paying attention to my driving the day I hit you. But if I hadn't run into the back of your car, we might never have met."

Michael put his arm around her shoulders and pulled her close. "And that would have been terrible."

"Anyway," I said, "Pauley still lives at home, and occasionally Aunt Emily washes his clothes. She says that whatever grease and paint isn't on Pauley's clothes must be running through his veins."

We had been traveling north along the Kona coast. "We're coming up on Pu'ukohola Heaiau, or 'The Temple on the Hill of the Whale' as it's called in English," Rob said into his mouthpiece. "It was one of the last sacred structures built here before outsiders took control."

"Look at those high rock walls," I said. "From up here it seems to be about the size of a football field."

"That's pretty close," Simon said. "Kamehameha the Great had it constructed. It's hard to tell from the air, but it sits high on a hill. Enemies coming either by land or by sea were spotted long before they reached the area."

"It looks like there's a long rock path leading down to the ocean," Aunt Edith said. "There's even a wall along part of the path." She had her nose pressed against the window pane.

"No mortar was used in the walls or pathway," Rob said. "Spaces were filled in with smaller rocks. Over time, water erosion caused the rocks to become smooth."

We circled the area one more time, and then headed southeast toward Hilo.

"That's Mauna Kea down there," Michael said, pointing to the volcano below us. "It means 'white mountain.' Unlike Mauna Loa, which is south of here, Mauna Kea is dormant and is the taller of the two. In winter, there can be up to four feet of snow on it."

It was my turn to tap him on the shoulder. "And just how did you know all that?"

He turned his head and smiled. "Richard told me when we took the helicopter ride last weekend."

On the east side of the volcano, I could see small streams running down the hill. Some of the landscape had eroded and formed gullies. Black piles of earth were heaped haphazardly along the trek to the sea.

"Hilo is up ahead," Rob said. "It's the second largest city on the Big Island and overlooks Hilo Bay." We were all straining our necks to see down below. "In 1984, a five-mile-wide lava flow from Mauna Loa came within a mile of town."

"A little too close for comfort if you ask me," DeLana said.

"Pretty scary," Rob replied. He made a slight turn. "It's too bad you don't have more time. Amanda and Denny and I come over to Hilo pretty often. It's fun to walk around town and browse through shops and museums."

"The Pacific Tsunami Museum is a must-see when you're in Hilo," Simon said. "Not only do the exhibits show what has happened in the past, but they work to make the island safer for the future."

"I'd like to tour it," Aunt Edith said. "I was Pauley's age when that devastating tsunami hit down there. Terrible, terrible thing."

Rob nodded. "It killed over 160 people here and a few more in Alaska. Some of them were children."

"That's awful," DeLana said. "I know they didn't have the sophisticated warning systems back then that we do today, but didn't people see the wall of water coming?"

"That's one of the heartbreaking things about it," Simon said. "A breakwater dam had been built across Hilo Bay in the early 1900s, and it helped secure the coastline to some extent. However, in this case, it gave the islanders a false sense of security. Officials here knew that a 7.8 magnitude earthquake had occurred in the northern Pacific near the Aleutian Islands. What they didn't know was that a ten-foot-high tsunami was heading this way."

"Or they just didn't think the waves would get over the dam," Rob said. "And then, in a little town up north of here, adult ignorance cost some children their lives."

I looked at Simon. "What does he mean, their 'ignorance'? Surely everyone did what they could to protect people from the water."

Simon sighed. "It was a weekday and kids were in school. In the town Rob's referring to, it was about lunchtime, and the students were outside playing. All at once the water along the shore was sucked out to sea. Nothing was left except sand, rocks, and lots of fish flopping around." He paused. "I guess people thought it was free fish for the taking, and that's what they did. The kids, along with adults, ran out there and started gathering up fish, shells, whatever."

My eyes grew wide. "Then the water came back in," I said. I shook my head. "Those poor people!" Since I was a teacher and often in charge of young lives, my heart ached for the souls lost that day.

From there we flew north toward Waimea and circled the Parker Ranch. Black Angus cattle, like the type Grandpa had at the Circle K, were roaming the pastures with white Charolais. There were many buildings and corrals dotting the landscape.

"How big is that ranch?" Aunt Edith asked.

"About 150,000 acres," Rob said. "It's one of the largest and oldest ranches in the United States."

"It's more than just a working ranch," Simon said. "They have all kinds of activities going on that draw tourists here year-round. Among other things, they have rodeos on the Fourth of July and Labor Day. Riders from all over the world come to compete."

"Noel would have a big time then," I said. "He travels all over the place competing."

"Noel has won a passel of ribbons and money too," Aunt Edith said with pride.

"Maybe the two of you can come for the Labor Day event," Simon said. "Hint, hint."

I smiled at him. "That would be nice, but not possible. I'll be back in school by then. Most Oklahoma schools start back in mid- to late August. It would be great for Noel, though." I looked out the window to our left. In the distance I saw a tall mountain enshrouded in mist. "Is that Haleakala over there?"

"That's it," Rob said. "It's beautiful up there."

"Yes, Simon and I went to Maui to visit his grandparents a couple of weeks ago. While we were there, we traveled to Haleakala. The view was breathtaking."

We flew back to Sky Kings Over Hawaii to pick up the guys. As Simon had predicted, both Dennis and Trip were elbow-deep in engine grease assisting the mechanic repairing the engine. Richard had a secret desire to learn to fly a helicopter, so he had taken advantage of chatting with one of the pilots who had stopped by for his paycheck.

Before we knew it, we were all back at Amanda and Rob's eating a splendid meal. Around 7:00, all the visitors were at the airport checking in for our respective flights. After hugs and promises to keep in touch, Trip and Ella walked to their gate. The rest of us were on our plane by 8:00 ready to fly back to Oahu.

Simon and I were sitting halfway back next to a window. "I hope you had a good time this weekend," he said. His hand was wrapped around mine, and he was doing the finger-bending thing.

My eyes were stinging, and there was a lump in my throat. When we had been boarding the plane, it dawned on me that this would be my last flight with Simon. The next plane I'd be on would be taking me back to Paradise and away from him.

"Allie?" He looked at me. I wanted to tell him that I had enjoyed the weekend very much. The words wouldn't come.

I guess he suspected what was on my mind. He placed my hand in his other one, and then wrapped his arm around my shoulders. "It's going to be fine, Allie; don't worry."

I nodded then laid my head on his shoulder. I didn't mean to let the dam loose, but the tears started flowing. Though I tried, they wouldn't stop. They spilled over and splashed onto Simon's shirt. He didn't seem to mind.

❀   ❀   ❀

At school the next morning, I was in much better spirits. Aunt Edith and I had picked up Rowdy and Precious at Evelyn's the night before, and they were excited to see us. We were glad to see them too. When we got to the apartment, the four of us shared bowls of butter pecan ice cream before turning in. It felt good to have the dachshunds curled up around my legs on the bed. A good night's sleep did wonders for all of us.

The students were excited about the field trip to the library. It was only six blocks away, so I hadn't made arrangements for a van. When we arrived, the director gave us a short tour of the facility. As I had asked her to do, she made a point of telling them that with a library card, they were welcome to come use the computers any time. Since they only had five available for public use, sometimes there was a waiting list. She pointed to the juvenile book section and child-friendly reading area across from the computer station. She encouraged them to use it while they waited their turn on the computer.

Four of the children didn't have a library card, so the librarian signed them up. All ten students checked out books for their job report. Instead of going straight back to school, I let them do their papers there. It proved to be a good decision, because many of them gained research experience while using the reference materials.

We walked back to school and arrived just before the noon bell was about to ring. Though many of them had finished their reports at the library, most said they planned to reread their books and do some final touchups at home.

After they left, I went down to check my e-mail. There was message from Frankie in my inbox. The subject line read, "We solved it ... sort of."

When I opened the message, Frankie had written that if I wanted details, I needed to give him a call.

I glanced at the clock on the wall and then pulled out my cell phone. It was 5:10 p.m. in Paradise. His cell phone rang two times before he answered it.

"Sort of, huh?" I said.

He didn't say anything for a few seconds. "It was the craziest thing, Allie. We've had our eye on Tack Dunbar and two of his scroungy cohorts for days. Despite that, two tailgates went missing Friday night, then two more early Sunday morning."

"Yeah, I heard from Riley that one of them was our pastor's."

"Yes, and he was pretty ticked about it."

"I take it that Tack had alibis for those times. He's sneaky; you know that."

"You're not telling me anything. Yes, from about 9:00 Friday night until closing time at 2:00 a.m., he was keeping a seat warm at the Barfly Bar and Grill up near Big Cabin. His two buddies were seen there until midnight, and then one of our guys followed them home. They live together in an upstairs apartment on Main Street."

I thought about that. "Maybe one or both of them snuck out the back way and met up with someone else."

"The tailgates had already been reported stolen before then," Frankie said. "All we can figure is that there are others involved."

"Do you think Tack is ram-rodding the group? I'm sure your guys have been trying to watch from afar, but maybe Tack sensed he was being followed and had someone else do his dirty work."

"We haven't made a secret about following him and his friends around town. But we didn't want to be accused of harassment either, so we've tried to lay low when possible."

"Well, your e-mail said you had solved it, sort of. Did you make some arrests?"

He started laughing. "Well, no, but we have recovered all the missing tailgates."

"Really? I would have thought that they would have been sold quickly."

"They may have been," he said. "That's the beauty of it."

I didn't get it. "Okay, I'm confused. Spill it."

He chuckled again. "You know the old steel-girded bridge at the north edge of town?"

"Dream Maker Bridge? Of course I do. Every teenager in the area knows about it."

"Yesterday Carl Floyd spotted Tack heading up Highway 66 in that direction. His pickup had a tarp over the bed, so he took off after him. After a couple of miles, Tack turned onto the bridge road. The dispatcher called me, and I jumped in my car and headed that way."

"When Carl caught him, did he have tailgates in the bed?" I asked.

"He didn't exactly catch him," Frankie said. "Carl told me he was about forty yards behind Tack, who was running sixty-five on that old gravel road, when he heard a loud *pow!* One of Tack's front tires blew out. Carl said that Tack started weaving all over the road trying to get control."

"So after Tack's pickup came to a stop, Carl got out and arrested him," I finished for him. Frankie didn't say anything. "But wait, you said no arrests were made."

"You're getting ahead of yourself, Miss Detective. Tack didn't gain control of his truck. He took out the new side panel that the state just replaced last week."

I knew that numerous complaints had been called into the State Department by various residents about the rickety section on Dream Maker Bridge. "You mean that after two years of calls, they decided it was time to come out and fix it?"

"They finally made it."

I shook my head and frowned. "Well, if Tack got stuck on the bridge, why didn't Carl arrest him?"

Frankie didn't say anything for a moment. "Because his pickup soared off the side of the bridge."

My frown turned to a look of surprise. "Good grief! It's at least a thirty-foot drop down to the water."

"Yes, plus some. When I arrived, Tack's truck was lying upside down and wedged nose-first into the muddy bank below. The bed was hanging over the edge of the bank immersed in the river. Tack isn't a favorite with any of us, but Carl was pretty shook up."

I got a sick feeling in the pit of my stomach. "Did Tack make it out alive?"

"Yes, and I assume he wasn't hurt too badly. He managed to climb out and disappear before anyone saw where he went."

Tack and I had had our differences through the years, but I didn't want him to die. "He's always landed on his feet," I said. "He's been suspected of I-don't-know-how-many crimes over the years, and he always weasels out of it."

"Yes, but someday we'll get him," Frankie said. "When the pickup landed on its top, the tarp broke loose. Though we can't prove they were actually in Tack's truck, three brand new tailgates were spotted floating down the river. Whether or not we get a charge against Tack for the theft, at least we recovered the stolen property for the owners."

"What about the other ones? I'm sure Grandpa and Uncle Clarence want their tailgates back too."

"We found both of them last night, along with all the other missing tailgates. A tip came in that they were hidden in an old shed on the Berkley place. Mr. Berkley let us search it, and sure enough, all the missing parts were there."

"At Mr. Berkley's?" He was a sweet old guy who was at church every Sunday morning and Sunday night. "You don't think he was involved, do you?"

"No, with his arthritis, he's been wheelchair-bound for years. The thieves probably thought that the tailgates wouldn't be found in his shed. The lock was so rusted all they had to do was give it a quick snap with a crowbar and it would have released."

"Well, good work, Detective Janson," I said. "The folks in Paradise can rest easier tonight knowing that you've solved this crime."

He chuckled. "Even as bold as Tack can be, I don't think he's stupid enough to try a stunt like this again. But like I said earlier, I wouldn't be surprised if he had already collected money for those tailgates from a chop shop somewhere. Since he can't deliver the goods, he may be running from someone meaner than us."

"You might still be able to pin this on him. One of his cohorts may get cold feet and confess."

"We're going to keep the pressure on all of them. But, until something else breaks, I feel like justice was served."

"I hope it's served here as well," I said. "Rocks are still being thrown off bridges, and it's getting old."

"Just hang in there. Simon and his team will catch whoever is doing it. Their luck is bound to run out soon."

I glanced at the clock on the wall. "I need to get to the newspaper," I said. "I'll probably see you this weekend."

"You all have a safe flight home. It will be good to see you. You've really been missed."

"Thanks. I've missed you too."

After we hung up, I realized I was homesick for my family. With the mention of Dream Maker Bridge, I couldn't help remembering an incident that happened there when I was twelve years old.

Noel, his brother Tate, and their sister, Summer, had arrived for their summer visit at the Circle K. Jamie, Noel, and Frankie always stuck together during those weeks. If you saw one of them, you saw all three.

Frankie was the only one old enough to drive, but he didn't have his own vehicle yet. Uncle Clarence would sometimes loan them his old pickup to use. It wasn't the most reliable truck in the world. The tires were worn out, and the spare wouldn't hold air half the time.

One day the boys wanted to go fishing below Dream Maker Bridge. Dad wasn't keen on having them out there without some way to get help if they needed it. He gave his cell phone to Jamie to take with them. I heard Dad tell him the night before to be sure to put it on the charger before he went to bed.

Dream Maker Bridge was a legend around the county. It was said that if you strolled over it with your sweetheart then dropped a coin over the side into the river, you'd fall in love.

Frankie had parked the pickup on the side of the road near the bridge. They started home around 5:00. When they drove across the bridge, one of the tires ran over a piece of barbed wire. The tire blew out, and the spare was flat.

Jamie called home, and I answered the phone. "Hey, snotface, I need to talk to Mom," he said. Though we didn't make it a habit of calling each other names, he was still mad at me. I had caught him and Kami Fisher smooching on the couch the previous Saturday night, and I told Mom about it. I heard that Dad gave Jamie a "setting a good example for your brother and sister" lecture. He also made him clean out the garage, which took several hours because it was in pretty sad shape at the time.

"She's not home from Paradise Petals yet, BB brain," I said. Though she tried to be home by 5:00 most evenings, Mom had called to say she'd be late because lots of orders had been coming into the shop all day.

There was a lot of static on the line, but I heard Jamie tell our cousins something about Mom not being here. "We had a ... ride ..." The phone was really breaking up.

"Allie ... hear ... said?"

"Yes, booger breath, you said you had a ride home." I looked at the clock. He was supposed to have been home by 5:00. "And you'd better hurry, or I'm telling Dad you were late." I waited for a response, but the line was dead. It wasn't the first time he had hung up on me.

Dad got home from Kane Energy around 6:00 carrying in two pizzas. Jeff and I didn't waste any time piling slices onto our plates. When Dad asked where Jamie was, I shrugged and told him he called to say that he had a ride.

Dad dialed the cell phone he had loaned Jamie and couldn't get through. "I'll bet he didn't charge that phone last night," he said. I realized from his tone that he was worried. It would be getting dark soon. "You keep an eye on Jeff, Allie. I'm going to Dream Maker Bridge to look for the boys."

Dad walked to the door, and at that moment Jamie and my cousins came strolling in. They looked beat, and their pants legs were wet and muddy up to their knees.

"Where have you boys been?" Dad asked. "I was just heading out to look for you."

Jamie pointed at me. "I called Miss Priss over there and told her that we had a flat on Uncle Clarence's pickup and needed a ride home." He glared at me. "Since Mom wasn't home when I called, I asked Allie to call Grandpa to come get us."

I glared back at him. "That's not true! The phone kept cutting in and out, but you said you had a ride home. Don't blame this on me, Jamie Kane!"

Frankie and Noel knew enough to stay out of this brother-and-sister face off. Dad questioned them and found out that Jamie had indeed asked me to call Grandpa. I didn't think it was fair, but I was the one who was grounded for a week.

I stopped daydreaming and grabbed my purse. It was nearly 1:00. If I didn't get a move on, I was going to be late getting to the *Hawaiian Star*. I walked around to the driver's side of my car. A piece of white paper had been folded and stuck in the door handle.

I took a couple of tissues from my purse then stuck the purse under one arm. Using the tissues, I unfolded the paper. A short message had been scrawled on it.

Dear Miss Kane,
    A warning to you—be careful on the west side of the island. You could encounter a falling rock.
                                      A Concerned Competitor

A concerned competitor? Evidently this person was trying to tell me that several people were involved in the incidents. What kind of competition did he mean? Were they competing to see how many people could be hurt? Killed? I shuddered at the thought.

I opened the car door and laid the note in the seat. After that, I pulled out my cell phone and called Simon.

"Isn't this a nice surprise," he said after he answered.

"Guess what someone left me?"

CHAPTER 17

Simon met me at the *Hawaiian Star*, and I gave him the note. I needed to write my article about the hula competition for Wednesday's edition, so I was glad he offered to do all the legwork and get the note to the lab.

When I walked past Mr. Masaki's office on the way to mine, he hollered at me. When I stuck my head around the door, he was slipping on a sports jacket.

"You look nice today," I said.

He straightened his pale blue striped tie. "Not my usual attire," he said. "I'm attending a funeral at 3:00 for one of our retired city councilmen." He picked up a manila folder lying on the corner of his desk. "Mia Cunningham has the flu. We're all glad there was a happy ending to your cousin's story, and I'd like to get a nice piece in Wednesday's paper." He had a hand on each side of the folder and was thumping the bottom edge on the desk. "I know you have other things to finish up, but would you mind writing the final article?"

I looked at him and smiled. "I'd be honored. I spent the weekend with Michael and Richard on the Big Island, and they gave me lots of information to work with."

He smiled and handed the folder to me. "That's what I was hoping to hear," he said. "Mia did a fine job with the previous pieces, and all her notes are in there should you need to refer back to anything." He glanced at the clock on the wall, and then he walked around the desk.

"I'll get to work on it right away," I said.

He waved, then turned and headed down the hallway. I walked upstairs to my office.

While I was waiting for my computer to boot up, the phone rang. It was Aunt Edith.

"I just wanted to let you know that Pinky and a friend of his invited Evelyn and me to go motorcycle riding this afternoon," she said.

"That sounds like something you'll enjoy. Do you think Evelyn will?" She didn't seem like the motorcycle-riding type to me.

"Well, when I first invited her, she hedged a bit. But it didn't take much convincing when I told her that Pinky's friend thinks she's cute."

"Oh, so they've met before?"

"Well, not officially, but since Hooper and Pinky are best buds, she's seen him around the building a few times." She giggled. "Evelyn told me that she and Hooper rode up in the elevator together last week. When he pulled out a switchblade and began cleaning his fingernails with it, she nearly wet herself."

I could imagine the feeling. If Hooper looked anything like Pinky did, in the rough Hell's Angels' motorcycle gang motif, I'd have been nervous too.

"We're planning to ride along the west coast of the island," Aunt Edith said. "Would it be okay with you if the pups rode along in the saddlebags?"

Her question took me by surprise. "They've never ridden on a motorcycle, Aunt Edith." I didn't have a good feeling about this. "I'm not sure if they would stay put."

"Oh, they love the bike," she said. "I've taken them on short runs around the neighborhood a couple of times."

That's news to me.

"Pinky takes his dog with him all the time. He showed me how to remove the lids from the saddlebags and squish a soft hand towel down into each one. The pups set their bottoms on the towels, and then I push some washcloths in around their bodies. They're safe and sound in there."

I knew I had no right to object. After all, I had been imposing on her to watch the dachshunds while I'd been at work. I had no doubt that they made a safe riding team.

"Okay, if you want to take them with you, that's fine with me."

"We should be back home before you get here, but I won't be able to fix supper tonight. Luu and I have a date."

"Don't worry about supper. If Simon and I don't go out, I'll throw together something for us."

"Oh, got to go. Evelyn's knocking at the door."

"Have fun today."

It was already 1:30, so I set to work on the article about Michael and Richard and the family that had been rescued from the island. When I finished it, I e-mailed it to the copy editor for his review then set to work on the hula competition piece. I had just finished rereading it for the second time when Simon called.

"After I left you, I took the note straight to the lab and asked for a rush analysis," he said. "The technician let me hang around and watch. It turns out the paper was run-of-the-mill dime store stuff that can be found in stores throughout the Islands. No prints were on it either."

"Big surprise," I said. "The bad guys watch the same crime shows we do. They've figured out how to cover their tracks pretty well."

"Afraid so," Simon said. "I requested several uniforms to patrol along the west side of the island this afternoon. Maybe the 'concerned competitor's' tip will pay off in an arrest."

"I hope so." I was staring at the competition piece on my computer screen, but the words were a blur. "Hey, maybe I should take a little drive along the west coast today. This guy seems to be keeping an eye on me. He might get careless, and I'd get the chance to spot him." I pulled out the rock-throwing folder containing all my notes.

"That's not a good idea," Simon said. "My guys will be watching every bridge and overpass. Besides, I'm sure you've got your hands full at the *Star*."

I heard him say something, but the words didn't register. I started jotting down a checklist of clues regarding the case.

"Allie?"

"Sorry, I didn't hear what you said."

"Yeah, I realized that a couple of minutes ago. I asked if you wanted to have dinner tonight. Say 6:00?"

"Yes, that sounds good. See you then," I said, then we hung up.

I felt like I was on to something. I intended to wrap it up and drive out to the west side of the island. After the hula piece was submitted, reviewed, revised, and resubmitted, the afternoon was gone. The next time I looked at the clock, it was 5:15.

I called Simon to ask if we could meet at the restaurant at 7:00 instead of having him pick me up at the apartment. I still had work I needed to finish before calling it a day.

"That will work out better for me too," he said. "Another rock was thrown over Farrington Highway north of Makaha."

I knew I should have driven over there, I thought.

"But the time was off," he said. "It didn't happen until around 4:45."

"Do you think the guy might have had second thoughts about throwing it? Maybe he spotted some of those officers you sent out there."

"We should know soon. Marshall was told that a couple of patrolmen picked up one of the three guys. He had a lava rock in the backpack he was wearing. The rock-thrower and the other one got away."

"Motorcycles have an advantage," I said.

"Yes, and it's really frustrating. Witnesses said that the guy who threw the rock jumped on his little green Honda and rode down the bridge embankment. The one wearing a red baseball cap led the officers on a merry chase all over the streets of Makaha. Marshall said they almost snagged him, but then he turned east on a road near Wainae. It leads to a golf course up in the hills. We thought there was only one way in and one way out, but the rider knew something we didn't. He disappeared like the wind."

"Well, maybe the guy that was caught will give up his friends," I said.

"I hope so. See you at 7:00."

Simon and I had a nice dinner at the Red Reef Café, which was located a short distance from Waikiki. It had become a favorite of ours. Traci and Tommy had introduced me to it when I came for the summer school interview.

Neither Simon nor I had eaten anything since noon, so we went all out and ordered shrimp and oysters with a side bowl of their specialty greens that were grown in nearby Waimanalo. We enjoyed listening to a local band while we ate, and then he followed me back to the apartment.

As I drove toward the parking garage, I saw Aunt Edith and Mr. Omura standing in the dark shadows of the building. They were wrapped in one another's arms kissing each other like there was no tomorrow. She hadn't said a great deal, but I had suspected that they were becoming more than work associates or just friends.

After I parked the car, I walked toward the tower. Aunt Edith, Simon, and Mr. Omura were looking up at the sky and talking.

"Yes, it sure is a beautiful night," Mr. Omura said as I walked up. He and Aunt Edith were holding hands.

From the grin on Simon's face, I figured he had walked up and surprised them.

"Well, Luu, thank you for a great dinner and wonderful evening," Aunt Edith said. "I'll see you bright and early in the morning."

Mr. Omura turned toward her and kissed her on the cheek. "I enjoyed it too, Edith." I was standing next to Simon. Mr. Omura looked at us. "You two young folks have a nice evening." He turned and walked to his car. Along the way he was singing, "It's a hap, hap, happy day, since the clouds have rolled away, do di do do, do di do do ..." Aunt Edith started humming the same song as the three of us walked inside the building.

"I'm sure going to miss Luu when I go back home," she said during our elevator ride.

"I'm going to miss a lot of people too," I said, squeezing Simon's hand. "Did the puppies do all right on your ride today?"

"Oh, they had a great time. We all did. Evelyn and Hooper really hit if off."

Simon looked at me. "Pinky, Aunt Edith, Evelyn Hunter, and a new guy named Hooper took the dogs on a motorcycle trip today," I said.

"Where did you ride?" Simon asked her.

"We talked about going through the middle of the island but decided to ride along the leeward coast instead. We rode past Waianae and Makaha then up to the hiking trail beyond Yokohama Bay. It's beautiful up there."

Simon told her that a rock had been thrown near Makaha. Aunt Edith snapped her fingers. "Man, I wish we had been there to help out the cops!" The elevator door opened on our floor. "Unfortunately, Hooper and the police aren't the best of friends right now. They might not ride him so hard if he had been there to help." She started walking down the hallway.

Simon looked at me with raised eyebrows. I shrugged. "Don't know him," I said. I figured I had better find out more about Aunt Edith's new riding buddy when we were alone.

"Well, it's my bedtime, you two," Aunt Edith said, once we were inside the apartment. "I'm going to turn in."

After telling her good night, Simon and I walked onto the lanai. Like Mr. Omura had said earlier, it was a beautiful evening. Reluctant to let it end, we snuggled together in one chair and enjoyed the sights and sounds of the night. Around 11:00, we were both starting to yawn, so I walked Simon to the door of the apartment. He took his time kissing me good night, and that was fine with me.

On Tuesday morning I woke up earlier than usual. I had had a wonderful dream about Simon, so I was smiling when I climbed out of bed. Aunt Edith was still asleep, so I put on my robe and took the dogs out to do their business. After coming back in, I fed them, and then I drank some orange juice and took my vitamins before heading for the shower.

With extra time on my hands, I leisurely drove to school. It was the last morning I would be making the trip, so I wanted to enjoy every minute of it.

The students were more rambunctious than usual. I could understand that they were anxious to be out of school. A couple of times while they took turns reading their papers, I had to remind them to be respectful and attentive to their fellow classmates.

I had planned to take them out to the playground so that they could enjoy their last hour outside. When I mentioned my idea to them, none of them seemed enthused about it. In fact, Mareko and Seth suggested that we stay inside and read.

About that time, Miss Kahala walked into the classroom carrying a huge cake. "The students and I are going to miss you, Miss Kane," she said. She was followed by her secretary, Diane, who was carrying a punchbowl. Behind her were several of the students' mothers carrying bottles of soda, packages of paper cups and plates, and other assorted items. A couple of grandmothers and dads were also among the guests.

"So this is why you didn't want to go outside," I said to the students.

"We knew we were throwing a party for you, Miss Kane," Mareko shouted. All the students started clapping. I was surprised and very pleased.

Miss Kahala read the inscription on the cake. "To the Best Summer School Teacher Ever!" she read. "The students told me what to put on it." She stepped closer to me and lowered her voice. "Don't tell the other teachers, but I have to agree with them."

I smiled at everyone. "Thank you so much for a lovely party. And to the parents of my wonderful students, thank you for sharing them with me this summer. I've truly enjoyed each one of them and my time here at Prince Kuhio Elementary."

The kids started cheering again. They quieted down when I started cutting and passing around pieces of cake. The room was full of laughter and fun. Everyone seemed to have a great time.

After the room was cleaned up and the students had packed their backpacks, I asked the visitors to please step out into the hall. I wanted to spend the last few minutes alone with my students.

"Boys and girls, I want to thank you for allowing me to be your teacher for a month. You came here not enjoying books and reading but have grown into fine, confident readers." I paused for a moment. Tears were stinging my eyes. My heart was breaking because I knew I might not ever see these precious children again. But, determined to make our final minutes together happy and positive, I got a grip on my emotions.

I passed out "I'm Proud of You" certificates that I had made for them. As I hugged each child, then watched him or her walk out the door, I was blessed. Each little head was held high, and I had no doubt that they were more compassionate and caring individuals. They were no longer children who hated reading. It felt good knowing that I had played a part in helping them.

Mareko was the last one to leave. Before he walked out the door, he turned and threw his arms around me. "I'll never forget you, Miss Kane," he said. "Not ever!"

I put one hand on his head and the other one on his back. "I'll never forget you either, Mareko. You're a special boy."

He stepped back and hoisted his backpack higher on his shoulders. "I'll be a great third grader," he said. "The best one at this school."

I nodded and smiled. "I'm sure you will be." Seth had come back to the door looking for his friend. "You'd better get going now. Have a great summer, boys!"

They both grinned, and then started running down the hall. "We're out of school!" I heard Mareko yell.

"Yippee!" Seth answered.

I shook my head and smiled.

I packed away things I had used so that Traci could come back to an organized room. Shortly after noon, I closed the door to the classroom and headed to the office for the last time.

"I really meant what I said earlier, Allie," Miss Kahala said. "If you ever decide to move to Hawaii, which I know would make my nephew very happy, I would do everything I could to help you get a teaching job on Oahu."

I smiled at her. "I appreciate that. But I love teaching third grade at Elliott Kane, and I can't imagine teaching anywhere else." I handed the keys to the Malibu to her.

"Are you sure you won't keep the car another day?" Miss Kahala asked. "It's okay."

"No, Simon is probably already out there waiting for me, and Aunt Edith wants to take me to the *Hawaiian Star* on her motorcycle."

"You're a brave soul, Allie." She wrapped me in a hug. "*Mahalo* and aloha. It's been a joy having you here."

I hugged her back. "*Mahalo*, Miss Kahala. The pleasure has been all mine."

The phone started ringing. Diane answered it then told the principal that it was the call she had been expecting. Miss Kahala waved at me, then turned and walked toward her office.

I turned to leave. "Oh wait, Miss Kane," Diane said. "I almost forgot to give this to you."

She handed me a small, pink envelope. My name had been written on it in neat block letters. "Do you know who left it?" I asked her.

"No. When I returned to my desk after your party, it was lying on my chair."

"It's probably a thank-you card from one of the student's parents," I said. "Thanks." I waved good-bye to her.

As I walked out of the building, my heart was heavy. I had fallen in love with the school, staff, and students. It was hard knowing I'd never step foot inside the door again.

I slipped the pink envelope inside my purse. Simon was parked in the handicapped spot. He waved at me. The gloom lifted a little at the sight of him.

Along with about thirty other people, Simon and I had lunch at the deli. We sat at a table for two near the counter. Aunt Edith and Mr. Omura were having a serious conversation.

"Okay, Luu, here it is," Aunt Edith said. She handed him a recipe card. "You have to promise me that only you will mix up the batter. This is a family recipe from way back, and I don't want it handed out to anyone else." She cast her eyes at Berta.

Berta lifted her chin. "Humph!" she said. She turned around and started wiping down the back counter.

"I know that you'll need Berta's help with the frying, but only you get to see the recipe, okay?"

"I promise," he said. "Family recipes are very important. Only my eyes will see what goes into the batter." He looked at the card and smiled. "Ah. I never considered that ingredient." He took a step toward Aunt Edith and kissed her on the cheek.

She turned a couple of shades of red. All at once she grabbed the front of his apron and pulled him against her chest. She planted a big kiss right on his lips.

Mr. Omura put his arms around her and kissed her back.

Everyone in the place started clapping. I was too stunned to look away at first. When I did, I noticed that Berta didn't look happy. I suspect that Mr. Omura broke some hearts in his store just then. He wasn't bound to forget Aunt Edith for a very long time.

"The lunch was delicious as usual, Mr. Omura," Simon told him. He nodded toward Aunt Edith. "And the entertainment wasn't bad either."

Both Aunt Edith and Mr. Omura smiled at him. "Don't be a stranger, Detective," Mr. Omura said.

"I won't." Simon turned toward me. "I need to get back to work." He nodded toward Aunt Edith's motorcycle that was parked near the door. "You two be careful on that thing."

I smiled at him. "We will. See you tonight?"

"You couldn't keep me away." He pulled me toward him and kissed me. Aunt Edith and Mr. Omura didn't have a thing on us.

I watched him drive away. Aunt Edith walked out of the deli with her purse in one hand and her pink helmet in the other.

"I'm going to let you wear my helmet," she said, handing it to me. "Luu has one that he's going to let me use."

Mr. Omura walked out carrying a black helmet with a smoke-colored face shield. "It's not as fancy as yours, Edith, but it will help keep you safe."

She took it from him and slipped it on her head. "Thanks. I'll get it back to you in the morning."

He waved at us, then turned around and walked back inside the deli.

Aunt Edith climbed on to her bike, and then started the engine. After revving it up, she motioned for me to get on behind her.

As I was about to sling one leg over the seat, I heard tires squealing. I looked at the busy street running beside the deli. Two motorcycles came into view—one green, one black. The one in front swerved to miss a stalled car. The other one fishtailed his bike and almost hit a young boy riding a scooter. Both riders were wearing backpacks.

"That looks like one of the bikes Simon described that was at Makaha yesterday," I said.

"Hurry up and get on then!" Aunt Edith yelled at me. "We're going to catch those dudes!"

Oh Lord! I swung my leg over the seat. Before I could fasten the strap on the helmet, Aunt Edith took off.

She swerved the bike off the sidewalk and jumped the curb. My bottom nearly slid off the seat, so I grabbed her waist. My purse strap was wrapped around my wrist nearly cutting off the circulation. The pink helmet was bouncing around on my head. I felt like a bobble-head doll.

"Hang on, Allie! They're getting away!"

She shifted gears and pulled onto Beretania Street. We hit fifty miles per hour in about eight seconds. A few of the wiser, more cautious drivers saw us coming and pulled over to the side of the street. The others weren't an obstacle for us. Aunt Edith just dodged around them. I could see that the two bikers ahead of us were doing the same thing.

"We're coming up on Piikoi Street," I yelled. "Maybe the light will turn red and slow them down."

She nodded. The helmet was banging against my ears and giving me a headache. Since I figured we'd be slowing down at the Piikoi Street intersection, I reached up to try to clasp the chin strap. That's when Aunt Edith kicked the bike into the next gear. I grabbed her waist with both hands and clutched the seat with my thighs. Never mind the chin strap. I needed to hang on for my life!

As we got closer to the busy intersection, I could see that the traffic light in our direction was green. It was clear that the bikers we were chasing had no intention of slowing down. *Stay green; please stay green,* I thought. We were sure to get hit by a car if traffic started moving in the opposite direction.

About a block before the two bikers reached Piikoi Street, the light turned red. They buzzed right on through it. A small truck swerved to miss hitting them. A couple of other drivers hit their horns.

Aunt Edith never missed a beat. Still traveling at about fifty, we zoomed right through the light. Car tires squealed. I braced myself and shut my eyes. I half expected to go flying through the air at any second. Instead I heard someone yell my name.

I looked to my right and saw Marshall and Dave. Their cruiser was stuck behind another vehicle that was blocking the intersection.

Aunt Edith shifted again. All I could do was wave at them.

The bikers turned down a narrow alley that ran between two office buildings. The repaving of the blacktop was long overdue. Big chunks of asphalt were missing. It seemed like we hit every pothole.

I heard Aunt Edith laugh. "We might need to go back," she hollered at me. "I think we missed a couple of those holes."

I started laughing too. What else could I do? My ears perked up when I heard the *whoop-whoop* of a police siren coming from behind us. Ahead of us I could see the two bikers swerve to miss a convertible loaded with teenagers. A block beyond that, red lights were flashing.

"Thank you, Jesus," I said.

"It's about time we got a little help," Aunt Edith said, motioning toward the intersection.

Four police cars were crisscrossed on the street. Their occupants were leaning on the hoods. All of them had pistols drawn.

Aunt Edith started slowing down, then we stopped. I turned my head around and saw Marshall and Dave right behind us. I waved again. Marshall started grinning. Dave was shaking his head.

"I think Simon wants to talk to us," Aunt Edith said.

I turned back around. Simon was standing in the middle of the street in front of the four police cars. He didn't look too happy.

Aunt Edith started slowly maneuvering the bike toward him. When we were a few yards away, she pulled over to the curb and shut off the engine.

I removed the heavy helmet and plastered a charming smile on my face. As I walked toward Simon, I could tell he was trying hard not to grin. When I reached him, I leaned up and gave him a kiss on the cheek.

He put his hands on my shoulders and nodded toward Aunt Edith's motorcycle. "I was afraid you two would get into trouble on that thing." I winked at him. He pulled me against him. "But once again, you saved the day."

He stepped back. I could see that both bikers had been handcuffed and were being loaded into the backseat of one of the cruisers.

I nodded toward them. "I hope that one of those guys is the one Aunt Edith grabbed at Wahiawa," I said. "Do either of their bikes have a torn seat?"

Simon nodded to someone behind me. "Yes, there's a rip where a passenger would ride," Marshall said. He walked up beside me.

I looked around and saw that Aunt Edith had Dave cornered by their cruiser. I smiled. "She'd probably go over and give that kid a piece of her mind, if she wasn't preoccupied."

Both Simon and Marshall looked at the pair. Aunt Edith was giving Dave an earful. He was smiling and nodding his head.

"What about the other suspects?" I asked.

"They're in lockup as we speak," Marshall said. "All four of the guys have snake tattoos on the back of their necks."

"So everyone is accounted for except for the fifth person," I said.

"She came in about an hour ago and turned herself in," Simon said.

"She?"

He nodded. "Dahlia Hong is the sister of the leader." He nodded toward the guy who had been on the black bike. "She came in and confessed everything."

"Dahlia Hong is the dancer at the hula competition who was so helpful to me," I said. "I'll bet she was the one wearing the St. Louis Cardinals ball cap. She sure had me fooled."

"Well, don't be too hard on her, Allie," Marshall said. "From what she told us, she was trying to get the group to stop throwing rocks and turn themselves in."

"But she was seen at some of the crime scenes," I said. "She's an accessory to the fact."

"I think she foiled more attempts than we'll ever know about," Simon said. "She was hoping the game would end before someone really got hurt."

"The game?" I couldn't believe this. "They were playing a game?"

"Patterned after Sage Master," Marshall said.

"Dahlia said she has been ridden with guilt for days now," Simon said. "She also said she left a message at the school for you today."

I looked dumbfounded. "I didn't get any phone calls. When I checked my mailbox the last time, there wasn't anything in it." That's when it hit me. "Oh, good grief!" I opened my purse, pulled out the pink envelope, and tore open the flap.

Dear Miss Kane,

My brother is in over his head. He and his friends are involved in a horrendous game that is injuring innocent people. After talking with you the other night and reading your articles, I know you're a fair and compassionate person. I want to be more like that too.

Mahalo for helping me make things right—both for me and my brother.

Yours truly,
Dahlia Hong

Aunt Edith had walked up beside me and was reading the note over my shoulder. When we finished, I handed it to Simon.

"I don't understand what in the world gets into young people these days," Aunt Edith said. "What possible thrill could they get riding around throwing rocks on innocent motorists' cars?"

"It's beyond a dare or thrill," Simon said. "These brazen acts amount to psychotic behavior. Only someone disconnecting him or herself from reality could have done this." He looked at me. "I suppose you're going to go to the *Hawaiian Star* now to write an article about this for tomorrow's paper?"

"Absolutely! The capture of these guys couldn't have come at a better time." I paused. "But don't worry. I'll hurry to get it done so that we'll still have time for our last dinner together."

"Not *last*," Simon said. "Just the last one during *this* trip to Hawaii. Would you like to come with us to the station and listen while we interview these guys? It would give you some firsthand quotes for your piece."

"You bet I would!" I looked at Aunt Edith. "Do you mind riding home without me?"

She shook her head. "You go right on with your young man, and then go write your article." She motioned toward the motorcycle. "I need to go turn in my bike at the rental shop. Pinky said he'd follow me down there and give me a lift back to the apartment." Aunt Edith started to walk away then turned and looked at Simon. She pointed toward the two bikers sitting in the police car. "Simon, to quote one of my favorite judges, Isaac Parker, the Hanging Judge, 'this case is one where justice should not walk with leaden feet.'"

"I agree with the judge," Simon said. "I believe whoever presides over these trials will bring them to justice quickly."

Aunt Edith put her helmet on, then took Mr. Omura's helmet from me. "Glad to hear it," she said. She turned and walked back to her motorcycle.

"I'm ready if you are," I said to Simon.

We walked to his car and drove downtown. Inside the station, I took a quick look around while they processed the two riders. Simon showed me his office and introduced me to the chief. During our short conversation, the man had nothing but praise for Simon.

The two men had been put into separate rooms for questioning. Simon led me into a dim room with a one-way glass. The leader was sitting alone at a small table on the other side. He had waived his right to have an attorney present. I suspected he would regret that decision by the time Simon finished with him.

"That's the same guy I talked to when the first rock was thrown on H-1," I said to Simon. "I wonder if he's the one who put the rock on my car at school."

"The lab report says yes," Simon said. I looked at him. "The DNA from the Juicy Fruit wrappers also points to him. I just got definite confirmation on both this morning, but didn't think to tell you about it at lunch."

"So it proves he was at the locations where rocks were thrown," I said.

"Yes, and that will help get a conviction." He nodded toward the suspect. "He's Dahlia Hong's brother. Would you like to ask him a few questions before I tear into him?"

I smiled. "Oh, you bet I would!"

He reached for my hand and led me into the other room.

"Mr. Hong, I think you know Allison Kane," Simon said to him. He flipped on the tape recorder that was sitting on the table in front of the man.

Hong looked at me with contempt. "Yeah, I know her." He turned his head in dismissal. "She's been nosing around in my business."

I walked around the table and looked him in the eye. He seemed surprised at my boldness. "And believe me, it was a pleasure," I said to him. I glanced at Simon. He had a gleam in his eye as if to say, "Been watching a lot of cop shows lately?" I looked back at the suspect. "Are you the person who left the lava rock on my car?"

He snickered. "Yeah, but I didn't get any points for it."

I acted like it was the first time I had heard of the game. "Points?"

"Every rock had a point value," he said. "A thousand points were given for having the guts to do the act."

"The act?" Simon said.

"Yeah, courage enough to throw a rock off a bridge." He looked at Simon like he was the dumbest person on earth. I knew that Simon was just trying to get everything on tape.

"It was all about skill, man," Hong said. He leaned forward and put his elbows on the table. "I was going to be the next Sage Master."

Simon pulled out the chair across from the guy and sat down. "So how did this point system of yours work?"

The guy rolled his eyes. "Like I said, a thousand points for doing the act, two thousand if the vehicle was hit in the front." He smiled and puffed out his chest. "That was my idea. It takes more skill to hit the hood before the vehicle goes by."

"Oh yes, I can see how that takes more skill," Simon said.

Hong didn't pick up on the sarcasm. I looked at Simon. He had a coal-black gleam in his eyes.

"We'd get a thousand points if the rock hit the trunk lid. Five hundred bonus points were given if neither the windshield nor the back glass got broken. There were a couple of other ways to earn more." He leaned back again in his chair and crossed his arms. "We weren't really out to hurt anybody, but I heard on the news that it happened a couple of times."

His lack of remorse made my blood boil. "So it was just a game to you guys?" I said. "Innocent people were scared out of their wits! Rocks hit drivers' vehicles whose only crime was that they were in the wrong place at the wrong time. Though maybe not physically, they were hurt nonetheless. A toddler was traumatized by splintering glass and required stitches. That's just the tip of the iceberg. And it was all for a stupid, childish game?"

Hong shrugged again.

I leaned down in front of him. "I hope you get the maximum prison time allowed by law," I said. I straightened up and looked at Simon.

"He and his friends are looking at five to seven years at least," he said.

Hong looked at Simon. For the first time, I saw a flicker of emotion in his eyes.

"No way, man. Only one of us has ever been caught breaking the law. Community service and maybe a fine are all we'll get. You'll see."

Simon walked over to him and leaned down. His nose was just a couple of inches from Hong's. "People were hurt, scumbag. For days you were causing motorists all over this island all kinds of distress. Some of those people may sit on your jury." He stood back up. "I wouldn't count on just a slap on the wrist if I were you."

Hong put his elbows on the table, then cupped his face in his hands. "I need a lawyer," he mumbled.

CHAPTER 18

"Well, I hope all of them learn a lesson from this," I said to Simon. He was driving me to the *Hawaiian Star*. "And I hope that justice will be served."

"I'm sure it will be," Simon said. "It doesn't matter which judge presides over this case; he or she will be under a lot of pressure to issue a strong punishment." He pulled through the alley and stopped at the back door of the *Star* offices.

"Not that I'm complaining, but did you ever find out why no rocks were thrown on Sundays?" I asked.

Simon sighed. "Marshall asked one of the guys who was brought in this morning that question. He said that Sunday was their day of rest."

I shook my head in disbelief.

"Now go in there and write a dynamite piece, Miss Reporter," Simon said.

"See you tonight," I said. I watched him pull out before I walked inside.

I saw Mr. Masaki in the hallway. He was thrilled that the case had been solved. Though he usually wanted to chat a while, he seemed eager for me to go upstairs to finish the piece. He even escorted me to my office.

I scanned my notes and then reread all that had been written. I double-checked facts, dates, and figures, then finished the piece. Since Aunt Edith and I helped in capturing two of the suspects, it was easy to write.

I was finishing the last paragraph when Mr. Masaki stepped to my door. I looked at him. "Just about finished," I said. He nodded but didn't come in.

I printed off a copy of the story then handed it to him. He took it from me and glanced at it but didn't continue reading it.

I looked at him and frowned. "Is there something wrong with the story, Mr. Masaki?" I thought maybe it was too lengthy.

He shook his head. "I'm really not very good at this, Allison," he said. "I'm just going to ask you to shut your eyes and come with me."

Now I was really confused.

He smiled. "Please?"

I stood up and walked around my desk. He took my hand. "Okay, you've got to shut your eyes now."

I did as he asked. He led me down the staircase then toward the main offices. I could hear music in the distance and smell food.

"Okay, you can open your eyes now," he said.

I opened them and saw that we were standing in the doorway of the employee lunchroom. Every person on staff was crammed inside it.

"Surprise!" they all shouted together.

I was stunned. Mr. Masaki took my arm and led me into the room. Platters and bowls full of food covered the table.

"Speech, speech," a few started chanting.

I shook my head, but the chant grew louder.

"You're going to have to say something to quiet them down," Mr. Masaki said.

I nodded, then fluttered my hands up and down. Finally the room was still.

"I'm totally overwhelmed by your kindness," I said, motioning toward the food-laden table. "Though I haven't worked closely with some of you this past month, I've enjoyed being here."

Some of them started clapping. The copy editor said, "She means me, you know."

"Yeah, yeah, yeah," a couple of the reporters said.

I smiled at them. "Anyway, it's been an honor and a joy to work at the *Hawaiian Star*." I put my hand on Mr. Masaki's shoulder. "And to work for this fine man."

"Hear, hear," I heard someone say. Most in the room were nodding their heads.

"Now without getting all mushy, let's eat."

I was ushered to the front of the line and given a dinner plate. I started filling it with goodies.

Everyone found a seat in one of the chairs placed around the room. It was a pleasure to share a meal with them.

When the crowd started breaking up, I thanked them again. I headed upstairs to finish cleaning out my office. After shutting down my computer, I set all my files in a neat stack on the credenza. The sack containing the office supplies that Mr. Masaki had provided when I first arrived was still well stocked.

I sighed. "Someone will have some nice things to work with," I said to myself. I walked over to the big picture window to take one last look at the gorgeous scene that had been mine for the past month. In the park, kids and dogs were chasing Frisbees, and old couples were sitting on benches holding hands. The colors of the flowers were just as vivid as they had been four weeks earlier.

As I was turning to leave, I saw Sammy Cho come out of the laundromat. He was walking toward his car. I started waving my hands trying to get his attention. He looked up at the window and waved. He had a copy of a newspaper under one arm. Since I knew he was a regular reader of the *Hawaiian Star*, I figured it was our paper. He lifted it in the air and then gave me "thumbs-up" sign with his other hand. I returned the gesture. He smiled at me, and then he climbed into his car.

I looked at the puffy, white clouds in the sky. It was another glorious day in Hawaii. "Lord, this good-bye thing is getting too tough," I said.

Before I started bawling, I grabbed my purse and walked out the door. I couldn't bear to close it—that made it too final. With my head held high, I walked down the stairs.

"I can't tell you how great it's been having you working for me this month, Allison," Mr. Masaki said. We were standing together at the back door. "I don't suppose I could tempt you into staying the rest of the summer?"

I smiled at him. "I've had a marvelous time in Hawaii and loved this job, and you've been a terrific boss." I paused. That old feeling of wishing I could be in two places at one time swept over me again. "But it's time for me to go home."

He nodded. "I understand. As Dorothy from the *Wizard of Oz* said, 'There's no place like home.' But Hawaii and many of its people are going to miss you. You've left your mark here."

My eyes were burning. He draped his arm around my shoulders and hugged me. I was afraid I'd lose it for sure.

"Thank you, Mr. Masaki, for the liberty you gave me here. My skills as a journalist are far better now than when I arrived."

He stepped back. "Well, if you're ever back in Hawaii, please give me a call. You'll always have a job waiting for you here at the *Hawaiian Star*."

"I appreciate that." I waved good-bye to him, and then walked outside.

Simon was waiting for me. We were going to go to Richard and Kim's for dinner.

He had some casual clothes in his car. We were going to go to the apartment, change clothes, and pick up Aunt Edith. She was already dressed and ready to go when we walked in.

"You look lovely as always, Aunt Edith," Simon told her.

She leaned up and gave him a kiss on the cheek. "Thank you, Simon."

The puppies each had colorful bandanas tied around their necks. They met Simon and me with sloppy kisses and expected some petting in return.

"Yes, it's good to see you too," Simon said to Precious. He stooped down and picked her up. She lapped his face like he was her long lost friend.

Rowdy was in my arms. He was yipping and letting us know that he was ready to go.

"You can use Traci and Tommy's room to change clothes in if you want to," I said to Simon. He handed Precious to me then headed down the hallway.

"I made a big bowl of potato salad and whipped up an orange chiffon angel food cake to take," Aunt Edith said. "A little birdie told me you were missing having a piece at your mother's birthday party."

I smiled at her, then leaned over and gave her a kiss on the cheek. "Thanks. You're a sweetheart."

She reached for the pups. "Now you go on and get ready so that we can go."

I relinquished the dogs to her. "Yes, ma'am." I hurried to my bedroom to change.

Michael and Richard were taking turns tending the charcoal grill when we arrived. The aroma of thick, juicy steaks filled the backyard. Kim and DeLana were in the kitchen fixing side dishes. I could smell spicy marinades and bread baking when we walked into the house.

Simon carried the crate that Rowdy and Precious were in to the backyard. They were both whining and couldn't wait to get out of it to reunite with their friend, Mitzi. The Pekinese seemed just as pleased to see them. Charlie and Bethany jumped into Simon's arms as soon as they saw him. The two children kept him and the dogs busy.

Aunt Edith and I carried the cake and potato salad into the kitchen. We were seated and eating by 7:00. The evening was filled with amusing stories and lots of laughter.

When we got back home to the apartment, Aunt Edith went on in. Simon and I sat in the car for a while. Kisses were intermingled with conversation.

"Want to go to the beach tomorrow?" Simon asked.

"Sure, but don't you have to work?"

His arm was draped around my shoulder, and he was playing with my hair. "I'm taking the next two days off."

"Well, that's a nice surprise." My eyes were closed. I was enjoying the feel of his fingers in my hair.

"I had intended on packing a picnic lunch and stealing you away to our special beach," he said. "But then tonight Richard told me that he and Kim are taking Michael and DeLana to see the USS *Oklahoma* Memorial at Pearl Harbor tomorrow. Would you rather go with them?"

"Hmmm. It would be nice to see it, but I'd rather spend some alone time with you." I reached for his hand. "I'll have DeLana take some pictures of it for me. Aunt Edith has a date with Mr. Omura tomorrow, so I guess it's just you and me."

We were quiet for several seconds, then he pulled me closer. "Saying you're special to me is an understatement, Allie." He paused. "I've never felt like this about any other woman before."

I turned my head and looked at him. In the darkness, his chocolate-brown eyes were intense. Soft wisps of his cologne lingered on his shirt.

"You're very special to me too, Simon." *Okay, Allie, it's time to take the plunge*, a little voice whispered.

Simon beat me to it. "I love you, Allie. With all my heart."

Before I could reply, he cupped the back of my head with his hand and brought his lips to mine. My heart started beating like mad, and I was sure he could hear it pounding in my chest.

The next morning Aunt Edith was gone when I got up. She had left me a note that the pups had already been outside and had their breakfast. I guess they didn't read her note. They both were snooping around their empty dishes.

"Okay, I'll give you a little snack," I said. While I munched on a Pop Tart, they both had a little more kibble.

Simon was supposed to pick me up at 11:00. I had some time, so I decided to give Kristin a call.

"So what's on the agenda for today?" I asked when she answered.

"Hey, stranger."

"How was church camp?"

"Oh, I had a blast! I thought we had a great time when we were teenagers, and we did, but last week was fantastic!"

I smiled. "I'm glad to hear it. Did you pound the kids with water balloons?"

She started laughing. "I took your advice and stocked up on those super-sized ones from Wal-Mart. But you know what? Riley and a bunch of the other kids had some even bigger ones! They nearly drowned me during the water fight."

I started laughing too. "The younger generation is getting too smart for us."

"That's the truth. Hold on a sec." I heard her put her hand over the receiver and mumble something. "Sorry about that. Joey is rushing me to get off the phone. He and I were getting ready to head to the Circle K. Uncle Ken and the family came in last night." Mom's brother, Ken, his wife, Janice, and their children lived in Virginia.

"Really? They came a little early this year." They only made it back to Paradise twice a year—a week at Christmastime and a week around the Fourth of July.

"Yes, believe it or not, they're going to spend two weeks here this time."

"Well, that's nice. I love seeing them."

"Guess who else is at the Circle K?" Kristin said.

"Give me a hint."

"Your favorite cousin from South Dakota."

"Noel and his family are there? They don't usually make it until later in the summer."

"Yes, and he has a messed-up leg. He was gored by a bull during the big rodeo in Casper a couple of weeks ago."

"Oh, that's terrible!" I said. "Is his leg going to be all right?"

"He says it is, but you know Noel. He'll say just about anything to be able to get back on some bucking bronc or angry bull."

We talked more about the visiting relatives and other things that had been happening around Paradise. By the time I got off the phone, I had to hurry to get a shower. I had just put my cover-up on over my swimsuit when Simon buzzed from downstairs. Fortunately, I had already packed my beach bag.

When we arrived at our favorite beach, it was nearly deserted. Simon brought along a large umbrella. We lounged under it for a while, talking, drinking pop, and napping, and then we headed into the cool water to swim. The seagulls and other birds begrudgingly shared the surf with us. We walked from one end of the long beach to the other, stirring up tiny crabs that were hiding at the edge of the water.

We arrived back at the apartment around 5:00. I fixed supper for us. Aunt Edith and Mr. Omura came in around 6:00. Simon and I had just sat down to eat, so they joined us. After cleaning up the kitchen, the four of us played dominoes for a couple of hours. Aunt Edith and Mr. Omura kept us in stitches. When the guys got ready to leave, my sides were hurting from laughing so much.

After Mr. Omura left, Simon and I dawdled at the elevator. I kept coming up with something to say to keep him there.

He wrapped his arms around me. "I'll pick you and Aunt Edith up around noon tomorrow," he said. "That will give us plenty of time for a leisurely lunch and to get you both checked in for your 4:00 flight."

My forehead was buried in his shoulder. I nodded my head up and down. "She and I need to clean the apartment in the morning and get packed." My voice was muffled. "We should be ready by noon."

Still wrapped in his arms, Simon guided me to the elevator. He pushed the button. We were still intertwined when the door opened.

"I need to go," he whispered.

"I know." We released each other at the same time. He stepped onto the elevator and turned to face me. "I love you, Allie."

I nodded my head. As the doors started closing, I caught them with my hands. I shoved them open again. "I love you too!"

He kissed me, and then the doors closed. I leaned my forehead on them and cried.

The next morning, both Aunt Edith and I were up by 7:00. We stripped the beds, and I took all the linens downstairs to the laundry room. After two washers were going, I went back upstairs to start vacuuming. Aunt Edith had beat me to it. While she vacuumed, I dusted. When that was done, I mopped the kitchen and bathroom floors. I knew there was no need to clean the sinks and mirrors until after we had showered.

The dogs sensed that something was up because they were constantly underfoot. Rowdy decided to pull over the plant that he had attacked when he first arrived. Precious managed to get her paw wedged between the bedpost and wall in my room. It took every ounce of patience I had to keep from wringing their necks.

At 11:05, I jumped into the shower. The apartment was gleaming. All my stuff was packed except my makeup and what I intended to wear. Aunt Edith was showering in her bathroom. In the middle of mine, I ran out of hot water. I could hear her howling through the wall. The cold spray must have hit her about the same time.

At 11:45, I took the dachshunds out for a final potty break. They took their time saying good-bye to all the shrubbery and fence posts around the pool. When we returned to the apartment, Aunt Edith had already set her luggage outside the door. She wasn't around, so I figured she had gone down to say good-bye to Evelyn.

After putting the pups in their crate, I set them in the hallway by my luggage. I walked onto the lanai for one last look at Pearl Harbor. The sky was a brilliant blue, and the sun was high.

"Thank you, Lord, for allowing me to come to spend a month here," I said. "I'll never forget it."

I asked God to please bless Traci and Tommy's home and their new child, who would be arriving soon. I also asked for a safe flight for all of us.

There was a knock at the door. "I'm coming," I hollered. I closed and locked the sliding-glass door. When I opened the apartment door, Simon was standing there.

"Ready?" he asked. He was dressed in a red-and-white aloha shirt and beige Dockers. His hair was damp around the edges. If I hadn't already been in love with him, I would have fallen that second.

"How did you get in?"

"Pinky was walking toward the building when I pulled up." He motioned toward the luggage. "Is this it?"

"That's everything."

Besides the luggage I had with me when I arrived, there were two large boxes sitting there. They were full of things I had accumulated while I had been here. Aunt Edith had brought an empty suitcase with her. It was now filled with souvenirs for folks back home.

I turned around and took one last look at the apartment. I set the key that Tommy had given to me on the kitchen counter, pushed the lock on the doorknob, and then closed the door behind me.

We had been in the air nearly an hour, and I was still trying to get comfortable. The pilot had assured us that the flight should be a smooth one to Los Angeles. He also said that we'd make good time because we had a strong tail wind.

Aunt Edith was sitting in the window seat next to me. She had been talking a blue streak since we had left the airport. She talked about the fun she had had in Hawaii, about the crime we had helped solve, about Mr. Omura, the Garden of Eden, and lots of other things. She also mentioned how she would like to move into one of the garden condominiums in Traci's complex someday.

"I caught the super down at the laundry room the other day, Allie. He showed me one of the condominiums that was vacant. It was really roomy!"

While we sipped our soft drinks, she expressed concern about the pups and the crate of pineapples she was taking back to Paradise. They were all down in the cargo hold below our feet.

I assured her that both the dachshunds and the pineapples would be fine. I listened politely and contributed bits and pieces to the conversation. But my mind wasn't really on it. I had given her the window seat because I couldn't bear to watch as we flew away from Oahu and Simon. I was already missing, no, aching for him. I was exhausted too. It was probably more from emotional strain than from the physical activity of cleaning Traci's apartment.

I laid my head back on the headrest and put my hand on my forehead. I felt a finger tap my shoulder.

"Hey, lady," the passenger behind me said. "I'm trying to get a little shut-eye back here. Could you please stop flashing that light?"

I grinned then turned around in my seat. Michael and DeLana were sitting behind Aunt Edith and me. "You're going to have to deal with the flashes of bright light, sir," I said. "You're just jealous because it belongs to me and not someone else." I nodded toward DeLana.

"We're looking," Michael said. "We just haven't found the right one yet."

He leaned over and kissed DeLana. I turned back toward the front.

My thoughts once again drifted to the handsome detective with chocolate-brown eyes that I had left behind. I could still hear his voice whispering in my ear. "We won't be apart for long, Allie. I love you too much."

"No, not for long, my love," I whispered to myself. I looked down at my left hand. I gently touched the diamond ring that Simon had placed on my finger. "Not for long."

A NOTE FROM THE AUTHOR

Thank you for joining Allie, Simon, Aunt Edith, and the gang for another adventure. I hope you laughed, enjoyed the suspense and travel in Hawaii, and were blessed. Please watch for the fourth book in the series, *Secrets in Paradise*.

If you'd like to find out more about me and the Paradise series, please go to my Web site at www.terryerobins.com. There you can give me your feedback, sign up for the informative quarterly newsletter, print off the Kane and Winters family trees, and more. Printable reading discussion guides are now available there as well. If you don't have Internet access, you may write to me at P.O. Box 335, Chelsea, OK 74016. I love hearing from readers!

BIBLIOGRAPHY

Songs:

Author Unknown. "What a Mighty God We Serve." Copyright Unknown.

Carmichael, Ralph Richard. "We Are More Than Conquerors." Communique Music Co. Copyright 1983.

Hall, Darryl and Oates, John. "Maneater." RCA Records.

Hill, Mildred J. & Hill, Patty S. "Happy Birthday." Copyright 1893.

Mullins, Rich. "Awesome God." Edward Grant, Inc. Copyright 1988

Negro Spiritual. "Jesus on the Mainline." Copyright Unknown.

Pober, Leon. "Tiny Bubbles." Granite Music Corp. Copyright Unknown.

Van Beethoven, Ludwig. "Moonlight Sonata." G. Schirmer, Inc. Copyright 1894.

Wagner, Richard. "Bridal Chorus." Copyright 1847.

Television Shows & Movies:

All Quiet on the Western Front. Universal Studios. 1930.

CSI: Crime Scene Investigation. CBS, New York. 2008.

Full House. ABC, 1985.

Six in the Morning. KOTV, Tulsa, OK.

The Poseidon Adventure. Twentieth-Century Fox Film Corp. 1972.

The Tonight Show. NBC, Los Angeles, CA.

The Wizard of Oz. MGM. 1939.

Books and Magazines:

Good Housekeeping. Published by Hearst Communications, Inc. New York, NY.

Scriptures (King James Version):

Psalm 89:14 Justice and judgment are the habitation of thy throne: mercy and truth shall go before thy face.

Acts 16:16–40 Story about Paul and Silas

Proverbs 3:5–6 Trust in the Lord with all thine heart; and lean not unto thine own understanding. In all thy ways acknowledge Him, and He shall direct thy paths.

Psalm 89:9 The Lord rules the raging seas. When the waves rise, He stills them.

Psalm 91:1–2 He that dwelleth in the secret place of the most High shall abide under the shadow of the Almighty. I will say of the Lord, He is my refuge and my fortress: my God; in Him will I trust.

Isaiah 9:6–7 For unto us a child is born, unto us a son is given: and the government shall be upon His shoulders; His name shall be called Wonderful, Counselor, the Mighty God, the Everlasting Father, the Prince of Peace. Of the increase of His government and peace there shall be no end, upon the throne of David, and upon His kingdom to order it and to establish it with judgment and with justice from henceforth even forever. The zeal of the Lord of hosts will perform it."

Psalm 34:7 The angel of the Lord encamps round about them that fear Him, and delivers them.

Related links:

Dec. 7, 2006: Breaking ground for the USS *Oklahoma* Memorial
http://www.youtube.com/watch?v=sVbSDUyhqI4

USS Oklahoma: Unable to stay—unwilling to leave video clip
http://www.youtube.com/watch?v=UymPXEOdvD4&feature=related

Dr. Jaggar and Isabel Maydwell (actors) at the Hawaii Volcanoes
National Park
http://hvo.wr.usgs.gov/volcanowatch/2006/06_06_01.html

For daily updates of the Kilauea volcano
www.hvo.wr.usgs.gov

DISCARDED

DATE DUE

5.28			
←			
2.17			